CW01466486

The Seven Rings

By Nora Roberts

Homeport
The Reef
River's End
Carolina Moon
The Villa
Midnight Bayou
Three Fates
Birthright
Northern Lights
Blue Smoke
Montana Sky

Angels Fall
High Noon
Divine Evil
Tribute
Sanctuary
Black Hills
The Search
Chasing Fire
The Witness
Whiskey Beach
The Collector

The Liar
The Obsession
Come Sundown
Shelter in Place
Under Currents
Hideaway
Legacy
Nightwork
Identity
Mind Games
Hidden Nature

The Born In Trilogy:
Born in Fire
Born in Ice
Born in Shame

The Bride Quartet:
Vision in White
A Bed of Roses
Savour the Moment
Happy Ever After

The Key Trilogy:
Key of Light
Key of Knowledge
Key of Valour

The Irish Trilogy:
Jewels of the Sun
Tears of the Moon
Heart of the Sea

Three Sisters Island Trilogy:
Dance upon the Air
Heaven and Earth
Face the Fire

The Sign of Seven Trilogy:
Blood Brothers

The Hollow
The Pagan Stone

Chesapeake Bay Quartet:
Sea Swept
Rising Tides
Inner Harbour
Chesapeake Blue

In the Garden Trilogy:
Blue Dahlia
Black Rose
Red Lily

The Circle Trilogy:
Morrigan's Cross
Dance of the Gods
Valley of Silence

The Dream Trilogy:
Daring to Dream
Holding the Dream
Finding the Dream

The Inn Boonsboro Trilogy:
The Next Always
The Last Boyfriend
The Perfect Hope

*The Cousins O'Dwyer
Trilogy:*
Dark Witch
Shadow Spell
Blood Magick

The Guardians Trilogy:
Stars of Fortune
Bay of Sighs
Island of Glass

*The Chronicles of
the One Trilogy:*
Year One
Of Blood and Bone
The Rise of Magicks

*The Dragon Heart
Legacy Trilogy:*
The Awakening
The Becoming
The Choice

The Lost Bride Trilogy
Inheritance
The Mirror
The Seven Rings

Many of Nora Roberts' other titles are now available in ebook and she is also the author of the In Death series using the pseudonym J.D. Robb.

NORA ROBERTS

The Seven Rings

THE LOST BRIDE TRILOGY

Book Three

PIATKUS

PIATKUS

First published in the US in 2025 by St Martin's Press,
An imprint of St Martin's Publishing Group
First published in Great Britain in 2025 by Piatkus

1 3 5 7 9 10 8 6 4 2

Copyright © 2025 by Nora Roberts

The moral right of the author has been asserted.

*All characters and events in this publication, other than those
clearly in the public domain, are fictitious and any resemblance
to real persons, living or dead, is purely coincidental.*

All rights reserved.
No part of this publication may be reproduced, stored in a
retrieval system, or transmitted in any form or by any means, without
the prior permission in writing of the publisher, nor be otherwise circulated
in any form of binding or cover other than that in which it is published
and without a similar condition including this condition being
imposed on the subsequent purchaser.

A CIP catalogue record for this book
is available from the British Library.

ISBN 978-0-349-43755-2 (hardback)
ISBN 978-0-349-43756-9 (trade paperback)

Printed and bound by CPI (UK) Ltd, Croydon CR0 4YY

Papers used by Piatkus are from well-managed forests
and other responsible sources.

MIX
Paper | Supporting
responsible forestry
FSC
www.fsc.org   FSC® C104740

Piatkus
An imprint of
Little, Brown Book Group
Carmelite House
50 Victoria Embankment
London EC4Y 0DZ

The authorised representative
in the EEA is
Hachette Ireland
8 Castlecourt Centre,
Dublin 15, D15 XTP3, Ireland
(email: info@hbgi.ie)

An Hachette UK Company
www.hachette.co.uk

www.littlebrown.co.uk

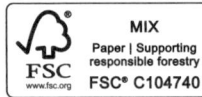

For Leslie and Amy,
friends and partners

PART ONE

—∿∿—

Madness

Though this be madness,
yet there is method in't.

—William Shakespeare

Prologue

In the 1780s, Arthur Poole sailed across the Atlantic, a young man with great ambition. His journey took him to the rocky, sea-lashed coast of Maine, and this new world he embraced as his own.

He worked and he learned and he thrived.

This young man of ambition and vision built ships, and built the beginnings of a business. To enrich and expand that business, he, shrewdly, married for money and position.

In time, like flowers in a fallow field, love bloomed there.

With an eye toward the generations to come, he built his business to last. And above that rolling, thrashing sea, he built a grand house, and one to last, with stone and cladded walls, and turrets rising, with massive entrance doors of the finest mahogany.

With his love of the sea, he added a widow's walk, and often stood there himself, watching his ships sail the fickle Atlantic waters.

His children drew their first breaths inside those walls, and played in the gardens, raced the wide halls, wandered the nearby woods, learned to ride, learned to sail.

Arthur Poole considered himself a successful man, not only a successful businessman, a man who'd risen from poverty to riches who lived on the cliffs above a village that bore his name. But a successful husband and father. A family man.

The family man held great pride in his children, and in the first-born of his twin sons, who'd courted and won the heart of a lovely (and wealthy) woman.

Collin Poole would marry Astrid Grandville not for advancement, nor money, nor social position, but for love.

On the last day of his life, Arthur Poole rode into his woods in the brisk fall air with his mind, as it often was, on the future. Wedding plans—the most beautiful and elegant wedding Poole's Bay had ever seen—entertained him. He thought of expanding the manor, making more room for the grandchildren to come.

But he would not attend his son's wedding. He would never see his grandchildren. On that brisk fall day, he fell victim to the dark magic of a mad witch who coveted what he had.

Not the family, not the business, not even his wealth. The manor.

Hester Dobbs would stop at nothing, certainly not murder, to become the mistress of Poole Manor.

And all who knew and loved Arthur Poole grieved what they believed to be a tragic accident, a fall from his horse.

When this death failed to give Hester Dobbs her desire, she murdered Astrid Grandville Poole on her wedding day.

And with that vicious slaying, with Poole blood on her hands, on her tongue, with Astrid's wedding ring now on her own finger, she laid a curse on the manor, on the future.

A bride in each generation of Pooles would die in the manor, and by her hand.

While she escaped the hangman's rope, she in her madness returned to the manor. On a night when the clock struck three, and the moon sailed full over the water, she sealed her curse with her own blood.

And leapt from the seawall to the unforgiving water below.

For more than two centuries, the manor stood, stone, wood, glass, watching the great sea. Inside its walls, it witnessed generations of first breaths and last breaths. As Arthur Poole had imagined, the manor grew and held his grandchildren, and their children, and theirs for generations.

And each generation knew tragedy. One bride lost to the twisted lusts of Hester Dobbs.

Until there were seven lost brides, and seven rings on the hands of the witch who killed them.

So within those walls, their spirits remained, as did Dobbs, as did others who either chose to stay or had yet to find their way beyond those walls.

There they walked, and they worked, and they watched.

And they waited for the one who could break the curse.

She came, a woman of Poole blood who'd known nothing of that family connection. She'd known nothing of her father's brother, his twin, or the heartless scheme to separate them after their mother fell victim to Dobbs's curse following their birth.

Nor did she know anything of ghosts or curses or the part she had to play.

But she learned.

She came to the manor alone—though she wouldn't remain alone—to learn of this newly discovered part of her family, to learn their history, to uncover how and why her father had been taken away from his brother.

How was it, though he'd never been to the manor before his own tragic death, that he, an artist, sketched it? How, though he'd never known of his twin, had he drawn a mirror framed with predators where he and a boy who looked like him stood on either side of the glass?

And as she learned, she walked and worked.

When the mirror called to her, she stepped through the glass. She witnessed the death of seven brides, and grieved for them. She witnessed the theft of seven wedding rings, and swore to retrieve them.

With what she'd once believed impossible now her reality, Sonya MacTavish understood the rings were the key to breaking the curse and forever banishing Hester Dobbs from the manor.

For all those who'd come before her, for the house she'd made her home, for those seven lost brides, she vowed to stay and hunt and fight.

Even as death woke all around her.

Chapter One

The dead filled the manor, but not as the spirits Sonya had grown used to, even fond of. They filled it now with blood and broken bodies, with agony and despair.

She felt their pain and their fear as her own as she looked down at Astrid Poole and the spreading red stain on her white dress. As she looked up at the first Collin Poole's body swaying above his bride from the noose he'd fashioned through his grief.

And beside the first bride, the last, as Johanna Poole's broken and bloodied body lay at the base of the stairs. And beside her, his hand over hers, the last Collin Poole, the husband who'd outlived her by decades before falling to his death down that same grand staircase.

Though he'd lived longer, grown older, Sonya saw her father in that face. Now grief, instant and fresh, joined the pain and fear.

Needing the life, the warmth, she gripped Trey's hand. "It's Collin. It's my father's twin."

"Yeah, just the way I found him."

To Oliver Doyle III—lawyer and lover—Collin Poole had been family. Remembering that, Sonya put her arms around him.

"I'm sorry. So sorry." Then she squeezed her eyes tight. "God, God, can you hear them? Can you hear all of them?"

"I hear them. Owen." He turned to his friend and Sonya's Poole cousin.

"Hard to hear anything else, unless you add in the dogs howling."

"Put me down." Cleo gave Owen's chest a nudge so he set her on her feet. "I dropped a glass. None of us are wearing shoes, so watch where you step."

She moved to Sonya, took her closest friend's hand and found it as icy as her own.

"I'll clean it up."

At Owen's words, Cleo shot him a fierce look. "Don't you go anywhere. Don't you dare."

"We have to stop it." Unable to help herself, Sonya pressed her hands over her ears. "She's torturing them. We have to stop it."

"Fear feeds her," Cleo reminded the rest. "I'm really trying not to give her a goddamn crumb, but . . ." She trailed off, looked up the staircase. "Oh Jesus."

Johanna stood, as did the shadowy figure with her. Even with the din, they heard the snap as her head jerked. Her lifeless body tumbled down the stairs as it had on her wedding day.

"She's killing them again. All of them. Everyone's dying again. We have to stop it," Sonya said. "Fuck fear." And her anger burned out fear as she swiped tears from her face. "She's making them feel it again, tormenting them to scare us."

Even as she spoke, the first Collin Poole, the noose around his neck, leaped off the stairs. The rope snapped, and so did his neck.

"Brutal," Owen muttered. "I'm in for a round of fuck fear."

"A circle, join hands," Cleo ordered.

"Why?"

"Look, Owen, I'm an amateur, but unity counts. What did you do when Pye ran off and up to the Gold Room door when that bitch was having another one of her fits?"

"Went after the cat."

"You sang. So, hell, sing. Everybody, sing."

"You want us to sing?"

She shrugged at Trey. "It's better than standing here just watching and hearing all this. Clover uses music to communicate with us, so what the hell."

"What are we singing?" Owen wanted to know, and took a firm hold on her hand and on Sonya's as Astrid Poole, a hand pressed to the bleeding wound, staggered down the steps.

"I can't think of every damn thing."

"Are we pissed?" Trey demanded, and let that fury ride as the man he'd loved like a second father tumbled down the steps.

"Damn right." Tears might've fallen, but Sonya repeated, "Damn right we're pissed."

"Then try this." He lifted his voice over the cries, the weeping, the howling. "Keep you in the dark, you know they all pretend."

His voice, which had once led a high school garage band, rang true as Owen's joined it.

Digging for lyrics, Sonya came in on the verse with Cleo. "Send in your skeletons."

It sure as hell fit the moment, she thought as they sang words of defiance and challenge. Words with no fear.

Lights flickered on and off; doors slammed. But slowly, gradually, the sounds of torment lessened.

When they reached the bridge, and she sang about being the hand that would "take you down," she meant it.

By the time they finished, the house had gone quiet. No one lay at the base of the stairs; no one swayed from a rope above them.

"Foo Fighters." Owen gave Trey a fist bump. "Inspired choice."

"I figured 'The Pretender' was a solid choice because that's all Dobbs is. A pretender trying to be mistress of the manor." He brought Sonya's hand to his lips. "You okay, cutie?"

"I will be." Since Yoda pawed at her legs, she bent down to pet him. "You had a time of it, didn't you? All you guys had a hell of a time."

"So did my girl," Cleo said as the black cat wound between her legs, then Owen's. "They all might want a little fresh air. I could use it myself."

"Just leave the door open," Sonya suggested, "let the air in. I'll clean up the glass."

"I've got it," Trey told her. "Stick with Cleo."

As Sonya herded Yoda, Trey's Mookie, Owen's Jones outside with

Cleo and the cat, Trey walked back to the kitchen for a broom. When he returned, Owen stood looking down where they'd seen Collin.

"You saw him fall."

Owen nodded. "Yeah. I had this sick feeling maybe he'd just taken the leap, tired of living without Johanna. Or worse, that Dobbs did it to him."

"He tripped. I had the same sick feeling, but he tripped. He was half-asleep it looked like, not real steady."

"He'd had that cold deal for a few days."

"Yeah, so not real steady. But something startled him. I think he saw—"

"Johanna," Owen finished. "At the bottom of the stairs. Whether he really saw her, or imagined it, remembered finding her that way, it unbalanced him just enough."

"I don't think it was Dobbs. He just lost his footing, and he went down."

"He had his hand over hers. When we saw him just now. I don't think he did it on purpose, but I think he was okay with it. Dobbs made a mistake showing us that, because I feel better about it. Believing he just lost his footing, but he was okay with it."

"We're going to beat her, Owen."

"Oh, fucking-A right we are." Now he grinned. "I've got plenty of songs in me."

Clover, the sixth bride and Sonya's grandmother, chimed in with Rihanna's "Don't Stop the Music."

"You got it, babe. And on that note, I want breakfast. I've got to get up in an hour anyway." Owen glanced toward the open door. "What are the odds of talking Cleo into making some predawn omelets?"

"You tell me. You're the one sleeping with her."

"I give it fifty-fifty, and I bump that up if I have coffee waiting."

Trey carried the broom and the dustpan of broken glass back to the kitchen. "Make the coffee," he advised. "Everyone needs time to settle. This was different from knowing we've got a house full of ghosts. It was seeing them die, hearing it, feeling it."

"Dobbs is quiet now. It had to cost her a lot of energy to pull that off."

"She wanted to hurt them. Everyone in this house, alive or dead, wants her out. The only way we know of is to find the rings. Take them back. Break the curse, get her gone."

"And Sonya's seen all seven brides now. How they died."

"Exactly. It's going to get worse from here, Owen." He sat at the kitchen island, shoved a hand through his tousled black hair. "We can't be here twenty-four seven. But they both live here, work here."

With the coffee going, Owen got out eggs, cheese, bacon. If he couldn't talk Cleo into making breakfast, he'd toss some together.

"I get the worry. I've got it, too. But truth?" He looked at his lifelong friend across the counter. "I don't know any two women—hell, people—who can handle it better than they can."

"When the mirror shows up, it doesn't give her a choice. Sonya has to go through."

"And you can't go with her." Owen, Poole-green eyes steady, handed Trey a mug of coffee. "I can, if I'm here. But you and Cleo, you have to wait on this side. That's a tough swallow for a guy whose nature, and skill set, has him helping people and fixing things."

"It's goddamn hard to take it on faith you'll come back through again."

"Here's the thing." Owen got his own coffee. "Considering it's framed in predators, it looks like it could eat you alive, but you gotta figure it's on our side, or why show Sonya what she needs to know to get that bitch out of here?"

"I tell myself that. Like I tell myself, from what we know or believe, Collin and Sonya's father used it to communicate with each other. Maybe they never knew exactly how or why."

"Sonya's dad probably never did, but Collin had to figure it out after your dad did the genealogy. Once he knew he'd had a twin taken away, given up for adoption, he had to figure it out."

"And by the time he did, and decided to contact Andrew MacTavish, MacTavish was dead."

"So here we are," Owen added. "Collin leaves the manor to his brother's only child. You fall for her. She gets her pal to move in with her, and I fall for her. There's a kind of symmetry going. I don't know what the hell it means, but, man, it's going."

He heard the sound of dogs racing through the house.

"Let's see if she's fallen enough for me to make those omelets."

Until she'd followed Sonya in the move from Boston to Maine, the only times Cleopatra Fabares recalled seeing the sun rise was after an all-nighter—work or play.

As for cooking breakfast—or anything else—that fell into the pretty-much-never area of her life.

But that was then, this was now.

She'd taken up Sonya's offer of moving in, of making Collin Poole's turret art studio her own without a second thought. But with the caveat she would also be in charge of the food shopping and cooking.

That posed a long, wide learning curve for the Louisiana-born artist and illustrator, but—surprise—she learned. And more, she enjoyed it.

And since the three a.m. wake-up call, and all that followed, stirred up her appetite, Owen didn't have to work hard to persuade her to make omelets.

She bundled up her mass of burnt honey curls, sent Owen out to the herb garden for parsley and tarragon. And got to work.

It gave her something to do—and more, gave Sonya more time to smooth out.

Her friend still held a lot of anger, and Cleo was all for the mad. But Sonya also looked a bit pale yet, and her deep green eyes showed a fatigue that came from more, far more, than interrupted sleep.

She carried the load, and while the rest of them could help, did help, they couldn't take it from her.

This helped, Cleo thought. Not just food, but the company, the routine. Trey and Sonya feeding the pets, Owen getting out plates and flatware.

Just the movement, the life—and the unity—helped.

When the oven timer dinged, Sonya walked over to take out the bacon. Trey put bread in the toaster—and watched Sonya.

Afraid she'll break, Cleo thought as she slid the third of four omelets onto a platter and put it in the warmer.

But she won't.

Any more than he or Owen would after witnessing a man they'd loved and respected die.

None of them would break.

When the last pat of butter she melted in the skillet began to foam, she poured in the egg-cheese-and-herb mixture.

"I think I'm going to paint out back today, do a study of the garden. The wisteria on the pergola."

"You don't need to stay near the house for me, Cleo."

"I can if I want, but what I want is out back. Unless you want to blow off the day and go sail the bay in my beautiful little boat."

"I've got a couple of jobs to juggle in with the Ryder Sports account. No day off for me."

"Next weekend."

Sonya smiled, but it didn't reach her eyes. "Next weekend sounds good."

With the last omelet on the platter along with bacon and toast, they sat together at the table while all four pets caught a predawn nap.

"These look amazing, Cleo."

"You'll convince me of that, Son, if you eat some."

"I will. And I'm sorry I'm being such a drag on everything."

"You're not," Trey objected, and deliberately lifted an omelet from the platter onto her plate.

"I feel like one. I . . . I've seen pictures, and he—Collin—was older when he died than my dad, but still, somehow, I wasn't prepared for how much they looked alike. It had to be worse for you and Owen, but I can't seem to shake that part yet. And we haven't heard anything from Clover since right after it stopped. She always has so much to say, and I'm worried she's—"

As she spoke, the tablet on the kitchen counter rang out with Elton John's "I'm Still Standing."

When tears sprang to Sonya's eyes, Trey reached for her.

"No, no, it's relief. It's exactly what I needed to hear. So are we, Clover." Now she forked off a bite of omelet, sampled it. And when she smiled, meant it. "And this is as amazing as it looks."

They ate while three dogs and a cat slept, while music played on the tablet. By tacit agreement, they didn't talk about what had happened, not yet. The time would come, but for now they let that rest, too.

"You've got a knack, Lafayette." Owen polished off the last of his omelet.

"I believe I do."

"You can give your knack a break tonight. How about I pick up something from the village?" Trey asked.

"Wouldn't hurt my feelings a bit," Cleo told him. "More time to paint, once I decide between a moody watercolor or a dramatic oil."

"How do you decide?" Owen wondered.

"Whim." She slanted him a look out of her amber eyes. "I do enjoy living on a whim."

"I'm glad you're taking the summer to paint for yourself." Sonya leaned back with her coffee. "And you're going to have a big bang of a show at Bay Arts this fall."

"We'll see about that, but it makes me happy. When fall comes, I'll be ready to go back to earning my living and illustrating. Oh, I forgot to tell you, I got the sweetest note from Burt Springer after I sent a copy of his granddaughter's favorite kids' book signed by me and the author."

"He's a sweet man. I really like working with him again. I don't live or work on a whim, but freelancing is taking me to many new places. A year ago, I couldn't have imagined running my own graphic design company."

"And kicking ass at it."

She grinned at Trey. "Yes, I am. I couldn't have imagined it, or imagined living in a big, gorgeous, haunted Victorian on the coast of Maine. Having a favorite cousin," she added with a lift of her coffee mug to Owen. "Or being with you, a third-generation lawyer who'll pick up dinner and tell me I kick ass."

Sonya shook back her hair and sighed. "Nothing Dobbs can do changes any of that. And she's not going to stop us. Cleo's said it before, and it's true. We bring the light and the life to the manor. We're going to keep right on doing that."

"Middle of the year's not too soon to start planning a big, bust-out holiday party at the manor."

Sonya pointed at Cleo. "No, it is not."

"Man, they're going to have us hauling around furniture again." Owen rose. "I'm going to take off, but I'll deal with the dishes first. Molly probably had a rough night, too."

Cleo rose with him, then took his face with its night's worth of stubble in her hands. Kissed him enthusiastically.

"You're more a savory sort of man, Owen, but you got just enough sweetness in there. The sun may be up, but me? I'm going back to bed."

"After a full breakfast and, what was it? Two cups of coffee?"

"Nothing stops Cleo from sleeping when she's ready to sleep," Sonya told Owen.

"Unlike my friend here, who, though it's still shy of six in the morning, will go to work."

"Things to do, people to please."

From the tablet came Johnny Cash and June Carter Cash's "Time's a Wastin'."

"That one ain't about work." On impulse, Owen grabbed Cleo, dipped her, and kissed her, also enthusiastically.

"Well, if that's what you've got in mind."

"I've always got that in mind, but Jones and I also have things to do and people to please."

"Add me to that list." Trey got up. "I'll give Owen a hand before Mookie and I take off. I'll grab a shower and change at my place. I'll be back with dinner. Any requests?"

"Surprise us," Sonya told him.

"Done."

Now she cupped his face, looked into those deep blue eyes. "I could've gotten through it without you, because that's what I need to do. But I'm really glad I didn't have to."

She wrapped her arms around him and held on a moment. "Really glad." She pressed her lips to his. "I'm going to go up, pull myself together, and get to work."

"You'll call if you need me."

"I will."

"I'm going to let Yoda and Pye out for a few minutes before I go back to bed. We'll all be up soon."

Of course all four pets raced out when Cleo opened the door. She stood there a moment. "Looks like a lovely day to paint *en plein air*. She'll be fine," she added, still looking out at the lawn, the garden, the woods beyond. "She's committed to this, and when Sonya's committed, it takes a hell of a lot to shake her off."

She turned back. "It's why she stuck with Brandon even with all her doubts about marrying him. Finding him rolling around naked with her cousin in her own bed?" Cleo snapped her fingers. "Done. She might have forgiven him if he'd been contrite, but she'd never have gone back to him.

"I'm only using that asshole as an illustration so maybe you'll worry a little less. She not only won't give up, but when you push Sonya into a corner? She'll come out swinging. Last night? A mistake."

Cleo pointed up to indicate the Gold Room and Hester Dobbs. "Her very big mistake."

"Why is that, especially?" Owen paused as he loaded the dishwasher.

"What she did before, to the seven brides? She has to pay for that. She needs to be stopped. But that happened before. Even though Sonya went through the mirror and saw it all happen, it already happened. Last night? Last night Dobbs hurt those we've all come to care about. That was immediate, that was now."

"She just needed to shake off the sad and find the mad again."

Cleo smiled at Trey. "You know her. I'm just saying this as someone who's known and loved her longer, she won't break. And she won't stop."

"There are times that's just what worries me."

"She needs this house and everything in it—with one exception—as much as this house and everything in it need her. We have the light on our side, and I have to trust that."

"Just do me a favor? Stick close today."

"I can do that. Now, y'all let Yoda and Pye back in before you get on, will you? I'm going to go get the rest of my beauty sleep."

As she walked out, Cleo trailed a finger over Owen's cheek.

Watching her go, Owen shook his head. "That woman's got me, inside and out and back again. And she's right, Trey. Everything she said was right."

"I know it. I'll deal with it. You, too."

"Yeah, me, too. Text me when you're ready to get the food. I'll meet you."

When Sonya came out of a long, hot shower, she found Yoda in the bedroom. A pair of cropped leggings and a roomy T-shirt lay on the neatly made bed.

Gripping the towel around her, Sonya breathed back tears.

"Thanks, Molly. Those are just right for today."

The young Irish housekeeper from so long ago continued to serve. More out of love than duty, Sonya not only felt but truly believed.

As Jack, the boy who'd died in the manor before his tenth birthday, came out to play with Yoda when no one was watching. And Jerome tended to yard work, Eleanor to the plants in the solarium.

Their spirits, and others she couldn't name, continued here, as much a part of Lost Bride Manor as the wood and the glass.

She had a duty to them, and to the seven brides. To Astrid, Catherine, Marianne, Agatha, Lisbeth, Clover, Johanna. For them, even more than for herself and Cleo, she would damn well hold the manor.

It would stay Poole Manor, as it had always been.

For them, she thought as she dressed, she'd stay, she'd work, she'd fight, and she would, somehow, take back the seven stolen rings and break the curse.

If it meant waking at three a.m.—the hour when Hester Dobbs had hurled herself from the cliff wall to seal the curse—then she'd wake at three a.m. If it meant walking through the mirror again and again to witness some horror, then she'd walk through the glass.

And somehow, she'd find the way to take those rings off the fingers of a dead witch.

Though she'd yet to dry it, Sonya pulled her brown hair back in a tail. If she had a call for a virtual meeting, well, she had her emergency makeup in her desk.

As she started out, Yoda jumped up to follow her through her sitting room and down the long hallway. She saw that Cleo's bedroom door stood open a crack. To let Pyewacket come and go as she pleased.

Because she knew her old college roommate well, she expected Cleo could likely sleep until nearly noon.

She wished she had the same talent.

Instead, she walked to the far turret and the library where she kept her office.

She glanced at her mood board, then continued to the desk that faced the wide doorway.

So quiet now, she thought as Yoda wiggled under the desk to keep her company. She could hear the sea roll outside, had come to love the sound of it slapping against the rocks. The morning sun streamed through the windows. On the sill, Xena, the African violet Cleo had given her on the first day of college, thrived, its pink blooms drinking up that sunlight.

Here, in the two-level library, books and beauty and history surrounded her.

She'd been productive here, and would continue to be. She'd done good work, and couldn't ask for more.

She had this room, this house, and all in it—and a ridiculous amount of money to live the life and do the work she wanted— because Collin Poole had chosen to give it all to his twin's daughter.

Death had given her this life, and she couldn't forget it.

She booted up her computer.

Emails first, read and answer. Do any updates or changes to previous work before moving into current jobs.

Then she pressed her fingers to her eyes.

"Oh God, Clover. I need to say all this, and I hope you'll listen. I'm so sorry for what she put you through. I'm sorry for everyone, but especially you. She took your life, and Charlie took his. She stole not just your ring but all your dreams. The home you and Charlie wanted to make here. The art he wanted to make, the gardens you wanted to plant. All the children you might have made."

Taking a breath, Sonya steadied herself. "And last night, hearing it and seeing it and feeling it all happening at once, it twisted up in me. If none of that had happened to you, to any of you all the way back to Astrid, and forward to Johanna, I wouldn't be here.

"I wouldn't have this. I can't make it all not happen, but I swear I'll find a way to make it right. Whatever it takes, I'll make it right for you, for all of you. You're the reason. You're my father's mother. You're my family. I'm going to make it right for my family."

The tablet played Taylor Swift's "Invisible String."

Sonya dashed a tear away, vowing it would be the last shed for the day.

"Yeah, yeah, that's right. It ties us together. All of us. And I promise you, I won't break it. Keep playing, will you? Whatever you want. I think the music's good for both of us."

And settled, finally really settled, Sonya opened the first email, and got to work.

Chapter Two

Sonya took her first break when the cat wandered in, sat, stared at her.

"Time to go out? Well, when you've somehow housebroken a cat, you have to respect that. And I could use a caffeine boost. Let's go, kids."

She walked downstairs, let Yoda and Pye out the front door. Stood a moment in the gorgeous sunshine looking out to sea and the boats plying it.

She went back to the kitchen for a Coke, then stood at the back door to look across the lawn and gardens and toward the thick green woods.

And turned when she heard footsteps.

"You beat my noon estimate by just over twenty minutes. And you're dressed and loaded up. Before coffee."

Cleo set down her Guerrilla Box, folding easel, and stool.

"I've still got coffee in the system from our insanely early breakfast."

Ready for the day in a wide-brimmed hat, cropped pants, and loose tee, Cleo filled a water bottle. "Yoda and Pye can keep me company. If they want to come back in, I'll take care of it."

"All right. It's gorgeous out, so they might as well enjoy it. So, drama or dreamy?"

"I know drama's my natural default, but I think today calls for dreamy."

"We had our share of drama for the day already."

"And there's that. See you later."

Sonya got the door for her. "Enjoy."

"Oh, every minute."

Sipping her Coke, Sonya watched her friend walk toward the pergola while Yoda pranced and Pye slunk over to greet her.

It looked, Sonya thought, like a perfectly peaceful spot on a perfectly peaceful day. You'd never know that vindictive viciousness existed here.

"But I know," she murmured.

She walked through the quiet of the house, into the library, where the music played.

She sat, and opened the next file.

By midafternoon her brain started to fuzz.

"Okay, maybe I need an hour, and some fresh air."

Since the sun shined bright, she grabbed her sunglasses and a ball cap. Not as romantically sexy as Cleo's painting hat, she thought as she pulled her ponytail through the back, but it would do.

She went out the front and to the seawall. The wind whipped just enough to blow at her tail of hair, and to whisk the clouds from her mind. The sea rippled with that wind so the boats on it rolled, and the waves crashed like thunder on the rocks.

Far out she caught a flash, then the leap and dive of a school of dolphins.

Her life had changed, she knew, completely and inevitably, that frigid winter day in Boston when Oliver Doyle II had knocked on her door to tell her an uncle she'd never known existed had left her all this.

And more.

She wanted it more than she'd ever imagined, this great, grand old house and everything in it. Ghosts included.

She turned now to look at it, how strong it stood, how fanciful. And saw a number of windows open.

Molly, she thought with a smile, letting the fresh air in. She wasn't alone in her deep need to tend and protect Lost Bride Manor.

She believed, strongly, one way to do that was simply to live, to do what came next.

She walked, rounding the house to where the gardens they'd planted late in spring thrived in summer. Here the wind softened to a breeze, warm and fragrant with the flowers she'd helped plant.

The cat sprawled on the roof of the Victorian doghouse—complete with turret—Owen had built for Yoda. As she walked, Yoda eased out his brindled hot-dog body, stretched. Both animals joined her as she walked back to where Cleo painted.

On canvas, twisty vines wound up and over the pergola, and dripped, a blooming fountain. Behind it, the green, green woods stood like a misty secret. Below it, spent petals scattered.

It all stood under a sky so blue and pure it all but broke the heart.

On a sigh, Sonya said, "Cleo."

"Dreamy works."

"It's so lovely. It catches in my throat."

"When the hydrangeas really get going, I'm going to do a study of them. Same method. First, one of the bed where we put the goddess. And I think some small studies of individual flowers. Anyway, nearly done. I think."

"Breakfast was a seriously long time ago. I'm going to put a snack together."

"I could use one of those."

"Good. I'll let you know when it's together. We could snack on the deck."

The cat and dog followed her inside and watched avidly as she put a fruit and cheese tray together.

"You'll get yours, too."

As she added glasses of ice and a pitcher of lemonade, a door from overhead slammed three times, like bullets.

Sonya's phone played "Rude" by Magic!

"Yeah, she's all that. But we won't be bullied."

She put a dog biscuit and a handful of cat treats on the tray, lifted it.

The door opened as she walked to it.

"Thanks."

After she walked out, it closed gently behind her.

So much good here, she thought. So much more good than evil.

She set the tray on the table on the deck and started to call to Cleo. But Cleo was already packing her Guerrilla Box.

"Good timing. The bitch is slamming doors."

Cleo pulled sunglasses out of her pocket as she walked to the deck. "It must kill her—metaphorically—to see us both working and enjoying it. And boy, did I."

After setting everything down, Cleo sat, let out a long, satisfied sigh. And the sky-blue toenails peeking out of Cleo's sandals reminded Sonya she hadn't had a pedicure herself in too long.

"I'm going to miss illustrating by the end of the summer, and want a good, interesting, fun job. But for now, this is heaven for me."

She reached for a cracker, loaded it with Camembert.

"Snacking on the deck on a perfect summer afternoon doesn't suck either."

"It does not." Cleo lifted the glass Sonya poured. "To more of this."

"Lots more of this."

"It seems Jack couldn't resist the day either."

Sonya snapped up straight. "You saw him?"

"No, but he was out here. I had a ball wing past me, with Yoda chasing it. But when I turned around—and it took me a couple of seconds to register—nothing. But for—oh, I don't know how long—I could hear Yoda racing around, and I heard Jack laugh. It was eerie, but at the same time . . ."

"It made you smile."

"It did. And I forced myself not to look around again because he's obviously not ready. But here's a kid who died over a century ago out in the yard playing fetch with the dog and laughing. It says a lot about us being here."

Sonya sampled some pepper jack. "And why we're here. Not just me. Yeah, things happened before you moved in, before Trey and Owen spent nights here."

"But it's escalated since."

"It comes and goes, but yes. She's gotten worse, and more of the others have made themselves known. On that part, I wasn't receptive—at all. Thought I was losing it when I'd find the bed made, dishes done, Clover's musical interludes, all of it."

"The portraits in the closet."

Such a jolt, Sonya thought, sipping lemonade, and such a strange joy to find those framed portraits in the studio's storage closet.

"Some by Collin, some painted by my dad. And we're back to Marianne Poole now. The third bride."

"I checked the closet when I got up. No Catherine. Yet."

"But one day we'll open that closet and find her. And if Owen's right, there'll be one more. Astrid, another painting of Astrid. The one in the foyer isn't part of the series."

"More than that?" Cleo plucked a raspberry. "First, Owen's right. And part of the reason he's right is one of them has to paint her. Your uncle or your dad, and it needs to be hung with the other six brides."

"I know—or have to accept—we'll find them when we're supposed to. In the meantime, I'm thinking about doing a full-house search—which, considering the size of the place, all the closets, drawers, trunks—all of it—could take frigging years."

"I'm in." After selecting a small branch, Cleo nibbled on tart green grapes. "You know that. We can draft the men, so that makes four of us. What are we looking for, Son? Do you think you'll find the rings that way?"

"No, way too easy. Add we know she's wearing them, all seven of them. But maybe, if we do a thorough search, we'll find . . ."

"A clue?"

Sonya had to laugh at herself. "It sounds very *Scooby-Doo*, but yeah. The house, the mirror, the residents—past and present—keep doling out pieces. Maybe we'll find more, and maybe a way to put those pieces together."

"I repeat, I'm in. This house is full of treasures, and every time we poke around, I find something I adore. But."

"You're going to be logical, aren't you?"

"In my way. We have a houseful of people who lived and died here over a couple of centuries. And Dobbs has been collecting the rings over that time. If any of them knew how to find the rings, get them back?"

"They'd have found a way to tell us already."

Clover went with U2 and "I Still Haven't Found What I'm Looking For."

"It doesn't mean we won't," Sonya murmured. "But yeah, you're right, the solution's not going to fall in my lap."

"But we look. Something may trigger something else. In fact, I say we finish this up, then pick a room and get to it."

Sonya looked back and up. "Which one?"

Studying the house, Cleo ate another raspberry. "I'm voting for Collin's office. He was the last person to live and to die here, so that's one reason. We've concluded his death was an accident. He didn't die by her hand, her will, her damn black magic. That's two."

"I've gone through it some, but not deep and thorough. It feels intrusive. And that's silly, I know."

Cleo gave Sonya's knee a pat. "It's sensitive, not silly. We'll be respectful."

"It's a good place to begin. Sort of starting in the more now, then working our way back. And it would give you a sense if you wanted to turn it into your office."

"It would. So?"

"Let's get on it."

"I'll take my stuff up to the studio, and meet you there."

Sonya took the tray back in, wrapped it for later, then made her way down the main hall in her labyrinth of a house to Collin's office.

A lovely room, really, she thought. Roomy, good natural light, a view of the side gardens. A big, beautiful old desk and a good leather desk chair, and a second for visitors. Shelves holding books, mementos, photographs. None of which she'd had the heart to touch.

And the painting of the manor with her father's signature in the corner.

How often, she wondered, had Collin looked at that painting and thought about their grandmother's cruelty? Separating orphaned infants, demanding her own daughter claim the child she chose to keep as her own.

Patricia Poole had never paid a price for that cruelty. Maybe her daughter paid it, locked in a world of her own delusions.

But if any answer to the rings lay with either of them, they were beyond her reach.

So she'd start with Collin himself.

She sat at his desk, and did what she hadn't pushed herself to do before. She used the passcode Trey's father had given her and opened the computer.

When Cleo came in, she carried a couple of boxes.

"I thought there might be some papers that should go to Deuce and the legal team. Or other things you might want to pass through them."

"Bound to be. The desk file drawers are full of paper files."

"Then I'll start there."

"He paid bills here. And kept perfect records. I've got all his passwords." She tapped the sheet she'd taken out of the middle drawer. "I put the list there so it'd be handy whenever I made myself do this."

Cleo sat on the floor, opened the deep file drawer. "Everything labeled and in alpha order. I'll put what it seems like you wouldn't need in a box for the Doyles to vet."

"I think I'm going to print out his records and do the same with those because we'll need to wipe the hard drive. We should donate the computer. Neither of us can use it."

"Here's a thought on that. Wipe the hard drive, yeah, but maybe set up the computer in one of the sitting rooms upstairs. Like a guest office. Something Trey or Owen, or one of the family on a visit, could use if they have a need for a desktop."

Lips pursed, Sonya nodded. "Taking ownership and making a purpose for another room. Good idea."

"But that desk stays here. It's beautiful. If I do use this room and you want to move your dad's painting—"

"No, I'd like it to stay here. I've got correspondence on here, too. Emails, business, family—and that's often one and the same, obviously. He kept a calendar on here, too. Birthdays, anniversaries."

As she scanned, Sonya's heart gave a quick lurch.

"Cleo, he has my birthday on here."

"He thought of you."

"He did. Mom's birthday's here. Her and Dad's anniversary. He thought of all of us."

"How does that feel?"

After taking a moment, she smiled. "Good. It feels good."

"Correct answer. Son, I'm keeping the files on house insurance, truck info, appliances, and all that. But he's got files on his health insurance, doctors, dentist, which I'll put in the box."

"Yes. Cleo, he has a file on me."

"On you?"

"My schools, from kindergarten on, the house we shared our senior year of college, my degree, internship, employment. My duplex in Boston. He's even got some of the accounts I worked on. My engagement announcement. When I resigned from By Design, when I started my company."

Her heart broke a little when she saw his scribbled note.

"He's got a note here, Cleo. *Start the new year off fresh. Contact Sonya.* He died before he could start fresh."

"And thought of you," Cleo repeated. "Kept track of you, and it doesn't feel intrusive."

"No, it doesn't. I'm just sorry it all happened the way it did. He wasn't alone. Not just because of ghosts. But he had the Doyles. He always had the Doyles."

"But he could have had you, and your mom."

"Yes."

"He kept track of you, and he left all this to you not just because you were his twin's daughter, but I think because he liked what he saw. He trusted you."

"He's got other notes here and there. My engagement announcement. He adds: *Could and should do better.*"

Cleo's laugh was sharp and wicked. "Points for Collin."

"When I started Visual Art by Sonya? He's written *Going places.*"

"He got that right, too."

"I feel, doing this, seeing this, I'm getting to know him a little. The thing is, Cleo?" She swiveled in the chair to look down at her friend. "We'd have liked him. Me, Mom, you. We'd have liked him."

"Son, we do like him."

"You're right. Okay." She let out a breath, swiveled back. "Okay. Let's keep going."

They went through another file, then another as time ticked away. When it struck her, Sonya stopped, sat back.

"We haven't heard from Clover since we started. We're going through her son's things, through his life, really, file by file."

It came from the music room, from the old Victrola.

Cleo lifted a finger.

"I know that one. My grand-mère sings it. 'God Bless the Child.' It's Billie Holiday. If you ask me, she's talking about Collin, and I guess your dad. But you, too, Son."

"But she doesn't want to be right in here while we do this. And that's okay. I keep getting a clearer, better picture of him, and doing this adds to it. This file here? It's a list of nonprofits he gave to annually. We're going to keep that going."

They spent nearly two hours at it, reading, printing, separating, boxing.

"Even though we're keeping it, I'm going to wipe the hard drive. Meanwhile, the shelves. You should go over all that, see what you want to keep, if anything."

"I'll Cleo it up some, maybe shift some things to other rooms. But I'm loving that brass sextant, and that old time and tide clock. The truth is, I've got a fondness for him, and I'll like having things that he liked in here."

Clover went with Hall & Oates and upbeat with "You Make My Dreams."

Cleo patted the phone in her pocket. "Well, he sure helped make mine come true."

Sonya put an arm around Cleo's shoulders, and felt, for a moment, all three of them connected.

"I've got another idea. The cabinet there."

"It's wonderful. I'd use it unless you want it somewhere else."

"No, it's perfect in here, but right now it's full of photo boxes, and they're full of photos or newspaper clippings, things he printed out from articles. I haven't gone through them all yet. We'll store them somewhere else for now. But later?"

Sonya went to the tall, beautifully carved cabinet, opened both its doors. She took out a box at random, set it on the desk.

"A lot of snapshots, and some more formal portraits. Spans decades and generations, from what I can tell."

"I bet he planned to organize all of them by category at some point." Lifting her hands, Cleo spread her fingers. "Who doesn't have a project like that waiting for the time and the mood?"

"Exactly. More photos stored in the attic. So we could make a gallery. Go through them, pull out the best, go back as far as we have. A Poole family and friends photo gallery."

"I'm liking that idea."

Green eyes flashed determination with some defiance mixed in.

"And, when the time comes, we use the Gold Room. After we evict Dobbs, I still wouldn't want to use that room for guests. It's just . . . I just don't. But a room, that room, dedicated to photos, and you know we'll find tintypes, and probably miniature portraits. If there are any family members we can't find, maybe we can reproduce portraits."

"I say, this is genius. I'd white sage the room first. Three times. Then we clean it out. Get whatever we want in there out of storage, and make a gallery. And we turn the dark to light."

"I know he didn't live here, but he was born here. I'm going to put up some pictures of my father, as a little boy, and one of my parents' wedding photos."

"More genius," Cleo began, even as Clover blasted out Tina Turner. *You're simply the best.*

"Let's take a few of the boxes into the dining room. Big table."

Sonya pulled another out. "We'll pour some wine, sort through. The ones we think we might use go in one box. Ones we won't, the other."

"I'm for that, especially the wine. We won't recognize everyone, though."

"Unsure, first box. Owen may know, or Deuce or one of the older Poole cousins."

"This is a plan, a very solid plan. And it's one more way to turn what she pulled last night on its ass."

By the time the men arrived, Sonya and Cleo had photos spread out, others in designated boxes, and had just poured a second glass of wine.

"What's all this?" Trey asked.

"Sonya's genius idea. Once we kick Dobbs back to hell, we're going to do a Poole Family and Friends Gallery in the Gold Room."

"Look at this, Trey." Sonya pulled one out of the gallery box. "It's your dad with Collin, at, I'm guessing, late teens or early twenties. You look so much like him. They're at the beach somewhere."

"Couple of buff studs," Cleo added as Trey grinned over the photo of Collin and Deuce wearing swim trunks and standing on the sand in front of the ocean.

"They used to talk about this. This has to be when they were in college, and drove down one summer to—I think—the Outer Banks. They tried to learn how to surf, and failed, but had a hell of a good time."

"I guess you might not have a clue, yet, as to how many photos are socked away in this house." Owen scanned what was spread around the big table. "How far back are you going?"

"Back to Arthur Poole."

Now Owen scratched his jaw. "You do realize they didn't have cameras back then?"

"They did miniatures, and I bet we'll find some. Then you have tintypes. But we're going to need your help to put names with faces."

He gave Sonya a shrug. "I'll help where I can, but not until I eat. We got lobster rolls."

"Excellent choice." Cleo rose. "We should eat on the deck. What did you get to go with them?"

"Potato salad," Trey told her, "coleslaw, and at our favorite chef's insistence, lemon bars."

"Bree knows what she knows." Cleo patted Trey's cheek as she moved by. "Where's the rest of our pooch family?"

"They're all outside. Including the cat." Since he didn't intend to settle on a cheek pat, Owen pulled her in, took her mouth.

"Mmm, since you're that hungry, you can help me set things up on the deck."

"We're really having fun doing this." Sonya rose and put her arms around Trey as much for the hug as the kiss. "We actually started— well, after work—going through and clearing out Collin's office so Cleo can use it."

"That's good." He drew her out to the kitchen, where he got a beer for himself and one for Owen.

"I hope you think so when I tell you we have a good-sized box of papers we weren't sure what to do with, and decided to dump it on the Doyle lawyers."

"That's fine. We'll take care of it."

"I went through the computer files. I'll tell you about that over dinner. It's mostly just sweet, and Owen should hear it, too. But I'm going to wipe the hard drive when we're done, and we're going to set up a kind of guest office in one of the sitting rooms. Anyone who stays here could use it if they need or want to."

"More fine." Studying her, he sipped his beer. "You've been busy."

"I needed busy today. And ending with the photos, and the plans for them? As Cleo so elegantly put it, it turns what Dobbs pulled last night on its ass."

"You know what one of the apparently endless things I find most appealing about you is?"

"Oh, do tell."

He ran a hand down the tail of her hair that reminded him of rich maple syrup.

"You always bounce back. Whatever gets tossed at you, you bounce back from it and keep going."

"And here I thought it was my elevated sense of style and winning personality."

"Those make the list."

In that moment, something in the way he looked at her had her heart trembling.

Owen burst in from the deck. "Take-out containers won't do it for her. She wants bowls and shit."

And the moment struck him, he looked from one to the other as he pulled out serving bowls. "What?"

"Just admiring the lady."

With the moment broken, Sonya shot out a smile. "You'll want serving spoons. And since it's Cleo, she'll want some hot sauce."

And since she knew Cleo, Sonya added cloth napkins.

While they sat on the deck in the warm evening breeze and enjoyed the feast, Sonya and Cleo filled them in on the day.

"So after I worked and Cleo created her magnificent and dreamy watercolor, we decided to tackle Collin's office."

"So I hear." Owen bit into his lobster roll.

"Sonya took the desktop, I took the file drawers. Your uncle was an organized and efficient soul."

"He was an artist, sure, but also a businessman. Pooles, by and large, tend to be organized and efficient."

"He didn't break that rule. Every appliance in the house, all the electronics, the water heaters, the furnaces, all filed with date of purchase, manuals. If there'd been any maintenance or repairs, it's in there."

"That's just SOP."

On a laugh, Sonya shook her head at Owen. "Cleo doesn't keep any of that."

"Why do I need a manual when I'm going to call somebody to

fix something anyway? And if somebody fixed it, then it's fixed. But knowing Sonya, I kept all that."

"The computer files. Correspondence. I printed out emails I thought someone might want a record of, or just for sentiment. He had a file on me. You're not surprised," she said to Trey. "Did you know?"

"Figured. I knew from my father he'd kept track of you. Being he was efficient, he'd have kept a file. Does it bother you?"

"No. It gave me the feeling if I'd needed it, really needed it, he'd have stepped in to help. He added little notes here and there, and that felt . . . sweet. He also had a file of his annual donations, and I want to continue those. Is there a way to make them in his name?"

Touched, Trey put a hand over hers. "We can arrange that, sure."

"Great. And all that led us to the photographs, which is where you came in."

"I like the office," Cleo added. "I put off using it because I didn't know if it would feel right. But spending the time in there today, it did. And I'm better off not mixing office stuff with art. I tend to get scattered that way."

"Really?"

Cleo gave Owen the hard eye. "Amusing."

"If you were efficient along with everything else, you'd be perfect. Anybody who wants perfect is stupid. I'm not stupid."

She lifted her wineglass, sipped. "And somehow, strangely romantic. In any case, we had a damn good day."

"One door-slamming incident's all she managed."

"Oh, she shook the walls a little on the third floor." Cleo waved it off like a gnat. "Weak sauce."

"She'll never be stronger than the two of you." Because he believed it absolutely, Trey lifted his beer in a toast. "Meaner, but not stronger. You're doing more to squeeze her out every day. Sitting here like this, having a good meal, dogs—and cat—in the yard. It counts."

"Going through Collin's office counts, too," Owen decided. "Needs to be done. He loved that desk—who wouldn't? Solid mahogany, custom-made for one of the Pooles—can't remember right off, but late eighteen hundreds, near the turn of the century. Pristine condition."

He started to take a drink, then set down his beer. "You're keeping it, right? In the office."

"Are you worried because it likely weighs a metric ton and we want you to move it?"

"I am," Trey said immediately. "My back and I are definitely worried about that."

"There's that, but mostly, come on, man, it's freaking magnificent. It suits the room, the purpose."

Genuinely amused now at his passion, Cleo arched her eyebrows. "Then you'll be pleased I feel the same. I fell for it at first sight. Now I have two magnificent desks. And this one, you don't have to muscle up or down stairs."

"Good. That's good." But he kept those green eyes on her amber ones. "And the cabinet in there. Jacobean."

"Also staying."

With that, he relaxed enough for another swig of beer. "That's the right choice."

"Look at that, will you?" Trey nodded toward the yard where the dogs, after a break to flop awhile, were up and running again. "I just saw the cat jump on Mookie's back."

"Hitching a ride," Owen said with a grin. "And Mooks's as into it as she is."

Cleo let out a roll of laughter as she watched. "Just *How about a ride, big guy*. And he's giving her one."

Chapter Three

They lingered awhile over lemon bars and cappuccino, then settled in the dining room.

Between Owen and the Poole family book Deuce had made for Collin, they identified some.

"I can't be sure on a bunch of these. Most of them are from before I was born. Clarice or Connor are better bets. Maybe Mike," Owen added, as he considered his cousins. "Maybe, but I'd try Clarice first. She's more into all this."

"I could invite her over to look through them. But there are more boxes, so it wouldn't be quick work."

"Better you give me a box or two, and I take them to her. She'll get to them. It'll pull her right in."

"No rush. I'm going to get another box," Sonya decided. "If we can go through those. I'll use one box for the ones we know, one for ones we'd like to frame and put up but don't know, and you take that to her. Third box for what we don't plan to use."

"Poole efficient," Trey commented.

"Can't help it."

"Give me one. I'll have my parents look through."

"That'd be great. I'd love to have names for all of them eventually, but we can start this way. I'll go grab another box."

When Sonya went to the office to grab another box from where she'd stacked them on the desk, one sat apart. And she recognized the photo lying on top of the box as one of Johanna.

"All right, Clover, this one next."

Her phone rang out with "It Wasn't Me."

"If you didn't . . ." She picked up the photograph. "Johanna? Maybe. Whoever, this one next."

She carried it back to the dining room.

"Clover—and it's still playing on my phone."

"She went with Chuck Berry," Owen observed.

"While I couldn't have said that, I got the *it wasn't me* right off. This box was set aside from the others, and this photo on the lid."

"Johanna." Trey took the photo. "Maybe she's giving you an assist now, too."

"Or Collin," Owen put in.

"That's a good thought." Cleo pointed at him. "If Collin's still here—and of course he is—he'd weigh in on this. At least it seems he would."

"Whoever did this, wants this box next."

She sat, opened the lid, and immediately saw more photos of Johanna, of her and Collin, of both of them with Trey's parents.

"Oh, is this you, Trey? On Collin's hip?"

"Yeah, my parents have a copy of this shot. Johanna's holding Anna, and Collin's got me. It couldn't have been long before their wedding."

"This definitely belongs in the gallery."

Sonya started to lift a pile out, then dug deeper.

"Wait! Tintypes, and yes! Miniatures, framed." Lifting more, she spread them out carefully. "It's—God."

"The seven brides," Trey finished. "They're all going to be here. And these weren't stored like this, not when we did inventory."

Looking through, he shook his head. "Not like this. I'd remember it. We didn't go through every box, just identified photos, but there wasn't one just like this."

"It may or may not be a clue, Son, but it's a major find, and a huge help with the gallery."

"It's Clover," Sonya murmured, and she picked up a photo. "Clover and Charlie on their wedding day. I saw this—dreamed, saw them in this meadow, dancing at their wedding."

"They look so happy. Young and happy," Cleo added.

And Clover played Dylan's "Wedding Song."

"We'll frame this. It'll go in the gallery, but before that, we'll put it out, and with Collin and Johanna's wedding photo, and any we find."

"Like this one. Lisbeth, right? The fifth bride. Formal wedding shot." Owen held it up.

"Yes. God, she's radiant even in a photo."

"I've got Agatha and Owen. Very formal. A handsome couple," Cleo said. "Oh, here's another—his second marriage—Owen and Moira. You know, I have to say they both look happier."

"I've got a tintype here," Trey offered, "and it's Marianne and Hugh Poole."

"The miniatures. Catherine—second bride. Not from her wedding, but there wouldn't have been time, since she died on her wedding night. And Astrid—they must've had this done before the wedding. Maybe as a gift to Collin, because you can see enough of her dress. It's her wedding dress.

"We have them all. All seven brides."

"And more," Trey added. "More photos. One of Clover in front of the manor."

"How can women carry all that around?" Owen wondered. "That's a baby mountain."

"We have steel spines," Cleo told him. "There's snow on the ground—a lot. Snow in her hair. She's laughing."

Cleo played "Cosmic Charlie."

"I don't think the Grateful Dead's a pun here," Owen observed. "Great song."

"It couldn't have been long before the twins were born. Patricia Poole missed these," Trey said. "When she tried to erase Clover and your dad from Poole history, she missed these. Or whoever she sent in did, since she wouldn't set foot in the manor."

"I won't exclude her from the gallery."

"Wouldn't hurt my feelings if you did," Owen told her.

"I won't, because she's part of the history. An ugly part, but part.

However I'm going to put up the most unflattering picture of Patricia Poole we find."

Trey grinned at her. "You can be mean."

"Damn right, I can. But I'm not going to think of that, or her, now. We have all the brides here, and I'm going to hunt for frames to suit each photo we choose. Of them and everyone else.

"And when that witch is gone, we're going to hang them and turn that room into something good, something positive and important."

A series of doors slammed; the chandelier overhead swayed as if in a brisk wind.

Sonya merely snarled at the ceiling. "Yeah, I'm talking about you. You're on your way out, so get used to it."

Once again, Trey laid a hand over Sonya's. "It might take her a while."

"Tonight, next week, next freaking year, she's going. And I have another goal now with these photos."

"You're going to need a plan, measurements, a grid," Owen said. "Once you decide how many you want up, all those different sizes and shapes. How you want them. You have to map it out."

"My company's called Visual Art for a reason. I can map it out. But I wouldn't mind your input. That goes for everyone here. I mean everyone," she said, raising her arms to encompass the manor. "All suggestions welcome."

"I'll have plenty. But now? I'm heading up." Cleo looked at Owen as she rose. "How about a ride, big guy?"

She started out, then laughed when he got up, swept her up, and carried her.

"It's a hell of a thing you're doing, Sonya. It's a hell of a thing you'd think of doing it."

"I owe them." Gently, Sonya ran a fingertip over photos. "All of them. Even Patricia. If she hadn't done what she did, my grandparents wouldn't have had the son they loved. My dad, my mom, me, we wouldn't have had our life in Boston. I might not even have been born, but if I had, I would've had a different life.

"I like my life. So I owe them."

She smiled at him. "I'll sort through more tomorrow, and make that box for Clarice, one for your parents. I didn't realize how late it got to be. So why don't you come upstairs with me and remind me one of the reasons why I like my life, right here, right now."

She woke at three, but not to walk. She heard the drifting piano music, the quiet weeping, the murmurs and sighs of those who couldn't rest.

Though the mirror didn't pull at her, she sat up, then squeezed Trey's hand when he took hers.

"I'm awake," she told him. "I'm aware. I want to see Dobbs."

He rose with her, and they went to the terrace doors together.

She stood, Hester Dobbs, on the seawall. Her black dress swirled, her dark hair flew in the brisk Atlantic wind. She faced that sea, as she had night after night for over two centuries.

And to seal the curse on the manor, on the brides to come, she lifted her arms to the sky. And leaped.

"Does she feel it?" Sonya wondered. "Every night? Does she feel the wind whipping around her? Does she feel the fall, and her body breaking on the rocks? The pain of that? That one instant of shock and frigid water lashing at her?"

"I think she does. I think she has to."

"Has to?"

"For it all to hold, Sonya, for her to keep her grip on this place. Maybe she wasn't mad when she bespelled Collin Poole back then. Maybe she was only half-mad when she killed Arthur Poole."

Turning, he nudged Sonya back to the bed.

"She was sure as hell crazy when she killed Astrid and laid the curse. And coming back here, to seal that curse with her own blood? There's no sanity left."

"You think she wants to feel it, every night. Over and over."

In bed, he drew her to him. "Yeah, I do."

"Because, in her madness, she sees it as power. Her choice, her blood. And through it, she remains in the manor. In her madness, that's all that matters. That's all there is for her. Mistress of the manor, forever."

"But she's not." He brushed a kiss on her forehead that struck her as both soothing and confident. "And she never will be."

"No, she won't. It's quiet again. The house is quiet again."

"Can you sleep?"

"Yes."

Closing her eyes, she slid into the quiet.

In the morning, Sonya's decision to use the gym came partly from a need for routine, and partly from simple defiance.

But she found herself grateful Yoda and Pye wanted to come with her.

When she opened the servants' door, they walked through with her, and down the stairs. She angled off from storage areas, from the home theater, and into the well-equipped gym.

Her uncle, she thought, had known how to perfectly design the manor, making it his own all while respecting its history.

"And that's just what I'm doing."

She looked over at the rack of free weights, nodded.

"We're going to keep the muscles in tune. This battle may be more mental than physical, but it's all connected, right? At least that's what that overly perky and impossibly ripped trainer keeps saying. So I'm going with an advanced session today."

She switched on the TV, chose the app, the program.

"Fifty-six minutes? Well, Jesus! Maybe that's a little ambitious for—"

As she spoke, the servants' bell began to ring, and kept ringing.

The Gold Room.

"Go ahead," she called out. "Go ahead and waste your time and energy. Me, I'm putting mine to good use."

She started the session.

"I may regret it," she muttered, "but I'm doing it."

Twenty minutes in, slicked with sweat, she regretted it. But she kept going. Part of it, she could admit as her muscles burned, was that incessant ringing.

A half hour in, she took a break to guzzle water like a camel, to towel off some sweat. And noticed the ringing had stopped.

Bolstered by the fact she'd outlasted Dobbs, she pushed play, dug down, and finished the routine.

Maybe she had to lie on the floor in a groaning puddle for a minute, but she'd done it.

Yoda came over to lie down beside her. The cat curled on a weight bench and watched her with mild disdain.

"Which one of you is going to help me up?"

Since neither volunteered, Sonya raised to a sitting position and ordered herself to finish with a ten-minute stretch.

She considered herself an Amazon when she made it back upstairs without limping.

When she walked back to the kitchen to refill her water bottle, it surprised her to see Cleo sitting at the counter with coffee and a Toaster Strudel.

"You're up early."

"Not as early as you, obviously. Did you shower in your clothes?"

"Muscle Up routine." Still a little breathless, Sonya pressed a hand to her heart. "Brutal. But she kept ringing the damn bell. Dobbs gave up. I didn't."

"That's my Sonya. I, on the other hand, am up because I have a yen to take a sail. You could come with me."

"Wish I could, but I'm already going to be late for work, since I plan to take a shower for a couple hours."

"Such a responsible soul. I, again on the other hand, am taking *The Siren* out for a sail. They're calling for thunderstorms late this afternoon, so I'll get in my sail, go by the grocery store and other errands, and be back home to paint in the studio before the storms hit."

"I have to point out there's responsible in there, starting with the sail." Deciding she deserved a reward, Sonya opened the fridge for a

Coke. "It wouldn't be responsible to have a gorgeous little Sunfish and not sail it."

"You're right. We're responsible girls. So let's just be girls tonight, since Owen and Trey both have work this evening, I have a plan."

"Tell me the plan before this sweat rolls off me and leaves a puddle on the floor."

"A big, giant girl salad for dinner. A solid session sorting the photos. Then a big, giant, buttery, salty mountain of popcorn, a bottle of wine, and a girly movie in pj's."

"And this is only one of the myriad reasons we're friends. I'm in. And now I'm also in the shower. Enjoy your sail."

After a blissful shower, Sonya tossed on sweat shorts, a tee, then decided the hell with her hair, and pulled it, still damp, into a tail.

When she sat at her desk, and Yoda scooted under it, she rolled her slightly aching shoulders.

"I feel strong and freaking righteous. Okay, Clover, let it rip."

The tablet rocked out with Destiny's Child and "Independent Women Part I."

"And that's damn right. I am."

As she booted up her computer, her phone signaled a text.

The Ryder Sports group with a request. For a video call at ten.

"Well, crap."

She answered in the affirmative, then pulled out her emergency video call makeup.

"Independent, yeah, but no business meetings with a naked face."

With a little time to spare, she dealt with emails, started work on a proposal for an ad campaign for a local business.

"Okay, Clover, music off for now."

And rolling her shoulders again, entered the call.

Burt Springer greeted her first. "Good morning! Thanks for making yourself available on such short notice."

"Never a problem. It's good to see everyone."

And everyone, Sonya noted, included Miranda Ryder, the steely and steady head of the company.

"We've got some progress reports to discuss, but before we get to that, we have an angle to run by you. The visuals you created, using regular people rather than models, wearing Ryder gear, using Ryder gear in their everyday lives, are the heart of the campaign. We'd like to expand on that."

"All right."

"Take the young man on the Ryder bike, heading to work in his business suit. Is he local? Available?"

"Eddie—he works for Doyle Law Offices. He's interning there. As for availability, I can certainly contact him. I do have several more photos of him."

Maybe muscle and mind did connect, Sonya decided, as she thought a step ahead. "But you don't want the same look. A different outfit, different day, different activity? Is that what you're after?"

"Got it in one."

"Casual clothes, heading out to meet friends for pizza. Out for an evening—sunset ride—with a date? Like that."

"Sunset ride with a date?" Livvy, public relations, put an index finger to each side of her head. "That's a winner."

"We'd like him to wear Ryder shoes, Ryder gear. You get his sizes, we'll provide them," Burt told her. "Then there's your lovely and generous friend, Cleo."

"I can speak for her, and say she'll be happy to. More yoga? Different poses, different outfits. Maybe something outdoors. She has a gorgeous little Sunfish. She already has a Ryder PFD, but you could add to that."

The banging started overhead. Sonya fisted a hand under the desk as Yoda squeezed between her feet.

Miranda Ryder's eyebrows shot up. "Is there a problem, Sonya?"

"They're calling for thunderstorms."

"It sounds like the storm's inside the house."

"It really does. Let me say, I think this is a terrific angle. I'm sure I can engage the same photographer, and I'll contact Eddie. I can already give you Cleo's sizes. Which others do you want to add?"

The banging stopped abruptly as she started the list. And the door-bell began to bong.

"Sorry, just give me one minute."

She rose quickly. Though she knew it was Dobbs, she looked out the window first. Then moved over to close the library's pocket doors.

It at least dulled the sound.

"Sorry again," she said when she sat back down. "It's a glitch I really need to fix. Old houses." She added a smile.

"Maybe it's haunted," Burt said with a quick laugh.

"Oh, no question about that." She added her own quick, and casual, laugh. "It adds to the ambiance."

She took notes, added her own ideas and vision. And when the house fell quiet again, felt as she had in the gym.

She'd outlasted Dobbs.

It took over an hour, and included a couple of bitchy door slams, but she got through it. And felt she'd barely missed a beat.

When she ended the call, she sat back, closed her eyes.

Clover congratulated her with Gaga and Grande and "Rain on Me."

"Yeah, I made it through that storm." Reaching down, she gave Yoda a rub. "We did. Now I've got a lot of unexpected work to do. Good for me! Calls first, Clover. I need to get Trey's mom and her camera on board."

But she stayed as she was another moment, eyes closed. Because she could see it. See how she'd work the series.

In sports, in life, Ryder's got you.

She pulled up her contacts and started making calls.

Halfway through, Yoda gave her The Look.

"Okay, I'll let you out. I need another caffeine boost anyway."

She let him out the front, then wound her way back to the kitchen.

A ball sat on the island, and made her laugh.

"Fine with me, Jack."

She got a Coke, and after tossing the ball outside where she knew Jack and Yoda would play fetch until the dog was worn out, she went back up to work.

And sent a text to both Trey and Owen. It seemed smart not to phrase it as a request, but a fait accompli.

> Ryder's decided to expand on the visual campaign. More photos! Which Corrine will take. And she'll work out the schedule to suit everyone. Meanwhile, I'll need your sizes. Shoes, pants, shirts. I promise, it'll be painless. And you get to keep the gear!

Setting her phone aside, she made the next contact by email. Glanced at her phone when it signaled. Owen's response was:

> Come on, man. Seriously?

She just smiled, wrote the email. And Trey's came through.

> Why are you doing this to me?

She sent the email, then answered both texts together.

> Yes, my favorite cousin, seriously—free shoes! And you both did this to yourselves by being so handsome and photogenic. And to thank you, I'll learn how to make another manly meal suitable for summer.

Owen came back fast.

> Pulled pork sandwiches, hand-cut fries, roasted corn on the cob. Strawberry shortcake.

If you think I can be bought with a meal, Trey responded, you're probably right.

> Done. Saturday!

Without a clue what all that meant, she texted Cleo.

> Can you see if your mom or grand-mère have recipes for
> pulled pork, hand-cut fries, roasted corn on the cob, and
> strawberry shortcake? If not, I'll try Bree, my mom, or Mr.
> Google. Then can you pick up what we need for all of it?
> For four people. I'll explain later.

> They have recipes for everything. Pye and I just finished our lovely
> sail. I want to hear the explanation. Home in a couple hours.

Sonya acknowledged with a heart emoji, then went back to work.

Once she finished setting up the new Ryder project, she shifted back to other clients.

Who knew that less than a year since starting her own business, she'd have an actual client list? And work, a nice flow of it, that challenged and satisfied.

And if that client list continued to grow, and the work continued to flow, she'd start thinking about—possibly—hiring an assistant. Part-time, and remote would be best, considering.

She cast a look at the ceiling.

At least for now.

She'd give it a few more months, then if—fingers crossed—the business earned and needed it, she'd start looking for the right person.

Yoda came back up, and instead of wiggling under her desk, just flopped down on the rug and went instantly to sleep.

Ten minutes later, with the library windows open, she heard Cleo drive up. She let the sleeping dog lie and went down to help Cleo bring in the groceries.

"It's a lot," Cleo said. "We had some of it, but it's a lot." She handed Sonya two cloth grocery bags. "Why are we making pulled pork and all the rest?"

"Actually, I have to make it because it was my deal. But I'm counting on your help. Oh, you got flowers, too."

"I got flowers, too. Took two more paintings into Bay Arts, bought the cutest pair of sandals I don't need but want, stopped by the bakery, so we're having double fudge brownies with our popcorn."

As she reeled it off, they walked through the house, set things down, walked out for the rest. Like Yoda, Pye decided it was time for a nap and trotted upstairs.

"Now, why did I buy a boneless pork shoulder?"

"I bribed Owen and Trey. Ryder wants more photos."

Cleo frowned. "Is something wrong with what they have?"

"No, everything's right, so right they want more. This includes you. Other yoga poses—free outfit. Outdoor setting. Maybe you sailing *The Siren*, or lounging outside with a book. Free outfit either way.

"You're in, right?"

"Sorry, I lost track after *free outfit*. Of course I am! Fun. Which isn't the reaction you'd get from either Owen or Trey. So food bribery." She offered a hand for a high five. "Smart."

"I hope I think so Saturday when I try to pull this—ha-ha—off."

"I'm getting free outfits so I'll be your sous chef. Now, let's get the rest of this put away. I'm ready to paint."

"I'll take care of the flowers. I've put a good day in so far. Long virtual meeting to get this rolling. She tried to screw it up."

Cleo glanced back as she put things in the pantry. She didn't have to ask who. "How?"

"Banging, slamming, doorbell ringing. I said stuff about thunderstorms, then electric glitches, old houses. I guess they bought it—because we just kept going."

"That's what we do. We keep going. Let me know before if you come up to the studio."

"Sure. Why?"

"I'm working on something I want to keep to myself for now. If you've got the flowers, I'm heading up."

"I've got them. I'll knock off when you do. Or if you work later, I'll come down and start on the photos."

"Works."

Cleo glanced outside at the first rumble of thunder. "And I beat the storm. A good thunderstorm's like good music. It energizes."

Thunder grumbled again as Cleo left, and Sonya tended to the flowers as the storm built. Yoda came down and stuck close as she placed the fresh arrangements.

While Clover played Springsteen's "Thunder Road," she carried arrangements to her bedroom and to Cleo's.

Though Molly had closed the windows to prevent the rain from coming in, Sonya couldn't resist.

She threw open her balcony doors, let the wind whip. Wrapped in it, she watched the storm lash and slash over the sea.

The angry sky hurled lightning so the air snapped. The lightning called the thunder that roared—a pack of lions—over sea and land. Rain drummed in a mad rhythm outdone only by the crash of waves on the rocky shore.

"It's beautiful, and it's terrible." Because he trembled a little, she picked Yoda up to cuddle. "And it's real power."

She kissed his nose. "Let's go put the new mood board together. And don't you worry. The manor's stood against countless storms."

She glanced up as she carried the dog out with her.

"And it's going to keep standing."

In contrast to the afternoon storms, the evening moved smooth and quiet. And ended with laughter and sighs as the credits rolled on a clever and frothy rom-com.

Comfortable in pj's, Sonya let out one more sigh. "Just what I needed. How about you?"

"Bull's-eye. I love men, and I'm especially fond of the two who come around here. But there's just nothing like a girls' night. This one hit all the marks."

"One more left to hit." Sonya reached for the wine bottle and poured the last of it into their two glasses. "How about we take this wine, our faithful companions, and have ourselves a walk around outside?"

"The perfect nightcap."

Yoda scrambled up when they switched off the TV, then raced down the steps from the second floor of the library. Danced in a circle.

Pyewacket took her time. She stretched, she considered, then poured herself off the couch like water from a jar.

When they reached the front door, the dog shot out like a cannon-ball while the cat slunk out and into the shadows.

Sonya breathed in the night.

"Everything's so clear now. We've got the moon, the stars, the sea."

"And our own little stars with our fairy lights. They bring the joy. We've had a good day, Son," Cleo added as they began to walk.

"Damn good day. We hold on to good days, and we're going to keep piling them up. I like knowing we've got that box of photos for Clarice Poole to go through, and one for the Doyles."

"It's fun going through them. Looking at the hairstyles, the clothes. You know what'd be nice? If when we really start digging through — trunks, drawers, closets—we found some photos of the staff who've worked here."

"Oh! We'd put them in the gallery! There's bound to be at least a few somewhere. The manor wouldn't be the manor without them. We'll start looking."

When they reached the back, Sonya stopped. "Speaking of looking."

Lights sparkled on the pergola; solar lanterns and lamps glowed.

"We did good work here, Son. We had a hell of a foundation, but we added to it."

"In all my dreams about living in a big old house, I never imagined I'd have the ocean out front and all this back here."

"It's a jewel, and we're going to keep polishing it."

Yoda let out a growl, a snarl. At Cleo's feet, Pye arched her back, hissed.

Out of the shadow of the house it came, eyes glinting red.

"Sweet Jesus." Cleo grabbed for Sonya's hand. "Is that a wolf?"

Dark as the night, it stood between them and the manor. The pretty lights glinted on fangs, long and sharp.

"It's not real," Sonya managed, because she wanted to believe it.

"Real or not, it's in the way. Back up slow. I don't think throwing wineglasses at it will do much. We need a rock, a big, thick stick. Something."

As they took a step back, the wolf, dark as the night, stalked forward.

Yoda's barks grew vicious, guttural in a way Sonya hadn't known he had in him.

"We have to stay calm," she said as she struggled not to just cut and run. "She wants fear."

"Hard not to give it to her. But . . . why didn't it just jump us from behind? Maybe it can't. Just can't."

It looked at her, Sonya thought, with a kind of feral hunger that turned her blood to ice. "I don't have it in me to test that theory."

In that moment, to her shock, Yoda, snarling, snapping, charged forward. "Oh God, no."

Even as she rushed after her dog, the cat streaked by her.

Both cat and dog leaped, and what had been the wolf dissolved into smoke.

Because her legs gave way, Sonya sat on the grass. "She didn't expect that. She didn't factor that in."

Yoda sniffed at the smoke, sneezed twice, then hurried over to Sonya.

"They protected us." She gathered Yoda into her arms. "A little dog and a snooty cat."

"She wanted us to run." Cleo picked up Pye and stroked. "It was close, but we didn't. She wanted us to scream—again hair's breadth, but we didn't. And you're right, she didn't expect a sweet little dog and a slinky cat to fight."

"But they did." Steadier, Sonya got to her feet. "A damn good day."

"That's right." Stepping over, Cleo tapped her glass to Sonya's. "Here's to us and our fierce defenders."

With a nod, Sonya drained her glass.

Chapter Four

Sonya plowed through the week, juggling work projects, taking virtual meetings, and completing a mood board for the additional Ryder project.

She stood studying it when Cleo came upstairs.

"I just checked the Friday spaghetti sauce I've got simmering. I got enough going it'll do for lunch tomorrow if—"

She caught sight of the board. "Well, you work fast."

"They need the basic pose ideas to get the wardrobe. Mood and activity matter as much as sizes."

"You've got this guy decked out in ski gear, skis included, and a crapload of snow."

"They want some winter sports shots. They're doing a model search and hiring a photographer. One of the Ryders has a chalet in Switzerland, so skiing, sledding, snowman building, and so on. And they want my input."

"First, they really respect your work and your brain. Second, they're seriously going all out."

"They do, and they are."

"And this would be me at the tiller of a small sailboat, and again, doing yoga in a garden."

"It would."

"I approve."

"Good, so did the powers that be."

It would work, Sonya thought. It would not just slide right into the campaign already begun but boost it up.

"They should finalize wardrobe next week, and ship it. Here. Corrine and I will sort through. Meanwhile, I'm shutting down early. I'm going up to the attic, start that full-house search at the top."

"Give me a half hour and I'll pitch in. While we're searching, we can find what we'd like to set up the guest office."

"Already there—thinking-wise." She smiled when she heard the sound of a ball bouncing down in the main hall, and Yoda's scramble after it. "And it looks like Yoda's occupied, thanks to Jack. I'm going to grab some sticky notes. I can slap one on pieces and places I've been through."

"That's an organized and efficient plan, as usual. I've got some bankers boxes in the studio. We can put a couple together just in case."

Sonya got her sticky notes, a pen. They walked up to the third floor together, and Sonya paused on the landing to look past Cleo's studio to the Gold Room.

"She's been quiet since the big bad wolf."

"In there spinning her webs," Cleo muttered. "Like the toxic spider she is. Hardly any banging around in there the last day or two. All right then, about a half hour."

While Cleo walked down to her studio, Sonya continued up to the attic.

Daunting was her first thought when she scanned the large and crowded area. And hadn't she put off really dealing with it for that very reason?

"Pick something," she told herself. "Start."

She chose what she thought Cleo would call a chifforobe. And a huge piece Owen would, no doubt, identify by period and type of wood.

She opened the doors first. And found absolutely nothing.

One side had a series of drawers. All empty. As were the two larger drawers at the bottom.

She closed the drawers, put a sticky note on one of the doors.

Still, maybe she'd move the piece down to one of the bedrooms. Once the house was fully hers—with no Hester Dobbs looming.

"It makes a statement."

She moved on. Nightstands, a small dresser, an elegant little slant-top desk.

She backtracked, and instead of just leaving the notes, wrote possible destinations for each piece.

She started to move through to the trunks for a change of pace, then pulled off one more dustcover.

Another desk. Handsome, she thought, and just a little feminine with the way it curved. Drawers in both sides, one in the middle. She'd need Owen for the type of wood, but it had a kind of brindle finish to her eye.

Like Yoda.

She opened a drawer, and to her surprise found a box of stationery. The pale pink pages had a flowing script header.

Miss Lisbeth Anne Poole

"Lissy," she whispered. "This was your desk. You sat here, right here, writing letters. And surely dreaming of your wedding day."

Sonya lifted out the stationery, set it on top of the desk, opened another drawer.

"Oh! They never cleaned it out. Owen and Moira. Couldn't bear it, I guess."

She found notepaper where Lisbeth had drawn hearts with her name and Edward's inside. With their initials inside. Where she'd practiced writing *Mrs. Edward Whitmore, Lisbeth Poole Whitmore* in perfect cursive.

She found hairpins and clips, pencils, a fountain pen and a bottle of ink. A small box holding theater stubs, playbills, a pretty pink stone.

Then the photographs. A framed one of Lisbeth and the young man Sonya recognized as Edward in a tarnished silver frame. One of Lisbeth with her parents, one with friends—Sonya recognized the woman who'd been in the music room the night she'd seen them. The woman in the blue dress.

"We'll keep your things, Lissy. We'll polish the picture frame and set it out. And we'll use the desk. It's going in the guest office."

She noted it on the sticky note, started to move on.

One of the dustcovers slid to the floor.

"I see. Thanks." She wound her way to the chair, one with that same finish and an inlaid fabric pad with pastel pink and blue flowers.

"It's perfect, of course it is. This is her desk chair."

As she ran a hand over its back, she felt the pull.

And saw she now stood in front of the mirror. The glass blurred with color, and she heard music. Something tinny and far, far away.

"Now? Here?" She looked back, wishing for Cleo, but the pull proved too strong.

"All right, all right. I want answers, so . . ."

She took a breath; she stepped through the glass.

Someone sang about hearing a nightingale's song.

Sonya felt dizzy, out of place, everything stayed blurred, but the voice singing: *I'll be warbling love's old sweet tune.*

Then she heard a voice, young, bright, join the other.

In the valley of the moon.

And her vision cleared.

Not the attic, but the desk and the chair. And Lisbeth Anne Poole. Lissy singing along with a record on a small Victrola as she filled her fountain pen with ink.

She wore a green dress—it might have been velvet. Long sleeves, a nipped-in waist. Her hair, tied loosely with a green ribbon, spilled down her back as she sat at the desk in a bedroom with wallpaper of big, rosy pink flowers that faced the gardens and the woods.

But snow fell, thick and steady, beyond the windows, and a fire crackled cheerfully in the hearth.

Stepping closer, Sonya caught her scent—young, sweet, floral—as Lisbeth began to write.

Dearest Dina,

You won't believe it! I hardly believe it myself.

I'm engaged!

Edward took me on an afternoon sleigh ride. Its snowing to beat the band here, and we had such a time with the horses prancing, their bells jingling! Everything was so white and pretty.

Then he stopped, and he took my hands, and he kissed them both.

Oh, Dina, my heart just flew!

He said he loved me, that I had his heart in my hands. He promised to love me to his last breath and beyond.

Can you imagine?

Then he took the ring out of his pocket-oh, its a pip, Dina-and he said: Marry me, please, Lissy. I think I'll die if you won't.

I was laughing and crying and pulling off my glove.

Yes, yes, yes! I don't know how many times I said yes, but I couldn't stop. At least I couldn't until he kissed me.

With the snow falling all around us, he kissed me. Oh, my heart, Dina, my heart!

I love him so very much.

Edward had already gotten Papa's permission, of course. When we got home, Mama and Papa had champagne waiting to toast us. They love Edward, too. I am the luckiest girl in the world!

They're going to throw us an engagement bash of bashes here at the manor. You must come. Say you'll be in my wedding party, won't you? Oh, I don't know how I'll wait to be Edward's bride.

Do come for the party, Dina, my dearest friend, and stay a few days at least.

The party's in three weeks, and you must come! Write back soon.

Your happy friend and bride-to-be,

Lissy

Taking an envelope, she wrote out a name, an address, and humming to herself, folded the letter into it.

Smiling, she held up her left hand to admire the sparkle of her engagement ring.

"Oh, Edward." She sighed and pressed her right hand to her heart. "We'll be so happy, forever and ever."

Then she shifted in her chair, looked around, looked at Sonya.

"Who's there? Is someone there?"

And shivering, she rubbed her arms as if chilled.

She doesn't see me, Sonya realized—not like the night in the music room. But she senses me, feels me.

And something else.

Something cold, something dark, like a shadow suddenly blanketing the room.

Dobbs, somehow here, watching, Sonya thought, as she, too, watched.

"You can't scare me today! Not one bit."

But she got up quickly and, taking the letter, hurried from the room.

The shadow stayed, and the cold with it. Then seemed to drift out the door.

Sonya stepped over, laid a hand on the desk.

Then she turned and went back through the mirror.

Everything tilted and went gray.

Arms grabbed her, pulled her in.

"Sonya, oh God. You weren't here, but the mirror was. You're cold, and Jesus, so pale."

"I'm okay, almost. Need to sit."

She braced a hand on the chair, sat. And Cleo knelt in front of her.

"It wasn't like it's been before, exactly. It didn't take me here. I mean, I didn't go back and stay in the attic. Maybe that's why I feel more off."

"Let me help you downstairs. You can lie down. I'll get you some water."

"No, no, it's passing. It was the desk, this chair. I went where they were. They were Lissy's. I went to Lissy's room. Deep pink flowered wallpaper, windows facing the garden. Her room."

"You can tell me, but let's go downstairs anyway. Your color's better. I bet you could use some air."

"Yeah, I could."

She got up, but didn't mind the support of Cleo's arm around her waist.

"I took longer than I thought," Cleo began, "then I went down to stir the sauce again, let the pets out. When I came up, I saw the mirror, and I knew you'd gone through."

"I can't stop myself."

"I know."

"I saw Lissy. She was writing a letter to a friend. The same stationery I found in the desk. She'd just gotten engaged. She was so happy."

"Let's go out front. I want the sea."

When they went out the front, the air whisked away any trace of dizziness.

"I found things in the desk—her things. Photographs, too. And I thought how we'd use that desk and chair for the guest office. Then . . . then the mirror was just there."

Sitting on the seawall, with the dog racing joyfully to join them, Sonya told Cleo the rest.

"She felt you."

"I think so, yeah. Me at first, then Dobbs. Because at first she just looked puzzled, you know? Then she looked shaken. I felt Dobbs, too. I wonder, did she feel me?"

Sonya looked up at the windows of the Gold Room.

"I hope she did. I hope it worries her. I'm fine now. I guess you didn't notice the desk."

"Not really, no."

"It's beautiful and it's perfect. I think I was meant to find it, and find her things in it. Hairpins, ticket stubs, photographs."

Clover tried Tom Petty's "American Girl."

"Yeah, she was." And for some reason the song, the connection made Sonya smile again. "Probably very typical for her age and time. Something very sweet about her, with some sass built in."

She glanced over as she heard the sound of a truck coming.

"It's Trey. I guess I have a story to tell again."

She got up and trailed behind Yoda's joyous run, and the happy wrestling match when Mookie leaped out of the truck.

"Owen's a couple minutes behind me."

He leaned down, kissed Sonya. "How'd the day go?"

"Productive, and with some mirror time at the end. Don't jump to worry." She lifted a hand to his cheek.

"Too late."

"I'm here, I'm fine, and I learned a little bit more."

"I'm calling for cocktails on the deck. I'm making my mama's serious lemonade—it includes gin. Trust me on it," Cleo added. "Go on around back, and I'll bring out adult beverages."

When Cleo walked off, Trey took Sonya's face in his hands and gave it a long look.

In response, she batted her lashes.

"You're okay," he decided.

"Actually, I'd rather go through the mirror than face off against a smoke wolf."

"Is that what you're calling it?"

"Why not?"

Hand in hand, they began to stroll.

"When I go through, I see something to put in the file." She tapped the side of her head with her free hand. "Or hear, or feel or learn. And I did. Since Owen's on his way, I'll wait and tell you both. And how did your day go?"

"Productive. Busy and productive, so I'm going to enjoy that adult beverage and a weekend without clients."

"Problematic ones?"

Since she obviously wanted the distraction, he obliged her.

"Well, there's the one who brought in a list of changes to her will, most of which negate the changes she made to her will about three months ago and refer back to changes made maybe six months before that."

"And there'll be a list coming in another few months?"

"Oh, absolutely." He said it with a kind of cheerful acceptance that Sonya thought all but defined him. "What's your productive?"

"Updates, testing, working up the package for Bay Arts. And finishing my mood board for the Ryder additions—and their approval of same."

With the dogs racing in the yard, and Pye climbing onto her favorite perch on the mansard roof of Yoda's doghouse, they walked up to the deck.

"We should have wardrobe by the end of next week."

Reading his expression, she laughed and hugged him. "It really won't hurt, and it'll be quick. Your mom's so good."

"I'm not going to ask what I'm wearing because I don't want to think about it."

"Then we'll move on. Cleo dropped the photos we put together last night at Poole Shipbuilders, for Clarice. And after work I started in the attic, and found more."

She watched the dogs bullet toward the front of the house seconds before she heard the truck. Cleo came out with a tray holding four glasses.

"I remember that lemonade," Sonya said. "Owen just drove up."

"It's memorable. I texted for Owen's ETA before I started mixing. He said five minutes. And I said: 'No beer, come to the deck.'"

After stepping up and onto the deck, Cleo set the tray down.

"The perfect summer cocktail at the perfect spot on a perfect evening."

The dogs raced back; eye-patched Jones strutted. Owen followed, and sent an aggrieved look at the group on the deck.

"Why can't a man have a Friday night beer?"

"Because you're going to have a Friday night cocktail. And if you don't like it, you can go get your prosaic old beer."

When he stepped onto the deck, Cleo handed him the fourth glass. He frowned at it.

"There's basil in here."

"And mulled strawberries, and gin added to lemonade. You can knock it, but not until you've tried it."

He took a sip, then shrugged. "It's not bad."

"That'll do." Cleo sat.

"Sonya went through the mirror," Trey told him.

Owen looked at Sonya. "You okay? You look okay."

"I'm definitely okay. Sit, relax. I'll tell you. I decided to start the serious search in the attic. I'm marking pieces I've been through with sticky notes. Cleo, I didn't tell you about this gorgeous chifforobe. I think it's a chifforobe. We'll want that downstairs."

"So it begins," Owen muttered.

"It's never going to end in this house," Trey added.

And there, she thought, that (almost) cheerful acceptance.

"But the real find was the desk and desk chair. I want you to take a look at it, Owen. You'll know what it is, besides beautiful. I was thinking of it for the guest office, but now? I'd love to put it back in Lissy's room, if I can find her room. The wallpaper . . . I didn't recognize it."

She held up a hand. "And I'm getting ahead of myself. I know it was Lissy's desk because I found some of her things in it. Writing paper, hairpins, photographs, and so on. Then someone helpfully pulled the dustcover off the chair that goes with it."

She took a drink. "Then, the mirror was there. Just there, and I had to go through."

She told them all she'd seen and heard and felt.

"She didn't see you like she did that night in the music room?"

"No." She shook her head at Trey, then turned to Owen. "I was the ghost, like we were at Lissy's wedding."

"More, she didn't see Dobbs, and neither did you," Trey continued. "But you felt her, and you think Lisbeth felt her, too."

"I'm sure of it. It got cold, and dark. I don't mean the light changed, but the air, it just felt dark, dark and heavy, where it hadn't."

"Sonya was really pale and shaken when she came out. I was on the point of texting both of you when she did," Cleo told them. "I didn't know how long she'd been in there, over there. Whatever the hell it is."

"I always feel a little off for a minute after, but this was more— going in and coming out."

"Because you didn't stay in the attic. You didn't go just back, you went where the desk was."

"Yes!" Pleased and relieved he understood, Sonya reached over to squeeze Trey's hand.

"I want to see this desk." Owen got to his feet. "In the attic, and uncovered, right?"

"Go on up, the three of you." Cleo rose. "I've got a couple of things to do for dinner. We can eat when you get back. Go show him, Sonya. Bring Lissy's stuff back down, and we can take a look at it after dinner. I left the boxes up there."

Jones, as always, went with Owen. The other four-legged creatures decided to tag along.

Owen stopped in the kitchen to sniff at the simmering sauce. "Smells good, but it doesn't look like pulled pork."

"That's for tomorrow." Cleo smiled, and made it sultry. "We have plans for you."

"Chifforobes," he muttered, and kept going.

"Probably not." Sonya patted his shoulder. "It's huge, and I don't know where I want it yet."

When they reached the library, Trey turned in. "Hold on a minute." Walking over, he studied the mood board, hissed out a breath. "This is one time I wish you weren't so damn good at what you do. So I'm still not going to think about it."

Owen took another moment. "We keep the gear?"

"You keep the gear."

"Good deal."

They continued up.

"If you don't count the wolf, she's been pretty quiet. And that was a quick, if intense, scare."

"You said it poofed when Yoda and the cat went at it."

She nodded at Trey. "That's right."

"That tells me the illusion can't stand up to a fight."

"Yet," Owen added.

"Yet."

They all paused on the third floor, and the sound of a staticky hum.

"No, you don't." Owen bent down and picked up the cat as she started down the hall. "Almira Gulch is in there, brooding and plotting."

"Almira who?"

Owen glanced at Sonya. "*Wizard of Oz*. Margaret Hamilton rocked the old Kansas biddy and the Wicked Witch of the West."

He carried the cat up the steps and made the turn into the attic, then set her down.

"That chifforobe? She's a monster, and a beauty. Cherrywood," he told Sonya. "Probably late eighteen hundreds."

"Needs a big room."

"Yeah, it does."

"That's the desk?" Trey pointed. "And the chair. That's burl wood, right, Owen?"

His eyes landed on it with admiration. "Burr walnut, and talk about a beauty. It's a kidney desk."

"Because it's curved," Sonya realized. "I see that. And that was the chair she sat in."

"Same wood, same era. Victorian. And if you hadn't changed your mind about using this for a desktop, I'd've changed it for you. The style's too delicate. It's plenty sturdy, but you want something that looks sturdy."

"More businesslike," Trey agreed. "No putting a desktop on something like this."

"I can't argue that. It was in front of the window in her room so she could look out while she wrote her letters. This stationery, this pen. She was using both, writing to someone named Dina. Miss Dina Triburn, in New York."

"Triburn?" Owen glanced back at her. "We've got Triburn relatives—distant cousins. My brother Hugh's connected with a couple in New York."

"She saved some theater tickets, some playbills. A few are from New York. So she visited there. And these photos. I'm thinking the one of her and Edward might be from the engagement party she wrote Dina about. It wasn't on her desk when I saw her."

"He's wearing a tux," Trey observed. "And that looks like an evening gown, so you're likely right."

"The mirror was right there. It hadn't been, but I felt it, and I turned, and it was right there."

She picked up one of Cleo's boxes and began to put Lissy's things inside.

"I think at some point they just moved this up here. After she died. They couldn't box up her things inside it. So they left them and brought the desk up."

"The family bedrooms would've been on the second floor."

"True, but, Trey, the wallpaper's changed. I've been in all of those rooms, multiple times. I've never seen that wallpaper."

"You've got a good eye," Owen commented. "Why not take another look now?"

"It's been over a hundred years," Trey pointed out. "Some of the wallpaper's changed. I know Collin did a lot of remodeling. Except for the short period Charlie and Clover lived here, the house stood empty for a generation when Patricia Poole refused to live here. Or, hell, be here."

"Threatened or warned off, take your pick, by Hester Dobbs. Okay, maybe." Sonya lifted her shoulders. "It can't hurt to look. I'd love to see it where she had it. It just feels like the right thing to do."

They went down to the second floor and began to study the rooms facing west.

"More centered than these, or those on the far end of the hall. Not the one my mother used. That has a sitting room, and this one didn't. I think . . ."

She opened another door, walked in. A guest room now, with its own small en suite and windows facing the gardens and the woods.

"You know, this feels right. The angles. The view. It's not snowing, and the woods are a hundred-plus years older. But the fireplace. It's the same mantel and surround. Where the bed is—a different bed, but the same place. The wallpaper's different, but it has the same tonal qualities. Hers was deep pink—rose-colored flowers over cream, and this is cream-colored flowers and vines over rose."

Sonya nodded. "This was her room."

Sonya's phone played Katy Perry's "Teenage Dream."

"Yes, she was, just a teenager, and one with dreams. We'll put her desk back by the window, where she dreamed some of those dreams."

They went back down to where Cleo had a platter of antipasto on the kitchen island along with a bottle of Chianti.

"We're going Italian tonight, start to finish. From antipasto through the gelato."

"Looks fancy." Owen snatched a marinated artichoke heart. "Tastes good and fancy." He looked down at Jones. "You guys have to settle for your usual. I'll feed them."

Trey crossed over to set the box he'd taken from Sonya on the dining room table.

"And I'll pour the wine. We found Lissy's room. The desk just belongs there. So, a Saturday project."

"I've got to work awhile in the morning. I can be back around noon. One, latest," Owen qualified. "I'm feeding these guys outside."

"Good idea." Sonya turned to Trey. "Working this weekend?"

"Client-free weekend. So it looks like I'm working in the attic."

"Which is much appreciated." She handed him his wine. "Mmm, Cleo, what did you do to these mozzarella balls?"

"Marinated them. I amaze myself."

"Join the crowd."

Owen came back, glanced at the platter, then the stovetop. "How long that's going to take determines how much of this I'm going to eat."

"About twenty minutes. Maybe fifteen."

"Good enough." He took one of the little plates and loaded it up.

"This is nice. A little bit fancy on a Friday night, it's nice. Thanks, Cleo." Sonya lifted her glass in a toast. "And everyone, forget all about this when I try making pulled pork tomorrow."

"Don't forget the hand-cut fries."

"I'm trying to, Owen. Really trying to."

"Use the mandoline."

She let out a laugh. "You want me to play a musical instrument while I make French fries?"

Shaking his head, he walked into the butler's pantry, rummaged around, and came back holding a tool with a long, flat surface and a leg he folded out to make an incline.

"How is that a mandoline?" Sonya wondered.

"Can't tell you, but it is."

"You adjust the blade there," Trey told her. "Then you just slide the potato down, and it slices them."

Impressed, Sonya frowned at him. "How do you know this?"

"My mom has one. I've been drafted into slicing stuff now and then. You use this guard so your hand doesn't hit the blade."

"Okay, I'll try playing the mandoline."

"Water's boiling," Owen told Cleo.

"I see that." She added the pasta, gave it a stir. "It's time you kissed the cook."

"Is it that time?"

He obliged her.

Chapter Five

After the meal, they had cappuccinos and gelato on the deck, and lingered until the setting sun turned the woods to fire.

As the garden and deck lights twinkled on, Trey stretched out his long legs.

"Nice night. Nice spot to spend some of it."

"One of my favorites, but I still want that seating out front."

"Working on it," Owen muttered.

"You shouldn't be so talented." Cleo shook back her hair. "We're due for some rain tomorrow, but Sunday looks to be perfect. Perfect for a sail, and I think it's time we had one on *The Horizon*."

"We could do that." He glanced over. "You're bringing the cat, aren't you?"

Since Pye currently curled on Owen's lap, Cleo just lifted her eyebrows. "She's proven seaworthy."

"How about we take them all, an afternoon sail?" Trey suggested. "Then we drop them at my parents', take you out to dinner."

"That sounds wonderful." Completely content, Sonya closed her eyes. "Really wonderful. Almost as good as this, right here and now."

They lingered longer, with the stars bright diamonds overhead, with conversation quiet and lazy and the sea a rhythmic murmur to the east.

When they went upstairs, Sonya opened the balcony doors.

"It's warm enough, isn't it?"

"Sure."

"I love the sound of it. I didn't know how much I loved the sound of it until I heard it, night after night. Now I wonder how I could ever sleep without it."

With the evening air streaming in, the stars sparkling, they looked out to sea.

Then she turned to him in the open doorway, slid her arms around him.

"It feels good. Cool air, warm body. I'm glad we have the weekend. I'm glad you're here."

"It's where I want to be."

She tipped her head up to welcome the kiss.

Warm lips meeting, sliding, parting.

She rose on her toes, and her hands took his face, then glided up into his hair.

It all aroused her, the warmth and taste of his lips, the texture of his skin, his hair, the feel of his body pressed to hers as the night air danced around them.

Her fingers got busy on the buttons of his shirt.

And the pounding, like slamming pistons, clanged from the third floor.

With a mix of longing and defiance, Sonya pulled him closer. "No, don't listen. It doesn't matter. She doesn't matter right now. She doesn't exist right now."

"Just you and me."

"Yes." Spreading his shirt open, she ran her hands over his chest. "Just you and me." Her lips curved before they met his again. "And a couple of dogs snoring on the floor."

"Just how I like it." He drew her shirt over her head. "And here you are, with me, in the moonlight."

Ignoring the insistent banging from overhead, he held her close, felt her heart skip a beat or two against his.

Just how he liked it.

And when he ran his hands over her, that heartbeat increased, as did his. Outside, the waves rose and fell, their rhythm steady and strong as he changed the angle of the kiss and deepened it. The air seemed to sing as it wafted over the sea and shimmered into the room.

He'd thought he'd known how much he'd wanted her, almost from the first moment, but it was nothing to what he felt when she was with him.

He barely noticed when the pounding stopped, and only thought: Dobbs can't win against this, not against what's real. Not against love.

He picked her up to carry her to the bed, and she smiled, laid a hand on his cheek.

"Just you and me," she repeated.

They undressed each other, taking their time, taking that time for lips to meet again, and again, for hands to stroke, to linger. For trembles to turn to sighs.

With the sea air came the wash of moonlight and that beat, that steady beat of water against rock.

His eyes were like the night sea, deep and dark. No man, she realized, looked at her exactly as he did. No man, she felt certain, seemed to understand the whole of her as he did.

And with him, as with no other, she could let herself give all she had, let herself take, all she wanted.

His hands, so strong, so sure, thrilled her. Kisses, long, slow, deep, set her blood to simmer. The bed groaned as they moved together, reaching, taking, so quiet murmurs and sighs grew breathless.

As urgency climbed, as hands and lips became more insistent, she welcomed the ache of need.

In the moonlight, with the music of the restless sea surrounding them, she opened for him.

When they were joined, when they were locked together, the world spun away. Like the waves, she rose and fell. She let herself give, let herself take, until there was nothing else.

In the morning, Sonya dressed for the work at hand in sweat shorts, a tank, and her oldest sneakers. She wound her hair, clipped it up.

She armed herself with packs of sticky notes.

With Owen and Trey she began a systematic search, going through dressers, bureaus, armoires, drawers in occasional tables and stands.

For the most part, those drawers proved empty. But here and there they found a stray pen, notepaper, the occasional photograph.

In one she found an old tea tin.

"Pretty sure this is Russian. Ah . . ." She attempted to pronounce the name on the hinged red tin. "Zvetouchny. Probably butchered that. But there's English, too. 'Packed by the Consolidated Tea Company in New York.'"

She gave it a light shake. "Something's in it that's definitely not tea."

When she pried up the lid, she found the tin filled with marbles.

"They look old." Owen poked a finger in to roll them around. "The tin and the marbles."

When he glanced over at Trey, Trey just lifted his shoulders. "Don't look at me. I don't know anything about marbles, less about old Russian tea."

"Well, the tin's very cool, and the marbles are pretty."

Sonya started to close the lid again when Cleo wandered in.

"And here she comes, practically an early bird."

"All y'all were buzzing my subconscious. I might as well have set an alarm."

Cleo had also dressed for the task in little denim shorts, a pink tee, and pink sneakers.

"Whatcha got there? Oh, look at those!"

"Know anything about marbles?" Trey asked her.

"Not so much, but I know rocks and crystals, and some of these are agate, some aventurine, carnelian. There's some with mica flakes—see how they glitter? Oh, look here! This one's got a lion inside, and here's one with a bear in it.

"I'll take these down," Cleo decided. "See if I can look them up. We should put them in a glass jar. They're too pretty, too full of energy—I swear, it's popping off them—to stay closed away. And the tin's a little treasure in itself."

"All yours," Sonya told her. "I've got a few things in that box going down. We haven't found much yet. We're doing this area first, then I figured—"

"Do it all organized? How about I bring the chaos, and maybe the luck?" Head angled, Cleo circled a finger in the air, then pointed. "I'm going that way."

After setting the tin of marbles in the box, Cleo wove through and picked her spot.

Well used to Cleo's methods, Sonya continued on. She hunted through the drawers of a small dresser she thought must belong in a nursery or toddler's room, and thought she might use it when she had children.

"These must be diaper pins." She held up a pair of large safety pins. "And some sort of a . . ." She shook the tiny silver dumbbell. "Baby rattle."

Clover joined in with Smokey Robinson and the Miracles.

"'Ooo Baby Baby.'" Grinning, Trey took the rattle and gave it a shake of his own. "In the box, right?"

"Absolutely."

"While y'all are playing, I think I brought that luck. Unless you hate this desk, Son."

Straightening up, Sonya worked her way over to Cleo. "I do not hate this desk."

"Tulipwood," Owen supplied. "Art Deco-y, I'd say. You got a nice tooled leather top."

"Sturdy, but not chunky." Sonya ran a hand over it. "We wouldn't want chunky. It'll fit, won't it? It's big enough but not overwhelming. We'll find a chair and use this as the core piece of the guest office."

Trey moved in, tested by lifting one end. "Easier on the back than a lot of the others, so I love it."

"Cleo and I can take the drawers to make it even lighter." Sonya gave the middle drawer a tug. "This one's locked."

Cleo opened the drawer on one side, and Owen the other. Both were empty.

Trey sat on the floor, managed to angle himself under the desk.

"I've got it. Key taped to the bottom of the drawer."

He brought it out, a small gold key on a thin gold chain. Then slid it into the lock, turned.

Inside they found a book with a red leather cover. The engraving on the center gold plaque read:

Marianne Louise Poole

"It's Marianne's—a diary." With care, Sonya lifted it out.

"And pressed flowers. From her bouquet, I bet." Cleo set them on the top of the desk.

Sonya opened the book and read.

"'I begin this diary, given to me by my dear mama, on the morning of my wedding. In a few hours I will be Mrs. Hugh Poole. Marianne Louise Poole, the wife of the man I love. Today marks the beginning of my new life.

"'In the days to come, I will write here my thoughts, my life, my joys, and though I cannot imagine any on this glorious day, my sorrows.

"'I will keep my diary, and the ones that follow, in the desk in the pretty sitting room, my pretty sitting room as mistress of Poole Manor. As I vow to be a good and loving wife to my husband, I also promise to be a good and caring mistress of the home that will become mine.'"

Sonya carefully turned the page, and continued.

"'Others have lived in the manor, have tended to it before me. I sometimes think I can hear them, or sense them as I walk through to learn my duties here. I feel a welcome from them, except . . . I think my nerves over the great responsibility make me foolish, as I do feel something that does not welcome.

"'I will not dwell on that, or on the war that rages through the country. Today I become a bride. Here I vow with all my heart to be loyal and loving, to be kind. To remember, always, this happy day when my love, always my love, becomes my husband.

"'I will pack this book in my trousseau, and the next I write in it, I write as a wife.'"

"I hope Hugh read this after she died. He loved her."

"He kept it," Cleo pointed out. "Kept it locked here in her desk, so I think he did. Read the last entry, Sonya."

Sonya turned to where the red ribbon marked the last entry.

"'Though I have been ordered, quite firmly, to remain in bed, I have slipped in here for just a few minutes. I find some quiet and calm in this room, and in writing my thoughts in this book.

"'I suppose I waddled like a duck here from my bed, and must admit even that short journey tired me. The midwife believes I carry two, and this I know is true. I feel my babies, and often think they play energetically together already. Even while they keep me awake there is such joy for me in those fierce movements.

"'Soon I will be a mother. At times it seems only days have passed since I became a bride. At other times it seems years since I carried these precious lives inside me.

"'Hugh is so attentive. He sits with me as often as he can, and brings me the news from the village and beyond. He rarely speaks of the war unless I press him. I know he is troubled, and I know Atlanta has fallen. We have hope the battle and the blood will end soon.

"'But here, I am safe, my babies are safe. Soon, I'm assured, I'll hold them in my arms, see their faces, count their fingers. As I love their father, I will love them always.

"'When I do, it will be the happiest day of my life.'"

Sonya let out a sigh.

"She barely had any time to hold them."

"It matters that you have this," Trey told her. "That you know, however short, she had a good life here."

"It does. You're right, it does. I'll read through the rest later. Maybe there's some clue in there. Something she wrote down she saw or heard or felt that could help. Meanwhile."

"We take the desk down."

"Yeah, and find a chair."

When a dustcover slid off a chair, Cleo walked to it. "I think we just did. I've got it."

Once they had the desk and chair in place, they brought up the monitor and keyboard.

"The printer's small, but I still don't want it sitting out. We'll find something for it."

"Good luck with that. Jones and I have to take off. We'll be back later. Three hours, maybe four."

Sonya checked the time. "I guess I'd better put that pork on. It cooks for hours."

"Want help?" Cleo asked her.

"I think I've got this part, but I'll send up an SOS if I run into a wall. I'll come back up."

She walked down with Owen, the dogs, the cat, while Trey and Cleo went back to attic duty. Then she split off to go back to the kitchen.

Odd how quiet and still the house felt, she thought, and pulled up the recipe on the kitchen tablet.

"Okay, Clover, I could use some confidence music as I transform this hunk of meat."

Sia's "Unstoppable" fit the bill.

It took longer than she'd anticipated—but what cooking deal didn't, in her estimation. Eventually she had chunks of spice-rubbed pork browned up, then swimming in beer.

She hauled the Dutch oven to the wall oven, slid it inside.

"That's supposed to do it for about three hours. Fingers crossed."

She set a timer on her phone, then looked around the kitchen.

"Molly, I hope you don't mind cleaning up. I'd like to get upstairs."

Clover answered with Stevie Wonder. "Don't You Worry 'bout a Thing."

"Thanks!"

When she reached the second floor, she heard Trey and Cleo in the guest office, so walked down to it.

She saw a drum cabinet against the left wall, the love seat moved to the right, along with a two-tiered piecrust table topped by a pretty lamp that favored the deep green wallpaper with its pink and white roses.

"Still looking for the right desk lamp," Cleo told her, "but that works for the printer. And it looks better with the love seat here."

"No coffee table. It'd crowd the room. Maybe an occasional chair there."

"Reading my mind." Hands on hips, Cleo glanced around. "And I'm thinking—we get nice light in here—maybe bring up one of the potted plants from the solarium. There's that big African violet—the purple one."

"I like it! And I'd like a mirror in here, a wall mirror."

"I guess we're going back up. But before we do."

Trey reached for the box and took out a stack of paper. "Kids' drawings."

"We found the stack of them in a drawer," Cleo said. "Cute mostly, and mostly what you'd expect. Crazy, colorful scribbles, or drawings of houses with big yellow suns, stick people. But there's one."

"Signed *Jack*." Trey took it off the top of the stack.

"Our Jack, you think? Oh."

He'd drawn the manor, and well for a child so young. The turrets, the big entrance doors, the shades of the stones. The weeping tree at the corner, not as tall, but leafy green as it was now in summer.

He'd drawn a boy—himself, no doubt—and a large spotted dog in the front yard. Both looked up.

On the widow's walk stood a figure in black, all shadows, arms lifted. Though her face was indistinct, she clearly looked down at the boy and his dog.

In one of her lifted hands, she held a bolt of lightning.

"He saw her," Sonya murmured. "He saw Dobbs. Look at the sky, how he brought in storm clouds. It's clear over here, but you see the storm moving in."

"He had talent, and yes," Cleo agreed, "he saw Dobbs. He couldn't have drawn her otherwise. He had to be frightened. I wonder if his parents believed him, if he told them."

"Probably not," Trey decided. "Placated him, reassured him. He's got a few more in there, and she's in a couple of them. Standing on the seawall, at night."

"He saw her jump." The thought of a little boy seeing such horror hurt Sonya's heart. "What an awful thing for a little boy. We'll keep them all. I can get a kit and make a protective book. We'll put it together, keep it in the library."

"That's a nice idea." As he handed her the stack, Trey kissed Sonya's cheek. "Something the mistress of the manor would do."

"I'll put them in the library for now. Meet you back upstairs?"

After she put the drawings on a table in the library, Sonya went to her desk. She took out a sketchbook, a spare pack of colored pencils. She carried them down to the kitchen, set them on the island with a note.

For Jack.

"I hope he'll take them."

Since she was there, she took a peek at the simmering pork. Hoping for the best there, she closed the oven door and went back upstairs.

As she passed the third-floor landing, she glanced down the hall. Red light eked out of the Gold Room to outline the door.

"Watch how much you matter," Sonya said, then turned her back and continued up.

Cold air rushed after her so her breath came out in clouds as she continued the climb. Though her belly quivered, she kept walking, and followed the sound of Cleo's voice to the attic.

"This isn't what I had in my head, but I'm all about this chair. How do I miss pieces like this on other go-throughs?"

"You're looking for something else every time. This, the ballroom, the basement, all the storage areas are like some big, never-ending bazaar."

"That's exactly it. Well, we'll see what Sonya thinks of this one."

So saying, she turned and sat in the chair with its high, straight-lined back framed in wood, set her elbows on the curved arms.

"Looks comfy," Sonya decided as she worked her way back to them.

"Is comfy. I had something more office-like in my head, but this?"

"Unique, pretty. The wide stripe pattern reads practical, but the shape says interesting. Add that rose color will work with the wall-paper."

"You're cold," Trey said when his arm brushed hers.

"Just Dobbs blowing cold air. Like a little chill's going to spook me." But she leaned against him a moment for the warmth. "I'm saying yes to that chair."

"I guess I'm hauling it down."

With a smile, Sonya squeezed his right biceps, widened her eyes, said, "Oooh."

"It's a good thing I like the way you're reclaiming rooms."

When Cleo rose, he lifted the chair. Gave one annoyed grunt, then carried it out.

"Trey said this is all like some endless bazaar, and he's right. Every time, new treasures. So, lamps, wall mirror?"

"Yeah, but I'm sticking with the process. Systematically."

"You know I love a good process, but systematically doesn't work for me up here."

"You go your way, I'll go mine."

They high-fived, separated.

Sonya uncovered what she thought qualified as a hall rack—enormous with a storage seat—empty. She imagined people had hung their hats, coats on the brass hooks, stored boots inside the seat.

She found a washstand, and immediately wanted it in one of the bathrooms. Pretty hand towels on the bar, she envisioned, an old bowl and pitcher, a tiny vase of flowers.

In her search through the drawers she found a small box. It held little silver bars, very tarnished. The monogram etched in each read HCP.

"Hugh Charles Poole," she murmured. When she heard Trey coming back, she called out to him. "I found these in this washstand—that's also going down somewhere. They're monogrammed. I don't know what they are. Not nail files, they're silver."

"Collar stays."

"Collar stays?"

"Yeah, mostly plastic now, I guess." He pointed at the invisible collar on his T-shirt. "They give the collar structure."

"He used this stand. Marianne's husband, Owen and Jane's father. Lisbeth's grandfather. Maybe in his dressing room. He used these in his shirts. All these things."

She set the box on the stand, looked around.

"People used these pieces of the manor day after day, night after night."

"Don't hate me," Cleo said as she came through holding a lamp with a clear glass dome. "But I think this would be the perfect desk lamp for— What's wrong, Sonya?"

"Collar stays." She shook her head, swiped at a tear. "It's weird what will hit the emotions. Hugh Poole's collar stays. And that lamp is perfect. I'm adding on a project."

"I hope it includes this." Cleo set the lamp on the washstand. "It belongs in the bathroom near my studio."

"Also perfect. Display cabinet. There's bound to be one, glass front. Maybe two of them, or one big one. We'll know when we find it. I want things like the collar stays—once I polish them up. Lisbeth's fountain pen. Little everyday things, important things, personal things. In the Gold Room, with the photos."

"A walk through Poole history," Trey said. "That's a good project, and I think you're finding these things so you can do just that."

"And I think this is why you're here, Son. Why this is your house, and your quest. It's a quest, the seven rings."

Hands on hips, Sonya looked around. "Not getting very far on that."

"Farther than anyone else," Trey corrected. "The portraits in the music room. They're part of it. The mirror, what you've seen on the other side of it. Those are reasons why something like these"—he picked up the box of stays—"why it matters to you."

"It does matter, so let's keep going."

When Owen returned, he found Sonya in the kitchen taking the next step in pulled pork. Removing the lid.

"Smells like you know what you're doing."

"You don't have to know what you're doing if you follow directions. Remove lid, cook another one to two hours. So I'm going with an hour and a half."

As the dogs decided to greet Jones with madness, Owen opened the back door. Three dogs and one cat bounded out.

"How's the search going?"

"Well, we haven't stumbled across seven wedding rings, but it's going well in other areas. I'll show you the guest office on the way up."

"Any interference?"

"She tossed some cold air at me, and that's about it." She turned, and noticed what she'd missed. Her hand reached up to her heart. "Oh, he took them."

"Who took what?"

"We found kids' drawings. A nice stack of them. Some were Jack's." She filled him in as they began to walk.

"Seeing Dobbs? Bound to give a kid some nightmares."

"And a grown woman, too. I got a sketchbook and some colored pencils, left them on the kitchen island. They're gone."

Owen said nothing for a moment.

"That's a damn nice thing to do."

"It's all I could think of. It's hitting my feels, Owen. I didn't know it would hit them so hard, finding all the little things we're finding."

She led the way to the guest office. Owen stepped in, took stock.

"Looks good. Chair's a winner. So's the floor lamp."

"We just found that one. I think it's Tiffany."

"Probably. Desk lamp's no slouch, but the drum cabinet? The champ. Burr walnut, like the desk. Pristine. Doesn't look like you guys need me. Maybe I'll get a beer and sit on the deck."

She gave him a finger poke in his rock-hard belly.

"Fat chance. I want a wall mirror right there. And we're finding things like baby rattles, collar stays, an antique yo-yo, an old cocktail shaker, a silver pocketknife engraved 1916. And I want more."

He paused at the third floor, looked down at the red glow around the Gold Room door.

"She's stirring around in there."

"It's been like that for hours. She doesn't like what we're doing, which just makes me want to do it harder."

"I'm on board with that."

When they reached the attic, he let out a laugh. "Man, you've been through a lot, that's some pile of dustcovers."

"It's a system. It's working. And if there's anything you want—"

His eyebrows drew together as he shoved at his dense brown hair. "Don't start that."

"Owen, if and when I manage to switch things around, furnish every room, I'm still not going to be able to use everything. We've still got the ballroom to go through, the servants' quarters, the basement."

"My house isn't finished. And I'm barely there as it is."

She would, Sonya determined, wear him down on this issue.

"You can earmark things for down the road. Anyway, if you want to start over there—"

"Got some mirrors here," Trey called out. "I don't think they're what you're looking for, but they're mirrors."

"Let's see."

She made her way over.

"Hey," he said to Owen, then looked at the three small mirrors he'd uncovered. "Got some wear on the glass."

"That just adds to the charm. I love the etching, the flower motif, the shapes. All different, but the same feel. Hang the three together, it's a statement."

"Okay."

Curious, Cleo wandered over. "I love them! Hang these, and we've transformed a room. A good day's work. I've got a couple bowl-and-pitcher sets on the other side of the attic. And we've got the trunks to get through."

"What happened to a good day's work?" Owen wondered.

"Day's not over," Cleo told him.

"The trunks can wait. I've got about an hour before I have to shift to kitchen duty, and I'm sticking with my system. But I want to see the bowls and pitchers."

When they walked to the other side of the attic, Owen scanned the space. "You know, all this? It could take months. Literally months."

Trey just shrugged. "You going somewhere?"

When Cleo let out a laugh and Sonya's rolled with it, Owen let out a sigh. "Doesn't look like it."

Chapter Six

Sonya decided to keep what she thought of as the everyday treasure box in the Quiet Place—the guest room where Cleo had her spill-over clothes. They'd add to it, no doubt, on the next search.

Maybe nothing, so far, provided any insight on recovering the seven rings, but every piece gave her more insight on the Poole family.

And yes, she thought again, it mattered.

But it was time to return to the now, and the now meant dinner.

It struck her.

"Shit, shit! I forgot the cake. I probably should've made the cake first."

"Not according to my mama. The shortcake'll get soggy. I'll handle the cake."

"Really? All yours. I have to make the fries—did you know you're supposed to soak the potatoes?"

"Now?"

"No, after I play the mandoline, which I'm about to do. Then, the barbecue sauce. I didn't even know you could make barbecue sauce. Why would you make something you can get in a bottle? A deal's a deal," she reminded herself, and got to work.

While the pork rested on a cutting board, she started slicing scrubbed potatoes.

"Okay, this is easier than I thought."

As Cleo slid a baking pan into the oven, the dumbwaiter in the butler's pantry rumbled.

"Oh God." Sonya actually felt her blood run cold. "I haven't touched that thing since the rat incident."

"Nothing says you have to now. I can get Owen and Trey."

"No." Her pulse pounded, but Sonya steeled herself. "I told them to go out and have a beer on the deck. They can't be here twenty-four seven to deal with things like this. But . . . stay close."

"Right beside you."

Sonya stepped in. "She's been quiet today. It'd be just like her to . . . Screw it, and her." She yanked it open, prepared to slam it shut again.

Inside she found a kitchen appliance.

"It's a deep fat fryer," Cleo identified. "I didn't know we had one. I was going to help you make the fries in a skillet. This is better."

"You know how to work this?"

"No. That's what the internet is for." Cleo hauled it out. "It's clean as a whistle. Thanks, Molly."

On an exhale, Sonya pressed a hand to the heart she hadn't realized hammered. "I'm going to need a big drink after this. Maybe now."

"Why not both?"

With the fries soaking, she started on the sauce, measuring, whisking. Praying a little.

"You actually like all this?"

"I do. Just another creative outlet," Cleo claimed. "And I've got this fryer figured out. Team effort on the fries. I've got the cake, you've got the pork."

"I'm hoping I've got the pork."

"Cake's done."

"That was quick."

"Shortcake." Cleo pulled it out. "My first."

With the sauce simmering, potatoes soaking, Sonya picked up her wine. "I left a sketchbook and colored pencils out for Jack. He took them."

Struck, Cleo laid a hand on her heart. "Oh, Sonya, that's so sweet! Art runs through your family, and his potential got cut off so young. We're doing good things here, Son. We're bringing the light. Before it's done, we're going to damn well blind her with it."

She opened the back door. "Start up that grill in about ten minutes," she called out. "We'll prep the corn, then dry off the fries, get them going."

Sonya had to grin. "You're definitely the captain of this ship."

"Goddess."

"All right, goddess, I'm going to pull the pork."

It worked, and so did the fryer.

While the pets ate, the four of them sat down to what Trey called a summer feast.

"You know, you're now the pulled pork queen." Trey took another bite. "This is amazing."

"I made barbecue sauce. It's going on my résumé."

"Damn good fries, too."

Nodding at Owen, Cleo ate one. "Team effort there, including Molly, who sent up the fryer."

Sonya sampled one herself. "You know, they wouldn't have had something like that when she worked here. I mean when she was alive."

"She watches," Trey said. "She learns."

"I'd say they all do." Owen studied the house as he ate. "That includes Dobbs."

"Maybe. But I think so much of her is stuck in the past. She doesn't care about today," Sonya added. "Not about things like kitchen tools, technology. It's all about power, and how and when to use it."

"She has to know how to use it again," Trey pointed out. "So I'd say you're both right."

"I don't think she understands why I'm here. She just wants me out. All of us out. But I don't think she believes for a minute I can recover the rings, break the curse."

"Let's keep it that way."

Surprised, she looked at Trey. "You think that, too."

"She's been here over two hundred years. Us? Everyone who's been here before? Temporary inconveniences. Annoyances."

"I'll go with that. But not the brides," Owen pointed out. "You don't murder an annoyance."

"No, not the brides. They're usurpers, rivals—and disposing of them is a way to either hold on to or increase her power. Sonya's a Poole, but not a bride."

Following, Sonya nodded and took another bite of a—yes, excellent—pulled pork sandwich. "So I'm an annoying inconvenience. One she wants gone, but not so much a threat. Won't she be surprised?"

"This Is War" played on Sonya's phone.

"Yeah, it is."

"Thirty Seconds to Mars. Nice choice," Owen decided.

"And I say she's had enough of our time this lovely evening. When do we set sail tomorrow?" Cleo asked.

"Can you get up before noon?"

"I can, with the proper incentive."

"Sunday breakfast at ten."

"Ouch."

He laughed at Cleo. "I'll cover that. Hoist sails by noon."

"That sounds . . ." Sonya sighed. "Just frigging awesome."

"I can't say it'll be awesome, but there's live music at Maloney's tonight."

"Maloney's?" Cleo frowned at Owen. "Is that the bar off Water Street?"

"Yeah. It's not exactly a dive. More of a joint. They get a band in on Saturday nights most of the summer."

"Who's playing?" Trey asked.

"Tin Roof."

"Ah." Nostalgia made him smile. "We were them once."

The insult lived in Owen's eyes. "Come on, man, we were worlds better."

"Maybe a few continents better."

"Either way, live music on a Saturday night."

"Dancing?" Cleo wondered.

"I take it you've never been inside. No room for it," Trey told her. "Unless you hop up on the pool table."

"Pool table." Cleo slid a glance toward Sonya. "What do you think?"

"You made a cake."

"Won't take me ten minutes to put it together when we get back, if you're up for it."

"I can be up for it. I need to change."

"Trust me." Trey shook his head. "You don't."

"It may be a joint, but I have my standards. Ten minutes."

"Twenty," Cleo corrected. "I have my standards. What about the rest of the family?"

"A couple of hours—take my word, that'll do it," Owen said. "Jones will keep them in line. And if he doesn't, you've got a houseful who will."

"All right. Twenty minutes." Cleo rose. "You boys can clear."

When they went inside, Trey sat another moment. "Tin Roof at Maloney's."

"It's Saturday night."

"And Sonya, especially Sonya, could use a couple hours away from Dobbs, rings, responsibilities."

"Seems to me."

"I was going to suggest a drive to the village and a walk in the park."

Owen grinned, and sang, "Old man, look at my life."

And Clover picked up the Neil Young tune on Trey's phone.

"So, Maloney's and a mediocre garage band it is."

Sonya kept it casual with Molly's choice of linen pants in faded green and a cropped white tee. She put her hair back in a sleek tail, added dangles to her ears and white sneakers on her feet.

Cleo came out of her room in a short black leather skirt and snug black tee she'd paired with platform sandals.

"Did Molly pick that?"

"No. I explained I always wear leather when I go to a joint."

As they started down, Clover added Megan Thee Stallion with Nicki Minaj and Ty Dolla Sign's "Hot Girl Summer."

On a laugh, Cleo took Sonya's hand. "That's one musically eclectic grandmama you got there, Son."

"She's all that and a Ferris wheel."

Trey took one look at them and shook his head. "Maloney's never had it so good. Okay, you guys," he addressed the pets. "Stay out of the liquor cabinet and no wild women. Present company excepted."

Sonya bent to give Yoda a rub, and ended up rubbing all three dogs and giving Pye a long stroke. "See you later."

They piled into Trey's truck. "I'm the DD," he told them. "And I should warn you, the wine's questionable."

"Wouldn't be the first time I've had a glass of questionable wine." Sonya looked back at the house.

The sun would soon set, so she'd left lights on. And she trusted Jack with all the pets. A couple hours in a bar with live music, mediocre wine, and pool sounded just fine.

"I get in ruts."

"Tell me about it," Cleo said from the back.

"I don't have to tell you. I probably don't have to tell anyone in this truck. I'm saying it's nice to be pulled out of my comfortable-ish rut for an evening."

She added a big smile.

"Maybe we could play some pool."

"Sure. Have you ever played?"

"Sort of. Hit the ball with the stick so it goes in the hole."

"I think that's golf," Owen said.

"Kind of the same, but you don't have to hit it as hard or walk as far."

"That's one way of looking at it," Trey decided.

"Music won't start for about another half hour. We'll have a game first."

"I guess you play," Cleo said to Owen.

"Now and then. We'll go easy on you."

"Sounds like fun."

They parked on the street and walked into Maloney's, where the sound system played Led Zeppelin's "Hot Dog." Over the bar with its eight stools and mountain man–bearded bartender, the O's and the Yankees slugged it out in the third. No score.

Tables crowded the space with a kind of bump-out for the pool table and a juke. The walls—fake logs and thick gray mortar that possibly had been white once—were decorated with signs for various beers and clever sayings like:

sorry, i'm drunk.

Owen signaled a waitress with purple hair, a nose ring, and sleeve tats, pointed to a table. She sent him a wink and, pursing lips of dark, dark red, blew him a kiss.

"We've got a reservation if you want that game."

"I love having friends in low places." Cleo set a hand on her hip. "I'll risk the wine. Coming into a place like this and not drinking— unless you're the DD—is just rude."

"Got you covered. Rack 'em, Owen."

While Trey went to the bar, Owen began to rack the balls. "We're playing eight ball. Simple rules. One team has solids, the other stripes. You have to sink all your balls into the pockets, then declare which pocket you'll sink the eight ball in. Hit that in before you sink all your other balls, you lose. Sink it in a different hole than you called, you lose."

"That's a lot of losing. But you win," Sonya qualified, "if you put all your balls in the holes, then the eight one. That black one."

"That's it. We play teams. We can do you and Trey, me and Cleo."

"Girls against boys." Cleo walked over to study the cues. "It's classic."

"Whatever. Let me show you how to hold that."

"Can I knock at them first?" Sonya took down a cue. "It'd be like a handicap, right? With the black one in the middle, it'd be harder to get it in a hole right off, and maybe I'd get one of ours in to start."

"You got it. Listen, but if you do hit the eight ball in on the break, that's a win."

"But why—" She broke off, gave a frustrated wave of the hand. "Never mind."

"You don't want the cue ball—the solid white one—to go in,"

Owen explained. "Not on the break, that's a loss. Through the game, if it goes in, it's a scratch, and the other team shoots."

"This is complicated."

"It's really not, once you get going. If one of the solids or stripes goes in on the break, you shoot again, and you can declare solids or stripes. Then you've got to hit a ball from that group with the cue ball, or the other team shoots. As long as you make a shot, get your ball in, you keep shooting."

"What if I hit one of the others—not mine—in?"

"Once you've called solids or stripes, unless one of yours goes in, too, that's a turnover."

Cleo blew out a breath. "Maybe you can walk us through it as we play."

"No problem. Sonya wants to break," he told Trey.

"All right." He handed Cleo and Sonya their wine. "Abby is bringing your beer and my Coke. You want to try to hit the cue ball right here, cutie." He held his finger over the table. "With a good, solid smack."

"Okay." She took a sip of wine, laughed. "*Questionable* is high praise." Then handed the glass to Cleo. "I remember you hold the stick like this."

"Something like that. Let's chalk it up first."

He did it for her, then adjusted her hold on the cue. "You want smooth, with a follow-through."

"Okay, here we go."

She slid the cue a couple of times, then rammed it into the cue ball. With a clatter, balls rolled, fell into pockets with a thump. Three found homes, then four. Then the eight ball dropped smoothly into the right-side pocket.

"Oh! Is that the win or the loss?"

Owen just eyed her narrowly.

"That was not a lucky shot," Trey said.

"It sort of was. I haven't played in a couple years." She took her glass back from a hooting Cleo. "I guess it's like riding a bike."

"Friend." He looked across the table at Owen. "We've been hustled."

"You a shark, too?" Owen asked Cleo.

"I taught Sonya everything I know, but I admit, the student became the master."

"Rack 'em, Trey. And no mercy."

The band opened with "One Eyed Bastard" as the women won the game. They exchanged fist bumps and exploding fingers.

"I'd be humiliated," Trey decided, "if the two of you weren't so damn good."

"I'm humiliated anyway, but I'll live with it."

They went to their table, and Sonya studied the band. Four guys, one girl. Probably college age, though they looked younger to her, with a lot of floppy over-the-eyes hair, ripped jeans, and combat boots.

Then they rolled into Bon Jovi's "You Give Love a Bad Name."

"That song's older than they are," Sonya pointed out.

"A classic's a classic" was Owen's opinion. "But the lead guitar's no Richie Sambora."

"Who is?" And Trey let out a quick laugh and rose. "Take a seat."

His pregnant sister, Anna, did just that. "Whew! We took an ice cream walk after we had dinner out. Then Seth says, 'Hey, let's drop in here for a set.' And who do we find?"

"You look wonderful," Sonya said. "Glowing."

"Pretty sure that's sweat. There's a nice breeze out there, but I'm running hot these days."

"Sweat or not, looking good, Mama. How's she doing?"

"Feisty, Owen, the girl is feisty."

"The best kind," Cleo said.

"And you"—she gripped Cleo's hand—"and you, too"—then Sonya's. "The nursery mural is beyond fabulous. I swear I can't count the number of times a day I go in there just to look at it."

Trey pulled over two chairs, crowded them in, as Seth brought Anna a glass.

"Bottled water on ice, as ordered. I just had an impulse to stop by, check out the band. We're always looking for entertainment options at the hotel."

Leaning over, she kissed Trey's cheek. Then she put Seth's hand on her belly. "The way she's dancing in there, she may be a rocker."

"Let's discourage any facial piercings. Cleo, we stopped into Bay Arts to deliver a few pieces Anna finished, and saw your paintings. They're wonderful."

"Thanks. There's so much around here that insists I paint it."

"Good for us. We bought one, the one of the bay, the boats, the two boys about to cast off in a little sloop."

"*Boys on the Bay*," Anna supplied. "I loved how they looked ready for adventure."

"We're having one tomorrow," Sonya told her, and adjusted the volume of her voice when the band took a break. "On *The Horizon*."

"We've got room for two, and what?" Owen calculated. "Two and two-thirds more, if you're interested."

"I'd love it. Don't know how I'd handle it at this stage, but I'd love it. Except—"

"We're booked at my parents' tomorrow. My mom's birthday."

"Next summer you're on. Meanwhile, Trey said you're going through storage at the manor, changing some things."

"Mostly adding," Sonya told her. "We think of it as reclaiming rooms."

"I think that's great. And I heard additional photo shoots for the Ryder project are happening." She sent a snarky sisterly smile toward Trey. "I bet you can't wait."

"Shut up."

"Not a chance. Mom's already got ideas. I've got one now. Home, Daddy. This baby mama's tired. I do have some more things for the website, Sonya. I'll get in touch next week."

"I'm ready whenever you are."

"We've got it," Trey said as Seth reached for his wallet. "I think we can spot you a glass of water and a Coke."

"He needs a guys' night."

"Anna."

"You do," she insisted, and turned to Trey and Owen. "He does. He's working more hours so he can take daddy leave, and getting things ready around the house."

"We're up for that." Owen looked at Trey. "Poker, Friday night. My place."

"Yeah?" Seth smiled. "Yeah, that'd be great. I'm in. Come on, babe, let's go home and put our girl to bed."

"And I'm down for that. Talk soon."

"They're so pretty together," Cleo commented. "Not just the looks, which rank high for both. It's the easy rhythm."

"Mom says Anna came home with stars in her eyes after their first date, and the stars never went out."

"Which doesn't mean we can't skin him at poker. Pull in Ace and Deuce if they're not busy. I can get Mike."

"Leaves us out," Cleo observed.

"Guys' night. You two can watch sappy movies."

"Which we will," Sonya assured him. "Now, we've gone over our two hours."

"Strict."

"Yes, my favorite cousin."

"I'd object, but I'm not sure I want to sit through another set. I've got it." Owen waved Trey back and went to pay the tab.

"I'm going to sharpen up my skills. We need a rematch."

"Adorable." Sonya examined her nails. "Just adorable. Remember, you have many other exceptional skills."

"Right. Where'd you learn to play pool to teach this one how to play?"

"My daddy. He's such a quiet, unassuming sort of man. People who didn't know him would think, oh, there's an easy mark. He'd let them talk him into a game, eight ball, nine ball, cutthroat, whatever. Then he'd quietly, unassumingly wipe the table with them."

"Good to know. When he visits again, I won't suggest a friendly game of pool."

"Play poker with him, prepare to lose your shirt."

"I'm pretty good at poker."

When Cleo just smiled, Trey nodded. "So noted." And rose when Owen returned.

Once they got in the truck, Sonya settled back. "This was a very fine idea."

"We still have cake coming." Owen nudged Cleo. "Right?"

"Let's have it up on the widow's walk. What do you say, Son? Up there under the stars, the moon, with the ocean rolling below."

"I say another fine idea."

They came home to delighted dogs, and a cat who allowed them entry.

Since Yoda still had a ball in his mouth, Sonya laughed.

"Good time with Jack."

"I'll let them out awhile."

"While Trey does that, I'll whip some cream. Sonya, cappuccino?"

"All over it."

In the kitchen with Cleo, Sonya got out cups. "It really was a good time. I keep telling myself to get out more."

"You do fine. You hit your comfort zone. We like to party, but we were never party girls. We're having ourselves an excellent weekend. Doing our search, fixing up rooms, having a fine meal, going out for pool and music. Tomorrow taking a sail."

"And Monday back to work."

"It's what suits us. Trey, just in time. Why don't you and Sonya take the coffee up. Owen and I can bring the cake."

They made their way up, and as they passed the third floor, Sonya looked down the hall.

Quiet and dark. Saying nothing, she kept going, but she'd felt it. Eye of the storm, she thought, and it would blow in before long.

But not, she promised herself, right now. She'd take that calm, even if it proved a false one.

When they reached the widow's walk, she stood under the stars, the moon, with the ocean rolling below.

"Worth the trip."

"Do you come up here much?"

"Not as much as I should. It always takes my breath. Cleo talks about painting from up here. She probably will."

She moved to the rail, breathed in the night. "Do you think I'll ever get used to it? I hope I don't. I hope it always takes my breath."

"You may get used to it, but that doesn't mean you'd take it for granted."

"I couldn't." She turned, smiled at him. "The same goes for you. I may be getting used to having you haul furniture or just being here when I need you. But I don't take it, or you, for granted."

"Here's where I want to be. You're why I want to be here."

She stood, her back to the sea, and the moonlight streaming.

"Sonya, it's only been a few months, but . . ." He trailed off as he heard Owen's voice.

"Jesus, Lafayette, I've got it."

"But?" Sonya prompted.

"Here's where I want to be," he repeated.

He reminded himself it wasn't the time or the place to say more.

He stepped to her, kissed her, soft, gentle. "You're why I want to be here."

Chapter Seven

Shortly before noon, they arrived at the marina with three dogs, a cat, a cooler of drinks, and enough food to sustain humans and pets for a serious sail.

"With all this, Owen," Sonya said as they started to unload the truck, "you might need a bigger boat."

"I think she'll handle it."

When he gestured, she followed his direction. "Well, she's a beauty, and I should've expected no less."

With her catch-all bag on her shoulder, Pye tolerating the leash, Cleo tipped down her sunglasses. "A wooden sloop. You went old-school."

"Classic."

He'd painted it navy blue, a rich choice with the gleaming teak decking. The brightwork shined.

Cleo pulled out another bag while Sonya wrangled two dogs and took yet another bag. Jones stuck with Owen as he and Trey hauled out the cooler.

Once they'd transferred everything, Sonya looked around.

"You built her."

"Had some help."

"Slave labor." Trey tapped his chest.

"And my brother, our uncle Mike. At thirty-eight feet I can sail her solo, but there's room for crew. Galley down below if you want to stow the food before we cast off."

"We'll do that."

Belowdecks, Sonya turned to Cleo. "Not just a galley, a little lounge."

"Look at the equipment. Classic build, and state-of-the-art electronics. Pooles don't stint." She opened a door. "The head's so cute it doesn't feel right calling it a head."

Sonya looked in, saw clean, saw white and wood and chrome, including a small shower.

"That's one minor concern off my list." She opened another door.

The stateroom was mostly bed with, she noted, storage as its base.

"Nice. Nice, clean, and efficient, with style tossed in. The man's got vision."

"He just keeps racking up those points," Cleo murmured. "Let's get this food put away, and set sail."

When they went back up, Trey finished putting the last pet PFD on Yoda. "I can turn my first mate status over to you if you want."

"I'll take it." Pleased, Cleo walked over to cast off. "On your orders, Captain."

"Day's wasting. Cast off."

When they motored out of the slip, Cleo moved over to Owen. Sonya caught a few words of conversation as she sat on one of the benches and prepared to enjoy herself.

"They're talking engines, rigging, draft, whatever. If she wasn't already hooked on him, and *The Siren* didn't seal the deal, *The Horizon* would. It really is a beautiful boat."

"Took him several years from design to maiden voyage. Weekends, evenings, vacation time, but he got just what he wanted. And Cleo? She knows what she's doing outside of a Sunfish?"

"Oh yeah, she does. Bet you do, too."

"Born and raised by the bay. But I've got no problem demoting myself to second mate."

On Owen's orders, Cleo hoisted sails. From her seat, Sonya watched the white mainsail rise, billow, and snap as it filled with air.

"Gorgeous." She tipped her face up as *The Horizon* streamed on the wind and water.

At the wheel, Owen heeled into it, let her fly. Jones moved up to the bow to stand and let his short, ragged ears do the same.

Obviously up for an adventure, Yoda joined Mookie on the starboard side to watch the water. In her pink PFD, Pyewacket stretched out on the bench like a sunbather.

"Born sailors," Trey commented, and Sonya laughed.

Adjusting her sunglasses, she looked up at the cliffs where the manor stood over the shore and sea.

"It's beautiful, from every angle. You know, I always imagined living in a big old house. Something interesting, something with history. I even collected pictures of houses for a while. Victorians topped my list, but Tudors, Colonials, whatever caught my eye. Nothing I imagined ever came close to the manor."

"It was meant to be yours."

"I feel that more every day." She nodded to Cleo and Owen. "She's trying to talk him into letting her take the wheel."

Amused, Trey gave the brim of her ball cap a tap. "I can tell you, he doesn't give it up easy."

And when Owen did, shoving his hands in his pockets and stepping back, Trey thought: Yeah, he's sunk. Completely, totally, absolutely sunk.

After a few minutes, Owen left her at the wheel and crossed the deck to the cooler.

"Is it beer o'clock already?" Sonya asked him.

"I don't drink when I drive, don't drink when I sail." He pulled out a Coke. "Want?"

Trey wagged his fingers, and Owen passed drinks over.

"You're not driving the boat," Sonya pointed out.

"For a few minutes. She's got it."

"Can I have a turn?"

Studying her, Owen took a long drink. "Have you ever handled a thirty-eight-foot sloop?"

"No."

"There's your answer."

He walked back to the wheel, but didn't take it. Instead, he turned on music.

Sonya took out her phone, tapped the camera for a shot of Cleo, white sundress billowing, at the wheel.

He let her handle the wheel for an hour. When he took it back, she headed to the cooler.

"That was a thrill. If I wanted a sloop, I sure as hell know where to go." She pulled out a bottle of water. "This boat is A1." She sat, lifted her face to the wind. "Now I need to talk Owen into sailing down to New Orleans sometime."

"How long would that take?" Sonya wondered.

"Oh, a week or so. He said the two of you sailed down to New York a couple years back, Trey, to visit his brother."

"Good times—and that's only a day or two at sea."

"We could start with that. He said he's going to head to somewhere called Pirate's Cove in a bit."

Trey laughed. "We named it that when we were kids. It's a nice spot, some out of the way. We lobbied—and hard—for permission to build a small dock. He must be ready to eat something, and to give the animals a pit stop."

He took his time, and when Sonya saw the cove—a small scoop out of water and land near the lighthouse—she stood.

"That's so charming. Cleo, you have to paint it."

"Right there with you."

"Hold that thought," Owen called out. "Drop sails."

Since Cleo already had her sketchbook out, Trey rose.

"I got it."

As she watched Trey and Owen work together, Sonya took another picture. She thought she might try her hand at doing it in chalk, and frame it for Trey's office or apartment.

When Trey secured the lines to the dock, Sonya started below-decks.

"I need a few minutes to finish this," Cleo told her.

"Take your time. I'll get the food. Looks like a picnic on a little rocky beach."

More rocks than beach, she noted, but that added to the charm and the sense of isolation.

She could see boats sailing on the bay, a couple of water-skiers, a paddleboard or two. She decided that added to it all as well.

Freed of the PFDs, the dogs leaped from boat to dock and onto the beach. Leading the way, Jones strutted toward the line of gnarled and wind-twisted trees.

"He and Mooks know their way around," Trey assured her. "Yoda will stick with them."

"Yeah, he will. Cleo?" she called down from the dock. "What about Pye?"

"She won't wander from her boys, or me. And absolutely not from her boyfriend."

"What can I say?" Owen put a selection of cold drinks in an insulated pack. "I'm a female magnet."

"Female felines anyway. Ten more minutes."

Owen angled to look at the sketch, at the tumbled rocks where the water lapped, the narrow crescent of sand, the twisty trees climbing the base of the cliff.

"Fast work."

He left her to it, joined the others on the beach.

"You can still see the manor from here." Happy, relaxed, Sonya leaned against Trey. "Look how the sun glints off the windows when it hits just right. You and Owen came here as kids?"

"Yeah, in Connor's fourteen-footer, we'd explore, eat junk food. When we were teens, we'd bring girls here. This time of year, you can swim if you're not afraid of cold water."

Not afraid, she thought, but distinctly not interested. "I'll pass there."

"There's a cave." Owen spread out a blanket. "It's pretty cool."

"Another pass."

"Girl."

"Yes, I am." She sat on the blanket to set out food. "We've got sandwiches, a variety of chips, fruit, raw veggies and dip."

Pye came back to climb onto a rock and gaze out over the water as if she owned it. Sonya glanced back to see the three dogs follow her out and engage in a sniffing contest.

When Cleo joined them, she ignored the food and started another sketch.

"I want one from here. Sweep of sand and the rocks in the foreground. Boat at the dock, the bay beyond. I'm going to sail here and try some painting on this beach. Maybe do one all the way to the far cliffs and the manor."

"Got binoculars in the bag if you want a close look."

"No." She shook her head at Owen. "I like this perspective. The single boat here, alone, the manor on the cliffs in the distance, alone."

"How about the cat?" Trey wondered.

"Not for this one, but in another? Sitting up there on the rock, gazing out. Mistress of all she surveys. Just doodling ideas here."

Once again, Owen angled to look. "She calls that doodling."

"She does," Sonya agreed.

On a contented sigh, she munched on a potato chip. Then looked up and over at the manor.

And gripped Trey's hand.

"Do you see that? The manor. Do you see that?"

"Yeah."

Something dark flew, then vanished. Then flew again.

Trey pulled the binoculars from the bag, and brought it all closer.

"It's her big-ass bird." He passed the glasses to Owen. "It flies out— her window, the best I can tell."

"Yeah, I see it. Flies out, then poofs. Then again."

"I need to see." Sonya took the glasses, and the view popped closer so quickly, she jolted. "Why is she doing that? There's no one there to try to scare, to threaten."

"She's practicing." Cleo set the sketchbook aside, reached for half a sandwich. "When no one can see. Or none of us can see—she thinks."

"None of us can see her fail. She's trying to increase her distance."

Trey took the glasses back to check again. "That's my take. She's trying and not getting anywhere with that."

He put an arm around Sonya's shoulders. "She doesn't want you to
see her practicing, wasting her time and energy."

"Because," Sonya said slowly, "she wants us—or at least me—to
believe her power's, if not unlimited, more than we can counter."

"And she'd be wrong." Picking up the sketchbook again, Cleo drew
a quick sketch of Dobbs from memory. And managed to show the
frustration as well as the madness. "Because she's losing."

"She's losing," Sonya agreed. "Every day we're there, she loses a little more. Every painting of a bride we find and hang is a loss for her.
Every room we use, another loss."

"Hey, cutie."

Trey turned Sonya's head toward him, and kissed her.

"Smart women," he said, "are so damned attractive."

"She scares me," Sonya admitted. "But—"

"You scare her right back."

"Yeah. It's good to know."

"Another arrow in the quiver's how I see it." Owen jutted his chin
toward the manor. "When we figure it all out, you're going to put one
right through her heart."

"That's the plan. She's stopped." Pleased, Sonya leaned back against
Trey. "She ran out of steam, gave up, needs to recharge. Whatever,
she's stopped. Probably up there having one of her tantrums."

And the thought of that pleased her even more.

They ate, lazed on the beach, and as the afternoon waned, stowed
everything away to leave the quiet spot exactly as they'd found it. As
they sailed, sliding along with other boats now, Sonya glanced at the
manor from time to time.

But saw nothing except the great house on the cliffs.

They docked in the early summer evening, and made *The Horizon*
shipshape before they stepped back on land.

"That was really wonderful." In the truck, Sonya relaxed. "A perfect summer Sunday sail."

"She's got running lights," Cleo pointed out. "Maybe a sunset sail sometime."

"We could do that."

"We could drop these guys off at my parents', walk off our sea legs before dinner."

"A man with a plan. Bay Arts is still open with its summer hours. I wouldn't mind going in for a minute, getting a look at the new pieces Anna wants on the website."

"Walking's not shopping," Owen warned.

"Often while walking, I find I might see something that says: *Buy me!*" Stroking the cat, Cleo smiled. "That's not shopping either."

"One step at a time. We'll drop these guys off."

When they reached the pretty Victorian, they found Deuce and Corrine in the garden sipping cocktails.

The dogs immediately made themselves at home, greeting their hosts, then wandering around the yard. The cat reserved judgment until Deuce walked over and gave her a long stroke.

She purred.

"She's such a flirt." Amused, Cleo stepped over to kiss Deuce's cheek. "But so am I. Corrine, your garden's so beautiful."

"Next to my kids, my pride and joy. And don't the four of you look windblown and sun-kissed. How about a cold drink? I'm having a Bellini, and Deuce is sticking with his G&T."

"I'd love a Bellini."

Echoing Cleo, Sonya held up two fingers.

"I could use a beer."

"I'm with Owen. I'll give you a hand, Mom."

"As if I can't put a few drinks together. I know you have plans for dinner, but I want to say I made a big bowl of pasta salad, and Deuce is grilling chicken."

"Your pasta salad." Owen pointed at Corrine, somehow elegant in her cropped khakis and pale blue T-shirt. "His grilled chicken?" Owen spread his arms, looked at the other three. "Come on, man."

"And there's a boule of sourdough made fresh this morning."

"You guys can go on if you want. I'm sticking."

"It sounds wonderful," Sonya said. "If you're sure you—"

"Settled. I'll be right back."

"You made her day." Deuce looked after his wife, pushed back the brim of his ball cap over his gray-streaked hair. "She made that pasta salad—enough to feed an army—hoping you'd stay. And I've got plenty of chicken marinating because I hoped the same."

He gestured to chairs on the generous back porch. "Let's have a seat. How was the sail?"

"Couldn't have been better," Sonya told him.

"That's good to hear. I thought I'd come by one day next week if that's good for you. I have paperwork for you to look over and sign regarding the donations you want to continue."

"You're welcome anytime, paperwork or not."

"Collin would be so pleased you're doing this."

He glanced back as Corrine came out with a tray carrying two frothy flutes and two pilsners.

"This is so nice," she said when Trey got up to take the drinks from her. "Summer goes by so quickly, and we're all busy. It's nice to have an evening like this."

"And your gardens are picture-perfect."

"They do make me happy. I did have a thought about gardens. I'm not going to insert work into the evening."

"It's not work if you love it."

Corrine beamed at Sonya. "It's not, is it? I need to see the wardrobe before I make any real decisions."

"Coming this week. I'd love to hear your thought."

"I'm told you've not only maintained the gardens at the manor but added to them. With Cleo doing some yoga poses outside, my thought is the garden at the manor."

"This is an excellent thought. The hydrangeas are really hitting gorgeous. And we have this statue. A goddess."

Corrine held up a hand. "Shots of Cleo with the flowers and the statue in frame. Don't hate me," she said as she turned to Cleo. "I think a sun salutation, at sunrise, would be fantastic."

Cleo winced, drank some Bellini. "I can take one for the team. But it better be an amazing yoga outfit. Got any ideas on those two?"

Corrine glanced toward her son and Owen, now talking baseball with Deuce. "Actually, I do have a few."

By the time Deuce started the grill, Sonya had a picture in her mind of how to put it all together.

In his Bermuda shorts and Red Sox tee, he grilled vegetables and chicken. It seemed so strange to her that this man had knocked on her door on a cold winter's day in Boston, and changed her life.

He'd helped her find family she hadn't known existed, helped give her a home she'd loved from first glance—and included a centuries-old curse to break.

He was the father of the man she'd fallen in love with.

When he set the platter on the table, she smiled at him.

"Thank you. Not just for the meal, but for everything you've done for me."

"You're welcome, and it's all been my very great pleasure."

With the reviving weekend behind her, Sonya faced the workweek with energy. She put that to use first with a workout. Every time the servants' bell rang, she chanted.

"Strong body, strong mind, strong spirit. I will kick your ass with all three."

She showered, changed, then flexed her biceps in the mirror.

"We've got this."

Mind, body, spirit united and focused, she walked into the library.

Then stopped at her desk when her heart took a quick leap.

She picked up the sketch, breathing slow as tears gathered.

Yoda looked back at her. If dogs could laugh, he laughed. He stood on his back legs as if ready to dance.

In the bottom left corner of the sketch, the careful printing read:

Jack

She had to swallow before she spoke.

"Well, this is wonderful. You really got him. The happy expression, the brindle coat, the squarish face, the weirdly cute proportions of those stubby legs and hot-dog body. Thank you, Jack. I'm going to frame this. I already treasure it."

She turned it so the model could see the sketch.

"Look at you! Jack drew you. Aren't you cute?"

Touched, grateful, she laid the sketch on the desk, and after Yoda wiggled under, sat and booted up her computer.

"Okay, Clover, I'm ready."

Jimmy Buffett's "Come Monday" started the day's playlist.

"And that's how we roll."

She got two solid hours in before Cleo shuffled down the hall.

"Hold on a minute. I want to show you something."

Cleo stopped. "Not a bad something, not before coffee."

"No, not a bad anything." Sonya took the sketch with her into the hall. "This was on my desk this morning."

"Oh, Son! It's so good, and how sweet is this? You have to frame it."

"I will. And I thought I'd get him an art kit."

"I could put something together, but a kit of his own's even better. I love this, what a good start to the day. Owen said we'd get thunderstorms late afternoon."

"How does he know?"

"He just knows. So I'm going to start on my summer edition of the tree out front, so I'm close to home. And I can't believe I'm having a conversation before coffee. Bye."

Since Yoda and Pye followed Cleo down, Sonya figured she'd let them out, and back in after she'd had her coffee.

She broke about noon for a Coke boost, a peach that tasted like summer, and some peanut butter crackers that tasted of childhood.

As she went back upstairs, she peeked out front. Cleo sat at her easel with Yoda napping nearby. The cat sunned herself on the seawall.

"And all's right with the world."

Seconds later, the doorbell bonged. Though Sonya's stomach jumped, she faked a yawn. "Boring."

Now banging joined the bonging, and she ignored it and walked back to the library.

"Getting under your skin, Hester?"

She considered that a small victory.

The little tantrums took energy, she thought, and she had no problem with Dobbs wasting hers.

She sat down at her desk to Twisted Sister's "We're Not Gonna Take It."

"That's right, we're not."

Her defiance meant ignoring the noise, and barely noticing when it stopped. She worked through the rumble of thunder, realizing she'd missed her afternoon walk.

She heard Cleo come in, and shortly after come up the steps.

"I'm in my studio for a while. Dinner's salmon with rice and candied carrots."

Eyes on her screen, Sonya shot up a thumb.

Before long, as the rain drummed, she heard the sound of the ball bouncing downstairs and Yoda scrambling after it.

Smiling, she thought again: And all's right with the world.

It stayed right through the evening, into the next day and the next. Sonya considered the routine a blessing, and broke it only when the Ryder wardrobe arrived.

"Oh boy, oh boy!"

With Cleo out running errands, Sonya carried box after box to the library, and considered that made up for the workout she'd skipped that morning.

She opened, unboxed, considered, admired. Then sorted by names on the labels.

By the time she'd finished, she thought her office space looked like a high-end sporting goods store.

When she heard Cleo, she jogged down the stairs again.

"The Ryder stuff's here."

"Oh boy, oh boy."

"That's what I said!"

They carried groceries and flowers inside, put groceries away.

Then Cleo looked at the armloads of flowers. "Molly, would you please take care of these?"

Clover answered for her with the Beatles and "With a Little Help from My Friends."

"Yes!" Cleo rubbed her hands together. "Let's go! I'm dying to see my yoga outfit."

"It's really pretty. I should tell you they switched the idea of you lounging to sailing."

"I'm fine with that."

"With Owen, on *The Horizon*. I got the idea when he let you take the wheel, sent them a photo I took. Corrine can come up with something more clever, but that's the idea."

"I want to see the outfit."

Cleo stopped at the library door and gaped.

"Holy shit!"

"I know. It took me forever, and I didn't even unbox the sports equipment." She pointed to the boxes beside the curving staircase to the second level.

"I'd say you should've waited for me to help, but I wouldn't have either."

"Your things are over here."

"Shoes?" Cleo pulled the lid off a box. "Oh, look at these cute boat shoes." And immediately took off her sandals to try them on. "Good fit, comfy, and they look good!"

She snatched up white pants cropped just below the knee, and being Cleo, stripped off her own to try them.

"And they fit," she stated before pulling off her shirt to try on a tank with horizontal navy-and-white stripes. "I need a mirror."

As she ran out, Sonya picked up her clothes and followed.

In her bedroom, Cleo turned in front of the mirror. "This works. I think I have to say it. I look shipshape."

"You do. I told them I didn't see Owen as a white pants sort of guy, so his are faded blue—bleached-by-the-sun look—and short-sleeved navy rash guard."

"Show off those pecs."

"You got it. Tan deck shoes. Now try this."

"Yoga! Okay, love the color. Dreamy lilac. Long sports bra instead of a tank."

"Show off those abs."

Cleo changed, checked herself from every angle.

"It's excellent, and I love the seamless tights. But I need a pedi—come close to matching the color—and a French mani. I'll book it today."

"They sent a yoga mat, too. It's like a sunrise color—goldy-rosy. No pattern. They don't want to detract from you, the garden."

"This is a hell of a good deal for me."

"Remember that when you have to greet the sunrise. Now take that off. I don't want anything to happen to it before the shoot. Let me know when you've got your nails booked, and I'll coordinate with Corrine."

Chapter Eight

On Friday, after a productive week, Sonya joined Cleo and her dreamy lavender toes at sunrise. And stayed out of the way as Cleo stepped on the mat.

"I'd like you to hold each pose just a few beats," Corrine told her. "And stay relaxed."

"I'm always relaxed at sunrise because I'm asleep. I'll start with a basic sun salutation."

"I want shots of each pose, from different angles. You know to ignore me. By the way? The toes? Fabulous touch. Whenever you're ready."

Trey and Owen stepped out, along with Jones and Mookie. Sonya just put a finger to her lips.

Hands in prayer, Cleo breathed in, lifted her arms, touched palms again as she arched back, held, then flowed down, palms on the mat, nose on shins. By the time she lifted to Ardha Uttanasana, she'd blocked out the camera completely.

"This is good," Sonya murmured. "It's so good. The light's perfect."

When Cleo ended in prayer, Corrine straightened from her crouch.

"Beautiful. I'd like another."

"I have to do three anyway. It's the right number."

When she completed the third, Corrine checked her camera screen, scrolling through shots.

"We've got it. You're a pleasure to shoot, Cleo."

"I'm going to start doing yoga out here, not at this hour, but this new mat handles the grass well."

"I gotta go," Owen called out. "Busy day, then poker night."

"Tomorrow," Corrine reminded him. "Ten o'clock. The two of you on *The Horizon*."

"I got it."

"And you." She pointed at her son. "In wardrobe in three hours for the on land. Tomorrow, two o'clock, wet suit. Waterskiing."

"I know, I know."

Sonya placated him with a pat on the arm. "How about some coffee, Corrine? And Cleo tried her hand at coffee cake."

"I would love that. I've got time, since Cleo's so easy to shoot."

"I've got to go, too." Trey leaned down, kissed Sonya. "I'll be back tomorrow after my mother tortures me. I'll bring dinner. I can buy it with my poker winnings from tonight."

"Expect a small order of fries," Owen told her. "Maybe a peanut."

"If I lose that bad, you're buying dinner." He kissed Sonya again, then Corrine. "Let's go, Mook."

"I'm going to do a little more, since I'm up and out here." Cleo stepped back into Mountain Pose, prayer position.

Since Yoda and Pye opted to stay out, Sonya led Corrine inside.

"I've said it before, but I really love the touches you've added to the kitchen."

"Credit Cleo the most. She really uses the space, which is why we have coffee cake she made last night."

Corrine set her camera on the table. "Would you mind if I walked down and looked at the portraits? The brides."

"Of course not."

"I'll just be a minute."

While Corrine walked down to the music room, Sonya made coffee, sliced cake.

Corrine came back, patted a hand on her heart. "Trey said you'd found more. It's eerie, and it's fascinating. I don't know the history by memory. Who's left?"

"Catherine. And Astrid. We think there'll be one of her, too. Like a set, a series."

"You're a brave woman, Sonya."

"I don't know if it's bravery." She gestured for Corrine to sit, joined her. "I do know I need to be here, and I need to do this."

"Isn't the definition of courage doing what needs to be done?"

"There's more. It's . . . The little boy who died here a hundred years ago? Jack. He drew me a picture of Yoda, a good one, left it on my desk."

"Incredible." Corrine rubbed her arms as if chilled. "Eerie and fascinating. I'm glad you're here doing what needs doing. Not just for the now, and I'm trying not to overstep, so I'll just say you and Trey look good together. But Johanna was a sister to me."

"I know." Sonya laid a hand over Corrine's. "I know she was, and I know how that feels."

"I'm glad you're here for her, Sonya. For Johanna."

"And now, I bet you'd like to see those yoga shots."

"Oh yeah, I would."

By the time Cleo came back in, Sonya was at her desk.

"I got caught up. I missed my chance to take a peek at the pictures."

"Be assured, they're terrific. We're sending what we both consider the best to Ryder—and pushing for our favorite."

"How about a hint?"

At her desk, Sonya lifted her arms up, looked up and pressed her palms together.

"Really? The first move?"

"Of the second round. Corrine said, and I agreed, your body was perfectly curved in both, but in the second round, you'd forgotten about the camera—and being awake at sunrise. There's a dreamy look on your face, the slightest smile. And the light's gorgeous. She'll send proofs later today or tomorrow."

"She's right about the camera. I got in the zone." She spread her hands. "And look at my outfit! While I wish I wasn't energized this early, since I am, I'm changing and going out to work on my summer tree."

Hand on hip, she studied Sonya. "You know, you've worked really hard and long this week. You should take a few hours, paint with me."

"I may have a new client."

"Really? Who? What?"

"My mother's doctor. Mom's been going to her for about fifteen years—I used her, too. Mom was in for her annual physical, and they chatted some. Dr. Lawrence asked how I was, and one thing led to another. The website is dated, plus, she's adding a new associate into the practice. I need to work up a proposal."

"I won't get in the way of that. But if you finish, or just want a break, come out. And remember, it's sappy movie night."

"I never forget sappy movie night."

"Big giant salad, fancy cheese and crackers, wine, followed by popcorn, more wine, and girl movie."

"The Friday night special."

Sonya worked while Cleo changed, while she went up to her studio to get what she needed.

As Cleo headed down, so did Yoda.

"Yoda's with me," Cleo called.

"Thanks!"

Then quiet as she read more about Dr. Nia Lawrence to spark ideas and direction for her proposal.

Potential new clients always pumped her up, and within twenty minutes she had a concept.

The doctor had a family practice, so play up the family vibe with calm, warm colors and clear, simple fonts. Photo and bio of the doctor in a drop-down, a photo of her talking to a patient. Short two- or three-line bios of staff, photos of them interacting with patients.

Our family cares for your family.

Something like that.

Office hours, office numbers, right up front.

She could absolutely make it look good, appealing. But that was nothing if it wasn't more user-friendly, and more accessible to mobile devices.

She could fix it, and spent the next hour working the concept into a plan, then added more time turning the plan into a proposal.

It took her more time to realize Clover had stopped the music.

And in the silence, she heard voices. Not close, not clear, but a murmuring, somehow female. With the voices, she felt a pull.

Not the mirror, she understood that immediately. But something that drew her, that pushed her to her feet.

She walked out into the hall, hesitated only a moment at the stairs. She could go down, call Cleo, but . . .

Drawn, she continued along the hall, walking steadily now, to the room where her mother stayed on visits. Instead of the flowering violet wallpaper Winter found charming, bluebirds flew across the walls. The bed, neatly turned down, had draping over its four posts and open canopy.

The room held an armoire she recognized from her Saturday search, a washstand with a bowl and pitcher, a small tufted chair and table, and a vanity with a mirror.

Logs snapped in the fireplace. The windows were dark with night, and the room was lit by candles.

A woman sat at the vanity, smiling into the glass. She wore a white nightgown with lace around the neck, a silk bow at the center, and a matching robe over it with the long sleeves gathered at the wrist.

Sonya had seen her before, wearing that nightgown as she walked, entranced, into the winter's storm, bare feet over the snow as Dobbs waited at the seawall.

Catherine.

Behind her stood a woman in deep green velvet, her sunny hair swept up, emeralds at her ears and another glowing at her throat against the sparkle of diamonds.

A pretty woman whose eyes seemed to shine with both tears and pride. Arabelle Poole, Sonya thought, brushing her daughter's hair on her wedding night.

"You look lovely." Arabelle leaned down to kiss the top of Catherine's head. "You made a lovely bride, my darling, and now you make a lovely wife."

"I cared so little about looking lovely." Catherine said it with a laugh in her voice as her eyes met her mother's in the glass. "I know it caused you frustration, my beautiful mama."

"Nonsense." But Arabelle's eyes laughed as she denied it.

"But today, and oh so much tonight, I want to be lovely for William. I love him so much, Mama. I never expected to love him so much, to know he loves me."

"He is a good man, and I trust will be a good and kind husband to my daughter. I wish both of you the happiness your father and I have shared."

Catherine reached up to take her mother's hand. "You and Papa, you are who I look to, always, to guide me. You must know William has great affection and respect for you both."

"And we for him."

Arabelle set down the brush and stroked her hands down Catherine's fall of hair.

"You and I have talked before about this night."

A faint flush rose into Catherine's cheeks. "Yes, Mama. I know the first time he makes me his wife there may be pain. I am not afraid."

"I believe William will be kind, and he will be patient. I believe you will find joy. This night, and all that follow, should never be merely duty, though it is for some. You, my darling, I wish joy."

"Don't cry, Mama."

"You were born in this house, and now you spend the first night as a wife in this house. I will miss you, Cathy, when you're mistress of your own home."

Arabelle's hand stopped, froze as it lifted once again to stroke Catherine's hair. The flames in the hearth stilled and held.

Catherine turned to Sonya.

"I never became mistress of my own home, or had a honeymoon in the spring. I had this one day, this one night as a bride, as a wife."

"I'm so sorry. I wish—"

"I am a practical woman. Wishes?" She fluttered a hand in the air, a hand where her wedding ring glowed. "Feathers in the wind. What's done is done. For this day, this night, for the first time in my life I felt beautiful. I found the joy my mother hoped for me. William was, as she believed, kind and patient. And more. For a few hours I knew desire, and what it is to be desired.

"I wonder if we might have made a child this night, if not for the dream."

"It wasn't a dream."

"No, no, not a dream. It began as one, or so it seemed. Dreaming of spring when we would make our crossing as husband and wife. Mr. and Mrs. William Cabot."

Rising, Catherine moved around her mother, gestured to the window.

"We had a winter wedding, both of us impatient to begin our life together. Such a storm, the snow, the wind, but it meant nothing to us in our happiness. Instead I dreamed of spring, and walked out of the manor and into the flowers, the green, the sunlight."

"A lie." Standing there, facing the young bride in white, Sonya felt the cruelty of it. "Her lie. Hester Dobbs."

"A lie, yes, and a wicked one. She waited for me out there, and laughing, I went to her. When she took my ring, the ring William placed on my finger only hours before? When I came to myself, oh, the terror! The horrible cold. I tried to run, I tried to call out for William, for my father, for Mama, but it was too late. And the tears froze on my face as I fell, as I died alone with my fear."

"She's evil, Catherine, and obsessed. She stole your life."

"This I can never recover. This nothing can change."

She held up her left hand where her gold wedding ring caught the candlelight.

"William put this on my finger, and made his promises to me. I made my promises to him. She took it for her own. It is not hers. None she took belong to her. This can be recovered. This can be changed."

"I want to get it back for you, to get all of them back for all of you. I don't know how."

"You will."

She walked back to sit under her mother's waiting hand. "Because you must."

She turned her face toward Sonya. "You must," she repeated.

Arabelle's hand came down; mother and daughter's eyes met with a smile in the mirror.

And the room changed back with sunlight streaming through the windows.

"Damn it." Sonya shoved a hand through her hair. "Just damn it."

She started to turn, then jolted when she saw Cleo in the doorway, phone in hand.

"Sorry. I didn't want to . . . interrupt, I guess."

"Did you see them?"

"No. I didn't see anything but the room, and you. I know you did. You were talking to someone. One of the brides?"

"Catherine. I need some air."

"Let me get you some water, and we'll go outside."

"I've still got some at my desk." They started out, then Sonya stopped in the hallway.

"Why did you come in?"

"Clover. That scent of hers at first. I'm painting, and her scent just filled everything. Then 'Help!' The Beatles, on my phone. So I ran in. I thought either Dobbs pulled something, or you'd gone through the mirror."

She waited for Sonya to grab her water bottle.

"I called out when I came in, but you didn't answer."

"I didn't hear you. I guess I didn't hear anything but them."

"Catherine and?"

"Her mother. Arabelle. Arabelle married Collin's twin, Connor Poole."

"I remember," Cleo said as they walked downstairs.

"It was Catherine's wedding night. That must have been her room once, or at least the room they used for that night."

They stepped outside into the summer sunlight, and Sonya let it warm her bones.

"Different wallpaper, different furnishings." She bent to rub Yoda. "The fireplace still wood-burning and the fire crackling. I could feel the heat from it. Candles, several of them. Oh, and two lamps. Oil lamps? Arabelle was brushing Catherine's hair. It was all so loving, so sweet."

She told her, trying to describe the feel of the room, the tone of the conversation.

"It's like you might talk to Winter, or I might with Mama."

"Yes, it was that connection, that bond. It was really lovely, Cleo. Then like with Lissy in the music room that night, everything stopped. It all stopped but Catherine. She looked at me."

"You spoke with her. I heard your part."

"She told me how much she loved William—William Cabot—and how she felt knowing he loved her."

As they walked to the seawall, Sonya tried to recount what Catherine had said to her, in detail.

"Like a dream." Cleo nodded. "That makes sense to me. She was spellbound, in a trance."

"Right up until Dobbs took her wedding ring. Cleo, she said she could never get her life back—that can't be changed—but that the ring doesn't belong to Dobbs and never will."

"All right, that's important. It's a kind of confirmation, Son."

Cleo tapped the moonstone ring she wore.

"Dobbs has the ring, but it's still Catherine's. None of the rings belong to Dobbs, so that part of *done* isn't done. We can take them back."

"She said I would because I must. What good does that do, Cleo? That doesn't tell me anything I don't know."

"Let's sit here, soak in some sun and this breeze like Pye. She's got the right idea."

Cleo sat on the seawall, drew Sonya down beside her.

"It hurts you to see her, speak to her, knowing what happened to her. It hurts me," Cleo added, "and I'm hearing about it all second-hand. You saw her die, Sonya, and now you saw her on her wedding night, all that anticipation and happiness. So you're hurting."

"I am."

"That discourages you. Why wouldn't it? Temporarily."

Sonya blew out a breath. "Temporarily."

"I know you, and I know once you settle again, you'll use all of it to add one more layer to your determination. You're allowed to feel sad. I'm sad, too. But she did tell you—us—something we didn't know."

Confused, Sonya frowned at Cleo. "I'm missing that part."

"Because hurt and sad. We've already said we have to accept, even through the mirror, the brides can't be saved. They died. Catherine told you just that. Her death can't be changed."

"Their spirits, their essence—whatever you'd call it—are still in the manor."

"That's right. So's Dobbs, so are the rings. But they're not hers, and—how'd you say she put it? That can be recovered. It can be changed."

"A brief how-to would've been helpful."

Cleo smiled because the comment sounded more like Sonya.

"I'm guessing if they knew the answer, they'd tell you."

"Yeah." Sonya lifted her face so the sea air blew over it. "And yeah, I'd already figured that. You're bloody well right about the hurt and sad, too. She was young, happy, in love, and eager to start her married life. She wanted kids, Cleo. It got to me."

She shifted to look at Cleo. "And now that I'm settling—thanks for that—I understand I'm not being shown these things just to hurt me, to make me sad. They strengthen the connection, and I guess that's important. If I don't feel that connection, that bond?"

"It's just a puzzle for you to solve. An exercise."

"Exactly. And when I think it through, there have been pushes for me to find the rings, but this is the first real confirmation, just as you said, that I can get them back.

"I will, because I must."

"You're bloody well right."

Sonya looked up at the Gold Room windows. "She's been pretty quiet all week. When she takes the next swing, it'll be a hard one."

"So we'll enjoy the quiet while we've got it."

"I'd better use it and get back to work."

Pyewacket leaped off the wall to follow as Yoda scrambled up. On the way, Sonya stopped to look at Cleo's painting in progress.

And admired the leafy, weeping grace of the tree, and the cladded turret rising above it toward a summer-blue sky.

"The shape of it, all those twists and curves. It looks ancient, in a really good way."

"I always wonder who planted it and when. Well, likely a grounds-keeper, but who of the household decided *I want this kind of tree here*."

"And you'll paint it again in the fall, then in the winter."

"Mmm-hmm. I'm calling the series *Turn, Turn, Turn*."

"To everything there's a season." And one of her father's favorite songs again. "Perfect."

"I should have another couple hours at it, at most, since Owen's probably right about afternoon storms."

"You get back to yours, I'll get back to mine. Thanks for being there, Cleo."

"Ever and always."

Owen wasn't wrong, but by the time the first bolt of lightning slashed the sky, Sonya knew Cleo worked in her studio. And Yoda had already deserted her to play ball with Jack in the main hall downstairs.

She'd finished her proposal, sent it off, then spent the rest of her workday on other projects.

As she started to shut down, Corrine sent her an email with attachments.

Hello, Sonya, I hope your day was as satisfying as mine. Three shoots, results attached. I had to reschedule the one with Eddie due to the weather. Let me know what you think when you get a chance to look them over. Corrine.

"No time like the present."

She opened the first file, studied the photos of Cleo she and Corrine had chosen.

Glancing at the time, she saw it was approaching after-business hours, but decided she'd send them anyway. Along with the others if they struck her as the right choices.

When they did, she shook her fists in the air.

"Wow! She did a hell of a good job."

Sonya sent a return email back saying just that, then composed another for her contacts at Ryder, and attached the day's work.

High on success, she jogged up to Cleo's studio.

As she approached, the door to the Gold Room creaked open. Through it, she heard the whisper of her name.

Clover warned her with Electric Six and "Danger! High Voltage."

"Yeah, don't worry. Not falling for it."

As she spoke, the door blew open. As it crashed against the wall, it seemed the storm had moved into the room. Even from a distance, Sonya felt the wind blow cold over her, saw the flash of light, smelled the ozone.

The floor trembled under her feet, and Cleo rushed out of her studio.

"Don't go near it!" Calling out, Sonya rushed to her friend. "She's trying to bait me, or us."

When the cat came out of the studio, hissed, Cleo scooped her up. "You stay with us."

Fog crawled out of the room, across the hall, and up the wall. Sonya watched the wallpaper curl and peel away, and the plaster beneath crack.

Yoda came on the run, snarling. Sonya headed him off, and like Cleo with Pye, grabbed him up.

"Nobody's going near that."

In what sounded like an explosion, they heard glass shatter. Shards flew out of the room to embed themselves in the cracking plaster.

So it bled from the wounds.

As it dripped on the floor, the hardwood shook, then opened like a pit.

"Jesus, that can't be real."

"It's not. It's not, but—" Cleo grabbed Sonya's arm and pulled her into the studio.

As they watched, the floor in the hall split and fell. Smoke billowed out; flames speared up, then licked their greedy way along the walls.

The laughter came, high-pitched and mad, as more glass shattered, as fire roared. The ceiling fell with a rain of charred plaster, flaming boards.

Dobbs glided out and down, black hair, black dress whipping in the wind she'd created.

"Your death is here, in fire and blood. And your bones will wash away in a flood. Here you risk a fiery death and will carry my curse to your last breath. This house is mine for all time."

Leading with fury as much as fear, Sonya grabbed one of Cleo's rocks, heaved it. Whether by luck or aim, it struck Dobbs in the center of her chest.

Had the house fallen around them, Sonya would've still felt satisfaction by the look of shock and—yes, it was pain—on Dobbs's face.

"Go to hell! This is my house!"

It all stopped.

Outside the studio, the floor, the walls remained pristine. The interior storm halted even as the one outside turned to a quiet rain.

"Holy shit! Holy shit! What did you throw?"

"I don't know, whatever was handy. I—God—I kept telling myself it wasn't real."

"But it felt real," Cleo finished. "We're shaking. All four of us."

Before she risked setting the cat down, Cleo moved to the doorway, peeked out.

"Nothing. No glass, no fire, no smoke or bleeding walls. And her door's closed again. You hurt her, Sonya."

"I did. I saw it."

Setting Pye down, Cleo picked up the stone from the floor of the hallway, gave a shaky laugh. "A hag stone. That's apt. Also known as a witch stone. It guards against evil, which is why I have a couple in here."

"I—I thought it was bigger when I grabbed it."

"Small but mighty, and obviously big enough. We were afraid, and Jesus, who could blame us? So she fed on that, came out to add more, and you let her have it. Wow. Her face."

Taylor Swift's "Bad Blood" played on Sonya's phone.

"Yeah, she's got plenty of that." Then Sonya narrowed her eyes. "Do you think she can bleed? That I made her bleed?"

"Damn solid hit from where I was standing, so I say yes. Jones tore a piece off her dress, so that means yes to me. I think . . ."

Frowning, Cleo turned the stone over in her hand. "I think there might be a trace of blood on here."

"It went through her. It hit, and went through her."

"Yes, it did."

Cleo put the stone in a small bowl, and from another, took a second hag stone.

"A fresh one," she said, handing it to Sonya. "In case. And, Son, I have to admit, I want—hell, need—a really, really big glass of wine."

"Me, too. Let's go get one."

"One other thing? She didn't come in here, neither did any of her nasty illusions."

"Hag stones?"

"And more. I like knowing she has limits."

"Again, me, too." As they started out, Sonya glanced back, and saw a canvas covered on an easel.

"You never cover your paintings."

"This time. Something I'm working on now and then, and not ready for anybody but me."

They both stopped at the closet. Sonya opened it and found only art supplies.

"I check it a few times a day," Cleo said.

"When it's time, Catherine will be there. Let's go get that wine."

Chapter Nine

After a quiet night, by Lost Bride Manor standards, Sonya gave Cleo the seal of approval on hair, makeup, wardrobe. Then she waved her friend off for the sailing photo shoot.

After shutting the door, she looked down at Yoda and Pye.

"Another attic Saturday for us."

When the doorbell bonged, Sonya just rolled her eyes.

"Oooh, doorbell ringing and no one's there. Scary."

As she started up the stairs, the servants' door creaked open.

"Eek! Creaky door opens. Terrifying."

She nudged it closed as she passed, grabbed another pack of sticky notes from her desk, then continued up.

On the third floor, doors flew open, slammed shut.

"You could always try rattling chains and moaning. Those are classics for a reason."

In the attic she found all the dustcovers removed and folded into neat stacks.

"Thanks, Molly. That does save time. And there it is! That's the vanity Catherine used on her wedding night."

Directly in her line of sight, so she concluded someone on the helpful staff had moved it to make it easy for her.

"Thanks. It's really beautiful."

She made her way to it and ran a hand over the wood. Wood that felt freshly polished.

"It's not too big, and I love the shape of the mirror. All the little drawers. Maybe we can shift some things around and put it back in the room. It feels right."

She opened drawers, and in the one on the left found a pair of hair combs.

"Oh, I wonder if these were Catherine's. I think they're mother-of-pearl—Cleo would know for sure. They're pretty, but simple, like for a young woman."

She set them on the top of the vanity, opened more drawers.

And found the hairbrush Arabelle had used to brush Catherine's hair.

"I saw this." Gently, Sonya ran her fingers over the bristles. "So soft. And I think this is ivory. Simple again. We'll put it on the vanity, I think, in remembrance. And Trey was right."

"About what?"

If it were truly possible to jump out of your skin, Sonya would have.

Brush in hand, Sonya whirled. "Jesus, Trey, you scared the crap out of me!"

"Sorry. I thought you heard me coming."

He moved to her, gave her shoulders a rub. "I called out a couple times. I guess you didn't hear that either."

"Didn't. Jump scare aside, hi."

"Hi." He leaned down, kissed her, lingered over it.

"I didn't expect you for a while. You either," she added, and rubbed Mookie. "Or you." She gave Jones the same greeting.

"I bunked at Owen's last night due to beer and poker. I left when he left, stopped off for a shower and a change."

Glancing around, he noted the folded dustcovers. "You're getting an early start on this."

"I credit Molly there. But I've already found a treasure. It's Catherine's. They're Catherine's," she corrected. "The combs, the brush, the vanity."

"How do you know?"

"I saw her sitting at it, saw her mother brushing her hair. Her wedding night. It was like the time I saw Astrid and the little party in the parlor, Lisbeth and that party in the music room. But I was aware, awake. I heard voices," she continued, and told him.

"You've seen five of them now, beyond when Dobbs took their rings."

"That's true. I hadn't thought of it, but that's true." As she spoke, she opened the rest of the drawers on the vanity, but found nothing. "All of them except Marianne and Agatha. And we found Marianne's journal. I've read most of it, and it's almost like seeing her."

"Logic—this logic anyway—says you'll see her and Agatha at some point. And, hopefully, talk to them."

"And maybe gain a clue. The rings aren't hers, don't belong to Dobbs, so I can get them back. I have to believe that."

She stood, scanning the attic.

"But it really helps to know it." She set the brush down, then pointed. "That armoire was in the room." She walked over to go through it. "No need for it now that there's a closet, and it's too big, but I'd like to move the vanity in there.

"Empty." She closed the last drawer on the armoire.

"I'll start over there. So, what was I right about?"

"Huh. Oh! About being meant to find these things. The marbles, the journal, the yo-yo, now the hair combs, the brush. It's more taking ownership, I guess. But for them. And I don't think Dobbs likes it."

He went through a highboy. "Did she act up some?"

"Definitely. You know she'd been mostly quiet for days. You had to figure she was planning something."

He stopped what he was doing to watch her as she opened one of the trunks.

"And what was it?"

"I was shutting down for the day when your mom sent some of the photos. Having you out playing fetch with Mookie? Genius, by the way. You both look great."

"What does that have to do with Dobbs?"

"I wanted to get Cleo, show her, so I ran up to her studio. I think maybe Dobbs was holding off until we were both up there."

"For what, Sonya?"

Enchanted by the dresses in the trunk, she didn't notice his tone.

"To cut loose. Big-time. Just opening the door of the Gold Room at first, and saying my name. As if I'd fall for that. We were having the storm, and then we were having the storm inside the Gold Room. Wind, thunder booming, then glass breaking."

As she went through the trunk, she relayed what happened up to the fire, the floor in the hall collapsing.

"And you didn't think you should call me, tell me you were in trouble?"

Now the tone got through. Holding the pink frock she'd seen Lissy wearing in the music room, Sonya rose.

"It happened fast, and things were, you could say, pretty damn fraught."

"And after, any time after? Like maybe, I don't know, when I texted you to ask how things were going?"

In Sonya's experience, Oliver Doyle III had a long, slow-burning fuse. Clearly, he'd reached the end of it.

"I would have, but—"

He interrupted in a tone so cool she felt the chill from feet away. And her hackles rose with it.

"You agreed to call me, Sonya, when there's trouble, and I need to trust you will."

"And I would have except for two reasons. The most important? We handled it. Which I'll explain if you just listen to the whole thing before getting mad. And second, which matters to me, you and Owen had a night off."

"From what?"

"From looking out for me, protecting me, which is why you left to come here when you knew Cleo was meeting Owen and your mom. As much to look after me as to help me go through all this—this stuff."

"So now I need a night off from you, like you're a chore?"

"No. Jesus." She laid the dress on a table, then shoved her hands through her hair. "You know that's not what I meant, and you're harassing the witness. I would've called if we'd needed you, and if you'd let me finish, I'll explain. You can cross-examine me after."

Now his tone heated up, and his hands went into his pockets. "This isn't a trial, and I'm not in lawyer mode."

"Sure feels like it."

"Damn it, Sonya. You're telling me, now, that you and Cleo were being attacked, that you were trapped with the goddamn house falling apart around you, fire, flying glass, and no way out of the studio."

"But none of those things were real."

"And you're smart enough to know that doesn't mean those things couldn't hurt you."

"But they didn't." She threw up a hand before he could speak again. "Just let me finish. Were we scared? Absolutely. It did seem like the house was falling apart, burning. It did seem real. Then Dobbs, she just, just glided down the hall over that freaking pit of fire."

"Jesus Christ."

"She started to cast another spell, I think. Or maybe she just likes talking in rhymes." Now she paced as she spoke while Trey stood still and annoyingly controlled.

"My death in fire and blood, she's going to wash away my bones in a flood, blah blah. And she ends with the house is mine for all time. Hers, I mean. It really pissed me off. I grabbed one of Cleo's rocks and threw it at her."

"You threw a rock at a dead, insane witch while the house was burning down."

"Yes!" Her fuse, not nearly as slow-burning, reached its end as she spun around to face him.

"Was I supposed to just stand there and go *Help! Help!* And it fucking worked, okay, so you can stuff your condescension. Cleo said it's a hag stone, wards off evil and whatever. Maybe, given the *logic* of the manor, that's why that particular rock came to hand. But it hit her, square in the chest, and it hurt her. It shocked her because she expected me to just stand there, helpless. It shocked her, and it hurt her, and she vanished. She vanished, and it all stopped."

He said nothing for a moment, then, "I need to see this rock."

She pulled one out of her pocket. "This is one like it. Cleo's keeping the other because we think it may have some of her blood on it."

"It went right through her," Sonya murmured as Trey took the stone and studied it. "It hit. I saw it hit, then . . . It was there on the floor in the hallway after."

She put it back in her pocket when he handed it to her.

"It's not very big, but it did the job. And ask yourself this, because I did. Why didn't she press the advantage and come at us in the studio?"

"Because she can't."

Now she took a moment. "You'd already figured that out. Good for you. Whatever Cleo's got going in there must work."

"Add that's where you've found the portraits. I don't diminish Cleo, but I think she's got some help there."

"I hadn't thought of that." She took a breath. "That sounds true."

He walked over, all the way to the attic windows, and threw one open. For the sea air, Sonya supposed. For a little cooling off.

She didn't think the same would work for her.

"I need to know you'll call me."

"I explained why I didn't. You can't be here twenty-four hours a day. You have work, just like the rest of us. Things you need to do outside that. Family and friends to keep up with. You have to trust *me* to know when to send out a distress call."

"Not just distress, Sonya. I'm sitting around eating burgers with Owen when you're going through this. I'm hanging out, bullshitting, and playing cards without a clue."

"And just what good would it have done to dump all this on you after it was over? Cleo and I went downstairs and had a lot of wine. Because we won the battle, Trey. We stood up to her, and we won."

"It won't be the last battle."

"No, and it's not going to be the last where you're not right here to fight it for me or with me. I want you in the war with me, Trey, just like I want you to trust me to fight."

"I do. I've seen you fight. That doesn't mean I have to like thinking about you facing off against her with a rock."

Visibly calmer, he moved back to her. "I don't want or need nights off from you. Being with you's what I want. No, I can't be here twenty-four seven, but I want you to call so I can be here. I want to know you will."

"If I had, you'd have dropped everything and come. Both you and Owen."

"Of course we would."

"And if I had, it would lessen my considerable victory. Plus, and I think it matters, I'd look weak to her, and that would give her one."

"It's not about keeping score."

Astonished, she threw her hands in the air. "Oh, hell yes, it is. At least on one small, petty hand it is. I hurt her, Trey. I saw pain on her face, and I'm holding on to that. That rock landed, and I think— I'm going to sound like Cleo because she put this in my head over wine—I think the intent behind the throw landed just as much. I wanted to hurt her, wanted to give her a scare, and I did.

"Come at me and mine, bitch, I'll come right back at you. Jones got a piece of her dress—and good dog, Jones. But I made her bleed. And if I get the chance, I'll do it again."

She took a breath, a steady one.

"She knows it now. She can worry about me now."

"You want me to say kudos, and I do. And I do want to see the rock you threw so I can get a nice, clear picture in my head of you throwing it. But I'm allowed to worry."

"You are, and I know you do. I didn't want you to worry last night. When it was over? I knew it was over for the night. I saw it in her face. I saw it, and I just . . . felt it."

"All right."

"All right?"

"Being annoyed you didn't call isn't at all the same as not trusting you to take care of yourself. And being glad you did."

She had to sigh, as this, this *reasonable* was why he rarely lost an argument.

"You weren't annoyed. You were pissed."

"Semantics."

"Lawyer."

"Irrelevant." He laid a hand on her cheek, and those deep blue eyes looked into hers. "Just understand, you're my first priority. Not work, not poker, not this house, not some curse. You. You're what matters."

"How am I supposed to stay irritated with you when you say that?"

"You weren't irritated. You were pissed."

"Correct. Now I'm not."

Sonya rose on her toes, put her arms around Trey's neck, and proved it with a long kiss.

Then she stepped back and picked up the pink dress. "This is Lisbeth's. She wore it the night I saw her in the music room."

Sonya brushed a hand down the skirt.

"When I first got here, and looked through some of the trunks, I thought all these wonderful clothes, packed away so beautifully. Historical. I thought I should donate them. A museum, a fancy costume shop or something, I don't know. Now I can't do it."

"Because you saw her wearing it."

"Yes. I can't have someone wearing it to a party or for dressing up. Or just behind glass or whatever at a place that doesn't know who she was. Who they were.

"Maybe it's stupid."

"I don't think so. They're not just clothes, they're memories."

"That's how I feel, and they belong here. So once I go through them, I'll pack them up beautifully again."

"You could display some of them. You've got plenty of room."

Intrigued, she brushed a hand over the dress again. "I could, and that's a really good thought. Maybe see if I can pick one from each decade or era. Sort of a history through fashion. I'll think about that. Meanwhile I just can't pack this away. So I'll hang it downstairs until I figure it out."

They worked together another two hours, found small things tucked away. A single white glove with a pearl button, a set of onyx studs, a little box with a lock of dark hair tied in a blue ribbon.

Sonya opened the drawer of a secretaire.

"Trey, come see this! A wedding invitation. Agatha's. Agatha and Owen. Still inside the double envelope. Look how beautiful. Gorgeous paper, elegant design. And the calligraphy. I couldn't do better with the tools I have today."

"Fancy," he agreed. "I wonder who saved it, and why?"

"I don't know, but it's the first thing of hers—that we know for sure was hers—we've found. You know, we're going to find something from all of them. Depending. I could get shadow boxes, one for each bride. And we'd have a way to display again, a way to represent each one."

"Owen and I could build those."

"That would make it even better. This box is full. I don't want to overload it. Let's take it down. I could use a Coke, and we should let these guys out for a while."

"Got it. Let's go, guys."

Trey hefted the box, and Sonya glanced back as they started out.

"We've made good progress here, but there's so much. We haven't gotten to the ballroom, much less downstairs, but still, good progress."

"You're good at making a plan, then following the steps, so that's what you're doing. Where do you want the box?"

"The Gold Room, but that's way down the list of the plan. I think the Quiet Place. We can use that space to sort through, organize, figure out how we'll display what we've found."

At the third floor, she paused briefly.

"She put a lot into that display yesterday. Collin never talked about her doing that sort of thing while he lived here?"

"No. Ghosts? Common knowledge, the whole lost bride thing, local lore. But I never sensed he was afraid here—the opposite, it was his home. And he never said anything about incidents like what you've had.

"But," he continued as they started down the staircase, "Collin was a man."

"Hey, looking for another fight?"

"No, so hold any feminist punch. Collin was a man, so she could consider herself mistress of the manor."

Sonya stopped at the base of the stairs. "Why the hell didn't I think of that?"

"That's what I'm here for."

"Am I the first woman to live here alone? Plenty of other mistresses, so to speak, over the last couple hundred years, but now it's just me."

"And it's just you after a long stretch of none."

"That's right, that's right. She scared Patricia off, then had the place to herself for a generation before Clover and Charlie moved in."

Foo Fighters expressed Clover's thoughts with "Home."

"It was and is yours," Sonya said. "But Dobbs, then Patricia Poole, changed that. And the manor was empty again until Collin came of age and made it his."

Trey set the box on the floor of what they called the Quiet Place, and looked at the old grandfather clock, its hands, as always, held on three o'clock.

"Then Johanna made the seventh bride, and Collin lived alone." He turned to Sonya. "And now you."

"The brides were obstacles, enemies, like you said. I'm more . . . competition. You remove an obstacle, you just have to beat the competition."

Thinking it through, she walked with Trey, leading the pets, to the kitchen. Opened the back door for the quick stampede outside.

"She's stuck in the past, right? In 1806, when she jumped to her death off the seawall. She exists after that, but her mind-set, her . . . culture? That's stuck in a place where women didn't own property, weren't in charge. I think . . ."

"I'd like to know what you think." Trey handed her a Coke.

"She wanted the first Collin Poole because he would own the manor. He'd inherit it."

"She made sure of that by killing his father."

"She tried bespelling Collin first, getting him to sleep with her, using that as her way to Poole Manor. But it didn't work, there was Astrid. So she removed the first obstacle, Arthur Poole."

Watching her, Trey nodded. "Why wait until after the wedding to kill Astrid, remove that obstacle?"

"I . . ." Sonya glanced up. "Let's walk outside, out front, sit on the seawall."

"Sure."

When they closed the front door behind them, Trey took Sonya's hand. "You don't want her listening."

"I'm not sure she can or does hear everything, but. And I like to keep an eye on her windows off and on. Anyway, I think she either needed or wanted the wedding ring. Cleo would say there's power in symbols, and she's not wrong. She took the ring, wears the ring."

"Because in her warped mind, it makes her a bride, and mistress of the manor."

"You've thought of this, too."

"Played around with it some."

He nudged her down to sit on the stone wall. The breeze whipped at her hair, and the strong summer light seemed to deepen the green of her eyes.

Poole-green eyes, he thought.

"Keep going."

"Still, it didn't work. They caught her, would have hanged her, but she got away long enough to come back here, stand on this wall, and with her own death seal the curse for generations to follow. More, she stayed, in her mind, mistress. Then in grief, Collin kills himself, his twin Connor inherits, marries Arabelle."

"But she didn't kill Arabelle."

"Same generation, plus, Arabelle would provide her with the next bride. She's got all the time in the world, right? Being dead. So there's Catherine. Another generation, another bride, another ring."

Sonya looked up at the windows. "Rinse, repeat. They all became obstacles in her mind, or steps to power. Brides—like Astrid. Pooles by blood or marriage. But me? I'm at best competition, at worst an interloper. An unmarried woman, living here alone. Well, with a friend—a female friend. As long as I stay that way, I'm a nuisance, but safe. Relatively."

She looked back at him. "Does that sound right to you?"

"It's logical, yeah. There's no guarantee Dobbs will follow logic. And I can tell you if he'd known there was this kind of risk, my dad would've done all he could to talk Collin out of the terms of his will."

"Then I wouldn't be here, I wouldn't have this place." She took his hand again. "I wouldn't have met you. Don't you think Collin knew, or strongly believed, when he made that will that the curse could be broken, and that I'd have the best shot of doing it?"

"I don't know, Sonya, but I know he was determined to give this to you."

She looked back at the manor, turrets rising, stones sturdy, a timeless, enduring beauty that held shadows and light.

"My father came here. Through the mirror, the way I've gone back to the past. I know he did. He painted the manor. But he never knew he'd been born here, that the woman who gave birth to him loved him, that he had a brother. A twin.

"But I know it, Trey, I know all of it, and Dobbs will find out I'm not just a nuisance, not just a competitor. I'm—and let's be dramatic. I'm her goddamn doom."

"You make me believe it because you do."

"And I do. I have moments, but I always come back to that. My house, my heritage, my job to do."

So he would worry, Trey thought. And he'd admire.

"You don't give up on things easy."

"I'd say we share that trait, and no, I don't. My mother pulled herself up after my dad died, and, God, it had to be hard. Brutal. But she did it. She did whatever had to be done and never quit."

"She's beautiful, your mom, in every way."

"Hundred percent. There are things I should've given up on before I did. Brandon for one. I was letting myself coast into a marriage part of me knew, just knew, wasn't right and never would be. I should probably have left By Design before I did, no matter how much I cared for Laine and Matt and them for me. Because I knew he'd never, ever stop undermining me there."

"I think you're wrong."

Surprised, she pushed her blowing hair back to study him. "Do you?"

"Yeah. I think you did all you could do in both of those cases until it was clear you needed to do something else. Then you pulled yourself up, and did it.

"It's admirable."

"Well . . ." A little flummoxed, she managed, "Thanks."

"It is. I've never had to fight that way, or change course like that. By and large, my journey's been pretty steady."

"It might help you're a steady sort of man. I've come to depend on that."

The dogs barked, then she heard the rumble of someone driving up the road.

"The rest of us are back." She pushed off the wall. Turning, she smiled at Trey as the dogs and the streak of the cat came around the side of the house.

"You know what else I've come to depend on with you?"

He sighed, but didn't really mean it. "Moving furniture."

"Got it in one." Then she waved as Cleo made the turn to the manor with Owen just behind her.

"How'd it go?" she called to Cleo.

"Absolutely great. Corrine was happy, so I'm happy. Plus, I got a nice little sail out of it." She waited for Owen to climb out of the truck. "Above all, we looked fabulous."

"Right." Owen looked at Trey. "Do you see me sailing, ever, in an outfit like this?"

"No."

"But thousands would," Cleo said, then pinched his biceps below the sleeve of the rash guard. "Stud."

"I'm going up, getting out of it."

"I'm doing the same, since I don't want to wear this to go on the hunt. Did we miss anything?"

"Nothing from our resident lunatic," Sonya said as they walked toward the house together. "But we found Owen and Agatha's wedding invitation."

"Big score. I want to see it."

"And the vanity I saw Catherine sitting at, plus the chair, and the hairbrush her mom used that night."

"Saw what, where?" Owen demanded, and opened the front door.

"I didn't have time to fill you in on yesterday. I'll do that while we change. You'll want the vanity back where you saw it, and them. We'll need to rearrange some to make that work."

"I do, and we will. Meet you back up there when you're ready."

Before Trey and Sonya reached the third floor, Cleo came running.

"You have to see this. It's Pye. I found it on the bed."

She held out the sketch for Sonya. "Jack. What a sweetheart. She looks appropriately slinky."

"And regal. The way she's stretched out in the window of my studio, he got her proportions, and the perspective. But he really got her 'tude. I love it."

"Me, too."

"We'll be up in five. I swear, I love this house."

"Me, too," Sonya said when Cleo dashed away. She looked at Trey, then took his hand again, squeezed. "How could I quit?"

Clover serenaded them with Freddie Mercury's powerful voice as they climbed past the third floor and to the attic.

"The Show Must Go On."

Chapter Ten

July rocked with storms and streamed with sun.

Sonya welcomed both.

Once the Ryder Sports team had approved and chosen the new photos, she selected some for the website, others for digital ads, television ads, billboards, in-store posters.

She mocked up a split screen. A girl in a Ryder bathing suit caught by Corrine in mid-leap off a diving board into a backyard pool, and a man on a ski slope, Ryder skis, parka, pants, gloves, helmet, boots, in the snow-drenched Alps.

Added a tag.

Then she got up, walked away, walked around, watered Xena, looked out at the sea.

Walked back.

"Yes. Yes. Yes. It works. It's right. *Anyone, anywhere, anytime. Ryder's got you.* It frigging works."

Sitting, she pored through the other shots for more. One with a photo representing each season. Snowboarding, Trey fielding a ball, Owen and Cleo sailing, a couple of teens playing touch football.

Whatever the season, whatever the sport, Ryder's got you.

And another split, sweaty Owen pumping iron and Trey playing fetch with Mookie.

At work or at play, Ryder's got you.

"We did this, we really did this. Good job, Corrine, good job, Ryder team. Good job, Sonya! And I've got another idea to try out."

Revved up and ready, she started working on it. As she made some headway, the doorbell rang. She started to ignore it as one of Dobbs's tricks, but Yoda scrambled up and ran out barking.

"Okay, okay, maybe somebody's actually there."

Though the interruption annoyed, as the new idea cooked, she went to the window, looked out. She saw a car, not a familiar one, in the drive.

"Hell, all right."

In roomy black shorts—Ryder's, of course—an old white T-shirt, and bare feet, she jogged down.

Opening the door, she found herself at a total loss for words.

Hair shining in the sun, khakis pressed, polo shirt blue to match his eyes, Brandon Wise, former coworker, former fiancé, lying, cheating, back-stabbing son of a bitch, stood smiling at her.

"Sonya, wow! What a place! And in the middle of nowhere. And you've got a dog."

Brandon eyed Yoda as Yoda eyed him, and Yoda cautiously wagged his tail.

Pye slunk down the stairs.

"And a cat." A shadow of irritation dimmed his megawatt smile. "You know I'm allergic to cats. Maybe you could put it away somewhere."

"No. What are you doing here?"

He shifted as Yoda gave his Ferragamo loafers a sniff. "I had some business in Portland, and decided to take a little detour to see you, see how you're doing. You must really ramble around this old place."

When he started to step inside. Sonya held up a hand.

"You're not welcome here."

Her tone had Yoda giving a quiet little growl.

"Come on, Sonya, don't be childish. I went out of my way just to see how you're doing."

He slid by her into the foyer.

Cats could growl, too, and Pye did just that. Upstairs, the iPad shouted out with Taylor Swift's "Illicit Affairs."

Ignoring it all, Brandon scanned the foyer, the turret sitting room, the main parlor.

"Looks like you fell right into it. I bet this old place is worth a mint. And it must cost another mint to maintain."

His gaze ticked up the big staircase, over again to the main parlor. She could all but hear him adding up inventory.

"Way too big for you, babe. And way into the hinterlands with no nightlife, no restaurants, no shops. You must be bored brainless."

He shot her another smile. "Aren't you going to offer me a drink?"

"No. You need to leave. I want you to get out." She pointed at the open door. "Now."

His smile—one she now knew had more smarm than charm—never wavered.

"Look, I made the detour because I wanted to congratulate you, in person, on the Ryder Sports job. As one professional to another."

"Okay. Now leave."

"Talk about sore winners." He laughed with it as he wandered toward the turret room. "Round walls. Weird place. Anyway."

He turned back to her where she stood flanked by the dog and the cat.

"You must have figured out by now that a project like the Ryder campaign's too big for one person. I've started my own company, and Wise Marketing's already taken off."

"Congratulations. Get out of my house."

He rolled right over her. "It was past time for me to shake loose of By Design. I'm pretty busy, but for old times' sake, I'm willing to help you out with Ryder."

Of all the things he might have said, that one hit the top of the irony bar.

"You have got to be kidding me."

He rolled right over that, too, and spread his hands. All reason and benevolence.

"I'm here to take some of the stress off you, share the load. In fact, I'm more than willing to clear the slate. Forget past mistakes, yours, mine."

He walked to her.

"How about we sit down, talk about it? I've missed being with you. Seeing you again like this . . ."

He started to reach a hand for her cheek.

"How about, once again, no? Try to touch me again, I'm calling the police."

"Yeah, I bet they're really on the ball down there in whatever it is, a hamlet?" He couldn't quite cover the sneer in his voice. "I just want to sit down, have a conversation."

Oh so reasonable, he spread his hands.

"We're both adults, and you've had more than enough time to cool off, come back to reality. And the reality is, we were good together, we need each other. Together we can put By Design in the ground."

"That's not my reality. I don't even think it's yours, but on the off chance it is, let me be really, really clear. I'm not interested in any association with you. At all. Ever. Now get the hell out of my house."

The look he gave her transmitted disappointed adult to stubborn child.

"There's that childish streak again. Honestly, it can be endearing."

He sneezed twice, gave Pye a vicious glare. "Now put that damn cat somewhere. We're going to sit down and talk."

He curled a hand around her arm, held on, fingers digging in, when she tried to jerk away. At her feet Yoda let out three quick barks and showed his teeth. Pye's ears lay back as she arched her back and hissed.

"Call off that ugly mutt and get rid of that cat."

"Take your hand off me, now. I'm warning you, Brandon, I can do worse, a lot worse than my dog and cat or the police. Get out of my house."

"Knock off the drama and bitchiness." Face set now, he tugged her toward the parlor. "We're going to sit down, and you're going to listen."

"No, and no."

She was on the point of kneeing him, hard, when Yoda's ball flew and banged into the back of his head.

A laugh followed it. A young boy's laugh.

"What the hell is that?"

"That's the *a lot worse*, and it's just getting started."

His head jerked back as if from a punch or slap, Yoda snapped and snarled. Pye took a swipe that scraped claws over his khakis.

Before he could follow through with a kick at Pye, Brandon wheeled back as if from a hard shove. And his eyes went wide with fear.

"Warned you."

"You hit me!"

"You know I didn't."

Then he jerked forward, looked behind him with a hand on his butt. And sneezed three times in rapid succession.

Enjoying herself now, Sonya smiled. "Nor did I just kick you in the ass."

A voice boomed out, female and full of rage.

Get out of our house, motherfucker!

Sonya's phone, the iPad upstairs, the one in the kitchen all boomed out with Tom Petty's "Don't Come Around Here No More."

"I'd take that advice." She strode to the door, pointed at the opening. And smiled again. "Run."

He managed a shaky stumble to the door, and kept going.

On the run to his car, he called out, "You'll regret this."

Another series of sneezes ruined his exit.

"I really don't think I will."

Sonya closed the door firmly behind him.

Petty continued to sing, but at a lower volume.

"I don't believe he will. Thanks for the assist, Jack, Clover. And you two." She crouched to scrub Yoda and Pye all over. "You're not an ugly little mutt, but my handsome hero. And you, a discerning and courageous cat."

She walked over, then just sat on the steps.

"I feel righteous. And shaky. Righteously shaky. I'm just going to sit here until the shaky part passes. Shit. If I don't call Trey and tell him about this, he'll be pissed at me. If I call him and tell him about this, he'll be pissed. But not at me."

She let out a breath. "So pissed either way, and I might as well call and tell him."

With Yoda snuggled beside her, Pye on watch on top of the newel post, she took out her phone. Since her hand trembled a little, she took a few more calming breaths.

"And I'll have to tell Cleo when she gets home. And Owen has to hear about it. Damn it, I have to tell Mom in case he tries to harass her."

She looked down at her dog. "Make one stupid mistake with one stupid jerk, and look what it gets you."

She called Trey.

"Hey, cutie. Everything okay?"

"Yes. It's fine, I'm fine, and I'm stressing that. But I wanted to tell you so we don't have a round about it, Brandon Wise was here."

"He came to the manor?"

"Yeah, he sort of bulled his way in, and—"

"I'm on my way."

"Trey, he's gone. I made him leave—with a little help from Clover and Jack. And Yoda and Pyewacket."

"I'm on my way," he repeated, in a tone that sounded absolutely calm. "Stay inside."

Since he'd ended the call, she sighed and put the phone back in her pocket. "Oh well."

She decided to sit just where she sat until she felt as calm as Trey sounded.

She didn't wait long. At home, Mookie rushed in to greet her, Yoda, and Pye. Sonya decided Steady-as-a-Rock Doyle had broken all the posted speed limits.

She'd seen him angry a handful of times, but now she recognized barely controlled rage.

"I know you're upset," she began. "So am I, but—"

His gaze shot down to her arm, seemed to burn there.

"You've got a bruise on your arm."

She glanced down. "Oh, it's nothing. It's just—"

"Sonya."

Her name, in a tone of utter patience with fury banked just behind it, had her swallowing any downplay.

"Let's sit down, and you can tell me exactly what happened."

"All right, okay."

She wasn't sure if he was in boyfriend mode or lawyer mode. Somehow it seemed like both. Maybe, she realized, he was always in both.

Already feeling she'd blown it all out of proportion, she sat in the parlor.

"You said he sort of bulled his way in. You didn't let him in, agree to let him come in?"

"No! I told him right off—when I got past the shock of him at the door—he wasn't welcome here."

"Those words?"

"Yes. But he sort of nudged me—"

"He put his hands on you?"

"Sort of. I mean he gave me a little nudge and came in. He started talking about the house, and he wanted me to put Pye away somewhere. He's allergic. I said no."

When she realized the words tumbled out of her too fast, she paused, breathed in, breathed out while Trey watched her. While he took her hand.

"Take your time."

"He . . . said I should offer him a drink. I said no, and I told him, again, to leave."

"Did he?"

"No. Trey."

"Sonya, we have good, strict laws regarding trespass in Maine. And if he put that bruise on your arm, that's criminal trespass. Tell me the rest."

She did, and watched the rage inch closer to the surface when she told him Brandon grabbed her arm. She hoped to lighten it up with the ghostly assist, but it didn't seem to work.

"He ran to his car, Trey. Sneezing. 'You'll regret this,'" she added, deepening her voice, adding the sneezes with three mocking *achoos*.

Before she could laugh, Trey nodded.

"And that's a threat. Criminal trespass, assault, harassment, and verbal threat. Do you have his contact information?"

"I guess, unless he's changed it."

"I need it."

"Why?"

"For the arrest warrant."

For a moment she could only gape at him.

"Oh, Trey, I don't want you to do that."

"Yes, you do." He held up a hand before she could argue. "First. Do you want him coming back here?"

"No, absolutely no. But I honestly don't think he will after this."

"Let's make sure. Next, do you want him, since he has his own company now, to trash yours with clients the way he tried to do with Ryder?"

"I—" She started to say he wouldn't do that, then realized, of course he would. "No, I don't."

"Then let Doyle Law Offices handle this for you. This is what I do, Sonya. Let me do what I do. You're going to file a police report."

"Oh Jesus."

"He knows where your mother lives, too, Sonya."

That hit exactly where he'd aimed. Hadn't she already considered he might harass her mother?

"All right." She shoved at her hair. Then shoved at it again. "I'm going to tell her about this. I don't want him bothering her, so all right. What comes next?"

"We call the cops. You file charges for criminal trespass, assault, and the verbal threat. I'll help you file for a protection against harassment order. You'll get it. He pushed his way into your home—what the law calls your dwelling place—without your consent, and after you'd denied him that consent. He ignored your demands to leave, he physically and verbally assaulted you."

"Holy shit. Well, God! A trial?"

"If he's smart, or gets a decent lawyer, he'll plead it down from a Class D misdemeanor, where he could do a year in jail and shell out a max of two thousand."

When her mouth simply dropped open, Trey gave her hand a quick squeeze.

"If he pleads down to Class E, he'd pay a fine and likely get probation instead of jail time."

It all left her a little dumbstruck. "I need to ask you one thing before I do all this."

"Go ahead."

"Do you want me to do all this because we're together? Is this personal?"

He leaned over, brushed his lips over hers. "Of course it's personal. And if I had a complete stranger come into my office, sit down, and tell me all this, I'd advise exactly the same."

She blew out a breath. "Okay, let's call the cops."

An hour later when Cleo came in, she rushed straight to Sonya.

"I passed a police car on Manor Road. Are you okay? What happened?"

"I'm fine, and I'll tell you. I really need some air."

"We'll go out on the deck. Trey, I left groceries in the car."

"I'll take care of it. I have some calls to make."

In the kitchen, Sonya stopped for a Coke. Offered one to Cleo. "And my day was going so well."

"What the hell happened? Dobbs?"

"No. I bet she enjoyed some of it, though. Brandon. Let's go out. Come on, Yoda, Pye, Mooks. Let's all go out."

"What did that slimy, limp-dicked bastard do now?"

"He came here," Sonya said as she led the way outside.

Cleo stopped in her tracks.

"Here? To the manor? What the hell is wrong with him? What did he want? You didn't let him in!"

"Last question first." Exhausted from it all, Sonya dropped into a chair on the deck. "No, I didn't, but he came in anyway. I don't know what's wrong with him, but he somehow thought he could talk me into hooking up with him again, personally and professionally."

"I need details. You must've called Trey. Did he kick the asshole out?"

"No, I did, with some help from Clover and Jack. And Yoda and Pye. He just showed up at the door, Cleo."

As she told the story yet again, Cleo pushed up to pace and curse, curse and pace.

It occurred to Sonya that Trey kept his rage locked down, and Cleo let hers bust free. And she loved them both madly.

"He thinks he's slick, slicker than spit. A polecat's asshole's more appealing. He put those bruises on you, and deserves a beatdown, good and proper."

Cleo threw her hands up. "Oh, why wasn't I here? I swear I'd've given him one."

"I guess he's going to get one, in the legal sense, because arguing with Trey on this kind of thing's like trying to bust up a boulder with a handful of overcooked angel hair."

Cleo stopped pacing. "What kind of beatdown?"

"Charges for criminal trespass—which up here is—Jesus, I think he said a Class D misdemeanor. Physical and verbal assault. And I'm getting a protection order."

Rolling her shoulders back, Cleo gave one sharp nod. "That sounds fine. I'd rather have some of his blood on me, but that sounds fine. I'm sorry I wasn't here."

"I wasn't alone."

Nodding, Cleo finally sat, and she took Sonya's hand. "I'm grateful for that, and they sure sent him off with his nasty tail between his spindly legs. Next time, don't open the door until you know who it is."

"As both Trey and the deputy reminded me."

"You need to tell Winter."

"I will. She'll be getting off work soon, and I want to wait until she's home."

"You're worn out."

"Dealing with him's exhausting. Jesus, Cleo, Jesus Christ, it's been a year since I caught him with Tracie and kicked him out, broke the engagement. How can he not be over it?"

"I'll tell you how I see it. He had these tendencies. He had them wrapped up tight, but they were there. You look back, you can see them."

"Yeah." Demoralizing, Sonya thought. And that was exhausting, too. "Hindsight's a good way to feel like a moron."

"You're not and you weren't. He romanced you, Son, and he was damn good at it. But he's a cake-and-eat-it sort, so he romanced Tracie, your own cousin, on the side. And maybe she wasn't the only one."

Sonya opened her mouth, closed it. Then just put her head in her hands. "Well, hell, that's one I hadn't thought of. And now do."

"Doesn't matter. Cheating's cheating. He played her, he played you, and when you booted him, he figured he'd talk you back. He couldn't because you're not a moron. Because you have self-respect and goddamn morals.

"I think that snapped something in him. He couldn't get his way with you, ends up with a broken engagement—which embarrassed him, made him look like what he is. A loser. Couldn't have that, so he did all he could to dump it on you. That didn't work either, not really."

"He pushed me out of By Design."

Lion's eyes fired as Cleo shot out a finger. "No, he did not! You made a choice, the right one. But knowing what happened, Matt and Laine lost a lot of respect for him. They couldn't fire him over cheating on you, but he knew, had to know, they looked at him differently. Thought less of him.

"Couldn't have that," Cleo continued, "so he sabotaged your work and worse. I bet he popped a cork when you resigned. But what happened? You started your own, and you did just fine. I'm betting that burned his conceited ass."

Wound up, Cleo circled both arms. "Then, holy hell, you get a whopping inheritance. Now the woman who dumped him's rich, with a big, beautiful house, her own company. It's burning and snapping and burning some more. But Ryder? You getting the Ryder Sports account over him? Woo! More, he gets canned because he went at you, lied right out loud."

"To sum it up," Sonya said when Cleo paused for breath, "I'm the reason for everything that hasn't gone his way since last summer."

"That's how his tiny dick and massive ego see it. Add jealous, because to him, you landed in a sea of roses, and he wants in. And you, being just another weak-minded female? He can talk you into it."

"Squeeze what he has out of my inheritance, steal some of the shine from Visual Art before he dumps me. That's the core, right? He needs to dump me. Get me back, get what he can, then break my heart and dump me."

"I've got a good feeling when you and the Doyles get through with him, he's going to give that up and go hunting for another ego boost and payday."

"It was never me." Not quite as exhausted, and no longer demoralized, Sonya sat back. "It's not me now either. I was just, well, a kind of mark, right? I checked off enough boxes for him, that's all. Is it crazy that makes me feel better about it all?"

"No, it is not."

"Good, because it really does. First there's Trey with his quietly simmering rage and wall of legal logic, now you with your loudly boiling rage and sensible psych evaluation. And to backtrack, my ghost and pet defense. I definitely feel better about all of it."

"Good, and when you tell Winter, you'll have a mama's fury and comfort."

When Trey came out, Cleo rose, and when he stepped onto the deck, walked to him. She wrapped her arms around him, pressed her lips firmly to his.

"Nice to see you, too."

"Anybody who goes after my girl, Sonya, they go after me. Anybody who stands for her, stands for me. Now, you sit down with her awhile. I need to put the groceries away and start dinner."

"I put them away; Owen's bringing dinner. We thought it was a good night for pizza."

"When isn't it? Then I'm going to go open us a bottle of wine."

"Opened, breathing on the island."

"I like a man who thinks of everything." Pleased, she kissed him again. "I'll just go get glasses, put together a little crudité."

When she went in, Trey sat. He took one quick study of Sonya, and smiled.

"Bouncing back, aren't you, cutie? You always do."

"If I start to worry, I just bring back a picture of his face when he ran out of the house. It's right up there with the picture of Dobbs when I hit her with the rock."

"Owen's up to date so you won't have to go through it again. And my dad's drafting a letter to the fuckhead."

"A letter?"

"Very formal, very legal. He's great at that. Basically, a cease and desist. Citing the harassment before the Ryder proposal, the incident here, the threat at the end of it. Legal action, blah blah, if such actions continue, if he disparages you or your company, and so on. He'll copy you when it's done."

"Covering all the legal bases."

"It's what we do. They're pretty steamed."

"They?"

"Ace was with him when I called, so expect—between them—the letter to be ice-cold and crystal clear."

"Thank you. Thank you for coming even when I didn't want you to, and for steering me through what I absolutely understand needs to be done."

"He needs to pay a price."

"He does, yes, he does. And you'll make sure he will. Now I have to go through it one more time. I need to go up, FaceTime with my mother. No," she corrected, "I'm going to bring my tablet down, do it right here, so she can see I have you and Cleo. It'll knock down some of the worry."

She came back with her tablet, and Cleo brought out wine and crudités.

"Here goes."

Winter answered with: "What a treat! After a long, busy day, a call from my baby."

Sonya's first response came with surprise. "Your hair!"

"Oh, right." Laughing a little, Winter lifted a hand to the shorter pixie style with its sweep of window bangs. "Saturday afternoon impulse for summer."

"I love it!"

Cleo leaned into view. "Me, too! Sassy Winter."

On another laugh, Winter shifted, looked sassily over one shoulder. "That's me, and I get a bigger treat with my two girls. And don't you both look wonderful?"

"Trey's here, too. We're sitting on the deck having wine. You should get a glass and join us."

"I don't mind if I do. Hi, Trey!"

"Hi. I like your hair, too."

"I wanted a change. It looks like you're having a beautiful day in Maine. It just stopped raining here. I don't see Owen."

"He's bringing pizza," Sonya told her.

"Sounds good. Too bad he doesn't deliver to Boston."

"Mom, I need to tell you Brandon came here this afternoon."

Winter paused in the act of lifting her wineglass. "He— What?"

"I'm fine, and with a little help from Clover, Jack, my dog, and Cleo's cat, kicked him out."

Winter took a breath. "What do you mean kicked him out? He came into your house? The nerve of that son of a bitch. I know damn well you didn't invite him in, so that's trespassing. I'm going to talk to my boss about charges."

"Already in motion," Trey told her.

"All right, of course. I'm taking a breath." After it, she drank some wine. "I want to know what happened."

So Sonya went through it one more time, and found it easier, as with some questions, Trey or Cleo picked up the answer.

At the end, Winter nodded, even smiled. "Clover and Jack. I bet they scared the crap out of him. And you stood up for yourself, Sonya. What a, well, dick. He can't stand your success, baby. The woman who kicked out his cheating ass a year ago is thriving, and he can't stand it. But there have to be consequences for this.

"Trey, can you lay those out for me? I'm going to take notes, and if you don't mind, I do want to speak to my boss about it."

"Sure I can, and I don't mind. Criminal trespass," he began.

He was winding it up as Owen and Jones came out. Since Cleo had left him a note on the fridge, he'd skipped the beer. Now he poured wine.

"Hey, Winter."

"Owen. Now the gang's all there."

Owen sent Trey a long, long look. Trey just shook his head.

"No, we're not heading down to Boston so you can hold my metaphorical coat while I kick his ass. Punches only hurt so long. My way's going to hurt deeper and longer."

"Why not both?"

"Counteracts the deeper, longer pain if we're arrested for assault."

"And here I sit agreeing with both of you. My gut wants that ass-kicking, Owen," Winter said. "But my brain has to agree with Trey. I'd like a copy of the cease and desist if that's okay. And don't worry, I honestly don't see him coming here. But if he does, he won't get in, and I'll call the police. I think being arrested and charged will shock him enough to make him stay away."

"It's the right thing to do."

"Then I'm more than ready to put all things Brandon Wise in a bag, tie an anchor to it, and toss it overboard."

"I like the visual. Now, you all go eat your pizza. I think I'm going to order one myself."

"I love you, Mom."

"I love you, baby. And that goes for everyone else. We'll talk again soon."

When Sonya signed off, she breathed out. "She's upset and angry, but she handled it well. She always does."

"Seems like you take after her there. And one more thing," Owen continued, "before you tie that anchor? If you ever change your mind about that ass-kicking, I'm available."

"I'll keep that offer in reserve. Now? Anchor tied, bag tossed. Splash! Let's have some pizza."

PART TWO

—∿—

Conversations

"The time has come," the Walrus said,
"To talk of many things."

—Lewis Carroll

Chapter Eleven

It didn't take long. Within a week, Brandon was arrested, charged, and transported to Maine. Trey sat in the courtroom as an observer, noted that the defendant had the wit to hire a local attorney, and had dressed in a suit that made him look like Mr. Clean-Cut and Successful.

The defense claimed the entire matter was a misunderstanding, a simple tiff between two people who had, mutually, ended a relationship.

The prosecution came out strongly in opposition. As Trey expected—as they took trespass seriously in Maine—the judge didn't buy the misunderstanding.

Trey watched, with quiet satisfaction, as Brandon shifted, even squirmed some, during the legal back-and-forth. Then found himself amused every time Brandon scribbled something on a legal pad, pushed it at his lawyer.

Scared, aren't you? Trey thought. And still think you know better than your own lawyer.

The judge granted bail, and granted the defendant permission to return to Boston until trial. But that was all the slack he ruled.

"This is ridiculous!"

At Brandon's outburst, Trey settled back with a very satisfied smile. He'd expected no less.

He watched Brandon turn to argue with his lawyer, and thought: Fear, more fear. He caught waves of it now.

"I'm not going to jail. Do you get that? That lying bitch attacked me!"

"Mr. Wise, you need to stay calm."

Trey saw the judge, who'd overheard the outburst as he had, raise his eyebrows. "Mr. Wise, calling the complainant names, particularly in my courtroom, won't help your defense. Counselor, please control your client."

"Your Honor, you have to understand! She's trying to ruin me! She's out for revenge because I broke our engagement. She won't let it go!"

"And yet you're the one arrested for criminal trespass in her home in a state other than the one in which you reside."

The prosecuting attorney got that dig in, and made Trey's smile widen.

"That's bullshit. I went to see her as a favor. I just wanted to— I only tried to—"

The judge slapped his gavel. "I will not have that language in my court. Counselor, if you can't control your client, I will hold him in contempt, and I will rethink granting bail."

The judge waited a moment while the defense attorney whispered in Brandon's ear. Then he brought down his gavel again.

"This hearing is adjourned."

Satisfying, Trey thought as he watched them lead Brandon out. Even more than a solid punch to the face.

Since Trey had faced off against the prosecutor in the past, he rose and hailed him.

"Got a minute, Derrick?"

"Got a few of them. Let's walk. I know you've got an interest in this one."

"I do. He's going to want to deal."

"Oh yeah." They moved into the hallway, stopped. "Scared of going to jail, and his counsel would have warned him, if found guilty, he could serve up to a year. He'll want a deal."

"And?"

"A thousand-dollar fine, a year's probation. I won't start there, but

I'll go there. If he contacts or attempts to contact the complainant again, he'll do time for it. That'll be clear, too."

"That's what I wanted to hear. Maybe you can let me know when it's set?"

"I can do that. Question? Is he as big an asshole as he seems?"

"Bigger. Thanks, Derrick."

"Sure. Grab a beer sometime?"

"Yeah, on me."

Satisfied the case was in good hands, Trey drove back to Poole's Bay.

When he walked in, Sadie, his father's admin, raised her head from her work. "So?"

"He didn't endear himself to the judge. He made bail, trial set for September."

"He best stay away from here if he knows what's good for him."

"He's too scared of jail not to. People like that? They think they can do anything, have anything, riding on good looks and surface charm. When they find out different, it's someone else's fault. But when they find out there are consequences, real ones? They roll into a ball and whimper. He's whimpering now.

"Is my dad busy?"

"He's between clients. Ace is in with him."

"Perfect. I'm going to have a word."

When he went in, he found his father and grandfather in the clients' chairs, drinking coffee.

Ace shoved up his glasses. "Don't tell your grandmother I'm drinking coffee in the middle of the day."

"Lips, sealed."

Trey walked over, sat on the edge of his father's desk. "Motion to dismiss denied, bail set at five thousand. Trial date set for September. The judge didn't take kindly to him calling Sonya a bitch in his court."

Deuce scratched the side of his neck as Ace muttered under his breath. "Jury trial?"

"Requested, yeah. The possibility of actually going to jail has him scared shitless."

"Good. Pushing in that house." Ace all but snarled it. "Trying to strong-arm a woman that way."

"Derrick Morley's prosecuting. Lowell Chase for the defense."

"Lowell's not bad," Deuce considered. "Morley's better."

"Yeah, and Morley agrees with my take. He'll ask for a deal to avoid jail."

"A little time in would teach him a lesson," Ace said, "but dealing means Sonya doesn't have to go through a trial. We'll bank on getting arrested, facing all this taught him that lesson, and he leaves that girl alone."

"After watching him today? I'm confident of that. If he was scared enough to run out of the manor, he's still running scared. The fact is, she won't be worth it to him after this. He'll twist it around in his mind, but pushing at her won't be worth the consequences now that he's had a taste of them."

"I'm going to agree. I've seen his type. Cowards under it."

As Trey nodded at his father, Ace spoke up.

"That girl's a jewel. And you ought to put one on her finger, boy."

"Ace."

Ace just sighed, turned to his son. "I don't know where this boy gets his snail speed from. It sure isn't from me."

When it rang, Trey pulled his phone out. "This sure as hell isn't snail speed. It's Derrick Morley. Yeah, Derrick, got news for me?"

He listened, nodded, said, "Uh-huh. Yeah, agree, quicker than I expected. I appreciate it. Let me know when you have time for that beer. Yeah. Bye."

He pocketed the phone. "The full fine of two thousand, eighteen months' probation. Mandatory anger management. Defense grabbed at the first offer."

"That's a good outcome," Deuce decided. "Done and over. Sonya can put it all away."

"She has, but this will help keep it there. I'm going to my office, give her a call, and let her know."

"Buy that girl a ring!" Ace called out as Trey left.

Trey just shook his head and kept going.

In her office, after speaking with Trey, Sonya just laid her head on the desk.

Clover tried Ariana Grande's "Breathin."

"I am, yeah, I am. And yeah, this has all taken too much energy, but now it's relief. It's like opening a vent so all that pressure's gone."

Sitting up again, she texted her mother, and since Cleo had gone off to paint at the cove, added her.

> It's done. He took a deal, pleaded guilty. 2K fine and eighteen months' probation, add mandatory anger management. If he contacts me again, probation's broken, and he goes to jail. We can all relax. Love you both.

Winter answered in seconds.

> Not only good news, just wonderful news. You stood up to a bully—more times than once—and the bully paid. I'm proud of you. And love you both bunches.

Relax, hell, Cleo texted on the heels of Winter's, celebrate! He got less than he deserved, but it'll do. Now, in our world, he will cease to exist. Love you both back.

"Okay, let's put that all away now, and get back to work."

She worked another two hours, and toward the end heard the bounce of the ball.

When it stopped, so did she.

She went down, found Yoda in the kitchen enjoying a beef stick.

The cat sat on a stool, washing herself. Which meant she'd likely had a treat, too.

And on the island, Sonya found a treat for herself.

Jack had obviously made use of the art kit she'd bought for him.

He'd painted the three dogs, sitting together in the backyard: Jones, with his eye patch and muscled little body; Mookie, floppy ears, goofy grin; Yoda, big eyes shining.

And the cat, sitting in front of her subjects like a queen.

He had the lush flow of hydrangeas to the right, and the lush green mystery of the woods behind.

"This is wonderful. And it's really good work, too. You got their proportions, and that's not easy. Most of all, it's just sweet."

She did what her parents had done with her childhood art. She put it on the fridge.

"This right here, things like this are a reminder why figuring out how to take Dobbs down and out is so important."

They'd done it with Brandon Wise, she reminded herself, and they'd damn well do it with Hester Dobbs.

When she opened the back door, both cat and dog decided to join her. With them, she toured the gardens. Then she went to the shed, got a basket, clippers.

Why have a garden, she thought, if you couldn't take some of it indoors? She took time to select what she thought would make a pretty arrangement for the table in the kitchen, and with one of Anna's vases in mind for it.

When she wandered around the side of the house, she nearly cheered.

"Look at this! We've got our first tomatoes. The little ones." She started to pluck them off, stopped.

"No, Cleo planted them. She should have the honor of picking the first ones. All three of them."

Happy and relaxed, she circled the house toward the sea.

And when she caught sight of a whale sounding, far, far out, deemed it a perfect day.

She imagined Cleo was sailing back by now, or had docked and was on her way home. She expected Trey might be finishing up work for the day, and Owen as well.

She knew Cleo planned a simple summer dinner, and that suited her just fine.

And considering all, she thought as she walked, it was time for a weekend barbecue, with the Doyles. Maybe her mother could drive up for the weekend and make it perfect.

Easy, family-style. Burgers and dogs, corn on the cob.

Thinking of it, she walked toward the seawall. The cat leaped up on it, gazed out as Sonya did.

"I should've brought the binoculars. If Cleo's sailing back, maybe we could spot her."

Pulling out her phone, she checked the time.

"No, she's in the car by now. It's later than I thought."

The phone in her hand exploded with Pink Floyd's "Run Like Hell."

"What? Why?"

The window of the Gold Room shot up, and the huge black vulture streamed out.

Dobbs had been practicing, Sonya remembered, and run like hell seemed like good advice. She dropped the phone, the basket, grabbed Yoda in one arm, snatched the cat off the wall with the other.

As she prepared to run, they both leaped out of her arms.

"No! Don't!"

When they ran toward the swooping bird, instinct gave her no choice. She ran after them.

To her horror, the thing shot downward.

With wild barks, Yoda leaped. Pyewacket leaped higher.

Those talons gleamed; the keen-edged beak opened.

The cat swiped. Still running, Sonya heard Pyewacket's quick cry of pain, and over it the scream of Dobbs's creature.

Smelled the sulfur as it dissolved into smoke.

"God, oh God, oh God."

Yoda nuzzled at the cat, who'd landed on all fours before she'd sprawled on the lawn.

Sonya expected blood, open wounds, or worse as she dropped down.

"Let me see. Yoda, get back and let me see."

She found no blood, no open wounds, but saw the pain in the cat's green eyes, heard it in her whines.

Internal injuries? Poison?

As Pye wiggled, tried to lick her paw, she saw it. The ice burns on both front paws.

"Okay. Oh, I know it hurts. I can fix it. You have to let me fix it."

As gently as she could, she picked up the cat, and looked up at the window with both hate and fury.

"You bitch. Going after a little cat."

Sonya heard an ugly laugh before the window slammed shut.

As she carried the cat, murmured to her, Cleo drove up.

She was out of the car like a bullet from a gun.

"What happened? She's hurt? What happened?"

"Ice burns, front paws. That vicious, bullying bitch. I know what to do, Cleo. I know how to help her. We have to keep her calm."

"I'll take her. I've got her. Go. Oh, Pye, I'm so sorry."

Sonya ran into the house, straight to the kitchen to put a bowl of water in the microwave, to get two soft, clean cloths.

"I know, I know, shh now." Cleo stroked Pye, cradling her as they came into the kitchen. "We're going to make it all better. Maybe I should take her to the vet."

"Let's try this first, it's nearly ready."

"It's hurting her. I can see it."

"I know, I know."

"Shh, shh now. Son, it looks worse than Trey's hand did that night."

"I know. Here, use this on her left paw. I'll take the right."

Pye didn't like it, struggled, while Yoda parked his front paws against the kitchen stool and whined.

"It hurts now," Cleo murmured, "but it's going to get better. Let us help now."

They'd applied the warmed cloths three times, and the redness had lessened to a painful pink, when they heard Trey shouting Sonya's name.

"In the kitchen! We're in the kitchen! It's Pye."

Two men and two dogs rushed in. Trey took one look at the setup. "Ice burns?"

"Yes. They're better. But—"

"Let's have a look." Carefully, he removed a cloth. "How many applications?"

"Two," Sonya said, then pushed at her hair. "No, three. This is three."

That told him they'd been severe. "We'll do a couple more."

"Let me have her."

"No, I—"

"Take a break, Cleo." Owen lifted Pye out of her arms. "I've got her. She'll hold quiet for me."

While Trey warmed the cloths again, Cleo swiped at tears. "Sorry. I'm a mess."

"She'll be fine," Trey assured her.

"That's right." Owen cradled the cat, kept his eyes on hers. Green on green. "You're going to be just fine. Might take me and Trey a little longer after the panic. Drive up, Cleo's car door's open, front door's open, Sonya's phone's on the grass along with flowers scattered out of a basket."

"It happened so fast. Clover tried to warn me, but it happened so fast. That goddamn bird. I dropped everything, grabbed Yoda off the ground, Pye off the wall, but—"

Because the men had a handle on it now, she covered her face with her hands. "They both jumped away from me, I couldn't stop them. They ran toward it, but I wasn't fast enough to catch them before . . . They both jumped at it. Yoda, those stubby legs, he didn't get very high, but God, Pye did."

She lowered her hands, struggled for calm. "She raked it with her front claws. It hurt her, I heard her cry, but I think she hurt it more. It screamed. It screamed, and it went to smoke."

"That's right, warrior cat, you hurt it more." Owen stroked a finger between Pye's ears. "Dobbs is no match for you."

"I'm so sorry, Cleo. I had the stone, the hag stone, in my pocket, but I wanted to get them inside, and—"

"Stop. None of this is your fault." Tears shimmered on Cleo's lashes. "Is it better? Is it any better?"

"Yeah." Trey unwrapped the cloths. "See? Another round or two. They're going to be sore and tender for a while, but it's easing up."

"Doesn't hurt as much now." Owen gave Pye another finger stroke. "She's starting to like the attention."

"She is." Cleo swiped at more tears. "Jesus, I'm a mess. It's better, she's better. Now I want to go up there, kick down the door to that room, and toss a bucket of water on that bitch."

"Not sure she'd melt."

Cleo sent Trey a fierce look. "Then I'll find a house to drop on her ass."

"In the meantime," Owen said, "why don't you offer Pye a couple of those treats. She's being a really good girl."

Because they knew the *t*-word, tails thumped.

"Good idea. Treats all around."

By the time they finished, Pye limped a little, but allowed the dogs to sniff at her as she went to the back door.

"She wants to go out, but . . ."

"She's good," Owen assured Cleo.

"Maybe I'll just watch her for a few minutes. Shit. I left my things in the car."

"I'll get them," Trey told her.

"Dinner." Cleo rubbed fingers on her temple. "I was going to do swordfish, blacken it, and I got some nice fingerling potatoes, and—"

"I can handle it, get it started."

"Oh, but—"

Ignoring that, Owen pulled a bottle of wine from the fridge, poured her a glass. "Take this with you."

"Maybe you could just prep the potatoes. You need to—"

Owen gave her a light shove. "Go away." He poured a second glass, handed it to Sonya. "Go away with her."

Because she didn't want Cleo to go alone, Sonya didn't argue.

"I know it wasn't my fault, but I'm still sorry."

"Me, too. But you have to be proud of her. Yoda, too, they went at it. We'll make her pay, Son. We made that asshole pay, and we'll make Dobbs pay."

"That's just what I said to myself before I went outside. She laughed, Cleo. After, when Pye was hurt, she made sure I heard her laugh."

"Is that right?" Amber eyes hot with fury, Cleo watched Pye leap onto the doghouse, then stretch out in the evening sun. "I might just try that bucket of water one of these days."

"We were all having a really good day."

"It hit a bump. A big, scary bump. We're over it."

"We'll eat out here in the sun," Sonya decided. "Keep an eye on Pye and the rest of them a little longer."

"I'm good with that. I'm just going to drink a little of this wine, make sure I've settled down. I want to get back in there. I don't trust Owen with those potatoes."

She could have.

When they walked back in, Owen had the oven preheating, the fish steak marinating, and the potatoes scrubbed, halved. He stopped mincing garlic to glance over.

"Figure you want some herbs here."

"Yes, I do. I'll go get them. I was going to do some asparagus."

"Yeah, I saw it."

As she went out, Trey put Sonya's flowers on the table.

Not the vase she'd had in mind, or the particular arrangement. But she found it very sweet he'd taken care of them.

He handed her the phone.

"Thanks. Thanks, both of you. I was in full panic mode."

"Didn't look it."

"Inside I was." She wrapped around Trey. "One minute I'm strolling around thinking about having my mom come up for a weekend, and your family over for a barbecue, and the next? Dobbs."

"You handled it. Both of you."

"And the cat's no slouch," Owen added. He tilted his head toward the refrigerator. "Got some new art."

"I found it down here before I went outside."

"It's pretty great," Trey said as Cleo came back.

"What's pretty great? I'm ready for pretty great."

"Jack painted our fur family." Sonya gestured.

"Oh! I didn't even notice. He really got the proportions, the perspective. This shows a lot more skill than you'd expect from a nine-year-old boy."

She brought the herbs to the cutting board, and Owen nudged her away. "I got it. These potatoes are mine."

"Fine." She walked over to take out the asparagus, and Trey stepped closer, studied the painting.

"He's been around a lot longer than nine years, though, so in some ways . . . You have to figure he could've gotten his hands on paper, pencils, even paints over the years."

"And practiced," Sonya realized. "Of course, why wouldn't he? The drawings of his we found upstairs are good. But the ones he's done for us? They're better. He's practiced, and improved."

She looked at Trey. "So has Dobbs."

"It's different for her." Owen tossed the potatoes in some olive oil with the chopped herbs, garlic, pepper. "She's stuck in a loop, jumping off the wall every night at three. I don't know about the rest of them, but he's not. Clover's not. Neither's Molly, for a start. They adjust, move with the now."

"That's a smart take," Cleo told him. "I like that take."

"Makes sense to me." Trey gestured toward the painting again. "Especially when you can see it."

"The brides. When they show me, bring me into their past, it's their past—like a loop. But when they speak to me, that past stops, it's like on hold."

"And it's now," Trey finished.

"I think this matters. I don't know how yet," Sonya admitted, "but it feels like a piece of the puzzle."

When the oven dinged, Owen put the potatoes he'd spread on a baking dish inside, set the timer.

"About twenty, stir them up, give them about another twenty. What's your spice deal for the fish?"

"That fish is mine." Cleo walked over, took his face in her hands, kissed him. Then got out a cast-iron skillet. "You can start the grill after the first twenty."

"I'll set the table. And add these." Sonya picked up the flowers. "Oh, Cleo, I forgot. We have three tomatoes."

"I saw this morning. I took a picture. I'll pick them tomorrow and figure out what to do with them. A couple more close to ripe, so we'd have five or six."

"You were right. This was just a big, scary bump, and we're having a really good day."

"Before Sonya sets the table, I'm dredging up that sack. We'll tie the anchor again," Cleo promised, "but I'd really like to hear how that asshole looked in court."

"Panic in a designer suit. Don't ask me what designer, but it had that look."

"He favors Tom Ford and Armani," Sonya murmured.

"Okay, probably one of those. I know his lawyer—he went local, which is the right thing. Not a slouch, but he couldn't control him. And the judge heard him call you a bitch. A couple of outbursts, and he and his attorney got a warning over contempt."

"And somehow," Cleo observed, "the day just got even better. That's all I needed to know. Tying on the anchor again, Sonya."

Sonya smiled. "Splash."

Chapter Twelve

Due to busy summer schedules, Sonya set the first Saturday in August for her family barbecue.

"That's actually better," Cleo decided. "It gives us time to come up with a menu."

"I figured burgers and dogs."

The manor chef looked appalled. "Absolutely not! We can do lots better. Think casual elegance."

"Casual-casual was my aim."

"Aim higher. Trey's whole family's coming, and your mama's driving up from Boston for the weekend."

"I'm excited about Mom coming, and worried."

"We're not going to worry." Cleo sat back in her office chair, pleased with the space, and thrilled she'd finished using it for the evening. "Just like with our open house, people, happy people, lots of light."

"I keep waiting for the light to go on in here." Sonya tapped the side of her head. "And I'll say, *Well, yeah, that's it. That's what I have to do to get the rings, kick Dobbs out, and all's right with our world.*"

"It'll happen when it happens. Right now, I'm pretty happy in our world. We'll be back upstairs tomorrow, doing our search for clues. It makes me feel like Daphne."

"I thought I was Daphne."

"You're definitely Velma—brainier. I guess since he's a lawyer, I'd have to cast Trey as Fred in our Scooby Gang."

"So Owen's Shaggy?"

Thinking, Cleo pursed her lips. "Doesn't quite fit, does it? Sonya, I didn't expect it to fit either, but I'm in love with him."

"You're in love with Shaggy?"

On a laugh, Cleo brushed a hand over her hair. "With Owen."

"I knew what you meant, and also knew that."

"Sonya, I mean all-caps love. I mean the-man-could-break-my-heart love, looking-ahead-to-having-his-babies love."

She'd known Cleo to be in lowercase love, but all-caps love meant the real deal. "Oh."

"I thought we'd just enjoy each other. Serious, but not too. It's been a thousand little things, and a bunch of big ones. The way he held Pye when she was hurt? Well, that just tied it up in a big, shiny bow."

"He's a really good man, Cleo. He wouldn't be my favorite cousin otherwise."

"I've asked myself if it's just because we're all in this situation together—the intensity, the proximity. But it's not." She lifted her hands, let them fall. "So I'm stuck."

"In the it's-all-about-me arena?" Sonya tapped a finger on her chest. "My best friend, my favorite cousin? I love it. Aside from that? You're good together, Cleo. From where I stand, you really fit. So, is it a problem?"

Cleo hunched her shoulders. "I don't know yet. On the practical side, I met him like five minutes ago. But I'm the first one to say love's not practical. The way you feel about Trey's not practical."

"Not even close."

"You know he loves you, Son. I swear, it's all over him."

"I think that. I feel that. We haven't said the word yet, and that word matters. But . . . If we're going by your time frame, I met him about six minutes ago. And he's a careful sort of man. Deliberate. I like that about him."

"Any reason you can't say the word first?"

"No. And yet?" She lifted her shoulders. "I don't. I guess I'm being careful and deliberate, too, about this."

"Because you want it to work, be right. I'm in the same place. So here we are, two smart, capable women. Stuck.

"It's not so bad being stuck."

"Sometimes it feels like—"

"Fate," Cleo finished. "And who am I to argue with fate?"

Yoda scrambled up with a bark and ran out.

"Speaking of fate, that must be the who and what of ours." Cleo pushed up. "They're running a little later than usual."

To make sure, they went to the door. Yoda streaked out, Pye slinked, and two trucks pulled up.

"I'm glad we talked about this between us." Sonya slid an arm around Cleo's waist. "It makes me feel more centered."

"Right there with you."

"There's something in the back of Owen's truck," Sonya noted as Trey got out of his, and Mookie leaped after him. "Oh, oh, Cleo, I think it's the seats for the front yard!"

"See that?" Cleo shook her head. "One more thing."

They hurried over as Owen let down his tailgate.

"What! You made two of them!"

He shrugged at Sonya. "Do the math. Four of us, two two-seaters."

"With the table between on each, and the weeper tree carving on the back. Owen, they're beautiful."

"Took a while," he said as he and Trey maneuvered the first one out. "With actual work to do in there."

"Worth the wait."

"Speaking of weight," Trey said, "they've got it. Where do you want them?"

"And be specific," Owen added.

"Okay, okay, over here." Sonya gestured vaguely, then hurried ahead with Cleo. "Two of them. Do we want them centered? I think we want them centered."

"With maybe a foot between. Eighteen inches max."

"Here! Right here. No," Sonya said and made both men give her a hard eye. "Just a scooch left."

"Define *scooch*," Owen demanded.

"Center the table here. Oh, that's wonderful. Even better than I imagined."

"I'm the one who said black locust, knowing it's a bitch to work with."

"There was a lot of cursing," Trey added. "I don't believe wood could actually do to itself some of what was suggested."

"Lost count of how many times I had to sharpen blades. But." Owen shrugged again. "They turned out. Let's get the other one."

"See that?" Cleo muttered. "He builds something like this, complains about it, then shrugs it off. He's perfect for me. What am I supposed to do? I'll get the beer."

Sonya stood and danced on the second spot. "Here. Right here. I can't believe you did two, and they're magnificent."

"They'll go a little more russet with age, and they'll last. Your great-grandkids will sit on them."

"So much what I wanted." Sonya ran a hand over the wide arch. "More than. The center table's genius. Thank you!"

She threw her arms around Owen and squeezed. "And you." Then Trey. "Slave labor. I have to sit! Try it out."

When she had, she butt-wiggled in, then sighed. "Yes! You said they'd be comfortable. Roomy, too. And the view."

"Be better with a beer."

Sonya just beamed at Owen. "Cleo's getting them."

As she spoke, Cleo came out with a tray. Two beers, two glasses of wine.

"Exactly right," she said as she set the tray on one of the tables. "An ideal spot for watching the sun rise. Not that I plan on doing that."

"Sit! Everybody, sit!"

As Trey handed Sonya a glass, the Gold Room window opened, slammed shut, opened, slammed shut. On the third time, it stayed shut.

"She hates this. Hates we're adding things to the manor, hates we're happy, hates we're here." She lifted her glass. "So here's to doing all of that."

"I brought you my grandfather's BB gun."

She nearly choked on the wine. "You brought me a gun?"

"A BB gun," Trey repeated. "It's old, obviously, but he kept it in good shape. It works. You could take it with you when you walk around. Something comes out of that window. You shoot."

"You want me to shoot Dobbs's evil bird? I've never shot a gun in my life."

"BB gun," he said again. "Not that they're toys, and should never have been. I'll show you how it works. The bird's a big target."

"We thought of getting you a slingshot for more of Cleo's magic rocks, but this seemed better. Point," Owen said, "pull the trigger. How about you, Lafayette? Can you handle a BB gun?"

"Pistol or rifle? My daddy had an old Red Ryder air rifle. We had to swear not to aim at anything but paper targets and tin cans."

"This is a pistol," Trey told her.

"I haven't shot a gun of any kind in a long while, but I do believe I remember how."

"I don't like the idea of having any sort of gun in the house."

"It's a just-in-case thing," Trey told her. "You could keep it in a closet, only take it with you when you walk around outside. Out here anyway."

He put a hand over hers. "She's practicing. Jones got a piece of her dress, you hit her with a rock, the cat hurt her flying monster. We can hurt her, and it. This is one way to do that from a distance. If she sends something after you, or them," he added, with a gesture to the pets, "you can hurt it."

"How about I keep it in the garden shed, in case. And I keep carrying one of the hag stones in my pocket when I walk?"

"She's got a good arm," Cleo put in. "Sad to say, better than mine. I'll take the air pistol. We'll keep it on the top shelf in the turret sitting room closet."

"That'll work."

He said nothing more about it until they were alone in her room with their dogs already settled for the night.

"I know the idea of bringing the air gun upset you."

"It more took me by surprise. I never thought of anything like that. It doesn't upset me as much as it makes me nervous. I've seen the movie," she added, trying to keep it light. "You could put your eye out with that."

He smiled, stroked her cheek. "Which is why you practice, use all the safety precautions. But start with the rock in your pocket."

"Rocks don't make me nervous." She studied him as she took off her shirt. "You're worried about me, but you should remember just what you said before dinner. Jones got a piece of her, I hurt her, Pye hurt her big, scary bird."

"Which is one of the reasons I worry. You said it pisses her off we're here—you're here—adding things. Basically, living your life. If that pisses her off, Sonya, how much more does it that you hurt her?"

"Point taken." When he pulled off his shirt, she moved to him, pressed her hands to his chest. Spread her fingers. "I think, honestly think, we're getting closer to the answers. I don't think she can know or understand that. She doesn't believe her curse can be broken. She's too full of herself to believe that. So I'm still an annoyance, a nuisance. I haven't graduated to competitor or enemy. Yet."

"You think you will."

"I don't know." She laid her head on his shoulder. "I think about it. What's the sense of time for her? How long have I been here, in her sense? She jumps to her death every night. Does that start the clock again, for her?"

"That's a theory."

"Yet she remembers, doesn't she, what came before she jumped, what came after? If for no other reason she has the rings on her hands to remind her."

"Maybe that's part of their purpose for her."

Sonya eased back. "And now that's a theory—they help her remember as well as add to her power. It starts to hurt the head trying to make sense of it."

"That's when you push it to the back of your brain and let it simmer there on its own."

"Is that what you do when you have a problem you can't solve?"

"It usually works."

Careful and deliberate, she thought, and eased back enough to link her arms around his neck.

"I do the same with work problems, so I'll try it with this. But I need something in the front of my brain. You could help me with that."

"That was my next idea."

"You have such good ones," she murmured as his mouth came down to hers.

It felt right, being with him. It felt right, loving him even without the word spoken. She embraced it, embraced him, and let herself be where the problems and puzzles and need for answers couldn't reach.

While the dogs slept, and the sea rolled, they undressed each other. Slipped into bed together. With the lights low, the breeze through the open windows stirring the air, she looked in his eyes.

And he reached for her.

While worries slept, her body awakened. Aroused by the touch of his hands, the seeking glide of them, she rolled with him to answer his needs with her own. Lips sought lips, hungrily now as passions broke through the quiet, and those rising needs heated the blood.

How quickly he could excite her, send her pulses throbbing and that sweet ache, that sweet and desperate ache, spreading through her.

And when his body, so surprisingly tough and strong, pressed to hers, she could only sigh his name. The hard planes, the seductive ripple of muscle formed such an enticing contrast to his smooth and steady nature.

Here, a man she knew she could rely on no matter what came. And here, a man who could stir her needs with a single touch.

"I want you." She grazed her teeth over his jaw as her hands gripped hard at his hips. "I want you inside me."

"Not yet." He captured her mouth again, stilling her words. "Not yet."

Instead, he took more, gave more.

His lips roamed down, down her throat, over her breasts while his hands stroked her toward madness.

Down her body, using lips, teeth, tongue to destroy her, giving her no choice but to surrender. To find a wild thrill in surrender.

Her moans turned to gasps, then her gasps to a cry of release. Breathless and blind, she shuddered.

And still he took more, gave more.

He'd wanted her like this. He hadn't realized how much he'd wanted her like this tonight, every night. Pleasured beyond reason. How he'd wanted her writhing under him as he built that pleasure again, built it higher.

The light gleamed low, but they were in the dark. He was with her in that dark that saturated mind and body until there was nothing but pounding, pulsing needs.

And she with him.

When his name, just his name, came through her lips like a sob, he rose over her, looked down at her. Her lips swollen from his, her face flushed with heat, her eyes deep and dark.

And he drove into her, into the hot, wet wonder of her, with an urgency he couldn't control or deny.

"Stay with me."

In the dark, a little longer in the dark.

She clung to him, her nails digging in, but he didn't feel the bite. Only the wild whip of need as he plunged deeper, darker.

When she cried out again, the sound took him to the edge of the dark, and over.

Though deeply asleep, Trey's instinct woke him as Sonya slipped quietly out of bed. When he started to get up, reach for pants, she shook her head.

"I'm sorry. It's not the mirror or anything. It's not a pull. I don't know why I woke up. It's not even three. Not quite three."

She looked toward the open doors. "I want to watch her," she realized. "I woke up wanting to watch her jump. I don't know why there either, but I do."

"Okay." He pulled on pants.

Always wary of night walking, Sonya wore nightclothes. With him, she stepped out on the balcony in sleep shorts and tank.

"She's already there. It's not quite three, but she's already there. Looking at the manor. At us?"

A different moon. A different night, he thought. A night that came and went more than two hundred years ago.

"I don't think at us. I think she's looking at what she sees as hers, what she's about to make sure stays hers."

The wind whipped the dark hair, the long black dress as Hester Dobbs turned to the sea.

Did she see her death? Sonya wondered. Did she look down at the rocks and see her body shattered, her blood splattered?

The death, the blood she used to seal the curse.

The clock struck three. She watched Dobbs climb onto the seawall, raise her arms.

Piano music drifted up the stairs. In the nursery a mother wept. In the servants' quarters, a girl from Ireland writhed in pain.

And Dobbs jumped.

"Every night. If I stop it, cut this loop, will Astrid stop playing her sad music, Carlotta stop weeping for her dead baby, Molly stop dying in pain, night after night?"

"I don't know." Leaning down, Trey kissed the top of Sonya's head. "But if you use manor logic, it seems like yes."

"I wish there was a way to make her just die there."

Trey started to draw her back in, stopped.

"What did you say?"

"That I wish she'd just die there." She sighed it out. "Die like anyone else would. For the sea to somehow wash everything she is away from here."

"Cut the loop here, on that night, at that time."

"Yeah, that'd be something—except she's already killed Astrid and taken her ring, started stage one of the curse. And in this time, she has the seven. I have to find them."

"And after you do?"

"I . . . I don't know. Happy ever after?"

"What's to stop the loop from starting again?"

Sonya stared at him. "That's a terrible thought."

"Maybe not. Maybe you woke up, we watched this so we could have this conversation. We find a way to get the rings, and while we're working on that, we figure out how to do exactly what you said. Make sure she just dies."

"As if the rings weren't enough of a puzzle."

"They're the key. Keys," he corrected, then looked out to sea. "This is interesting."

"You'd think so. For me, it's a what-the-hell moment."

He smiled at her. "We'll figure it out. And once you find the rings, we won't risk having it all start up again. It ends. Ends right here, on this night."

"In 1806."

"We'll work the problem. The mirror's part of it. But"—he turned her to face him—"when we find the answers, you don't go through it alone. Owen's with you.

"Come on." He drew her back in. "Let's get some sleep."

"You're putting this on back-of-the-brain simmer?"

"That's right."

She admired the ability, didn't think she had it.

And two minutes back in bed, dropped into sleep.

In the morning, she found Owen in the kitchen already at breakfast, which included a Toaster Strudel along with cereal and blueberries.

Heading for coffee, Sonya pointed at the pastry. "Risking your life?"

"I got permission. Fed our troops. They're outside. Used the gym for a quick one," he added. "She rang the bell. A lot."

"Typical."

"I think she came down there."

Sonya turned. "What? While you were working out?"

"Yeah. Got cold, lights started blinking. I had music on, and that went to static. I'm going to admit, the hair on the back of my neck stood up."

He took a bite of pastry, then picked up his coffee mug.

"Owen! What happened?"

"Just said. Except how Jones turned to the door, started growling. He's got a good one. When he started toward the door, it all stopped."

"Just like that?"

"Jones went at her before. I say she knew he'd do it again, and maybe get more than a piece of her ugly dress."

"Well. Good dog, Jones."

"Yeah, he is."

She sliced a bagel as Trey came in.

"I'm up for toasting bagels. That's as far as my breakfast skills go this morning."

"I'll take it."

"So." He got coffee, then sat beside Owen. "Got another theory going."

"About Dobbs? I need another hit of coffee first."

With fresh coffee, Owen continued to eat as Trey laid it out.

"Huh. Makes a weird kind of sense when you twist it around. You break the curse with the rings, okay, but you don't stop Dobbs from doing the same damn thing all over."

"It's depressing." Sonya set the toasted bagel in front of Trey, popped in another. "And annoying."

"But when you think of it, it rolls. And now that you thought of it, and it's rolling, we just have to figure out how."

"How what?" Cleo asked as she came in. As she, too, headed for coffee, Owen gestured to Trey. "Run it again for the late sleeper."

"Eight-forty-whatever on a Saturday morning is not late sleeping. What are we figuring out?"

"Dobbs," Sonya said.

"Oh, her." Cleo drank some coffee. "All right, brain will engage. Let's hear it."

As she listened, Cleo got out another Toaster Strudel. By the time Trey finished, she sat with it, and nodded.

"That's absolutely right, and it's so obvious now that you've said it, I feel stupid not thinking it all the way through before."

"I've thought about that. Why would it show me all it has—and Owen, too—if I'm not supposed to finish it? End it?"

"Very good point." Unlike Owen, Cleo used a knife and fork on her pastry. "We'll have to depend on that. And since we're starting before what's my crack of dawn, we should be able to finish going through the attic and start on the ballroom.

"And I've been working on the menu for the barbecue."

"What's wrong with burgers and dogs?"

Sonya leaned over, gave Owen a light punch on the arm. "That's what I said!"

"Trust me." Cleo pointed at the tablet. "You'll like it."

Through Saturday, they filled another box of mementos, shifted more furniture, then took a break with a sunset sail.

Cleo and Sonya spent part of Sunday afternoon at the hotel's ballroom for Anna's baby shower.

In anticipation of a girl, the room shined in pink and white with baby block balloons, centerpieces of pink and white rosebuds over cloths of white lace.

An arch of more balloons and flowers rose over the mommy-to-be chair.

They enjoyed the female energy—as Cleo called it. Pink champagne and pink lemonade flowed before, during, and after a lovely lunch finished with pink-frosted cupcakes.

They sighed over tiny onesies, tiny frilly dresses, laughed over games.

And Cleo won a basket filled with lotions, candles, bubble bath, and more by naming the most songs with *baby* in the title.

On the drive home, Sonya glanced over as Cleo hugged her basket. "How did you know all those songs?"

"Some from a childhood where people liked to sing, and the rest? Owen. Stick with Owen long enough and you end up knowing all the songs."

Cleo gave the basket a grin. "I got the best prize, and that was a lot of fun."

"It was. I just really loved the girly-girlness of it all. And Anna looked so happy. Ready to get back to the hunt?"

"We'll see what the men came up with, change into get-it-done clothes, then I'm ready to put in some time. Did you smell this candle? Night-blooming jasmine. Mmmm!"

"Show-off."

Before the weekend turned to weekday, they'd found small treasures in a carefully handwritten guest list, a menu for a garden party, and an invitation to a garden party hosted by Mr. and Mrs. Owen Poole.

Given the date—and a quick check of the Poole family history book—Sonya determined Owen and his second wife, Moira, would have been married two years.

She spent some evenings sorting through what they'd found, creating boxes for each bride or family group. She would do better, she thought, better than leaving it all neglected in drawers or forgotten in trunks.

What seemed too impractical to display, well, she'd have the individual boxes, something future generations could go through.

She wanted to think of others living in the manor, appreciating its beauty and resilience, having the connection with those who'd come before.

What they didn't find nagged at her. In all the hours of hunting, they hadn't found a wedding dress worn by any of the seven brides.

"I understand Astrid's," she said to Trey. "It would've been ruined, and Lisbeth's, likely the same. I can see Johanna's, Agatha's, because they died in their wedding dresses. I thought we'd find Marianne's, Catherine's, and I really hoped we'd find Clover's."

"Patricia Poole would have ordered anything that belonged to Clover removed, probably destroyed."

"You're right. I need to stop obsessing about it and get to work. You need to get to work, too."

"I do." Trey took his go-cup of coffee, called to his dog. Sonya walked with him to the door, kissed him goodbye, waved him off in a steady shower of rain.

Then she stood as the silence of the manor fell around her and looked up at Astrid's portrait.

"I'm not giving up, and I won't. Just putting it away for a few hours."

She went upstairs, Yoda at her heels. She sat at her desk, took a breath.

"Ready when you are, Clover."

When the music started, Sonya booted up and got to work.

Later, she saw Cleo make her sleepy morning trek to the kitchen, then her awake and ready return trip.

"Rain's supposed to stop in another hour or two, but I'm sticking with the studio today."

"On your secret project?"

"That's the plan."

"Check the closet."

"Always do."

Sonya barely noticed the rain, then only noticed when it stopped, as Yoda gave an apologetic little whine.

"Need to go out? Good time for a break and a caffeine boost."

She took him down, let him out. After she got a Coke, she took it with her to join him.

"Smell that? Fresh. We can take ten minutes in the fresh."

She got his ball from the shed, tossed it for him while the cat, who'd followed them out, watched from her perch on the doghouse.

"Okay, break's over. I need to . . ."

She felt it. Sly fingers curling in her belly. Tugging, pulling. Toward the woods.

"God. Not again, not there. I have to . . ." The ball dropped out of her hand as she started forward.

"Jack, Jack, please watch them. I don't know where I'll go, what I'll see."

Her body felt limp and light even as her heart picked up a fast, heavy beat. The wet leaves shimmered in the sunlight, and the shadows behind them seemed too deep and darkly green.

Compelled, she walked into the woods that seemed to close in all around her. The air, thicker, wetter, dropped over her until she felt it was an effort to simply breathe.

Here and there, a sunbeam sliced through the green dim, a misty sort of light that struck her as otherworldly.

She heard the stream bubbling, small animals rustling, the insistent call of a bird, shrill in the quiet.

And there on the path, the mirror, its blurred glass surrounded by predators.

She held back just a moment, looked behind her. Yoda hadn't followed. So she braced herself and walked forward.

Walked through the glass and into the past.

Where it was spring. The sun washed down through leaves tenderly green and just starting to unfurl. Rather than thick, the air felt light, breezy. Trilliums popped up to show their color as she remembered they had a few months before in the spring of now.

Ahead, a sleek gray dog flushed birds out of the brush. They rose in a cloud of feathers and annoyance into a sky of tender blue.

The two people walking the path stopped, looked up, and laughed.

The man, tall in his brown jacket and trousers, called to the dog. "Behave, Rex."

"He thinks he is." The woman spoke, her voice as light as the air.

She wore a long skirt of dove gray and a white blouse trimmed in lace under a deeper gray jacket, its sleeves puffed at the shoulders. Her hair, richly black, curled at the sides under a straw boater.

She recognized them now. Owen Poole and Moira, the woman he married and made a family with two years after the wedding-day death of Agatha.

"He's young yet, and full of energy."

Moira lifted her eyebrows as Rex leaped into the bubbling stream to drink. "So it appears."

As she started to walk on, Owen took her hand. "Moira, I wanted to walk with you here today to have a private word."

"We've walked here before."

"We have. In the past year we've walked together here, in the gardens, in the village. I hope you know how much those walks, those talks have meant to me."

"And to me as well."

"I wish to walk by your side for the rest of my life. To have you beside me, Moira. I've come to love you, love you deeply, and ask you here if you would do me the very great honor of becoming my wife."

"Owen." She pressed her free hand to her heart. "I never expected . . . I thought . . ."

He gripped that hand. "Tell me you feel more than friendship for me, though I treasure your friendship. Tell me, if not now, you might feel more in time."

"Owen, I'm . . . I'm breathless." She let out a dazed sort of laugh. "I couldn't—I wouldn't let myself believe you felt or could feel for me as I do for you."

He brought the hand he held to his lips, pressed a kiss on it as he looked into her eyes. "If you feel as I do, you are madly, wildly, desperately in love with me."

Tears sparkled as she laughed. "I am, and have been, and will be."

He drew her close, and from where she stood, Sonya could see her tremble into the kiss.

"Will you be mine, darling Moira? Will you make me the happiest man in all the world and be mine?"

"I am." She laid a hand on his cheek. "And have been. And will be."

She didn't tremble now, but gave a quick cry of joy as she answered his kiss.

The dog jumped out, shook the wet away, and splattered them both with it.

Laughing, hand in hand, her head tipped toward his shoulder, they walked on.

Sonya knew she wasn't meant to follow, had seen what she'd been meant to see.

She stepped back into summer and thick green, and looked down the path.

They had given each other words of love, of marriage, of the future in the very same spot where Hester Dobbs had killed Arthur Poole.

"It means something," she murmured. "It means love triumphs.

Light, no matter how the dark spreads, always pushes through. I needed to see that. And I need to remember it."

So she would, she promised herself as she started back down the path toward the manor.

Chapter Thirteen

Knowing the futility, Sonya didn't argue with Cleo about the barbecue menu. She didn't bother to debate or even question. Obviously, the impromptu sort of gathering she'd imagined had become a mini-event.

Instead, she focused on helping to make it work, and the excitement of having her mother up for a couple of days.

If she worried, and she often did, it centered on the mild annoyances Dobbs tossed out. Because that's all they were, mild annoyances. Ringing doorbell, slamming windows and doors, flickering lights.

Worse would come, and waiting for it kept her nerves on edge.

"I agree with you, Cleo, about the people being here, the energy they bring, but I'm worried about—"

"Food and drink are under control, Son."

"Not that." Maybe a little, she admitted. "No big blast of anything since the really big blast."

"Oh, her. Forget her for now. Whatever she throws, we toss back. Harder. And see, I made this marinade, and these flank steaks are going to soak in it overnight. Now, if you ever finish peeling those potatoes, we're going to make the best potato salad anyone's ever had. Creole-style."

"Sometimes I don't know who you are," Sonya replied.

With a laugh, Cleo put the steaks in the fridge. "I'm into this cooking shit, Son. It's like a drug. We're going to get this prep done, and when Winter gets here, we'll have some wine. Get her settled in, then I'm making that shrimp-and-rice dish Bree gave me the recipe for."

Nodding, nodding, Cleo studied her list again. "If we've gone wrong anywhere—and I really don't think so—Winter will save us."

"I just want her to have a good weekend here."

"Then we'll make sure of it."

Knowing her job, Sonya peeled, sliced, chopped, minced.

When all the make-ahead dishes were tucked away, she helped clean up.

"That's the hardest part done."

"Promise?"

Chef Cleopatra waved a hand. "Tomorrow's easy, just like I planned. And we've got a few hours before Winter gets here. I'm going up to the studio."

"I've got a little work I can deal with."

As they walked out of the kitchen, Cleo put an arm around Sonya's shoulders. "If you get that feeling like you did a few days ago, text me."

"Honestly, I don't know if I can."

"Try. I know it was a good, positive thing you saw, and really romantic on my scale, but try. Just *SOS* is enough."

"I'll try. It's never happened when my mom's here. I hope that holds."

Work pulled her in, and assured her she'd never find cooking and planning meals like a drug. Occasionally enjoying, even satisfying. But so was takeout.

Immersed in her first round of tests for the medical practice's website, she only pulled out when Clover played the Vogues' "Five O'Clock World."

Twice.

"Okay, all right. I got the hint. Ten minutes to finish running this through, and I'll shut down. Shit, there's a glitch. Make that fifteen. I can fix this."

It took twenty, but when she shut down, she felt she'd earned the weekend.

She walked down the hall to give her mother's room one last check. Fresh flowers—selected from the garden—stood in a small, squat glass vase on Catherine's vanity. She'd placed the hairbrush, a hand mirror there as well. As she had the round cobalt perfume bottle with the gold cap found in the attic.

She checked the bathroom. Fresh towels, fancy soaps, and the lovely old powder jar they'd found and she'd filled with bath salts.

The little things the house provided, Sonya thought, made all the difference.

She went down, doing a survey of each room. Floors and furniture gleamed under Molly's loving care. Flowers fresh from the garden or the florist, candles ready for the flame.

It all said not just beautiful old house, but home.

They'd found old frames upstairs, and she'd ordered others. Some photos she'd framed stood on shelves, on mantels, paying homage to those who'd come before her.

Cleo would say those little things brought the light, and Sonya had come to believe it.

Drawn by Yoda's happy barks, she wound her way to the kitchen. It sparkled. She'd helped make that happen. Had to have your hand in, she thought.

But it didn't just sparkle. There were the little things here, too. Cleo's suncatcher rainbowing the light, one of Anna's bowls filled with colorful summer fruit, the glass jar filled with sunny lemons.

It mattered, these things they'd brought to the house.

Content, she looked out the window. She saw the dog, racing with the red ball, and the cat, sunning herself on her doghouse perch.

And she saw the boy in his short pants and untucked shirt, hair tousled from the play and the summer breeze. The breeze carried his laugh to her as he took the ball from Yoda, winged it high and long.

"Perfect timing," Cleo said as she walked in.

At the window, Sonya held up a hand, curved her fingers in a *come* gesture.

Cleo hurried over. She let out a gasp, clutched Sonya's shoulder.

"It's Jack. Oh, Sonya, it's Jack. He looks so . . ."

"Happy," Sonya murmured as it all caught in her throat. "Just a little boy playing with his dog on a summer day. A happy boy with a happy dog."

As she spoke, Jack turned. He looked back at the house, looked at them standing behind the glass. Her heart leaped, her eyes burned when he grinned.

He took the ball from Yoda, rubbed the dog all over and into delirium. Then carrying the ball, he walked to the shed. Turning again, he gave a wave, then walked through the door of the shed.

And was gone.

"He let us see him." Overwhelmed, Sonya wrapped an arm around Cleo. "He let us see him, and see him happy."

"It's a sign, not only that he's come to trust us, and that's just huge, Son. Huge. But it's a sign the light's only getting stronger."

"I was thinking along those lines right before I saw him. I did a kind of walk-through, just making sure everything's perfect for Mom. I thought about the things we brought down, put out, the things we've brought in, and how all of that matters."

She started to open the door, call the pets in. Yoda let out his someone's-coming bark and raced around the house.

"I bet that's Mom now."

"Like I said, perfect timing."

They hurried to the front, rushed outside just as Winter took her weekender from the car and gave Yoda some love.

"There's that good boy! Oh, and there are those gorgeous girls."

She threw open her arms to pull both of them in. "Mmmm! So much better than FaceTime and texts."

"I'm so glad you're here! Come inside. Come in. I've got your case."

"I've got one more thing." She pulled a basket out of the trunk. "Bread basket."

"You baked bread? Oh, smell that, even through the cling wrap." Cleo took the basket.

"There's enough if you want to sample tonight."

"Oh boy, will we," Cleo told her.

"And plenty to put out tomorrow. Yes, you told me not to bring anything, but I really wanted to, and this was fun. Oh, look at your lawn chairs. They're . . . well, magnificent, like the manor.

"Owen built them?"

"He did. You'll try them out. We'll get you all settled, Mom, and have some wine."

Clover greeted her daughter-in-law with Dylan and "Winterlude."

"It's still a little jolt," Winter decided. "But a good one."

"I'll take your case up."

"I can unpack in five minutes, baby, then I'm really here."

"I'll put the bread in the kitchen, and pour the wine."

"Everything's beautiful, Sonya." Winter glanced around as they started upstairs. "This, to keep my nerves at bay, is how I picture you and Cleo. Living your lives, doing your work, being happy in this beautiful house."

"That's just what we're doing."

"I know you love it, and whenever I come here, I see why. And I'm back in my beautiful room. It's—the vanity. That's Catherine's vanity? The one you told me about?"

"It belonged in here."

"It's just lovely." Moving close, Winter ran her fingers over the top. "Absolutely lovely." She wandered over to the windows. "And look how your gardens have grown. Yoda's amazing doghouse, the woods so green and thick."

"We saw Jack out there just before you came. Cleo and I saw Jack playing with Yoda. I told you about Jack."

"You did." Without thinking, Winter hugged her arms. "You'll have to forgive the shiver that gives me."

Winter turned back, studied her daughter. "It doesn't give you one."

"No. But then I've had months to, well, connect, and to get used to what goes on here."

"It might take me longer, so I'd better unpack. Five minutes."

In less than ten, they sat outside, admiring the garden with wine and the tray of cheese and raw vegetables Cleo put together.

"I have to say again how much I love the hair. Sassy Winter."

Grinning at Cleo, Winter gave her head a little shake. "I needed a change-up. I can get so bogged in routine. Passed that one onto you, baby."

"Routine's productive. But yeah, a change-up now and then boosts the energy. We sneak in some. Like a family barbecue that won't be burgers and dogs, as Chef Cleo's going big."

"Go big or why bother? Plus, I get to show off my skills, 'cause I got 'em."

"She does," Sonya concurred. "It's almost scary."

"I'm here to help. Sous chef, line chef, bottle washer. Whatever you need."

Cleo lifted her wine, sipped. "You can join the party after dinner."

"We're having a party?" Sonya said.

"An ice cream making party. Peach ice cream for dessert tomorrow. I remember how my grand-mère used to make it. Churn, churn, churn. And there's an old ice cream maker down in storage."

"Well, God" was Sonya's opinion.

"I was going that way, then I thought: Wait a minute. Technology. So I bought us a new, improved, shiny machine. No rock salt, no hand churning. I got all we need to make it. It'll be fun."

"See, Mom? Scary."

And, Sonya discovered later, fun.

"This is a first for me," Winter admitted. "I didn't have a grand-mère who made ice cream."

"Me either," Sonya added.

"And I didn't know the trick about peeling peaches. Half a minute in boiling water, ice bath, and the skin slid right off. I'm putting that in the book, Cleo, for the next time I make peach pie."

With the peaches softened in sugar and lemon juice, they set up a line for mashing.

"A first for me. I've never mashed peaches. I never dreamed of mashing peaches," Sonya added, and laughed as the tablet played Snoop Dogg's "Peaches N Cream."

"We're going to love them after all this."

"Y'all got this. Mash, then strain. Solids there, juice there. I'm going to cook up the base."

A change of routine, no doubt, Sonya thought, but she enjoyed hanging out in the kitchen with her mother and her best friend.

And her grandmother, as Clover played tunes throughout.

So damn if it wasn't a party.

"Into the ice bath. Otherwise, it takes about four hours to cool in the fridge, and I don't wanna wait. And while that's happening, I say wine and we sit out front in Owen's fabulous seats."

"There's nothing routine about this." As content as her girls, Winter sighed as she looked out at the sea while the sky above softened toward dusk.

"Anytime you want to make that your room permanently, Mom, it's yours. Or the apartment if you'd rather the space."

"I can't think of much that fills my heart more than knowing you mean that."

"The *mean that*'s from both of us," Cleo added.

"Your saying it is a gift. I'm a city girl at the core of it. A working city girl. But I sure love coming up here, seeing the two of you, having this time. And I appreciate Trey and Owen giving it to us, though they didn't have to. You know how fond I am of them."

She sipped her wine. "To prove it, I'm making breakfast Sunday morning."

As dusk went to quiet night, they went back in.

"It's churning time. Takes about a half hour, and the peach solids go in right at the end of that. Anybody want a snack while it's working?"

"After that dinner, Cleo?" Winter shook her head.

"Look there," Sonya said as they stepped into the kitchen. "A tea service set up on the table. Molly did that."

"Yeah." Winter blew out a breath. "A little jolt."

So while the ice cream maker did its work, they had tea.

When it was done, Cleo transferred the ice cream to a freezer container.

"It looks like soft-serve," Winter noted. "And it's so pretty."

Sonya got three spoons. "I know it's not frozen, but we need to sample it."

"Fingers crossed," Cleo said, and crossed fingers on her left as she dipped in with the right. "Oh, it's good!"

"No," Winter disagreed. "It's fantastic."

"We did it! And there's plenty. I call for a bowl of ice cream for breakfast." So saying, Cleo put the container in the freezer.

"Who'd argue with that?" Winter slid an arm around each of them. "My girls. What a lovely home you've made."

Sonya woke in the night, listened to the clock strike three. Piano music drifted up, sad and sweet. Weeping added sorrow and grief. She heard, as she sometimes did, murmurs. Voices, sounds that seemed wrapped in cotton.

But she felt no pull, so lay listening awhile before sliding back into sleep.

And dreamed of a storm at sea, a sailing ship rocked by waves as rain lashed down and lightning split the sky. A man stood at the bow, clothes soaked, hair streaming wet, and defiance in his stance.

She heard him speak over the crashing waves.

"I built this boat. Pooles built this boat, and the sea will not take it. No storm will beat it."

Someone cried out: *Sir!* And he turned, looked back with eyes of Poole green.

"Stay the course, Captain. We're going home. We're going home," he repeated. "My wife waits."

And she did. She stood on the widow's walk in her white dressing gown. The rain hadn't reached the manor, but the wind blew strong to stream through her hair as she looked out to sea.

"Come home to me, my love." Laying her hand on her belly, she kept watch. "Come home to us."

In sleep, Sonya murmured, "Marianne."

In the morning, she thought of the dream, so clear in her mind.

Somehow, they were showing her pieces of the lives lived. The love, devotion, sorrows, and joys.

She'd hold them all. She'd write it all down as she had all the others. He had come home, Hugh Poole, home to the woman who waited with two lives inside her. He came home in the ship he'd built and named for her.

Grateful for the dream, she went downstairs to find her mother already sitting on the deck with coffee.

"You're up early."

"Routine. I fed Pye and Yoda. And though the ice cream tempted, I held off. Come join me."

"Be right there."

She got coffee for herself, then went out, sat. Sighed.

"I don't do this often enough," Winter said. "Sit out in the morning with coffee, even on weekends. It's always *You should do this, or that. Get this done.* I'm going to do a change-up there, too.

"Someone watered the pots before I came out," she added. "I thought to do it for you, so I checked them. It's such an odd thing."

"There's odd, and then there's Lost Bride Manor normal. We're pretty sure it's Eleanor. She waters the solarium plants."

"You seem well adjusted to Lost Bride Manor normal. I'm working on it. I have to tell you something."

"Is everything all right?" On alert, Sonya shifted to her, reached out.

"Yes. Nothing's wrong. I did something. I didn't mention it because it felt a little silly. Honestly, a lot silly. I have this picture I took of your dad holding you when you were a baby. The way he looked at you, and you at him. You were about three months old, and your eyes were already going green from that infant blue."

"I know the photo. You have it in your room."

"You'd been crying—I'd forgotten that. Just fussy, and he picked you up. I remember now like it was yesterday. He picked you up, and held you. He said, 'Daddy's got you, baby girl.'"

As emotion filled her throat, Winter paused a moment.

"You stopped fussing, and looked at him as he looked at you. It was love, and I snapped the picture.

"I love that picture. I made a copy, framed it. I told myself I meant to give it to you, but that's not what I really meant to do."

"Then what?"

"I took it out last night, and I put it on the dresser. I felt silly, but I said, out loud, that it was for Clover. That I'd brought it for her to have, to see her son holding his daughter. To see the love between them. And to see the man he'd grown to be."

"Mom. Mom, that's not silly. That's so kind, kind and loving."

"This morning, it wasn't there, but where I'd put it?"

With her eyes damp, Winter had to take a breath before turning to Sonya.

"There was a little frame, and inside a clover. A four-leaf clover that had been dried and preserved. More? When I picked it up, not jolted but so touched, my phone played. Alanis Morissette. 'Thank U.'"

"It's beautiful. What you did, what she did. It's beautiful."

"I started thinking how I wish I'd known her, then I realized, in a way, I do. I do know her. And I'm so glad she's here with you. I can't be, and it eases my mind knowing she can, and is."

In reassurance, Clover went to Colbie Caillat with Sheryl Crow. "I'll Be Here."

Smiling, nodding, Winter sipped her coffee. "It's going to be a beautiful day."

"Let's go wake Cleo up with a bowl of ice cream."

Laughing now, Winter rose. "Let's do that."

When Trey and Owen arrived, dogs in tow, Winter greeted both men with hard hugs, and the dogs with happy rubs.

"It's so good to see you. All of you."

"Like the new do," Owen told her.

"Thanks. Me, too."

Cleo put her hands on her hips. "I have a plan. I'm no Bree with a massive open house to run, but I have a plan."

"Chill some, Lafayette. It's a barbecue."

"What you call a barbecue, I call a fais-dodo, and where I come from, you don't stint on those. Table, long enough to seat all of us. Smaller one for a carving station."

"Carving what?"

She just pointed at Owen. "You'll find out. Another one for a bar. One more for dishes I'll keep cold on ice. Chairs."

"Why can't the food be on the table where we eat?" Trey wondered.

Cleo sent him a withering look. "Because there's too much food for that."

"I've seen the menu." Winter widened her eyes. "She's not wrong about that."

"People'll start coming around four, so, Sonya, you should start doing the tables up by three. I have drawings of what I'm after."

"Seriously?"

Cleo pointed at her face. "Look at my face. Don't I look serious? Music, Clover's handling it. Winter's in the kitchen with me. Son, you're on reserve there."

"Have I been insulted?"

Trey just lifted his shoulders. "I'm a little afraid to say."

"All right." Cleo clapped her hands. "Let's get cracking. Women, kitchen. Men, tables."

Sonya sent Trey a wide-eyed look as she followed Cleo. And Trey turned to Owen.

"When did she get so scary?"

"It's always been there. Something's wrong with me, man. Because I like it."

Once again relegated to chopping, Sonya took time between to study Cleo's drawings. And breathed a sigh of relief, as she'd kept it simple. Very pretty, but simple.

When the time came, she spread on the blue-and-white-checked cloths, cut flowers for the old blue mason jars. As she folded napkins, Trey came by.

"Looks nice. You, too."

"She gave me fifteen minutes to get my party on. I think she could out-Bree Bree."

She'd done her hair in a short, single braid, tossed on a yellow summer dress about the same shade at the black-eyed Susans on the table.

"Remind me of this next time I think, much less say, let's have a cookout."

"Actually." As he looked around, Trey skimmed a hand down her arm. "It feels right."

"It does?"

"Sure, a few clicks up from what I expected, but it suits the manor, and both of you. It's friendly, and it shows a lot of care. I think we've hit the end of our list, so I can give you a hand."

"Well, according to Cleo's illustration, which belongs in an art gallery, cocktail napkins on the bar table, dinner napkins—the extras—on the other tables."

"I can handle that."

"Later, I want to tell you a couple stories. Good ones."

"Okay."

"And you know what?" Sonya took her own look around. "You're not wrong. This does feel right."

When Anna and Seth arrived, Anna handed Cleo a large covered cake dish. "I know you said bring nothing, but who says no to mini cream puffs?"

"Not me. Go on out. Drinks are all set. There's wine, beer, and this evening's specialty, Bellinis. Lemonade, soft drinks, and water for you and the baby."

"Sounds . . ." Anna stopped as she looked outside. "Well, wow, that looks fabulous. Oh, there's Owen. I got a look at the new seats out front, and I want one."

"You'll talk him into it."

"If not," Seth said, "I'll bribe him."

"Sounds like the rest of the family's here. They were driving up together," Anna added.

"Perfect. Go sweet-talk Owen, and tell him to start the grill."

Outside, Sonya put herself in charge of the bar, poured lemonade for Anna, red wine for Seth. She made a Bellini for Corrine, another lemonade for Deuce—who was behind the wheel.

"A Bellini, my own darling?" Ace asked Paula.

"Who would say no? Sonya, everything's just lovely."

So was she, Sonya thought. Trey's grandmother exuded easy elegance like breath in her summery floral dress.

If she did a poster on handsome couples, the senior Doyles would be her first pick.

"What's your pleasure, Ace?"

She smiled at him, finding him so dashing with his steel mane, his bold blue eyes behind the silver-framed glasses.

"I have so many pleasures, including being right here, right now. But to drink? I see that one says hard lemonade."

"Cleo's grand-mère's brew."

"I'd trust Imogene, so I'll try it. This reminds me of being here a long time ago. Remember, Paula, coming to the manor after Collin had done some of his remodeling, but before he added the apartment? He had us over, just like this. The family."

"I do. Another lovely day. And I remember thinking he'd brought the manor back to life. Just as you have, Sonya. You and Cleo."

"Sometimes, like now? I think we were waiting for each other."

"Collin chose well in you." Ace took the glass she handed him, had a sip. His eyebrows wiggled. "Now, that's what I call lemonade."

Chapter Fourteen

Sonya thought of the summer gathering as an evening with family. The Doyles had become hers. Cleo's laser focus on food, drink, and presentation made it an exceptional evening with family.

Food ranked as top conversation topic at the start of the meal.

"Flank steak happens to be my specialty." Ace took his rare and nodded at Cleo. "I've met my match."

"It's hard to believe you didn't cook before you came to Poole's Bay," Corrine commented.

"I can verify that." With her wineglass, Winter gestured at Cleo, then Sonya. "Neither of them had the slightest interest. Oh, they'd pitch in."

"I'm an excellent chopper/stirrer," Sonya claimed. "And that's what I did a lot of for this spread, as that's what Cleo assigned to me. There's a lot of my knife work in that potato salad."

"Which is excellent. Zippy," Paula said as she took another bite.

"Creole. I had to order the Creole mustard, as you Yankees don't stock it locally."

"And what makes it Creole mustard?" Deuce wondered.

Cleo winked at him. "The zip."

He laughed. "Works. And your chopping, Sonya, really polishes it off."

"You have a flair for it," her mother said. "And you, to your credit—or mine, since I raised you—never failed to clean up after a meal."

"Now we have Molly."

"Oh boy." Seth hunched his shoulders at the mention of ghosts. Anna patted his arm. "I'll keep you safe."

"Molly's a jewel." Sonya smiled over at Seth. "And as benign as they come."

"She is," Winter agreed. "I can't say I'm used to all of it, but there's something about coming out of the shower in the morning, finding your bed made. And your clothes laid out."

"Something creepy" was Seth's opinion.

"She takes good care of the wood." Owen glanced toward the house as he sipped his beer. "She might have some help with it, who knows, but the furniture, the millwork, the floors? You've got to have some love in you to take that kind of care."

"There's one who waters the pots. Eleanor, right?"

"Right, Mom. Jerome—he stacks wood, I think he weeds, as we never have to. And we would. There's Rita—"

"You actually give them names?"

"Those are their names," Sonya told Seth.

"How do you know?"

"Clover told us."

"And it just gets creepier."

"Her musical stylings." Never one to pass up teasing his brother-in-law, Trey took out his phone, set it beside his plate. "Give Seth a tune, Clover."

Willing to play, Clover went with Blue Öyster Cult. "(Don't Fear) The Reaper" sang out.

"That's just . . . I don't know what that is."

"Communication," Owen told him. "Like the Creole mustard, it's got a zip that works."

"There's a kid," Trey pushed on. "Jack. He plays with the dogs, and the cat. Draws pictures. They've got one on the fridge."

"You've got a ghost drawing on your refrigerator?"

"He'd have been an artist if he'd lived." Cleo bit into a slice of Winter's bread. "He has talent."

"Was he a Poole?" Corrine wondered.

"Yes," Sonya told her. "He died when he was nine. A fever took him. When I first got here, he played tricks on me. I'd come into the kitchen, and all the cabinet doors would be open, the stools lying on the floor. And yes," she said to Seth, "it did creep me out."

"Finally!"

"But then I got Yoda, and, well, a boy and a dog. Most days when I'm working, I can hear them playing fetch down in the hall."

"We got used to each other," Cleo put in. "And built up trust. Sonya bought him an art kit."

"Nobody finds that weird?" Seth looked around the table. "Nobody?"

"It's life at the manor," Sonya said. "And the trust is important. He let Cleo and me see him in the yard with Yoda. Just a little boy in those short pants with the . . ." She gestured.

"Suspenders," Deuce murmured.

"Yes. I caught a glimpse once before, but he ran from me. This time, he turned, grinned, waved. It . . ." She pressed a hand to her heart.

"Misty moment," Cleo finished.

"I'll say again, Collin chose well." Ace lifted his glass. "Here's to the ladies of Lost Bride Manor."

"I'll drink to that." Seth lifted his, then looked at his wife. "But I'll tell you, honey, we're never moving from our unhaunted house."

"You'll be dealing with cries in the night soon enough." Ace added a wink. "From my great-granddaughter."

"Oh, that reminds me." Paula shifted. "I saw the mural in the nursery. Cleo, Sonya, it's just magical."

"That was the goal. But Cleo's got the lion's share there, too. I'm the designated assistant. It's like chopping."

"Sonya minimizes her artistic talents."

"My fine art talents."

"Which she has."

"She's got a painting she did of the tree out front in the, what is it?" Trey had to think. "The gift-wrapping room."

"Where once again we hauled furniture in and out," Owen remembered. "We're the designated muscle around here."

"You have a gift-wrapping room?" Anna looked back at the manor with delight. "I have to see it."

"We'll show you. And Cleo's using Collin's office, so a few changes there. We've found so many treasures, big ones, small ones, in storage. We're making use of them where it makes sense."

"Which involves hauling furniture."

"Strong and strapping," Cleo purred so Owen just shook his head.

"What's this I hear about a Poole family gallery? Corrine brought me and my own darling a few pictures to identify when she and Deuce couldn't."

"Poole Family and Friends Gallery. We're going to— Not to scare Seth again."

"No." He looked at Sonya with a plea. "Let's not scare Seth again."

"So I'll just say, when we have control of the Gold Room again on the third floor, we'll make it a kind of Poole history gallery. And since we're finding so many of those treasures stored away—hair combs, a kid glove, an old yo-yo, invitations, and more—we're going to display them."

Deuce looked down at his plate a moment, then lifted those blue eyes to Sonya.

"I didn't know what to expect or hope for that day I knocked on your door in Boston. A part of me still grieved the loss of my oldest and closest friend. I wanted, so much, to honor his wishes, and wanted to persuade you to at least consider coming here."

"You were honest, and that was persuasive."

"You gave Sonya, and me," Winter added, "family we didn't know we had."

"That was Collin's wish, or one of them. What I didn't know that day was you would honor not only his wishes but the dreams he had before he lost Johanna."

"They're my dreams now, too."

"Tell us about some of them," Corrine prompted. "What you plan."

"Oh, well. Top goal has to be finding seven wedding rings and how they'll move someone who won't be named at the moment out of the manor. In the meantime, we'll keep going through everything in storage, making use. Taking ownership, one room at a time."

"I now have a gorgeous vanity in the room I use when I'm here."

"It was Catherine's, and that was her room. We put it back. And we found a desk that was Lisbeth's, and it's in the room she had. Eventually, I'm hoping to tackle the servants' quarters, find a use for them, furnish them, and hopefully that lightens up the ballroom so we can open it again."

"We'd throw some blow-up-your skirt holiday parties with a ballroom."

Sonya grinned at Cleo. "Wouldn't we? And there's a space up there where we're talking about displaying some of the amazing clothes stored in trunks. A kind of fashion history. If Poole's Bay had a museum, or there was a way to help fund one, we could donate or lend—whatever it would be—at least some of them. They've been beautifully kept."

"A museum." Ace pursed his lips. "Hmm."

"Seed planted," Paula said.

"Let me give that some thought."

"Those are very fine dreams." Corrine's wistful smile matched her tone. "Collin and Johanna shared some of them. I may not be strong and strapping like some at the table, but I hope if you need an extra hand, you'll call on me. I'm a hell of an organizer."

"I can attest," Trey said.

When the meal ended, and Sonya got up to clear, everyone stood.

"No, please sit, relax."

"Absolutely not." Corrine continued stacking plates. "We all ate, we all help. Then, I'm with Anna. We want to see that gift-wrapping room."

"We can take a little break before dessert." Cleo led the way into the house.

"I heard a rumor about cream puffs."

"That's a fact," Cleo told Ace. "And they'll go perfectly with the peach ice cream we made last night."

"Homemade peach ice cream." Deuce pressed a hand to his belly. "Somebody should've told me."

"Just stack everything up for now," Sonya said. "A walk through the house, and upstairs, will help work up a dessert appetite."

It took time to bring it all in before Sonya could lead the way.

"I see changes already. Good ones," Corrine decided. "And you've framed some of the photos you found, too."

"With names and approximate dates on the back. You all really helped us there," Sonya told her. "You and Deuce, Ace and Paula. And Clarice Poole."

"I remembered this one." After giving Mookie a quick pat, Ace tapped a photo. "At a party when I was strong and strapping—and younger than these two. Michael and Patricia were already married, and living on the other side of the village."

He angled his head in thought. "Michael came, as I recall. Patricia, of course, didn't. A Poole cousin visited from New York or Boston, maybe Chicago. I danced with her a time or two. Julia—one of the Haverton line. Pretty girl. But not as pretty as my own darling."

He gave her a kiss on the cheek. "I do like dancing with pretty girls."

"I'd worry if you didn't."

"In any case, it wasn't long after this, if my memory serves, that Michael inherited the manor, and Patricia had it closed up."

When they moved to the music room, Anna let out a breath. "The portraits. Trey told us you'd found more, but seeing them's different than just hearing about them."

"Pretty girls," Paula said. "Well, this one."

"Agatha," Sonya supplied.

"More handsome than pretty."

"Sonya found her wedding invitation," Trey told them.

"I'm hoping we find others. It would be nice to display as many as we can."

"I still have Collin and Johanna's. You can have it."

"Oh, Corrine, I don't want to take—"

"You should have it. I knew Johanna's heart very well. She'd love what you're doing."

Clover spoke through Simon and Garfunkel's "Bridge over Troubled Water."

"We were that to each other, whenever we needed to be. So I'll be her bridge now."

Because she understood the bittersweet of memories and loss, Winter slipped an arm around Corrine's waist as they continued.

By the time they'd reached the third floor, Ace gave a *whew*. "You can forget how big this house is. I'd say I've worked up that appetite."

"My quad muscles have muscles," Cleo claimed.

"Let's show off your studio first." With relief, Sonya noted the Gold Room remained quiet and still.

"I haven't been up here in too many years to count," Paula said. "That magnificent view, and I love how you've made it yours, Cleo. It's just—"

She turned, saw the mermaid painting.

"Oh my goodness. Oh my! I've heard, but as Anna said, seeing . . . It's magnificent. She's magnificent."

"Mine," Owen said. "When can I take her?"

"Actually, now. She dried well. I'll get her ready for the trip tomorrow."

"About damn time." He draped an arm over Paula's shoulders. "You can come see her whenever you want."

Sonya itched to check the closet, but thought of Seth. She hung back when Cleo took the group across the hall.

Only paint supplies. "Not yet."

Trey waited in the doorway. "It hasn't been that long since you found Marianne."

"I know. I'm just impatient." Taking his hand, she walked into the gift-wrapping room.

"This is brilliant." And one hand on her baby mound, Anna turned a circle. "Absolutely brilliant. I want one."

"I knew it."

She laughed at Seth, squeezed his hands. "Don't worry. Mom will help me figure it out."

"After TBD Kate Miller."

"Definitely."

"This is your work." Deuce gestured toward Sonya's paintings. "Cleo's right. You do minimize it."

"I appreciate that, but—"

"No buts." Trey spoke firmly.

"She's her father's child in that she inherited his talent. Just not his passion for this kind of art. You painted that one in college. I remember."

"Cleo dug it out."

"They're all wonderful. That tree—you both painted it. It's got such presence," Corrine said, "such character. How old is that tree?"

"I'm not that old, youngster." But Ace studied the painting. "Planted before my time. She's a beauty."

"Cleo's doing the tree in each season."

"I love that idea, but, Mom, look at this! Look how they're using this armoire. The closet rod as a paper roll, the storage for wrapping supplies."

"You know we don't have one of those."

"We could get one, Seth. Or someone could build one."

Owen caught the look. "You know I build boats, right?"

Anna circled a hand over her baby mound. Maybe as habit, maybe as ploy.

"You can build anything. And Trey would help, wouldn't you, Trey?"

"He doesn't give me a choice."

When they started down for dessert, Sonya took a last look back at the Gold Room. Still and quiet.

By the time they returned to the kitchen, the dishwasher hummed and the counters sparkled.

All Seth could say was "Holy crap. Just holy crap. That's seriously spooky. And convenient."

So the manor remained quiet through dessert, and while they sat together on the long summer evening as the lights twinkled on.

Sonya watched the Doyles and the Millers drive down the lane with a sense of peace. They'd given friends who were family a lovely evening.

"Best barbecue in the history of them. My girls know how to throw a party."

"Wait until the holidays." Sonya hugged her mother. "You have to promise to come for Christmas."

"That's a promise I'm happy to give, and keep. And now I'm going up to luxuriate in my beautiful room. Pancake breakfast, ten o'clock. Good night, all."

"The rest of us should have a last drink out front." Cleo gestured. "I still need to unwind."

"I'll get them," Trey told her. "Go start unwinding."

The dogs raced out, and the cat meandered to leap onto the stone wall and look out at the moonlit sea.

As Sonya sat, she considered it the perfect end to a perfect day.

That night, she didn't wake at three, and slept dreamless. She didn't wake until nearly nine, and woke alone. No Trey, no dogs.

She quelled the desperate urge for coffee long enough for a rapid-fire shower.

She heard her mother's voice, and Trey's, and Owen's, as she approached the kitchen.

"I know Sonya doesn't tell me everything that goes on here. And maybe downplays some that she does. I understand why, and I'm doing my best to respect that. I also know she and Cleo are strong, smart women. But I need to know the two of you are looking out for them."

"You can count on that," Trey told her.

"It's more than strong and smart," Owen added. "There's a lot here that's on their side."

"I'm holding on to that, too. I wonder if the both of you have considered moving in—I mean all the way—at least temporarily."

"Mom!"

Winter winced, and went back to mixing her batter. "I'm sorry, baby. And part of me is standing here appalled I sound like I'm saying a woman needs a man to protect her. That's not it. It's the safety in numbers." She shook her head. "It's mostly that anyway."

"Trey and Owen both have work, just like Cleo and I do. And they're here, adding to our numbers, as much as they can be."

"We've got voices," Trey pointed out. "And I'll use mine to say we're here to look out for you."

"I don't—"

"And you look out for us," he interrupted. "That's how it works. That's the deal, Sonya."

"That's not what she meant."

"That's what I heard," Owen corrected. "Relax on it, cousin. We're in this together. We're not just here for the sex and free meals. Though they weigh heavy on the scale."

Trey had to laugh. "That's one way to put it. What Owen's saying is we're here for all of it. For you and Cleo, for the brides, for Collin. For the manor. And if it wasn't for that other weight, we'd still be here."

"I'm happy bearing that weight, but one way or another, we're all in."

Sonya gave up. "I need coffee."

"I worry," Winter told her. "Not every minute of every day, but I worry. When you have your own, you'll know worry's part of the package. And like the love, it never goes away."

Winter gave her a kiss on the cheek. "Get your coffee."

Trey waited until she'd taken the first couple of sips, then went to her, kissed her. "Good morning."

She studied him. "Do you ever lose in court?"

"Unfortunately."

"I don't see how."

Before Winter left that afternoon, Sonya asked her to take a walk with her outside.

"Am I in for a scolding?" Winter asked.

"No."

"Good, because that remains my job."

Sonya let out a laugh. "When's the last time you scolded me?"

"Memory fails. It's been a while. So, say what you need to. I'm here to listen."

"I know that. And what I have to say? First, I hate that you worry at all. Part of the daughter package."

"Understood."

"It's also understood you do, you would, even without all of this." She waved her hand back at the house. "And you're not wrong I down-play some of it, but I want you to know, to be absolutely secure in knowing, Dobbs isn't going to win. I'm not going to let her. She has weaknesses, and I'm starting to figure them out. I can use them. I have used them."

"It's still so hard for me to comprehend what she is, how she is."

"And I think that may be one of the reasons why she's lasted so long."

Winter glanced at the house. "Who wants to believe in the ghost of an evil witch? Who would unless they had to face her?"

"But I have, and I comprehend fine now, Mom. So does Cleo, so do all of us. I want you to remember a little boy who died so long ago drew us the picture that's on the fridge."

"It's adorable," Winter murmured.

"It is. Remember that Clover looks out for us, too. And there's Molly and the rest. I know more are with us than I can name. We're putting a centuries-old puzzle together, and that takes time. But we're doing it."

"You were always good at puzzles."

"The other thing I need you to know is I'm ridiculously happy here. I know, in my gut, this is my place. This is my house. I'm here for those seven women, for Collin, and for Dad, too. And I'm here for myself. You taught me, you and Dad, to stand up to a bully, for myself and anyone else."

"We did." Winter touched Sonya's cheek. "And did a damn good job."

"You did, and that's what I'm doing. I'm standing up to a bully."

"I'm still going to worry. But maybe I'll worry a little less."

"That's good enough."

"I should get on the road." She pulled Sonya in for a tight hug. "And I miss you already."

"Maybe sometime you could stay a little longer."

"I'm saving vacation time for the holidays. For your holiday bash, for Christmas to New Year's Day if my room's available."

"Really?" Simply thrilled, Sonya threw her arms around Winter again. "That would be so great."

"And since I will worry some, I'm inviting myself to Thanksgiving. Whether you have it here or, I suspect, at the Doyles', I'm coming."

"You know how much I love that. I love you."

"I do, and I do. Come on. Let's get one of the strong and strapping to bring down my suitcase."

"And you're taking home some leftovers. No cooking tonight."

"I won't argue with that."

Arm in arm, they started back to the house.

The week started rainy, and stayed that way. Sonya didn't mind a few days of the gloomy and the wet, and figured the gardens would drink it up. Now and again, the wind rose up to whip the rain against the windows, adding patter and drum sound effects.

She didn't mind that either.

She missed her walks, but the view through the library windows of lush green grass and stormy seas made up for them.

And she had the gym. After months of using the space and equipment, she'd learned to block out the ringing bell, the occasional banging, even the quick wash of cold air.

Yoda didn't appear to mind the wet either, as he'd race around outside, roll in the soaked grass while the cat slunk out, did what she had to do, and slunk back in again.

While she worked at her desk, she'd hear the ball bouncing, Yoda's scrambling. And to her pleasure, she might hear Jack's voice.

Good catch!

By midweek, with fewer distractions, she'd caught up on everything work-related.

She stood at the library windows, looking out at the roll and the toss of the sea as Clover played "Here Comes the Rain Again."

Those who predicted such things said the weather would break by late afternoon. And those forecasters promised a clear, bright day to follow.

So she'd designate that for a trip to the village. Make a hair appointment—it was time. Visit the shops, and her village clients, indulge in some shopping.

Still watching the sea, she pulled out her phone, called the salon.

With that done, no work to pull her in, Cleo tucked into her studio, she considered her choices for the rest of a rainy day.

She could curl up and read. She could give herself a facial, stretch out, and stream a movie. Or she could go up and make some headway in the ballroom.

She loved the idea of somehow clearing it out, making it shine, and holding a big bash of a holiday party. Why have a ballroom if you never had a ball?

Holiday Ball at the Manor.

Go fancy and festive. Like her mother, Collin had stowed enough holiday decorations to outfit a small town. They'd go through all that, pick and choose, get more. Hire Bree—absolutely—to coordinate, and Rock Hard to play.

Months ahead yet, and she didn't want to rush what was left of summer, but it would take months. And no amount of planning mattered if the ballroom remained crowded with stored furniture.

Decision made, she thought, and texted Cleo.

> My desk is clear. I'm going up to the ballroom to see what I can do.

> I need about a half hour, then I'll come give you a hand.

Sonya acknowledged with a thumbs-up.

At the top of the stairs she paused, and so did the bounce of the ball. "I'm going to the ballroom. Just letting you know."

At the third floor, she glanced down. All quiet in the Gold Room, and she refused to think: Too quiet. Nothing but the sound of the drumming rain.

Instead, she wondered if Cleo worked on the painting she kept under wraps.

To cut the gloom, she turned on all the lights, then maneuvered through to throw open the ballroom's terrace doors.

Somewhere in the mass of storage they'd find furniture Owen deemed suitable for the outdoor space. And for the holidays, maybe a couple Christmas trees in pots. Or—

She rolled her eyes at herself.

"Stop it. If you don't deal with what is, you can't get to what could be."

But she stood a moment longer, looking out at the gardens, the blooms heavy-headed with rain. The trees, deep and green, swayed in the wind like dancers.

It felt as if the world filled with their whoosh, the drumming rain, and the pound of the sea.

She breathed in the air, thick, wet, warm.

No, she didn't want to hurry the last weeks of summer.

She turned back, metaphorically rolled up her sleeves. She studied the forest of white drapes, like ghosts themselves.

"All right. Pick a spot. Get started."

With booms like cannon fire, the doors behind her slammed shut. The doors ahead of her slammed shut.

And the lights went off.

Chapter Fifteen

Not just rainy-day gloom, Sonya realized. Even that miserable light faded toward deeper. Not pure dark, at least not yet.

She tried to level her breathing, tried to remember Dobbs wanted her fear. Wanted to feed off her fear.

"Don't give it to her. Don't."

Cold swept over her like an ice floe. She watched her breath come in clouds.

Through Shawn Mendes, Clover urged Sonya to "Hold On."

"Doing my best."

As she started for the door, white-draped furniture slid across the floor. The draping billowed as whatever it covered seemed to growl its way over the floor.

It moved to block her, and she felt panic rising when she turned, and it moved again.

"It's my damn house! It's my damn stuff!"

But her voice wavered enough to push the panic closer to the surface.

Furious, she shoved a piece out of her way and started forward. It slammed back into her hard enough to knock her back, and nearly down.

She watched the ballroom doors begin to glow, and the elegantly carved wood bow out, bow in, bow out, and heard the deep inhale, exhale as it did.

Like some nightmare monster's breath.

Overhead, the chandeliers swayed, crystals clicking, snapping together in a sound like ice breaking. The ceiling that held them seemed to groan.

Heart hammering, Sonya pulled out her phone. Time to call in the troops.

One of the white drapes whipped out, slashed like a whip at her hand. The shock sent her phone clattering away.

Breath shattered now, Sonya dropped down, grabbed for it. It skittered away from her fingers.

Leave and live. Stay and die. Stay and die, and fill my throat with more Poole blood.

The voice whispered, more terrifying than a shout.

I am mistress of the manor. I am death to Poole brides. My curse took seven, and holds strong as the first. Run away from this place, and I will spare you.

She shook, from the cold, from the fear, but she shouted back: "Kiss my ass." She shoved a hand in her pocket, closed a fist over the hag stone she habitually carried now. "Show yourself, you bitch. You coward. I'm not going anywhere."

As she scrambled to her feet, the undraped display cabinet tipped toward her. Boxed in, unable to evade, Sonya planted her hands on it, pushed.

Her feet skidded as she lost ground, and lost it, she realized, because the cabinet weighed heavier than it should have.

This is going to hurt, she thought, struggling to prepare herself. It's really going to hurt.

In the cold, hard air, she caught the scent of a meadow.

The cabinet tipped back, just a fraction. Sonya set her teeth, pushed harder.

And nearly lost her grip when she saw Lilian Crest, Clover, her grandmother. With her young, pretty face fierce, blond hair streaming, Clover pushed with her.

"Push!" To Sonya, the voice sounded like music. "Come on! Harder!"

She bore down, gave it everything she had. Sweat trickled down her face, down her spine. Her breath came in gasps and pants.

Clover looked at her, bright blue eyes full of warmth. "I won't leave you. Don't give up."

"Won't. Can't."

"There's my Sonya," Clover said with a smile.

And the cabinet righted.

"Shove that up your ass sideways, bitch." Now Clover grinned. "She can't kill me again, right? I can't stay like all corporeal and everything. Takes it out of me, but you needed to see me so you'd fight."

Clover lifted her fists in a boxing stance.

"She'll crawl back in her hole now," she continued as Sonya simply stood, stared. "But she'll come back. Be ready. You're not alone."

"Clover."

"I really can't stay like this, but I just want to . . ."

When she wrapped around Sonya, Sonya felt the slim frame, the smooth skin. The warmth. She hugged back, hard.

"I have so many questions."

"I don't have a bunch of answers. Except, I liked you from the start. And then? I loved you. I love you. And well, shit, it's a real bitch, you know, but I need you. We need you. Don't give up."

"I won't. I just—"

But she faded away. Her scent lingered a moment longer, then that, too, faded.

As it did, the lights flashed on, the balcony doors swung open to the rain and wind.

And with a war cry, Cleo burst in the ballroom doors, Yoda and Pye with her.

"Sonya! I couldn't get them open." Running forward, Cleo shoved tables aside, and reaching Sonya, wrapped around her as Clover had.

"Did she hurt you? What happened? God, I couldn't get in!"

"I'm okay."

"You're freezing!"

"It's okay. It's over, and I'm okay. She stockpiled enough energy to trap me in here."

"I was about to text Trey, and the handle moved. It hadn't budged, but all at once, I could open the doors."

"We'll text him in a minute anyway. How long was I stuck in here?"

Cleo's hands moved over Sonya, still checking for anything that hurt.

"I don't know exactly. I was just finishing cleaning my brushes, and, Sonya?"

Out of breath herself, Cleo pressed a hand to her drumming heart.

"I think it had to be Jack. I heard a voice, a boy's voice, say, 'Sonya needs help.'"

"Jack."

"Yeah. Come on, let's get out of here. You should sit down, have some water. Then you can tell me what happened."

"Yeah, that sounds . . ." Shaking her head, she stiffened her spine. "No. Damn it, no. You know what? I came up here to do what I want to do, what I need to do, and I'm going to do it. I'm not giving up."

"Son, it's not giving up to sit down and recover."

Fury burned through the cold as she set her shoulders, balled her fists.

"The hell with that. I don't need to recover. She's done for now. She pulled out a lot of stops, and they didn't work. Again. So she's done for now. I'm going to do what I came up here to do. But I have to find my phone."

Clover used Bon Jovi to give the location with "It's My Life."

"That's right. Damn right. And I am going to live while I'm alive. Right here in *my* house."

"You're rubbing your hip."

"Oh, she shoved something at me. Maybe that stand there."

"Let's see." In the way of forever friends, Cleo just yanked down Sonya's shorts. "Ouch. You got a solid bruise."

"Yeah, and I feel it, but bruises fade. And she's the one who left the field. See that display cabinet? She tried to push it over on me."

"Well, shitfire! It's big, and it's heavy. You'd have more than a bruise."

"But I don't. And when we kick her crazy ass out of here, that's going in the Gold Room to display Poole mementoes."

"Okay, all right. It'll be perfect. But, Son—"

"You text Owen, and I'll text Trey. So they know where we are. Then how about picking a spot? We'll start the hunt, and I'll tell you what happened all the way through to the incredibly happy ending."

She tossed off a cloth, opened a drawer of a bureau at random.

"Oh, and look, look, right off the bat." She pulled out a long necklace, a rainbow of beads with white stars and crescent moons scattered in.

"How sweet is that? Love beads, right?"

Slowly, carefully, Sonya ran them through her fingers. "I guess. They're hand-strung. Clover's. I know it because she was wearing them."

"When?"

"I'll tell you," Sonya promised. "I think, I'm pretty sure this was hanging in the room—my room—where she had my dad and Collin. I didn't pay as much attention because—"

"You were focused on her, and what was happening."

"Trey's right, Patricia would have ordered whoever she sent up here to get rid of Clover's things. But they missed this. Just didn't find it. But she saved it for me."

Her phone played Annie Lennox and "The Gift."

"One I'll treasure." Sonya put it on. "Let me start at the beginning."

They started another carton, earmarked pieces, and made the kind of steady progress Sonya had hoped for.

Then Cleo stretched her back, pointed. "Look, the sun. We haven't seen that for a few days."

"And it looks terrific. We should go down. We did good work here, and these two probably need to go out. Plus, I think I'm ready for that sit-down now."

"How about we do that outside?" Cleo closed the terrace doors.

"I'm with you." Sonya checked the time on her phone. "It's nearly six. I didn't mean to stay up there that long."

"We did what we needed to do. I'll throw a quick pasta together for dinner. In a bit. I want the sit-down, too."

"Don't worry about dinner. We'll make some sandwiches or something. It's been a day."

She opened the front door for Yoda and Pye, then gripped Cleo's hand. "Look at that. Oh, just look."

A double rainbow arched over the sea.

"If that's not a really strong sign, I don't know what is. Get a picture."

When Sonya took a few, Cleo nodded. "Good. You need to paint that."

"I—" Sonya paused on her knee-jerk denial. "You know what? I will. Eventually. Let's get a glass of wine and have that sit-down out front."

They'd barely settled down when they heard the trucks coming.

"Ready to tell the story again?"

"Yeah." Sonya ran her fingers over the beads. "And don't mention that I forgot to bring that stupid BB gun out with me. Again."

Sonya rose as Trey, then Mookie jumped out of the truck. He held up a large take-out bag from the Lobster Cage. "Got dinner. Picked up a couple of seafood platters, and sides."

Now Cleo rose. "Bright blessings all over you."

"I'll put it inside."

Owen and Jones got out of their truck, headed over.

"So an incident," he said, studying them both. "In the ballroom?"

"That's right."

"If there was a battle, it looks like the good guys won."

"Also right." Sonya sat again. "And we're just now toasting our victory."

She saw Owen skim a hand over Cleo's cloud of hair, and still studying her, lean in to kiss her.

That's settled, she thought. He loves her. And knowing it added a little more warmth to the evening.

When Trey came back and the dogs occupied themselves with a wrestling match while the cat sat on the wall and observed, he sat beside her. Touched a finger to the beads.

"That's new."

"Actually, it's old."

"You said you weren't hurt. Either of you."

"No. I've got a little bruise."

"From what?"

"Let me start at the top. Another rainy day, all caught up with work. I decided I'd make some progress in the ballroom."

He listened, then held up a hand. "She trapped you."

"Slammed the doors, turned off the lights. It was darker than it should've been, so she added to that. But she either didn't or couldn't make it full dark."

"Couldn't," Cleo said. "If she'd wasted power trying that, she wouldn't have had enough juice, the way I see it, to bring on the rest."

"And what's the rest?" Owen asked.

"She moved the furniture, boxed me in with it. Shoved something at me—that's the bruise. I couldn't not be afraid."

"I guess you couldn't not be human."

Grateful, she tipped her head toward Trey.

"I started to text Cleo for help, but she knocked the phone out of my hand—used one of the dustcovers. She whispered the usual 'leave or die' bullshit—but there was more. I'll come back to it. I got down, trying to find my phone, then I'm nearly as pissed as scared and yelled at her. And this big display cabinet started to come down on me. I was boxed in, braced for some pain. Pushing, trying to push it upright. Not getting anywhere. And then . . ."

She touched the beads again. "Clover. Right beside me, pushing with me."

"Wait." Trey took her hand. "You saw her?"

"I saw her. I spoke to her, and she spoke to me. I don't think I could've done it without her."

As she told them the rest, a tear spilled out, and she pressed her face to Trey's shoulder.

"It was horrible, then wonderful. She hugged me. I felt her arms around me, I could smell her hair. She said she had to go, couldn't stay corporeal for long, that she loved me.

"Then she was gone, the terrace doors swung open, the lights came back on, and Cleo came into the room like a cannonball."

"I couldn't get in before. I pushed, I pulled, I banged on the door, shouted."

"None of which I heard."

"It was only a couple of minutes. I was getting my phone to call our cavalry, and the handle turned."

"What was she wearing? Clover?"

Both amused and baffled, Cleo turned to Owen. "Are you serious?"

"Yeah, and here's why. They cleared out her things, dealt with her body, and cleared out her things. Like she never existed. If she was wearing anything when she gave birth, and died, well, it was going to be messy. So what she wears, it's a choice, right? And part of the illusion or whatever it is—I can't explain it."

"All right," Cleo allowed, "that's actually interesting."

"A dress. Summer dress," Sonya remembered. "Colorful—pinks, oranges, some white. Swirls of color. Sandals." Sonya closed her eyes to bring it all back. "Bright pink sandals. Orange earrings. Double dangling balls. A lot of beaded bracelets, and this."

She touched the necklace. "She was wearing this, and after, I found it in the first drawer I opened."

"A gift," Trey said. "Something of hers she could give you."

"Yes. They must have missed it when they cleared her things out of the manor."

"I'll buy that." Owen nodded. "But that's not what she was wearing when Trey saw her."

"Because she dressed up for you," Cleo concluded. "Wanted to look her best, and in her own way."

To agree, Clover used Lady Gaga and "Born This Way."

"A summer outfit, too," Sonya murmured. "So she pays attention to the seasons."

"With her own unique sense of fashion." Cleo tapped Owen's cheek. "Excellent question as it turns out."

"Now that it's answered, go back to what Dobbs said to you. You said more than the usual," Trey remembered.

"I think it was. 'Leave and live. Stay and die.'" Concentrating, she relayed the rest. "Spare me," she said again. "She keeps warning me.

She warned Patricia, and Patricia ran. She keeps expecting me to. But she warned Patricia because she related, even liked her."

"She doesn't relate to you," Trey put in. "She doesn't like you."

"Exactly, so it's warning for a different reason. She didn't hold back and wait for Patricia to get married—at the manor—move into the manor, but scared her off because she liked her, as much, I'd say, as Dobbs likes anyone. But she wants me gone for a different reason. I don't think she can kill me."

"There's a happy thought," Cleo murmured.

"No, it's manor logic. She can hurt me, at least a little. Ice burn, and I've got a bruise on my hip that proves it."

"You're not a bride," Trey said. "You're not engaged and planning a wedding. You live here, so you're in the way, but not like you would be if you were the next gen of brides."

"I think she needs me alive, and needs or wants me gone, so she's doing whatever she can to make my life here too terrifying to stay."

"She doesn't get you at all."

Sonya gave Cleo a little laugh. "Apparently not. I have to leave, like Patricia did, by my own choice. I'm not going to."

Sonya sipped her wine. "And she's the one who lost the Battle of the Ballroom."

That night, she lay in bed with her head on Trey's shoulder.

"I know you worry about me, and I know it's stupid to tell you not to."

"Good. You're not stupid, so you won't."

"But I want you to take this to heart." She propped on her elbow to look down at him. "I am not alone in this. I not only have you and Cleo and Owen, but Clover made it clear. I know we've said it before, but this really brought it home. She was right there, Trey, right there beside me."

"Cutie, I'm factoring that in."

"Maybe try to give it a little more weight."

"If it didn't have weight, I'd do exactly what your mom said. I'd move in, all the way, and I'd find a way to work from the manor. And you need to factor something in."

"All right. What?"

"She's insane. At some point she could lose whatever control she has and go too far."

Sonya lowered her forehead to his. "I've thought of that. I have. And I balance that out with knowing I'm not alone. It's me for a reason, Trey. It's us for a reason."

"I know that, too, and it weighs on both sides. I also know you're all in on this. If I thought I could talk you out, I'd give it a shot. I'm pretty good at arguing a case."

Smiling, she rubbed her cheek to his. "So I've noticed."

"If I did that, successfully?" He reached up to toy with a lock of her hair. "I don't think you'd ever be Sonya again. You'd never forgive yourself, or me."

"You maybe, because I'd know you did it out of concern for me. But the rest? You're right. So how about don't do that, and let's never find out?"

"That's where I stand right now."

"Let's take the victory."

"The Battle of the Ballroom."

"That's right, and the sweet and happy ending that came after the battle." She brushed her lips over his. "We can make our own happy end to the day right now."

Lowering to him, she brushed her lips on his again, and once more before letting them both fall into the kiss.

When Sonya got out of the shower in the morning, she found Molly's choice laid out on the neatly made bed. Not her usual work clothes, but an easy, breezy summer dress she'd yet to pull out of the closet that season.

"You know what? That works. Casual, but put together."

She dressed, added the selected sandals, added the seed pearl drops

THE SEVEN RINGS 219

that always reminded her of tiny white grapes. On impulse, she added Clover's love beads.

Taking a step back, she studied herself in the mirror.

"It's like wearing a garden—in a good way. Thanks, Molly."

As she walked out, Cleo came out of her room.

"It's barely nine-thirty. Who are you?"

"Funny. Need coffee."

Sonya walked with her. "Or. You could come with me. I can wait. Shopping."

"Not today, Satan. I want to finish my summer tree before it's not summer."

"I thought you had."

"Nearly. You look good. Professional, but not stiffly business. Pretty but not frivolous."

"Apparently, that was Molly's plan."

"I can look pretty." Considering, Cleo nodded. "I could look pretty and meet you for lunch."

"That's a plan. One would work for me." Sonya paused at the library. "How about the casual place at the hotel?"

"Also a plan."

"I could text Anna, see if she wants to join."

"Yeah, do that."

"I'll text her now. I have to grab a couple of things. See you at one."

She sent the text, gathered her things. And read Anna's reply on the way downstairs. Detoured to the kitchen where Cleo stood, waking up her brain with coffee.

"Anna rain-checks. Almost-Mom checkup today. Just you and me?"

Still drinking, Cleo shot up a thumb.

Bending down, Sonya gave Yoda a scrub. "Be good for Cleo. And Jack," she added as she walked out.

On the way to her car, she glanced back at the house and saw the shadow at her bedroom window, as she had seen it the first time she'd come to the manor.

But now she lifted a hand in a wave, and the shadow lifted one in return. Sonya smiled as she drove away.

En route, she went over her agenda.

Gigi's, A Bookstore, Bay Arts. Depending on time spent in each, either the salon or the yoga studio. Lunch, the florist on the way home.

Calculating her walking route, she opted to park nearest the salon, as she'd end up there one way or the other.

As she walked, she noticed plenty of tourists, and found herself pleased she could recognize so many locals. Plenty of them, too, out and about. Three days of rain, she decided, and the sun pulled everyone outdoors.

She entered Gigi's, chatted with the owner—her client. She browsed, and thinking of the gift-wrapping room, the gift storage, let herself think Christmas.

As she came back to checkout, a woman and a teenage boy came in, both carrying boxes. Sonya caught the scent before they'd set the boxes on the counter.

"Delivery!" The woman tossed back a head of beaded braids.

"And just in time. We're running low. I'll check you out first, Sonya. This is Carrie, and her boy, Hogan. Carrie's Bayside Lotions and Potions."

"And the soaps smell amazing. I already use them, and I just picked up more. Sonya MacTavish." She held out a hand.

"Great meeting you."

"Sonya's Collin Poole's niece. She's up at the manor."

Carrie's large brown eyes widened. "Oh."

"Seen any ghosts?" her son wanted to know, and Sonya smiled.

"All the time."

"Don't know if I could do it," Carrie said. "As beautiful as that place looks up there on the cliffs, don't know if I could live there."

"Bet it's cool."

"It really is," Sonya told Hogan. "I don't suppose I could take some of these products right from here."

"Absolutely."

"It's crazy, but I'm doing a little advance Christmas shopping."

After studying her choices, she took out two cakes of soap in pale blue, a body scrub with blue flecks, the coordinating shower gel, body lotion, a pair of candle tins. Arranged them in a group.

"Add a good book, a bottle of wine, maybe a pair of pretty wine-glasses, put it together in a nice basket. My aunt will love it."

"Add a book and such." Gigi pursed her lips. "Maybe a fancy guest towel, too, or a bath pouf. That'd make a nice window display."

"Wouldn't it? I'll take all these, and if I can, another set like it in this scent." She picked up a deep purple soap. "Gorgeous."

Checking off her mental gift list, she gestured. "And one more set in the equally gorgeous fuchsia."

"You sure made my day," Carrie told her.

"Isn't hurting mine either." Gigi began ringing up the purchases.

"We love your products. They're lovely to use, lovely to look at. You make them all yourself. That's impressive."

"My sister and I."

"And?"

Carrie laughed at her son. "And Hogan's a big help when he's not in school. My daughter, too, and my sister's two girls."

"A family business, and a creative one. I imagine a lot of people would love to know more about it. If you ever want a web presence."

"We've got a website."

Behind his mother's back, Hogan rolled his eyes, and she said, "I heard that!"

On a grin, he lifted his shoulders. "Lame. Old, creaky, and lame. Not you, Mom, the website. We need to move into this century."

"Sonya's the one who pulled me into it."

Sonya gave her client a smile. "It's what I do."

"Web pages and like that?" Hogan asked.

"Web pages and all like that."

"Got a card or something?"

"I do." She slid one out of her case, handed it to him.

Nodding, he studied it. "Slick. We could use some slick. I'll work on her."

Pleased with the stop, Sonya walked back to her car to stow her bags. Maybe she'd bought more than she'd intended, but she had a gift-wrapping room with storage.

She strolled into A Bookstore. Diana rang up a customer while several others browsed the stacks, and Anita answered questions from one on the phone.

They both shot her smiles. Since they were busy, she put business on hold and did her own browsing. Ten minutes, two books, and another couple of gifts later, she walked to checkout.

"Busy morning," she said to Diana.

"The best kind. How've you been, Sonya?"

"Busy, so the best kind of good."

Anita finally hung up the phone and let out a long exhale. "Wow. Our online business has taken a jump since you took that on, Sonya. I'll thank you later, but now? Whew!"

She looked at Diana. "The customer wants the entire Sutton Grove series."

"It's a good one." Diana shifted to Sonya. "And it's twenty-three books."

"Double it. She wants a set for her brother and one for her grandfather. A pissed-off gift."

Sonya laughed. "I have to ask."

"They both argued with her that women can't write good, gritty, compelling mysteries. Joyce B. Landon writes the Sutton Grove series."

"Ah."

"They're good, gritty, compelling mysteries."

"They are," Diana agreed. "We're not going to have the whole backlist in stock."

"I told her we'd order. I'll get started."

"If you've got just a minute first? And maybe take one more to get me the first book in that series? I'll send you these digitally, but since I was coming in anyway, I printed out the T-shirt idea, and the bookmark."

When she walked out, again pleased, she decided she could cart her bags one more stop. Then juggled them as her phone signaled.

The readout said: Doyle Law Offices.

"Hi. It's Sonya."

"Sadie." Deuce's admin spoke in her crisp and bedrock Maine voice. "Eddie's not around, so I'm handling Number One. He wants to meet with you. He can come to the manor at noon."

Number One. Ace.

"Oh, I'm actually in the village now, and have an appointment in a few minutes. I could come by the offices later if he's free."

"When?"

"Ah, I'm supposed to meet Cleo for lunch at one, but I can cancel that and—"

"Hold on."

Sonya shifted the bags again, blew out a breath, and kept walking. Sadie came back on, brisk as ever.

"Ace says it's his lucky day when he can take two pretty girls to lunch. One o'clock at the hotel."

"Oh, that's— We'd love it. Which restaurant?"

Brisk turned almost amused. "It's Ace, two pretty girls, lunch. What do you think? The fancy one. One o'clock," she repeated. "Table for three. He won't care if you're late. But I will, so don't be."

So warned, Sonya moved a little faster.

Chapter Sixteen

Sonya wasn't afraid of Ace, but anyone who wasn't at least a little afraid of Sadie had ice water in their veins rather than blood.

She wasn't late.

Since her lunch date had chosen an upscale restaurant, she thanked Molly again for the wardrobe choice, and her hairdresser for the punch of style in long, loose waves.

She walked in and saw, of course, Ace Doyle had the perfect table by the wall of windows overlooking the bay, the boats sailing on it, the lighthouse in the distance.

And of course, he already sat at that perfect table in one of his sharp three-piece suits, complete with pocket square.

He rose when he saw her, then took both her hands, kissed both her cheeks. "You're a vision."

"I couldn't be less and have lunch with the most dashing man on the coast of Maine. This is a bright spot on a bright day."

He pulled out a chair for her. "These old bones are glad to feel the sun again. Now, what can I get you to drink?"

"It's been a busy morning. I'd love a Coke."

He turned to the hovering server. "My lovely companion would like a Coke."

"After I spoke with Sadie," Sonya began, "I wondered about Eddie. Is he okay?"

"More than. I sent him off to court with Trey today. We know

Sadie can handle all of us and then some. Eddie needs the experience, and some exposure to Trey's style of litigating."

"What's his style?"

Ace sat back as the server brought out Sonya's drink.

"There's an old saying for lawyers. When the facts are on your side, pound the facts. When the law's on your side, pound the law. When neither's on your side, pound the table.

"My grandson never pounds the table." Pride coated every word as he continued, "Facts, law, logic, reason are his tools, and he never forgets to give the emotions a little tug."

"Sounds like a good lawyer."

"Damn good lawyer. And here's my other date."

He rose again as Cleo came in, dressed for it in a sheerly layered mini with white flowers over ocean blue.

"Another vision. I'm the envy of Poole's Bay."

"Since you're the most charming man in Poole's Bay, I'd say we're the target of envy."

The server stopped by as Ace pulled out Cleo's chair. "I'll have sparkling water with lime, thanks. Since I just finished a painting, and I'm driving, I'm going to pretend it's champagne."

"What did you paint?"

"I finished the tree in front of the manor, dressed for summer. Fall and winter to come."

"I look forward to seeing all four seasons. And what made your morning busy?" he asked Sonya.

Whatever he wanted to meet her about would wait, she realized. Friendly conversation first, menus, specials, ordering—which included Ace's choice of a pull-apart cheese bread for the table.

By the time Sonya sampled her shrimp salad, she'd forgotten about the requested meeting.

He told stories that made her laugh or simply fascinated her.

"Not long after Collin took over the manor, before he'd done much clearing out or fixing up, he had a poker party. A kind of christening with cards, whiskey, and cigars. Let's see, there was me and Deuce, your cousin Connor, Larry—that's John Dee's dad, retired down to Florida. Friendly game, at a table he and Deuce had hauled up and set right in the big foyer."

The memory made him smile as he ate.

"Had a fire going in the parlor, some chips and whatnot to soak up the whiskey. Now, Collin, that boy had a good brain for business. Poole brain there. But he couldn't play poker worth a damn."

"More a chess man," Sonya said.

"That's a fact. Always thought he could bluff or draw to an inside straight. We're playing penny ante, which was lucky for him, but on one hand, the pot got healthy, and Connor raises it, and I raise that. Had myself a pretty full house, queens over nines. And Collin's sitting there with trash. I'm telling you, you could see it on his face. But he's getting ready to raise again."

He paused, tapped his napkin to his lips. "Now, he'd hauled his own stereo up to the manor. Just as he's about to bump that pot with that trash hand, lose his shirt again, Kenny Rogers starts singing. 'The Gambler.'"

"You've got to know when to hold 'em," Cleo sang. "Know when to fold 'em."

And Ace shot a finger at her. "That's right. Gave every man in there a good, hard jolt. He'd hauled that stereo up to the manor, but he hadn't set it up yet. It wasn't even plugged in."

"Clover." Sonya tossed back her head and laughed. "Looking out for her boy."

"Have to say yes. We didn't know it then, but I know it now. Turns out Collin took his mother's advice and folded."

"Who won the pot?"

He grinned at Cleo. "My full house beat Connor's heart flush. Good healthy pot, too."

Sitting back, he sighed. "For the most part after that, Collin stuck with chess."

"We'll set up a poker night," Sonya promised. "But you'll have to deal with women at the table."

"I never object to women at the table." He winked at them.

"And I'm glad both of you could come, indulge me for lunch. It's good to see friends so close. My best friend, since we were boys long ago? Oh, we got into some scrapes together over the time—and some no one, not even my own darling, knows about to this day. Best man at each other's wedding. I went for the law, he for medicine. Joe was the village doctor for more years than I can count.

"He lost his beloved to cancer about three years back."

"Oh." Sonya reached over for Ace's hand. "That's hard."

"For some, there really is only one. She was his. A year later, he retired, moved down to North Carolina to be closer to his youngest daughter and her family."

"You miss him," Cleo said.

"Like my right arm. We keep in touch. Emails, calls, even social media. His oldest lives in Bangor, so he travels up now and again, visits. Paula and I travel down once a year. But I miss having a beer with him after a long day, sitting around the poker table. I know the treasure of good friends."

He lifted his glass. "So I know that what I wanted to talk to Sonya about, she would talk to you about, Cleo. She'd want to hear what you think. You mentioned a museum, something to hold and display the history of Poole's Bay."

"I did."

"Well, I had a glimmer about that, and I gave it some thought. Talked to some people. The old school—kindergarten through eighth grade." He flashed a grin. "One of the places Joe and I got in some scrapes."

"Redbrick building," Sonya said, bringing it into her mind. "On the other side of the marina. It's on . . . what is it?"

"Gull Lane," Cleo supplied.

Ace sat back. "Not only a pleasure to look at, a pleasure to talk with, but observant about where you are."

"It's our community."

He nodded at Sonya. "You've made that so, and people notice. When they built the new schools—elementary, middle, high school—all before either of you graced this earth, they used it as a polling place, a meeting hall, for storage, for this, that, the other."

"And you think it could serve as a museum."

"It's a good, solid building. Not that it won't need work. Bringing it up to today's codes, dealing with lead paint, asbestos. It's why we haven't tackled it. It needs a purpose so that the work it needs means something.

"I can tell you it's sturdy, in and out. Took a little tour of it yesterday. All this rain? No leaks. Built to last. Now, it's village property, the building and the land it sits on, and that would remain. What it would need is funding. At least the pledge of it to get it moving through channels, to get a plan done."

He sipped his water. "The people I talked to are warm to the idea. We have a foundation, the family, and we'd make that pledge, a substantial one. I know a few others who'd cough up more."

He held up both hands. "Now, you've got to account for people being people. There'll be some squabbling on what goes in it, how's it all done."

"I bet some good and sensible lawyers could handle the squabbling."

He sparkled a grin at Sonya. "Wouldn't be the first time."

Sonya looked at Cleo.

"Son, you already know what I think."

"Yeah, I do." She looked back at Ace. "We're in."

"I had a feeling." He took both their hands, squeezed. "How about we talk about it a little more over dessert?"

Sonya hadn't been as excited about a project since she'd landed the Ryder account. Unlike the Ryder project, she knew this one could and likely would take years.

Ace had estimated three, with the initial several months—at least—dealing with those squabbles, legalities, plans, and budget.

But the idea of being part of a yearslong project in her home, in her community, just added to the excitement.

And still she felt a thrill a few days later when she opened an email from Carrie of Bayside Lotions and Potions.

Reading between the lines, she decided Hogan had pressured his mother, probably his aunt as well, to make the inquiry. The distinct lack of enthusiasm, coated in doubts and wrapped in politeness, came through clearly.

Carrie wasn't convinced her business needed what Sonya could offer.

"So I'll convince you."

She'd taken a look at their website, and the social media pages no one had posted on in more than six weeks, and decided Hogan's assessment of *lame* was high praise.

They obviously hadn't paid anyone who knew what they were doing to set them up. Design-wise, the page hit limp. As far as user-friendly, it didn't reach limp.

"You need me," she murmured.

She decided to take some time to show them why.

She went up to gift storage, arranged products on the hunt table, scattered some flowers, some of Cleo's crystals, took pictures with her phone.

She took them down to her own bathroom, arranged them on the vanity counter, took more, took some of individual products.

"Relax. Indulge. Enhance," she muttered. "Something like that."

Back in her office, she mocked up a web page, new header, new font, clear text, creative photos.

Carrie, it was good to hear from you.

The products your family makes are exceptional. I love using them, and enjoy giving them as gifts. In my opinion, they deserve a better showcase.

I've attached my idea for the design of your home page. It's just the look I envision. This is something you could absolutely do yourself—the photos, the dreamier colors, the clearer font. You're welcome to take this idea and run with it.

However, what I don't think you can do is improve the bones of your website, the setup, the speed, the need to have it work smoothly on mobile devices. I can offer you that service, and improve your social media exposure.

I don't want to overwhelm you, but I'd also suggest a logo design with consistency, that illustrates the creativity and care behind your products.

Please let me know if you have any interest, and I'd be happy to work up a proposal. Take all the time you need to discuss with your family.

Consider the attached a thank-you for introducing me to Bayside Lotions and Potions products.

All the best,

Sonya MacTavish

She sent it off, with attachment, and decided to take her break.

She found Cleo in the kitchen filling her water bottle.

"I'm about to head out. I'm going to stop by Bay Arts, then go over to Gull Lane. I want to do a painting of the old school."

"Well, that's a brilliant idea. And maybe include it in your show next month."

"Maybe, but I think we're mostly set there."

"I'm pretty damn excited."

"So am I. A fun start to autumn for me." Pausing, she sipped some of her drink. "I'm going to miss packing up my art supplies and going wherever I want to paint any day I want to. Sabbatical's about over."

"Cleo, you know if that's what you want, that's what you should do."

"I do know. But I love my day job. In fact, I got two offers. One I'm definitely taking, the other . . . I think I'm done thinking about it, and want that, too. Maybe."

"Well, tell."

"The author of Burt Springer's granddaughter's favorite book."

"*Jessie's Best Day*. I remember."

"I did two others for her, and she wants me for the next. I wouldn't start for a couple weeks, as she's still tweaking the text. Obviously, I don't want anyone else illustrating it."

"That's great. What's the other?"

"Different for me, so I really wanted to think it through. I knew what you'd think."

Sonya laughed. "Tell me what I'd think."

"You read Jonah T. Long."

"I do, as do millions of others. He's great. Terrifying and great. I've never talked you into trying one of his."

"Because terrifying. He's doing a YA."

"Really? Different for him, too."

"I guess. It'll be a three-book series. A trilogy. He wants chapter illustrations. Twenty chapters, twenty illustrations, plus an illustrated frontispiece, possibly a *The End for Now* sort of thing, and a cover design.

"He wants me."

"Holy crap, Cleopatra! This is huge!" On a squeal, Sonya shot both hands into the air, shook them. "It's monumental! You have to do it!"

"That's what I knew you'd say."

"Because you have to!" Grabbing Cleo's arms, she bounced. Because Yoda bounced with her, she laughed and let him out.

"Jonah T. Long's a perennial bestseller for a reason. He's had his books adapted into acclaimed films for a reason."

"So you've told me. Often. They're sending me the manuscript."

"Oh, oh, you have to let me read it. I swear I'll buy the book, but I have to read it."

"The thing is, to take the job, do the job, I have to read it. And draw suitably creepy things. Which I've never done. For a reason."

"But you could, and you know it. You'd crush it! Jonah T. Long wants you, Cleopatra Fabares! So obviously, he's seen and admired your work."

The enthusiasm was infectious, no question about it. Cleo only worried that infection would turn out to be a debilitating virus.

"My first thought was to have you read it, then tell me what I need to draw."

"You know it can't work that way. But I'm reading it!"

"I know it can't work that way, and hell, I'm taking the job anyway."

"Yay!" Sonya caught Cleo's face in her hand, tipped it right and left. "Cleo, you live in a house haunted by many, including the insane. You can't be scared of a book."

"Can, too. And you haven't read one of your horror novels in months."

"I know. But I'm going to read this one."

She grabbed Cleo again, hugged her, bounced.

"This is huge for you! It's going to be amazing."

"We'll find out. I have to go and grab what's left of the summer. And text my agent."

"Yay!" Sonya said again, then danced around the kitchen when Cleo left.

While Cleo crammed as much summer as possible into the end of smoldering August, Sonya pushed more work into her days to give herself blocks of time for her search. If nothing else came of it, she felt she honored her inheritance, the manor, her father's family history.

She carved out time to create a design for the Gold Room. Or what would be, when she claimed it, the family and friends gallery.

Twice she drove to Portland—and indulged herself by taking photos of the Ryder billboards with her design. With Burt Springer, she toured the Ryder building, donned a hard hat to walk through portions still under construction.

It took a week, and Sonya assumed some family wrangling, before Carrie of Bayside Lotions and Potions agreed to a revamped website, brochures, and new business cards.

Sonya considered it a victory for herself, and for young Hogan.

At the end of a workday, Cleo came to the library.

"Son, it's date night."

"I know. I'm just finishing up."

Turning, Cleo studied the mood board for the newest client.

"It's really pretty. I like the way you're playing up the natural magic, organic ingredients, family enterprise."

"Carrie's on board, but not a hundred percent."

"She will be by the time you're finished."

"That's the goal. And . . . Done till Monday."

She shut down so they walked through the hallway together, cat and dog in tow.

"Dinner at the Lobster Cage, a little local music at the village joint after."

Cleo paused at her room. "The high life in Poole's Bay. Ballroom work Saturday, and a Sunday sail."

"My kind of weekend."

Sonya continued to her room to find Molly had chosen a blue dress and added a short white jacket, as the nights already tended cooler.

"I like it. It's been a busy couple of weeks." She cast her gaze up, thought: And quiet, too. "It'll be nice to have an evening out."

She walked to the balcony doors first, threw them open. Looking out at the sea, she considered she'd been here now for six months, double the three-month trial she'd given herself when she'd driven to the manor for the first time.

Over six months since she'd taken that chance—on board, she thought, but not a hundred percent.

Until she'd seen the manor. Met Trey. And ended up losing her heart to both.

"You used to rearrange the bottles on the dresser, Molly. It unnerved me." She breathed in the sea air. "I want you to pick your favorite. Pick the one you like best, and it's yours. I want you to take it, have it. Sort of a belated half-year anniversary gift."

Guns N' Roses played "Sweet Child o' Mine."

"We're all in this together, Clover. And we're going to win this together."

She went in to shower, then spent time trying to duplicate the casual waves the stylist had given her at her last appointment.

Decided, close enough.

When she came out, the blue bottle with its little butterfly cap was missing. Six months before, she thought again as she dressed, that would have unnerved her.

Now it warmed her inside and out.

She took one more look at the sea, then shut the doors before she walked down to Cleo's room.

Cleo wore sizzling red with her strapped, mile-high heeled sandals.

"We look good," Cleo decided. "Make that good and hot."

"Well, really, we can't help it."

"So true."

Cleo picked up her tiny excuse for a purse, they linked arms and started down.

"I gave Molly the blue bottle with the butterfly."

"Aw."

"It made me wonder where she'd keep something like that. Or the hair combs you gave her last week. Another timeline? Some tucked-away place?"

"Now, that's a question."

"I hope she doesn't stay in that room. The room where she died. But I guess they don't stay anywhere really. Part of it, at least part of it's a loop for them, like it is for Dobbs. And will that loop stop when we break the curse?"

"I hope the sad and painful parts will. And, Son, we're easing some of that just by being here. We brought life here, and purpose and hope."

"That's not just a good way to think of it, it's the right way."

Yoda raced to the door, spun a circle, barked.

"I think our dates are here. And the playmates."

Mookie barreled in, and with Yoda immediately rolled into a mock fight. Jones strutted in, gave them a superior look with his good eye.

"That's a sight a man's grateful to see on a Friday night."

Sonya angled her head. "Playful dogs?"

"Beautiful women." Trey scooped her up for a kiss.

Cleo pulled Owen to her with a fistful of his shirt. "These two women are ready for a good meal and some potentially above average music to follow."

"We got Question Mark. That's the band," Owen explained. "Question Mark."

"I'm sure they'll do."

"I'm tonight's DD, so I have to listen to them without the benefit of beer."

"You'll get through it." Amused, Cleo took his hand.

"All right, Jack, you're in charge."

Also amused, Trey took Sonya's. "Really?"

"He's very responsible," she said as they walked out to Owen's truck. She glanced back, saw the shadow move by the library window. "They all are."

She settled in the back with Trey. "The days are getting shorter, the nights a little cooler. I might be sorry to see summer end, but I'm looking forward to seeing Poole's Bay in the fall."

"She puts on a show," Trey told her.

"I'll have weekends to paint that," Cleo put in. "A reward for going back into work mode. And a respite with color and beauty as opposed to the dark and creepy."

"It's a terrific book. Scared the crap out of me. And it has a lot of heart."

Cleo shifted to look at Sonya over her shoulder. "I get why you're so into his books. He puts you there, right there, makes you feel it. Which is exactly why I'd avoid his books like the seven plagues if I hadn't taken this job."

"What works so well in this story? The monster is so much just a regular guy, until he's not. And when he's not, he can still bring some of that through. Just a regular guy who happens to feed on the youth, energy, vitality of young people in a sleepy southern town.

"I loved it. I swear, you can feel the Spanish moss, smell the lazy river that winds through, feel the heat pressing down. I can't wait for the second book."

"Don't remind me I'm going to deal with this twice more."

"I could tell you it's fiction. Monsters aren't real." Owen gave a shrug. "But sometimes they are."

"Thanks for that. And since I already know that, I'm only going to work on it in the bright, bright light of day."

"Which is getting shorter."

At that, she punched Owen's arm.

"Just the facts," he said as he drove into the village.

"I'll save you, Cleo," Sonya assured her. "And your illustrations are going to crush it. We're also going to crush our own in-house monster, reopen the ballroom, and have one hell of a holiday party."

"You're feeling positive tonight," Trey commented.

"I am. I realized today I've passed my three-month mark, which was sort of my borderline when I came here. Give it a quarter of a year, see how it goes. Well, I know how it's gone, how it's going, and I'm going to make sure where it ends up. Meanwhile, I've got my bestie with me, I found my favorite cousin, have an adorable and faithful dog, met my biological grandmother. And."

She turned, took Trey's face in her hands for a kiss. "I found you. That's a lot of positive."

Now Trey laid a hand on her cheek. "That's why you'll crush her."

When they walked in, they found the restaurant doing a booming Friday night business. The pretty young hostess gave Trey her wistful smile before her gaze ticked to Sonya. With envy.

"Welcome. We've got your table ready."

"Speaking of crushing," Sonya murmured.

Trey gave her a poke. "Stop."

"We're full of facts tonight."

"Ian will be your server. He'll be right over."

"Busy night," Trey commented.

"Busy week. Your parents were in last night, Trey. It's always good to see them."

She passed out menus. Trey picked up the wine list to study.

"How about we try this chenin blanc? Bree mentioned it."

"If Bree gave it a yes, so do I," Sonya told him.

"I'll take my one stingy glass of it."

Ian came over, his face wreathed in smiles under his orange-streaked topknot of dark hair. "Hi, everyone. It's nice to see you all here. Can I start you off with drinks?"

"We're going to try this chenin blanc." Trey tapped the menu.

"Chef gives that top grades."

"So I hear. A bottle of sparkling water with it, Ian. How's it going?"

"Really well, thanks." He looked at Sonya. "I've got an interview in Boston on Monday. I really appreciate you putting in a good word for me with Green Engineering."

"Happy to do it. We're all about crushing it tonight, so I know you'll crush the interview."

"I'm sure going to try. And speaking of crushing it, we've got a couple of specials that do just that."

When he'd recited them, he left to get the wine and water.

"I'm going for that sea bass," Owen decided. "I'm not even going to ask what crisp paupiette is."

"French," Cleo told him. "I'm also going French-ish with the shrimp de Jonghe."

"I'm sticking with Maine. Grilled lobster tails. You?" Sonya asked Trey.

"I think . . . going with a favorite. Lobster ravioli. I'm firm on jalapeño hush puppies for a table app."

"Sold."

As they drank wine, shared the starter, Trey steered the conversation toward the proposed museum.

"I wanted to let you know Ace is making headway there."

"I had no doubt."

"A lot of threads to tie, but he's good at it."

"Poole Shipbuilders are on board. That's from the top," Owen added. "We'll pledge a sizable donation—amount still under discussion—put some of the Poole business history in, snag naming rights on one of the rooms or sections."

"Naming rights. I hadn't thought of that. I wonder . . . Why are you smiling like that?" she asked Trey.

"Pretty sure I know where this is going."

"Oh yeah?" She picked up her wine. "Why don't you tell me?"

"The Collin Poole and Andrew MacTavish Room."

"You know her," Cleo murmured. "And got it in one."

"He did." Under the table, Sonya squeezed his hand. "It honors them both, and it puts my father's connection to the manor right out there, where it belongs. I don't know how that sort of thing works, but—"

"I do." Lifting her hand, he kissed it. "We'll make it happen."

As they finished their mains, the redheaded missile that was Chef Bree shot out, nudged Trey, and plopped down.

Her face still flushed from the kitchen, she pointed at Owen first. "The bass?"

"You see any left here?"

"I do not. FYI, you're all sharing the Heaven on Earth and the passion fruit mousse. And you're welcome. You"—she leaned around Trey to point at Sonya—"good idea about the museum."

"You heard about it?"

"Word gets around. Pretty sure Ace Doyle made sure of that." She beamed at Cleo. "You did pretty well on the shrimp."

"I'd have done better if I'd bypassed the jalapeño hush puppies."

"No one can. Anyway, my news. Manny and I are making it official."

Trey managed to keep his jaw from dropping. "You're getting married?"

"What?" She snorted, slapped his arm. "Dude! No. Later for that if this works out. We're not just moving in together. We're renting a house together. Nice little bungalow a block back. Kitchen's been redone, so that pulled me—and all my gear. It's got a finished half basement that pulled Manny, and all his. We move in the second week of September.

"I'm revved."

"You're always revved," Owen pointed out. "But congratulations, right?"

"Right is right."

"That should make it easy for you to talk him and Rock Hard into playing in our ballroom for our holiday party at the manor."

Bree leaned past Trey again. "Seriously? I thought I heard that ball-room place was full of stuff."

"We're working on it. And we'll need you."

"Goes without saying. Bash in the Ballroom. I'll think about it. Gotta get back. Ian'll bring you cappuccinos after they clear. Later."

She zoomed off, and Sonya just grinned. "You know if I went for women, she'd give you serious competition, Trey." Then leaning over, she clinked her glass to Cleo's. "Another step in our holiday plans in place."

Chapter Seventeen

Midnight came and went by the time they drove back to the manor.

"Question regarding Question Mark," Sonya began. "Will they or won't they, at some point, reach up for the average bar?"

"No," Owen said immediately. "And let me make that hell no, with an exclamation mark."

He caught Trey's eye in the rearview.

"Yeah, I gotta agree with my former bandmate on that. The bass player's not bad, but a rock band's not held up by bass alone. Tell you what, we'll make it up to ourselves, hit the club in Ogunquit sometime soon."

"Maybe find out when Rock Hard's playing." Cleo shifted to look back. "See when Bree has a night off and she's going."

"I can do that."

"Sounds like a party. I wonder . . . No, not tonight." Sonya caught sight of the manor. Only the lights she'd left on glowed. "I wondered if Clover and her ghostly friends had a party like the time before."

"Maybe they did. Just wrapped it by midnight."

Laughing, she leaned against Trey. "I really like to think so."

When Owen parked, she got out. "I trust Jack took care of it all, but we'll let everybody out for a bit before . . ."

She trailed off, groped for Trey's arm.

"What is it?"

"I feel . . . The mirror. I feel it. I don't— I can't— There. There. Do you see it?"

It stood on the lawn, the glass glinting in the cloud-shadowed moonlight. Where it hadn't been, Trey knew it hadn't been, even seconds before.

"Yeah, I see it. What else do you see?"

Pressing a hand to her belly, she leaned against him. "The mirror. There's movement in the mirror."

"I can see that." Owen stepped up beside her. "Colors, dark, but colors against that, moving."

"I don't see anything but the reflection of the glass." In support, Cleo put a hand on Sonya's shoulder.

"I have to go. I can't not go."

"I know." Struggling, Trey leaned down to kiss her. "Owen's with you. Cleo and I will wait. Right here."

"We've got this. Whatever this is, we've got it."

Taking her hand now, Owen walked with her. Over the grass toward the mirror.

"Voices, I hear voices. Music and voices."

"I don't, not yet. Just . . . sound I can't make out."

"I'm not afraid," she said to convince herself.

"Good. You can protect me."

Together, they walked to the mirror and through.

When they vanished into the glass, Cleo vised a hand over Trey's. "I hate this. I hate we just stand here. We can't hear, can't see."

"Right there with you. The dogs are barking. Maybe you could let them out."

When she rushed over to open the door, he took another step. Pressed his hand to the glass.

On the other side of it, Sonya stood with Owen on the lawn. In a star-drenched sky, a full moon sailed over the rolling sea.

Throughout the manor lights glimmered and shone. Through windows open to what felt like any night in early summer, she heard music.

A male voice crooned. *When you were sweet sixteen.*

One couple laughed, a gay sound, as they danced over the grass.

Others walked, lit by moonlight and strings of Chinese lanterns. Men wore tuxedos, some more formal tails, while the women shined in sweeping gowns low and fitted at the bodice. Gowns of silks, satins in soft colors they wore with long gloves and the sparkle of diamonds, rubies, emeralds.

"Moira! Moira and Owen Poole. Over there. I recognize them. Do you see them?"

"Yeah, okay. Blue dress? Blue flowers it looks like running down the skirt."

"Yes! They're older than when I saw them in the woods. When he proposed. They look happy."

"Everybody does. Makes me wonder why we're here."

"I want to hear what they're saying."

She tugged Owen over, ghosts among the ghosts.

A few people applauded as they walked through, as the song ended and the dancers took a bow, a curtsy.

Moira patted her husband's hand. "We should go in now, Owen."

"You're not light-headed?"

"Not in the least. I just needed some air. You know how it is."

Her hand brushed lightly over her belly.

"She's pregnant. It's . . . I can't really pinpoint, but I know it's after Lisbeth's birth. The fashion. I've tried to pay attention to how it evolves. Owen, I think it's somewhere around the turn of the century, so maybe ah . . . I think it's Jack."

"I have to trust you on that."

"Why would we need to be here for that? They're happy. They don't know what's going to happen to Lissy."

"It wouldn't change anything if they did. They'd just grieve longer."

"You're right. I know you're right. I just—they're going back in. Maybe we're supposed to follow them, go in, up to the ballroom."

As they started to, she froze.

"What? Dobbs?"

"No. No. No." She lifted a trembling hand.

"Jesus, it's Collin. Standing right there by the mirror. He had to come through like we did, but from before. He looks, I don't know, my age maybe."

"Yes, about your age. But it's not Collin. It's my father. Owen, it's my father."

She knew it absolutely. They were twins, yet there were small, subtle differences. And she knew the man standing by the mirror, wearing ancient jeans frayed at the hem, a Boston University T-shirt, his hair tousled and in need of a trim, his face stubbled and in need of a shave, was Andrew MacTavish.

Her father.

Breaking away from Owen, she ran.

"Dad. Oh God, Dad!"

Running, her arms open to embrace him, she went right through him.

She gave a quick cry, more grief than shock. His body jerked as if someone had bumped him. Eyes wide, he looked around.

Looked, for a moment she believed, looked at her.

"Dad."

She reached out, but saw he stared through, not at her, then past her.

"Easy." Owen went to her, put an arm around her shoulders. "It's hard. Can't imagine. But you've got a chance to see him again."

"He felt me. I know it. He can't see me, but he felt me. We're ghosts here, but so is he. Why can I see him, but he can't see me?"

"Hell if I know, Sonya, and it sucks. Look, he's not afraid. He's more—"

"In wonder." A tear spilled out. "That's what he'd call it when he saw something that struck him. In wonder. It's the manor that strikes him."

Even as she spoke, so did Drew.

"It's a dream, just another dream. How can they be so damn real? How can I smell the salt air, feel the grass under my feet? Hear that music? What the hell song is that?"

Shaking his head, he stuffed his hands in his pockets, studied the manor.

"The most amazing house I've ever seen. And I keep seeing it. On the coast somewhere. Man, Winter and Sonya would love this place. One day, maybe."

Then his head turned. "Who the hell is that?"

"Dobbs." Owen gripped Sonya's arm firmly to hold her in place.

"I see her. So does Dad. He sees her."

"Not one of them," she heard Drew say. "Something else."

"She sees him, Owen. She's walking his way. She could hurt him. I have to—"

"She didn't. That didn't happen then." He kept his grip firm, and hoped he spoke truth. "It won't happen now."

Even as Dobbs glided toward him, Drew looked back at the mirror. "Sonya's calling me. Time to wake up."

Turning to the mirror, he stepped through.

"Stay away from what's mine." Dobbs slapped a hand toward the mirror only to fall back several steps. She cradled one hand in the other.

"Damn to you. Damn to all of you. I should've smothered the babe. Pick one, steal its breath. This one brings trouble. Brings trouble."

Her madness swirling like a cloak, she paced around the mirror. A woman nearby suddenly shivered and hugged her arms.

"This brings trouble."

With her face wild with fury, lips peeled back in a snarl, Dobbs balled her fist. She rammed it toward the glass but before she struck, pulled back, cried out in pain.

"Damn to you."

She opened her fist, scowled at her blood-smeared knuckles. Then the face of her fury turned dreamy. Her eyes shined as she held out her hands, as she smiled down at the four rings on her fingers.

"Four now, and the fifth tucked away in bed. Safe and snug, they think. Oh yes, safe and snug this night. But soon enough, soon enough a bride she'll be. And mine.

"Soon enough."

She dropped her hands down by her sides, threw her face up to the sky. "Safe and snug and warm, but here I bring the storm."

Laughing, she threw her arms up.

The wind swirled. Lightning flashed. Thunder roared. And rain poured out of the sky in a torrent.

On shrieks and laughter, people ran toward the house until only the three stood outside as the rain drenched the lawn.

"Soon enough." Smiling, smiling, Dobbs admired her fingers and what gleamed on them. "Death comes to the bride."

She lifted her face, shouted at the sky. "I am mistress of the manor, for all time."

On another whirl, she vanished.

"Hell of a show," Owen managed. "And what we came here to see. We're soaked. Time to go back."

"He heard me calling him. He went back for me."

"That's right. And we're going back." He pulled her to the mirror, and through.

To a dry, clear summer night.

"Jesus, you're soaked." Trey reached for her. "And crying."

"It rained, it rained on the party."

"You'll tell us, but we're going up." Cleo took her hand. "I'll help you dry off and change. Trey."

"Yeah, yeah. I'll make tea."

"I'm not driving now." Owen shoved at his dripping hair. "I'm having whiskey."

"I'll take care of it." As he walked to the house, Trey looked back. The mirror had done what it came to do, and was gone.

Not just soaked, Trey thought, not just crying, but so pale he wondered his arms hadn't passed through her. He watched her walk upstairs with Cleo as Owen followed with Jones in step beside him.

And he'd make goddamn tea.

"Stick with me," he told the rest of the pets. "Give them some space."

Not for the first time, he wished the mirror, and the manor with it, to the far reaches of hell.

Upstairs, Cleo drew Sonya into her room. And saw Molly, most likely, had already turned on the fire.

"You're shivering. Stand by the fire. You need to get out of those wet clothes. I'll get towels."

Because it was Cleo, Sonya let the last thread snap. She covered her face with her hands and sobbed.

"Oh, Son. Baby. Whatever happened, I'm so sorry." Wrapping around her, she stroked, she swayed. "Don't talk now. Just tell me if you're hurt."

When Sonya just shook her head, Cleo held her. "I've got you," she said, and let Sonya cry it out.

When the sobs tapered off, Cleo eased back. "I'm going to get you towels and dry clothes."

She turned, and saw while she'd comforted Sonya, Molly had taken care of the essentials. Towels, a sweatshirt, sweatpants, and thick socks lay on the bed.

"You're an angel," Cleo murmured. "I think that's literally. Here now, let's get you out of that wet dress."

Sonya let out a breath, drew another in deep, let it out. "Okay. Okay. I just needed to get that out."

When she'd stripped down, Cleo wrapped her in a towel, used the other on her hair.

"That's better. We can hit it with your hair dryer."

"It's better." But Sonya leaned her head on Cleo's shoulder a moment. "I don't know what I'd do without you."

"Lucky you don't have to find out, ever. Let's get you dressed."

Dry and dressed, Sonya tapped her face. "How bad?"

"Nothing ten minutes with cold compresses wouldn't fix, but in this case, I think you go as you are. Son, Trey's worried, and we're in the dark, so more worried."

"You're right, and I've steadied up enough now. Thanks to you."

"We steady each other. That's the deal."

Sonya managed a smile. "Best deal ever. Let's go downstairs."

Owen and Jones waited in the hall. After a careful study, Owen nodded.

"If I'd gone down before you were ready, he'd ask, and I'd tell him. You should do that."

"Damn it, Owen."

He scowled as he looked at Cleo. "What?"

"You just keep racking up the points."

"Yeah? What's my score?"

"Game's not over."

Downstairs, Trey paced the kitchen. He was a patient man. He'd been told, more than once, he had too much of that particular quality.

But his patience had just about reached its limit.

"Fuck this." He started out, then heard them coming. Pulling back some control, he poured whiskey for Owen.

Yoda ran over to Sonya, then rose on his hind legs as if to cheer her.

"That's a good boy." Petting him, she looked at Trey. "Sorry it took so long."

"It's all right." He knew the aftermath of a crying jag when he saw it, so pulled the patience back again. "Why don't you sit down? Why don't we all sit down?"

Still standing, Owen picked up the whiskey, drank. "That'll do it." He pointed at Sonya.

"A shot of that, tea chaser. I've got it. Sit with Cleo. You're the ones who went through it. Trey and I just wait."

"That's a tough gig."

"It damn sure is."

As she reached for the whiskey bottle, Owen closed a hand over hers. "Appreciate it." Then poured her a shot himself.

"Very much appreciate it," Sonya said as she took a seat at the table. Yoda crawled under to lie at her feet. "And I'm sorry you had to wait until I pulled it together."

Trey opted for coffee, and brought it with him to sit. "You were only gone about a half hour this time. Twenty-seven minutes, actually."

"I don't think we were there that long, were we, Owen?"

"More like ten. Ten, twelve tops." He sat with Jones on guard beside his chair.

"It's that weird time deal. It was a party," she began. "I think just after the turn of the century. Early nineteen hundreds. Moira and Owen Poole. Formal party, and I think spring or early summer. We could hear music from the ballroom, and we were out on the lawn. People were taking the air."

Sonya looked at Owen.

"Yeah, fancy clothes, lots of jewelry. Full moon, clear skies."

"That's right. A full moon, clear skies. Beautiful evening. Owen and Moira—older than when I saw them in the woods. She was pregnant. Not showing. It was their conversation. It had to be one of their youngest."

"Not Lissy?" Cleo asked.

"Going by the fashion, and roughly how much older they were, no. She had to be pregnant with Jack. And later . . ." She shook Dobbs away to tell it all in order. "They started to go back in, and we weren't sure if we should follow. Then . . ."

She had to pause, and lifted the tea Trey made her.

"Dobbs?"

She shook her head. "No, not then. My father. My father, standing there watching like we were. He was about thirty, not much more than thirty, I guess, wearing his old Boston U T-shirt."

She cleared her throat. "He looked sleepy. I mean, like he'd been sleeping. Sometimes, when a painting wasn't going well, he'd take what he called an inspiration nap. Five or ten minutes on this old sofa in his studio. He looked like that. He thought he was dreaming. He spoke out loud, and thought he dreamed it all."

"I've seen the pictures." Owen spoke to give Sonya time to steady again. "Yeah, they looked alike. At first, I thought it was Collin."

"He'd come through the mirror," Trey said. "Your dad."

"Yes, though we didn't see him come through. But there he was, and I called out to him, and ran to him. But he didn't hear me, and I went right through him. It's not like that for me and Owen, for each other. For each other we're there, ah, corporeal. But I couldn't touch my dad. He felt me, though. Felt something.

"He looked at me. He didn't see me, but for just a second, he looked at me. He sensed something. Then . . . Owen."

"Dobbs." He snapped his fingers. "Just there. Sonya's dad saw her, too. And said something like she wasn't one of them. The people at the party."

"He'd have noticed she was dressed differently, she looked out of place. He noticed things."

"She didn't. Notice us," Owen added. "She was focused on him, and she knew who he was."

"Your father," Trey supplied.

"It pissed her off, you could see it." Owen tossed back more whiskey. "Maybe she wanted to do something, but Sonya called him. Not this Sonya, kid Sonya, through the mirror. He said: 'Sonya's calling me. Time to wake up.' And he went to the mirror, went through before Dobbs reached him.

"That pissed her off even more. She took a swing at the mirror."

"It stopped her. I think it hurt her."

"Damn right. Bloodied her knuckles. She punched at the glass, but couldn't hit it, and yanked her hand back. I saw some pain as well as mad and crazy."

"She said she should've smothered him the night he was born. Pick one—like Patricia made her daughter pick one baby to keep. That he—my father—brought trouble."

"That would be you."

Sonya nodded at Cleo. "That would be me. I like knowing I give her trouble. She had four rings, and said the fifth was tucked into bed—Lisbeth. Soon enough she'd be a bride. She laughed, lifted her arms. Wind, thunder, lightning, rain."

Sonya heaved out a breath. "She poofed; we came back."

"You left out the rings."

"I said she wore four."

"No, I mean, before she lifted her arms up to do the crazy bring the storm shit, and during, they went all, you know, glittery."

Frowning, Sonya shook her head. "I'm not sure what you mean."

"Like glittery," he repeated. "Ah, sparking. Like you're welding something and you get sparks."

"I . . . Yes, when she had her arms up. I guess I thought that was just the lightning. I didn't notice anything before she lifted her hands."

"She went—" Owen wiggled the fingers on his left hand. "Down at her sides, and the rings started to glitter—it's the word I've got for it—and then sparks."

"She uses the rings to boost her power. I guess we knew that, or thought that," Cleo considered. "This feels like more."

"She doesn't just want the rings—the symbol of them." Trey spoke slowly. "A token of the lives she took, the brides she removed. She needs them."

Trey spread his hands. "She's dead. Yeah, she sealed the curse with her own blood, but she's dead. Dead's gotta be a big power suck. We already know, have solid evidence to conclude she has to take time off and on to basically recharge."

"The rings are a power source." Logic, Sonya thought. Manor logic. "She needs them for power, and maybe . . ."

"To exist," Trey added. "A big maybe, but a maybe. Get them back and—"

"Unplug a main source of power," Owen finished for him.

"Break the curse, and remove her. And by *remove*"—Cleo sipped her tea—"I mean destroy, obliterate, annihilate, with extreme prejudice. Bonus round if she screams in agony on the way out."

"And you keep racking up the points." Reaching over, Owen snagged Trey's coffee mug, toasted Cleo, sipped. Winced. "It's cold, man."

"So make some more."

With a shrug, Owen took the mug, rose to go to the coffee maker. Jones opened his eye, watched the journey. Satisfied, he closed it again.

"We learned more than I realized. I didn't put all this together."

"You took a hard punch, cutie. You saw your dad, right there, and you couldn't connect. You couldn't talk to him, or touch him. You couldn't have a moment with him."

"I don't understand why. He came through the mirror, just like Owen and I do."

Trey took her hand, pressed it to his cheek. "He didn't die here. He died in Boston. As far as we know, and it's pretty conclusive, he's never been here except through the mirror."

"So he couldn't be there the way Owen and I can. The mirror was in his studio—another place, another time. He saw that night—he told Mom he'd had a dream about this manor, and people walking around outside in fancy, old-fashioned clothes. He saw that night but not the way we did. So he couldn't see or hear me. But we could see and hear him."

"Because it all happened, at that time and place."

"I get it. It's enough to give you a migraine, but I get it."

"And even though he couldn't see or hear you, Son?"

She nodded at Cleo. "I saw him again, I heard his voice again. A kick in the emotional crotch, but also a gift."

Clover, who'd stayed quiet throughout, played Paul Simon's "Father and Daughter."

"He did love me."

"Does," Trey corrected, and Sonya pressed her face to his shoulder.

"He lit up when he heard you call through the mirror." Owen brought Trey fresh coffee and a mug for himself. "Here's a guy thinking he's having a pretty cool dream, but he lights up when he hears his kid, and he pulls out of it. I'm glad I got the chance to, sort of, meet him."

"He went back through the mirror. She didn't follow him," Trey pointed out, "because she can't. If she could do what you and Owen can do, Sonya, she'd have done it. Found a way to go through, go back, do what she could to make sure you never come here."

"She can't even touch it. The predators. I always wonder why you'd have a mirror with a frame like that. Weird, a little scary, really."

"To keep evil at bay," Cleo said. "Protection. Strong magic. And it invites you in, shows you what you need to know or witness or understand."

"More demands I go in. But . . . There's nothing about it in Marianne Poole's journal. The only time I saw it, other than as a vehicle to bring me in and out, was the day Dobbs killed Astrid. Astrid was at the mirror, *that* mirror, when Dobbs killed her. Her blood. Staggering back, her hand on the glass. Her blood on the glass."

"The first bride's blood, innocent blood on the glass even as Dobbs spewed her evil, stole the ring—the first ring. Blood's life," Cleo said. "Astrid's blood brought the mirror to life."

"That's a conclusional reach," Trey considered, "but I'll allow it. The mirror exists, we've all seen it. It has power. That's undeniable. Only Pooles can go through it—Cleo and I are blocked. So are the dogs, the cat. No way Jones would sit on this side otherwise. But Sonya's the one it pulls, not Owen."

"She's the one who needs to see. I'm just the muscle."

"More," Sonya corrected. "Glittery sparks. I missed them, you didn't. Trey, in his lawyerly way, brings the facts. Cleo, in her Cleo way, thinks outside the lines into the magic."

Steadier by far, Sonya sipped the last of her tea.

"Dobbs brought the storm," she continued. "She'll bring it again, and more, and likely worse. But the four of us together, the combination of strengths? We bring a perfect storm, a counterbalance."

Simple Minds reminded Sonya, "Don't You (Forget About Me)."

"Wouldn't and couldn't. Not you, Clover, or any of you. I saw my dad, and I'm going to take that gift and consider this a really good night. I could apologize for the meltdown, but I needed it. So thanks, all three of you, for holding me up."

"You need some sleep. We all do."

She nodded at Trey. "No argument on that."

They went up together. When Sonya finally slipped into bed, Trey drew her close.

"I need to hold on a minute."

"As long as you like. I know how hard it is for you to wait on this side while I'm on the other."

When he said nothing, she angled up to touch his lips with hers. "I had to wait on the other side twice while you were in the Gold Room. I think we're getting closer, Trey. That's not logical, really, but I feel it. And feeling that's going to help me sleep tonight."

"It's not illogical. We're piling up weight on our side of the scale. And you're here, safe. That'll help me sleep tonight."

He woke at three, listened to the clock strike, to the music, the weeping, the murmurs. But Sonya didn't stir. So holding her still, he slept with her.

Chapter Eighteen

After an understandably late start, Sonya thought they made good progress in the ballroom.

She found small treasures, as she'd hoped. A Valentine's Day card, both sweet and elaborate, to Lisbeth Poole from her Edward.

It promised they'd be sweethearts forever and a day.

Not a promise he could keep, she thought as she tucked the card and envelope in a box.

They found an old Maxwell House coffee tin holding rocks and pebbles. Though obviously a child's collection, Cleo pounced on it.

On her systematic journey through, Sonya found a beautiful piece Owen identified as a folding card table, in carved rosewood.

And immediately assigned it to the game room.

"I may suck at video games, but expand those horizons to cards, board games? Oh, I bet I could find some vintage board games on-line. We'd need a cabinet to put those in, or something with open shelves to display them. Display them," she decided immediately.

"I like it." Cleo adjusted the clip she had holding her hair up and back. "We find a pretty old jar, display those marbles. Arrange the other toys we've found."

"Exactly! Get games that've been around awhile. Ah, Parcheesi, cribbage, backgammon. Find a vintage poker set. For display and use. Anything new and shiny, that goes in a drawer. And there it is!"

Sonya used both index fingers to point at a bookcase with three glass doors. "Isn't that the same wood as the table? Owen, isn't it?"

He studied the case with a mix of admiration and despair. "Yeah, it's rosewood, and it's a beauty. It's not the same era as the table."

"We don't need matchy-matchy. We don't want everything to look all staged and set, but fun, comfortable. It'll go so well, and it's just right for what I have in mind."

"It's pretty big," Trey pointed out. "And the game room's one of the smaller spaces in the manor."

"You're right." Before she deflated, inspiration struck. "But there are bigger spaces down a level. We've got the gym, the movie theater down there already. It's a better place for a real game room."

"So down, let's see." Tapping his fingers, Owen pretended to calculate. "Four flights of stairs. I want to book hernia surgery in advance."

"Book mine while you're at it."

Sonya just patted Trey's hand because she could see it—how it could look, how it could be used and appreciated.

"Video games—we move a couch down there, a couple of comfortable chairs. Poker, that gorgeous old table, more chairs. The display for the games. A pool table, unless you fear us—an old one. And a vintage pinball machine."

"Pinball." Trey stuffed his hands in his pockets. "Damn it, hit a weak spot."

"A bigger weak spot with vintage," Owen agreed.

"Now you're caught in my web. But you can see it, right? Obviously, it can't be this minute, but it'd be great. Collin made good use of the spaces he opened up down there. But there's so much more. We shift the game room down there, expand it. And we do something else with the current game room."

"Such as?" Trey wondered.

"I don't know yet." She waved a hand in the air. "We'll figure it out."

Plan in place, to her mind, she put a sticky note on the bookcase.

"You know what this house is missing?" Trey asked.

Owen answered, "A freight elevator."

Grinning, Trey pointed at him. "Great minds."

After a productive weekend—with a spontaneous poker game on the table in the ballroom, the bliss of a Sunday sail—Sonya rose on Monday early enough to find Owen in the kitchen.

"About to head out. I got a workout in."

"I'm about to do that myself."

"That folding card table, the chairs we found, the backbreaker bookcase?"

"Yeah, yeah." She headed for coffee. "We'll enlist more muscle for that."

"You don't need to, seeing as it's already down there. The table, chairs, the bookcase."

"You and Trey already got it down there?"

Owen just looked at her. "Take a couple hits of coffee, think again."

She did, then her eyes cleared. And widened. "Oh. Ohhh!"

"Yeah. You got a hell of a team around here." He grabbed his go-cup, turned as Trey came in. "I canceled the hernia surgery."

"Huh?"

"Some of the residents already moved the future game room stuff down there. Catch you later." He went out the back, gave a whistle. Jones peeled off from his companions and fell into step with Owen.

"Huh?" Trey said again.

Sonya handed him her coffee, made another cup.

"Obviously my game room idea has sparked imaginations on both sides of the veil."

She switched cups, kissed him.

"Have a good day," she told him as she walked out.

Trey looked down at the coffee, then drank half of it standing where he was. Since he'd started early enough, he could get in a workout at his place before he went into the office.

He switched to a go-cup, topped it off.

He thought about Sonya, down in the gym, the damn bell ringing as she did curls or squats or whatever the hell. Down there with a dog and Christ knew who or what else.

Then she'd spend most of the day at her desk. Alone, but not alone. With Dobbs slamming doors and windows, or much, much worse. The mirror could pull her who knew where or when.

And there was nothing he could do about it.

He hated when he could do nothing. Day after day, he worked to find solutions for clients, to find a way through difficult situations, issues, obstacles.

But for Sonya, he had no system, no precedent, no clever argument to help pull her through the maze.

This house, he thought as he walked through it. He'd always loved it. He'd not only accepted but enjoyed knowing its history and that many who'd made it still existed inside it.

He stopped at the game room.

He'd always been welcome there. He'd had good times there. With Owen, Manny, other friends, with Collin. Dobbs had never tried to run them out.

But then, he—and they—hadn't been an obstacle, a competitor, a threat. Not then.

"I'm all of those now."

He hoped she knew it.

In the Quiet Place, the hands of the old clock stood at three. He could change them, but they'd only move back. Annoyed, he walked in, changed them anyway.

He paused at the music room, scanned the portraits. Five of the seven. What would happen when they found and hung the last two? No way of knowing, but by any logic, it had to matter.

He paused again at the base of the stairs, and looking up, heard doors creak open. Heard, and felt in his bones, the low hum from the third floor.

Dobbs baited him. Even knowing it, he took a step up.

Diana Ross sang out "Stop! In the Name of Love" from Sonya's tablet in the library.

"Damn it, Clover."

However much it grated, he did stop. Not because of the warning, but due to the reminder he'd made a promise to Sonya not to go into that room. He could regret the promise, and at that moment, he did. But he'd made it.

"The time's going to come she'll have to let me off the hook for that promise. The time's going to come," he repeated.

He went out, called Mookie. And with a last glance at the manor, drove away.

Winded but righteous after her workout, Sonya showered off the well-earned sweat. Since she had a couple of virtual meetings scheduled, she spent time on makeup.

She came out to find white cropped pants and a navy V-necked shirt on the bed.

"I guess you heard I'll be on-screen today. This works."

She dressed, added simple stud earrings, then wound Clover's rainbow beads into a modified choker.

"I like it. Very presentable. Okay, Yoda, time to go to work."

She'd held the first meeting before Cleo came down the hall.

Cleo stopped, yawned.

"Once I wake up, I'm going to take advantage of the day. I'm getting in a sail. I'll either paint at the cove or find another spot. Then I'll run some errands, buy the groceries—including the pork chops I'm planning to grill for dinner."

"That sounds like a full day."

"It is, so I'm leaving Pye here."

Sonya nodded, waited a beat. "You want to know if I'm okay without asking if I'm okay."

"I figure you're sick of the question, because I would be."

"I'm moving in that direction, so I'll just say situation normal."

"Isn't the rest of that: *all fucked up?*"

Sonya laughed. "Well, it's the manor, so some fuckery is expected. I'm good, promise. I'm going to FaceTime Mom after work, and tell her about seeing Dad. I wanted to settle in with it all the way before I did that. We'll both cry, and that'll finish the job."

"All right. I'm going down to wake up with coffee."

"Bring me a Coke when you come back? I'm about ready."

"Can do."

Yoda went down with her and the cat, another part of the morning routine. He'd have his romp outside, Sonya thought as she resumed her work.

He returned when Cleo dropped off the Coke. Sonya smiled her thanks as she continued her conference call with her first clients, the sisters of Baby Mine.

By the time Cleo came out, ready to go, she'd moved on to the final testing of another client's website.

"Have fun!"

"No doubt about it. Make sure to get outside for a while. It's one of those perfect days."

"On the schedule."

Clover used Van Morrison's "Into the Mystic" to wish Cleo bon voyage.

"Good one."

With music playing, and Yoda settled under her desk, Sonya sank into the work.

When her alarm went off, she got up. She paused at the top of the stairs as the ball bounced below.

"You can take him and Pye outside if you want. I'm going to be at least another hour."

She took a quick bathroom break, refreshed her lipstick.

When she came out, the manor held silent. Happy someone was enjoying Cleo's perfect day, she went back to her desk, reviewed her notes for the meeting.

"No music till we're done, Clover."

Forty-three minutes later, she sat back with a sigh.

"All done, and I'm ready for a snack and a walk outside. Which means I need shoes."

As she pushed up from her desk, stretched out several hours of sitting, she heard voices.

Not Cleo. Even if her friend had slipped into the manor without Sonya noticing, she recognized the deeper timbre of male voices.

Not Cleo, not Dobbs. She strained her ears, but couldn't make out words, just the sound. And now a quick—male—laugh.

She felt no pull from the mirror.

Picking up her phone from the desk, she put it in her pocket.

Her house, she reminded herself, and walked quietly out of the library. She turned, followed the sound of voices. And music, she realized. Bon Jovi. "Livin' on a Prayer."

So eighties? Nineties? Or beyond that.

Not from the nursery, and she gave a quick thanks for that, as the room held so much sorrow.

No, they came from what she thought of as a den. Where, she remembered, Owen had once seen himself playing chess with a younger Collin.

Pulse quickening, she stepped to the doorway—the open doorway, where she kept it closed.

A fire crackled in the hearth, and a light snow—thin as gauze—fell outside the windows.

Two men faced each other over a chessboard. For an instant, just a flash, her heart tripped as she thought she watched her father and Trey.

But no, though the resemblance struck hard, she watched Collin with his longtime friend, Deuce.

Deuce with his hair jet-black, no glasses over those deep blue eyes. He wore a sweater nearly as deeply blue, and smiled Trey's smile as he moved his bishop.

"Get out of that one."

"Oh, I will."

But Collin sat back first, sipped a whiskey as Deuce did the same. "How does it feel, old married man, to start planning a nursery?"

"Terrifying. Wonderful. And right back to terrifying."

"How's Corrine doing?"

"Still queasy most mornings, but they say that'll ease up. It's early days." He pointed at Collin. "Other than my parents, hers, you're the only one in this loop for now."

"If I don't know how to keep a secret, who does?"

"That's God's truth. All those years ago, sneaking in here as kids. If your grandmother had found out, our asses would've been in matching slings."

"But she didn't. And you were the only one who knew I planned to do just what I'm doing, since she no longer has a say in it. Live my life here. We keep each other's secrets."

"We do, always have."

Collin moved his rook, and with a nod, Deuce studied the board.

"You think I don't see that. But I do. You haven't mentioned plans for your next trip."

"I'd been thinking about talking you and Corrine into joining me for a trip to Ireland this summer. Your family homeplace. But now . . ."

"Now, with a baby coming? I think Corrine and I stay closer to home."

"I might do the same. I've got plenty of company."

"They're quiet tonight."

"Oh, I expect my night music later. Plenty of that during the day, too."

"Does your in-house DJ still favor rock?"

"They do."

Deuce moved the next piece.

His hand still on the knight. The flames in the hearth froze in place. The music stopped.

And Collin turned toward Sonya, smiled.

"Trey looks so like him, doesn't he?"

"Yes."

"We sat here like this countless times over the years, Deuce and I. No one ever had a better friend than I in Deuce Doyle. Thick and thin, he was there for me, always. You understand that bond."

"Yes. You . . ."

"Look like your father. I wish I'd known him better."

"Better?"

"We met, in a way. Through the mirror. As a child I thought of him as my imaginary friend. And later, a kind of dream. When I learned, from Deuce, he was real, that I had a brother, my twin, a mother who'd loved and wanted me, it was too late."

It no longer struck Sonya as odd she'd have a conversation with someone who'd died before she'd known he'd existed.

And there were things she wanted to say.

"I'm sorry. I think—I really believe—you'd have been there for each other, too. So I'm sorry for both of you."

"So am I. It's something that can't be changed. This night, with Deuce, was just before I met Johanna. I'd known love. It sits across from me here, but I'd never known what it was to love a woman with every fiber, every thought, every breath, and to be loved by her."

"She was beautiful. I don't just mean physically. The way Corrine talks about her, I know she was beautiful."

"Oh, she was. My life changed with that love, and changed again when I lost her."

She heard the wistfulness in his words, and still with it, the grief for what might have been.

"Deuce, Corrine, Ace, Paula, then Trey, Anna, Owen. They were here for me, always. Others, too, but those formed the core, the heart of my family."

"They're still here for you."

"That's true, isn't it?" His face softened with a smile. "In so many ways, I lived a fortunate life. You're my brother's daughter. I want to tell you, I didn't know the full extent of the danger here. Dobbs never troubled me, or not enough to worry me. If I'd known . . ."

He trailed off, shook his head. "I'm not sure what I'd have done. I couldn't share this with my brother. The manor, the business, all I inherited should have been half his."

"He had a good life in Boston, a fortunate life. He loved, and was loved."

"Yes, and that dulls the sting. I wanted you to have all of this. I needed you to, and felt absolutely certain, blood kin or not, you were the right choice. Know that I was proud of you, from a distance."

She started to take a step forward, but felt, strongly, she couldn't. Shouldn't.

"Why from a distance?"

"You had that good life. Weighed with grief, for my Johanna, for the brother taken from me, for all of it, I felt inadequate, intrusive, and cowardly." He looked toward the fire a moment, then back at her. "A mistake I hope you'll forgive."

"There's nothing to forgive. I'm grateful, beyond words grateful. I love the manor, and did from the minute I saw it. I love knowing I have more family, and the history of that family. You gave me an incredible gift."

"And a burden with it."

"A responsibility," she corrected. "But . . . is there anything you can tell me—the rings—how to find them? How to get them? How to stop Dobbs?"

"I don't know the answers. The portraits . . . something, but I don't know."

"The portraits of the brides. You and Dad painted them. When?"

He shook his head. "In dreams. It feels like dreaming. I can't stay much longer. I haven't been able to show you, speak with you this way before."

She saw frustration now as he lifted his hands. "It seems to me death brings as many questions as it does answers. I think, I can't know, it takes time to come like this."

"Johanna might know. Can you ask her?"

Grief filled his eyes. "I can't. We can't be together."

"I don't understand."

"The curse, the goddamn curse. It must be. At times I can sense her, almost feel her. I think I hear her voice, but I can't find her, or see her clearly, or touch her. It's a kind of torture. She stands in the way. Dobbs stands in the way.

"So much to ask of you, my brother's only child. Break the curse, Sonya. Find a way. You're the hope, the key, the answer."

The fire snapped to life, Jon Bon Jovi sang "Wanted Dead or Alive."

Deuce lifted his hand from his knight, grinned at Collin. "Checkmate."

Collin stared, cursed, laughed. "Well, damn it."

And they vanished.

Sonya stood a moment, fingers pressed to her eyes.

Then she went back to her desk, sat, and wrote it all out.

"Clover, are you with Charlie? Can you be with Charlie?"

Clover went back to Carole King. "So Far Away."

"Oh God, that's so cruel. And that's the damn point, isn't it?"

She went downstairs. She needed to get out, get the air, think. But stopped by the music room.

"The portraits—two to go—but the portraits are part of the answer. The rings are in the portraits."

She walked over, touched the ring on Johanna's finger.

"Yeah, okay, silly to think I could just take it out of the canvas. But then again, still two to go. Maybe when they're all here?"

She backtracked, went up to Cleo's studio, opened the closet.

Felt her hope drop.

"Not yet. What the hell are you waiting for?"

As she closed the door, Dobbs slammed furniture in the Gold Room.

"Oh, bite me."

She walked to the curved windows, looked out at sea and sky. Yes, a perfect day, and she'd go out and absorb just that.

As she turned, she noticed the open sketchbook on Cleo's desk, and the figures of a hulking mass of a man, the smiling face. A handsome face until you really looked. Then? Everything about it just a little off, as if it was still being formed. And what it would become would not be handsome.

And when you really looked, it had spider legs crawling down your back.

"Creepy. Well-done creepy." She glanced back at the covered canvas. "Whatever that is, I bet it's not."

She walked down, and out the front door. The breeze blew; the waves crashed. Boats plied the water under sunshine and a scatter of pretty white clouds.

Fingering the stone in her pocket, Sonya sat on the seawall, and just let herself be.

Before long Yoda raced around to her, the ball clutched in his mouth. The cat gave a leap and took her place on the wall.

"Jack didn't wear you out? Did he send you around because he thought I needed that happy face?"

She crouched down, petted him, rubbed his belly when he rolled it up in ecstasy.

"Well, he was right. It's just what I needed."

She took the ball, tossed it. While Yoda chased it down, Sonya reached out, stroked the cat, who undulated her body in approval of the attention.

She threw the ball until her arm ached.

"That's it for the day. Everybody, inside. Time for a snack."

When she reached the kitchen, the dog and cat treats waited on the counter.

"I'm on it, Jack."

She doled them out, made herself half a PB and J along with some fat purple grapes. After refreshing her water bottle, she took it all upstairs.

She could get another couple hours in, maybe a little more, before Cleo came back with groceries.

She picked up where she'd left off, but ten minutes later admitted she couldn't focus on work. Unfocused, work suffered, so she set it aside.

Instead, she pulled out a sketchbook and began to draw.

Two hours later, she looked up, blinking, as Yoda yipped and ran downstairs. A little surprised at herself, she studied the sketch.

She took the book down, set it on the table in the foyer, then went out to help Cleo.

"Tell me you got out and grabbed some of this day!"

"I did. My arm's rubber from tossing Yoda the ball. How was the sail?"

"Glorious. I ran into John Dee at the marina. He was doing some work down there. He sends his best. We're having those pork chops," she continued as they carried bags into the house. "The green beans I picked up at the farmer's market, along with smashed red potatoes."

"Smashed?"

"I wanted to try something new to me, and they look like fun. I'll get the last of them. You start putting things away. Then I call glass of wine time."

"I hear you."

Sonya did her duty. She didn't know why Cleo bought eggs when they had nearly a dozen, but she didn't question the cook.

Cleo came back with the last of the bags, and Sonya's sketchbook.

"Have you been sketching? I didn't open it, but it was right there."

"I have, and I'll show and tell over that wine."

"Pour that wine. I've got this. Good workday?"

"Yes, very good. And morc."

"Dobbs?"

"Barely a peep. Only when I went up to check the closet for Catherine. Nothing. But I saw the sketch on your desk. Very creepy. Creepy in an 'am I really seeing that?' way."

"It's coming along. All right. Show and tell."

"On the deck? Perfect day's moved to perfect evening."

They went out, sat. After taking a sip of wine, Sonya set the glass aside. She opened the book, handed it to Cleo.

"This is . . . Is this that room where Owen dreamed about playing chess with Collin?"

"Yeah."

"And this is Collin. Our-age Collin. With . . . Deuce. It's Deuce Doyle, isn't it?"

"Again, yeah."

"Okay, first, I'm going to say this is wonderful. You can see the bond like it's alive. A winter's night, two friends together over whiskey and chess, light snow, fire burning. Cozy room, lamplit. Beautiful."

Now she looked at Sonya.

"You saw this?"

"One more yeah. I saw them playing chess, talking. And like what happened before, it all went still. Collin spoke to me. We spoke to each other. It was sad and sweet and, well, lovely in its way. We would have liked him, Cleo."

Cleo gave her hand a squeeze. "Tell me."

Chapter Nineteen

As dinner prep got underway, Owen arrived with a bakery box. After a perfunctory greeting to Yoda, Jones collapsed under the table.

"He had a long day," Owen said. "I took him to work with me. Tour group, lots of kids. Being admired and fawned over gets tiring." He set down the box. "Chocolate chunk cookies."

He hooked an arm around Cleo's waist, yanked her in for a kiss. "What's cooking?"

"Grilled pork chops, smashed potatoes, and sesame green beans. We'll wait to start the grill until Trey gets here."

"Okay. I'll feed the horde when the Mooks shows up."

"I didn't know you did tours at Poole's."

He glanced over at Sonya as he got a beer. "Yeah, a few times a year. It's good PR. We do a couple days of them during the school year for students. Kids are a little scary." He downed some beer. "In a good way."

"What's good-way scary?"

"They ask a crapload of questions, and man, are the little guys literal. Like why doesn't the boat sink when people get in it?"

"Why doesn't a boat sink with people on it?"

"If you were serious about that, I'd go into buoyancy, floatation, displacement. But your average eight-year-old doesn't want the science."

"So what do you tell them?" Cleo asked.

"Even with people or cargo on it, it weighs less than the water it's on, and we build them to keep the water out, and the air—and people—in. That usually does it."

"When it doesn't?"

"You start talking about buoyancy, floatation, displacement until your average eight-year-old's eyes glaze over, and you've done your job."

Yoda let out a trio of barks, raced out of the kitchen. Jones gave a grunt, then went back to his nap. Pye, apparently wise to routine, sauntered over to the back door.

"I'll feed them, start the grill. Hey, Yoda, this way. Come on, Jones, pull it together."

Minutes later, Sonya saw Mookie, tail wagging, ears flapping, run to the backyard. Yoda greeted him as if they'd been parted for centuries.

Then Trey, T-shirt, jeans, high-tops. As all that thick raven-black hair was windblown, she decided he'd had his truck windows open on the drive from the office.

She watched him and Owen exchange a few words. Owen passed him the beer, and when Trey took a swig before handing it back, Sonya got another out of the fridge.

"Trey looks a little frazzled. He rarely does."

When he came in, she held out the beer. "You look like you could use this."

"Could. Thanks. Hi." He leaned down to kiss her.

"Trouble?" she asked.

"Hmm. No. End of day, hysterical client. This happens."

"Why don't you sit down?"

"I'm good. Grilling? I can set things up on the deck."

"Sit down a minute," she repeated.

His eyes sharpened. "Trouble?"

"No. But I want to show you something."

She picked up the manilla envelope she'd prepared, handed it to him. "It's for Deuce, but you should see it first."

"All right."

No more questions, Sonya thought. He simply slid onto a stool and opened the envelope.

She'd put the drawing on top so it was the first thing he saw when he pulled out the papers.

He stared at it for a long moment, then lifted his gaze to hers. His heart lived in his eyes.

"You didn't draw this from a photo you found."

"No."

"You saw this? Them?"

"Yes."

"The mirror?"

"No. The way it was with Astrid in the parlor, Lissy in the music room. That way."

"Horde fed," Owen said as he came in. "Grill's on. What you got?" He stepped over, looked over Trey's shoulder.

"That's . . . that's Collin and Deuce? Young. I mean, Collin's even younger than that time I saw him. It's a hell of a good drawing. And majorly cool."

He put a hand on Trey's shoulder as he spoke.

The connection, Sonya thought. Another set of lifelong friends. Thick and thin, as Collin had said, always.

Was it happenstance or fate, she wondered, that the two men here had come from the same bloodlines as the two men who'd played chess on a snowy night?

"Deuce will love it."

"I wrote it all out, as much detail as I could remember. I heard them talking. Well, I heard voices and followed them, and Bon Jovi, to the den."

And with no more questions, Trey set the drawing aside to read. When Owen did the same over his shoulder, Sonya left them to it to help Cleo. The kitchen fell quiet until Trey stacked the pages.

Clover filled the gap with Queen's "You're My Best Friend."

"Yeah, they were that to each other. He spoke to you, you spoke to each other."

"I got a chance to thank him. And a chance to see, in those few minutes, who he was. You can be told, but it's different when you can see for yourself."

"And he added to Dobbs and her bitch quotient," Owen added. "It's not enough to kill those seven women. Collin knows Johanna's here, but he can't see her, be with her. Same with the others."

"The portraits, the ones you've found. He told you they matter in all this."

"But not how, Trey. He just doesn't know."

"Painted in dreams. But your father's not here, Sonya."

"No. He's—at least part of him is in the house in Boston. My mother believes that. It's why she'll never move."

"But he came here," Owen pointed out. "We saw that for ourselves."

"Twin bond." Cleo spoke for the first time. "It's strong and it's real. Maybe they came through the mirror. Maybe they painted the portraits before they died, or after. Either way, they weren't revealed until now."

"Because now's the time," Owen finished. "And time's part of it. Could be they've been kept in another time. Weirder things have happened here."

"Five down. Or rather up," Sonya corrected. "Two to go."

"You have more pieces here." Trey tapped the papers. "If we believe Collin, and why wouldn't we, the portraits are part of the solution. And you hanging them in that room, on that wall, which it turns out will hold the series of seven perfectly? Not just a matter of honor and respect."

"That's right. That's good!" Nodding at Trey, Cleo continued to use a fork to more or less smash the potatoes she'd boiled. "You can believe everything happens for a reason or not, but that did. That happened for a reason."

"But I look at them, and I don't see the reason."

"Two to go," Cleo reminded her. "Then we will."

"I'm actually feeling fairly positive. Seeing them together—your dad, Trey, and Collin—just that warm, easy friendship. Brothers, really. That's a big positive."

"You captured that." Trey lifted the sketch again. "You didn't sign it."

"Oh, it's just a memento."

"It's art. It's a gift. Yours, and one you used to give a gift. Sign it."

"Don't be a dumbass," Owen added.

"Fine, sure. You build art," she added with a scowl at Owen. "I don't see you signing it."

"I put my mark on everything I build."

"I—really? Where?"

"Different places." He gave a typical Owen shrug. "Depends."

"Yoda's house?"

"Ah." He had to think about it. "Inside the turret. How long for those?" he asked Cleo when she slid the baking sheet of potatoes drizzled with butter, sprinkled with spices, in the oven.

"This size? About a half hour."

"I'll handle the chops."

"I'll set us up." Rising, Trey pulled Sonya in, held her close. "Thank you. This means a lot, not just to my dad, but the whole family."

He drew her back, tapped her chin with his finger. "Sign it."

After dinner in the garden, they enjoyed cookies on the front lawn as the first stars began to twinkle over the sea.

"It never gets old. The view, the sound. I'll miss sitting here when winter drops down." Sonya leaned around Trey. "Where's your mark on this, Owen?"

"You're sitting on it. Or it's underneath the seat where you're sitting."

"Why not where people can easily see it?"

"Then it wouldn't be mysterious. Trey had this brand made for me one Christmas. My initials—sign documents, you end up signing your initials everywhere. He took that and had it replicated inside the shape of Maine on a woodworking brand. Pretty cool."

"That is cool."

"I'm a cool guy," Trey said.

"Obviously. Speaking of Christmas—"

"Not yet."

Laughing, Sonya patted Trey's thigh. "Only that I need to get down there and go through Collin's decorations. It looks like enough to decorate the village."

"That's a fact."

"Since my mother has the same addiction, I'm used to it."

"Before you get any ideas," Owen said lazily, "Collin hired a crew."

"Then we'll do that. But we want our hand in, too. Right, Cleo?"

"Hundred percent. But before Christmas comes my favorite holiday."

"Halloween. Plenty down in storage for that, as well."

"And considering all, the manor needs to dress for Samhain. We should be able to handle that ourselves.

"It's really cooling off now," she added with a little shiver, "and this southern girl's heading for the warm."

"You're right about the cooling off. I'm for inside, and I want to check the closet again."

"We might as well all go."

Cleo shot Owen a look of approval. "There's that positive. Four of us, four times the positive."

"I know you check every day, Cleo," Sonya said as they started in. "And I looked after I saw Deuce and Collin. I don't know how positive I am, except I'm positive I want it to be there."

"Wishes don't come true unless you wish."

When they went in, started for the stairs, Mookie and Yoda raced up ahead like runners off the mark. The cat slinked between Cleo and Owen and bounded after while Jones restrained himself, staying at Owen's heel, and heard the hum before they reached the landing.

"She does that a lot lately," Cleo told them. "Just that low hum."

"She slammed some furniture around when I was up here earlier." As it had become instinct, Sonya closed her hand around the stone in her pocket.

"All right now." Cleo held up both hands as they turned into her studio. "Four minds, one positive thought. Sonya, open the door."

"One positive thought," she repeated, and opened the door. "Oh Jesus! It worked."

Catherine Poole Cabot smiled quietly, a bit shyly, though her green eyes held joy. Against a backdrop of snow, the sea beyond, she wore white silk. The artist's skill, Andrew MacTavish's skill, brought that sheen to the canvas. Stars glittered along the hem of the gown, on its poufed shoulders. White satin sashed the waist of a wedding dress trimmed in ermine.

She wore pearls around her neck, and her hair dressed high under the star-trimmed veil.

She carried roses, the faintest blush of pink against the white. A gold band, as simple as the dress was elaborate, circled the third finger of her left hand.

Catherine Poole Cabot, daughter of Connor and Arabelle Poole, wife of William Cabot, who died in her nightdress and bare feet in a blizzard of snow on her wedding night.

"I watched her mother brush her hair out. It must've taken forever to style that way, and nearly as long to take down and smooth out."

"It's beautiful work," Cleo said. "The light, the details. She looks lovely, and all her happiness is in her eyes."

"You know where we haven't gone before? The artist," Trey continued. "Your father, in this case again, had to see her in this."

"Dreaming, Collin said. Painted in dreams. I've had those dreams."

"And then there were six. We'll take her down." Owen stepped in to lift the painting. "Put her up with the others."

Sonya stepped back. "I know you're right about the space, the way it would fit seven portraits. And the one of Astrid in the foyer, too large, different style. But if there is one more to find, who painted it? They've each done three now."

"If you count it out, it would be Collin's turn." Trey stroked a hand down her back. "I guess we'll find out when we find out."

"She's like the others, painted in detail, with skill. The white dress, the flowers, the ring. Brides didn't always wear white in her time or Astrid's. I did some research," Sonya explained, "hoping for—I don't know what. Queen Victoria wore a white wedding dress, years after this, and that's when white ruled the wedding day. But both Astrid and Catherine chose white.

"Does it matter?"

"For the series, I'd say yes. It adds to the feel, the tone, the style. And," Cleo added, "that sense of innocence. I'll get what we need to put her up."

When they reached the music room, Cleo peeled off. Owen walked over to lean the painting against the wall.

"I wonder, cutie, if you dreamed this."

"The painting?"

"All of them. The way you chose this room, this wall, the way you spaced the first two."

"We switched out what was there, and then . . . I don't know. If I did, I don't remember."

When Cleo came back, Owen took the measuring tape. He measured from the corner of the wall to the portrait of Marianne, then walked to the other side, measured from that corner to Johanna's portrait.

He stopped, muttered to himself, eyes closed. Before Cleo could speak, Trey held up a hand, shook his head.

"Do the math?" Owen said. "Factor the space from that corner to the seventh painting, calculate the other side, the size of the paintings, the spacing between? It's exact. I'm telling you, man, you don't get exact by accident."

"If you were hanging seven paintings in a series?" Sonya said.

"You work with space so you know. I'd measure the wall, the paintings, calculate the spacing, do the math. Then I'd do the math again before I put in the first nail. You didn't do any of that."

"No. Maybe Collin did. Hell, maybe the manor did. Maybe, because I do work with space, I just saw the potential here. Or maybe I dreamed it."

"Let's put her up." Trey walked over to give Owen a hand.

When Catherine stood with the other brides, they all stepped back.

"It's stunning," Cleo said. "Visually stunning. The art, of course, and the subjects. It's also a history of fashion. You can see the changes generation by generation. The shape of the gowns, the sleeves, necklines. The hairstyles."

"Seven women spanning over two hundred years since the manor was built. Seven brides. There would be eight if Patricia hadn't taken the warning."

"Maybe she didn't want eight. Or six." Cleo angled her head. "Another reason she scared Patricia off? Maybe. Seven's a number of power."

"She got six with Clover," Owen pointed out.

"Yes, then one more for seven. Seven and two hundred years. Not six in two hundred and thirty or forty—I'm not doing the math."

"Thirty," Trey told her.

"Okay. But by skipping that one generation and waiting. Seven over the two hundred and thirty years since the manor was first built."

"When she first started to covet it," Sonya murmured.

"You don't actually think she'd stop because, what, seven's her lucky number?"

Cleo shook her head at Trey. "No. There are other numbers of power, and she got her two hundred years and seven. If that's something. She amassed that power. She's got no reason to stop, does she? And she's insane on top of it."

"She's not getting a chance for eight." Trey's eyes hardened as he scanned the portraits. "We find the answer. And if the answer, or an answer, is on that wall, we need, and we'll find, one more portrait."

"Commonalities," Sonya began. "Oil paintings in the same style. All wedding day portraits, all wearing white. All holding flowers, all wearing a wedding ring. Opposing that? Different backdrops, not all wear veils, two are pregnant—Clover visibly. Only two are Pooles by birth. Of the six we have, three died wearing that dress. Clover and Marianne died later in childbirth, and Catherine in a nightgown on her wedding night."

"Sometimes they're not wearing them."

Sonya turned to Owen. "What? The wedding dresses?"

"The rings, in the paintings. Sometimes they're not there. I'll walk by, glance in, and for a couple seconds, they're not there. Then they are."

"I know."

"It's happened a few times so I know it happened, right?"

"You've caught glimpses of their reality," Cleo decided. "Because they're not wearing them. Dobbs is."

"Interesting" was all Trey said.

"Weird, but you know?" Owen shrugged. "You get used to weird."

"Weird's one thing. Murder through sorcery's another."

Cleo raised her brows at Trey. "And on that happy note, I'm going up, let all this simmer."

"I'm with Lafayette. So's Jones."

Sonya lingered even when Yoda and Mookie followed the others.

"You see the rings."

"Yes, I see them."

"It has to mean something that Owen doesn't always see them—everything means something. It's the figuring out what that makes you crazy. And to think I always liked puzzles."

"Nobody solves a puzzle with pieces missing. And there's more missing here than one painting. If Dobbs is wearing the damn rings, and she is, how the hell are you supposed to get them back? And what are you supposed to do with them if you do get them? Why in all the time I spent in this house over the years didn't she pull any of her bullshit?"

Frustration built, spilled over.

"All that started with you. Why are you the one? The one pulled into this, the one expected to deal with it, solve the puzzle, find the rings, break the curse?"

"All I can say about the last part of that is because my father was born here, and that makes me a Poole."

"You're not the only Poole."

"No, but the house is mine."

"And all the baggage with it. All you didn't know about when you agreed to the terms of Collin's will."

"I know about it all now," she said, watching him carefully. "And

I'm still here. You're upset and angry. You'd already had a hard day before you got here."

"It has nothing to do with my day, and I'm fine."

"You don't get really angry often, not so it shows, anyway. So when it does, it does. And I'm getting a feeling you're mad at me. I don't know why."

"I'm not mad at you. The situation—there are six dead women on that wall, and one more to come. Not that long ago, Dobbs tried to burn the house down around you."

"It wasn't real. It—"

"Real enough, Sonya. What she can do is real enough she put seven women in the ground. Because of this house. Because of stone and wood and glass."

The house was more than that, she thought. So much more. So was her heritage.

"You think I should go. Walk away, close it up again."

"I think you should consider what it would do to you and your life if you spend it here, trying to find seven wedding rings. If this is what you want for your life, day after day, maybe year after year. Never being sure what Dobbs might do next."

It was one thing, she realized, for her to take it on. Her heritage, her legacy, her need to honor both. And another to expect him to do the same.

"It's a lot. And you've shouldered so much of it."

"I'm not talking about me."

"I am. You fix things. It's what you do. You help people—that's not just your job, it's your nature. So you've shouldered a lot of it. It's wearing on you. Do you need a break?"

"A break? From what?"

"From this." Sick at the thought of it, she held out her hands. "All this. From juggling work and worry, and the normal with the crazy. From me."

"What the hell do you take me for?"

She saw clearly she'd only made him more angry. And heard clearly, from the slamming doors, Dobbs enjoyed it.

278 ⌒ NORA ROBERTS

"I take you for someone who doesn't back down easy. Who manages to keep calm in a crisis. And maybe someone who's had enough of knowing another crisis is coming, at any time, from any direction.

"I know you care about me."

"Jesus." Shoving a hand through his hair, he turned, paced away. "That's a pale word for it."

"I don't want to lose you."

He spun back. "For fuck's sake, Sonya."

"Please. I realize I've been stupid not just saying it before. Words matter, and I haven't used them. I shouldn't have held them back until you're on edge. I love you, and I don't want to lose you. I love you, and I'd so much rather you took a break, stepped back for a little while, than stay because it's your nature to help."

"I don't need a goddamn break, and I don't need you to tell me you love me surrounded by stupidity."

Shock smothered even instinctive temper. "Trey."

"Shut up. Just shut up."

He turned to pace again. She might have slapped back if she'd had words, or just walked away if she hadn't been frozen in place.

"Just shut up and listen. There are other walls in this house." He flung a hand toward the portraits. "Other walls that can hold paintings of murdered women. She's got no reason to stop, Cleo's got that right. I'm damned if you'll be number eight."

"I never thought I'd say this to you, but you need to calm down. I'm not a bride."

"That's right, and that's a problem for me. As long as things are the way they are, as long as they are and you live in this house, you can't be."

"That would come under the category of my problem."

"And the stupid continues."

Her spine snapped as straight as a steel pole. "I'm not going to stand here while you call me stupid."

Turning her back on him, she strode to the doorway.

"I'm in love with you. Words matter? There they are. I started sliding the first time I saw you, standing out front in the snow. Wonder all over that face. That face I can't live without now."

She'd turned, and now stood in the doorway with her heart in her throat. "Trey—"

"I'm not finished. I haven't said those words because they matter. Because I knew once I had—"

"You'd make me so happy I'd actually feel stupid?"

"Sonya." He shook his head, shoved his hands through his hair again.

She could actually see it happen, could see the calm slip over him again.

"I haven't said them because once I had, it stopped there. I couldn't move on to what I want, what I believe you want. I knew that, I've been dealing with that, but tonight?"

He looked back at the portraits. "It just hit harder, that's all. What Cleo said—solid manor logic—Dobbs won't stop. You're an annoyance, an obstacle, so she harasses you, threatens. She could hurt you. But you can't become a competitor, Sonya. You can't give her the reason, the excuse, the power, whatever it is, to make you number eight."

He came to her now, took both her hands. "I want a life with you. I want you to marry me, for us to start a family because I love you. And because I love you, I can't ask you. I won't. And we can't have that life or that family."

"But you would, and we could, if I walked away from the manor?"

Shaking his head, he brought her hands to his lips. "No, that was wrong of me, and I'm sorry for it. I'd hate myself, and if you didn't resent me straight off, you would down the road. And you'd be right to, that's the goddamn kicker. You can't walk away from this. From them."

"I can't, no, I can't walk away from them. But I can want what you want. I do want a life with you, children with you. I want to fill the house with them."

Now he smiled a little. "There's a hell of a lot of rooms in this house."

"Well, maybe not every one. Trey, it's so much more than enough for me to know you love me, you want that with me. I can wait, because you love me."

She fell into the kiss, into the love, the promise. She held on to it, and him, while Clover serenaded them with Adele and "Make You Feel My Love."

She felt his, tasted it on his lips, knew it in his heartbeat, in the arms that kept her close.

And held her still when her head rested on his shoulder.

"We're in this together," he promised. "Whether it takes a day, a month, a decade. We're in it together."

Together, she thought. She looked at the women on the wall in their bridal white and made her own promise.

They'd find a way, the way, to free them, reunite those who wished it. And she and Trey would build that life together, right here in Lost Bride Manor.

Chapter Twenty

Despite the morning rain, everything looked brighter. To Sonya's ear, the whole world sang.

Coffee tasted even more wonderful. Her toasted bagel? Fit for the gods.

She recognized herself as a walking cliché, and didn't care.

She managed to work, even when she caught herself singing along to Clover's morning playlist.

She had to restrain herself from getting up and dancing to Queen's "Crazy Little Thing Called Love."

She restrained herself again when Cleo, with a vague morning wave, walked downstairs.

Ten minutes, she ordered herself. Give her ten minutes to get down, make coffee, drink enough to wake up.

She managed seven.

Cleo sat at the island, sleepily scrolling on the kitchen tablet, with coffee, her half a Toaster Strudel, her cup of granola-laced yogurt.

She gave Sonya a look with lazy lion's eyes.

"Trey must've been on his game last night. You have the look of a woman who's been very well laid."

"There was that." She glanced at Cleo's breakfast mug. "Drink some more coffee."

"I intend to."

"No, I mean now. Wake up!"

"You know the reason we've always been good roommates—now

housemates, Son? Because you know I don't like conversation before at least one full cup of coffee in the morning."

"Make an exception."

Cleo drank a little more. "This better be good."

"It's so good. The best. It's better than the best." She did a quick twirl. "Trey loves me."

Cleo sipped a little more coffee and gave her friend a long, lazy stare.

"Oh, such news." she said, flat-voiced, flat-eyed. "Bring out the band, cue the acrobats. Why, I'd never have known. Except for the way he looks at you, touches you, stands up and by you. I feel I might swoon from the surprise."

"Drink more coffee! He told me he loved me. He told me he's in love with me, and has been, and wants to get married and have babies."

"Whoa! Wait!" Cleo shot up one hand, downed more coffee with the other. "He asked you to marry him?"

"No. He said he couldn't, and he wouldn't because . . . Are you awake?"

"I am now. And I want details. Every tiny detail."

"Okay." Sonya dropped down on the stool beside her. "After you and Owen went up, I could tell he was upset, and pissed off about something."

She told her, every tiny detail.

When Sonya teared up, so did Cleo.

"It's like one of our girls'-night movies, only better. Son, he's such a good man. Such a really good man. The things he said to you— beyond all the sweet, sweet things? They make solid sense."

"You mean I can't marry him until."

"A fabulous dress and a piece of paper? They count, sure they do. But they're not worth the risk. I know both of you are traditional—"

"Like you're not?"

"Not as much." Cleo got up for another cup of coffee. "But I'm romantic enough to believe, all the way, that love matters more, and most. You have that, and we'll get you the rest. We'll work even harder now."

She came back, sat. "You know I love him, too, and I'm so happy the two of you found each other because, Son, the two of you really work. I believe you were meant to find each other, and would have regardless, but who knows when. If."

"If I hadn't come here. If I hadn't come here, and stayed. I think that, too, the way I think my parents would've found each other even if Dad had been raised here. That's what I've always wanted, Cleo, deep down in it. That kind of love and commitment, that kind of partnership."

"Now you have it."

Clover celebrated that with "Walking on Sunshine" as the rain drummed outside.

"I am! And it does feel good. I want it all for you, too, Cleo."

Cleo's smile came slow and easy. "Oh, I'm in no rush for the *all* part. I'm enjoying feeling what I never felt for anyone before. Owen's a very good man, too."

"My favorite cousin for a reason."

Cleo's smile turned into a knowing one as she sipped her coffee. "And so far has been consistently on his game."

"And with that, I have to get back to work."

"I'll be in the studio today, obviously. If it clears up, I may take it out to the garden."

Still walking on sunshine, Sonya started out. She paused by the music room, took a careful look. Six brides, six rings.

But she'd tried to puzzle out why more frequently Owen saw differently, now and then.

Because he was a man? Maybe? Because, even though he'd been a toddler, he'd met one of the brides? He'd met Johanna.

She decided to give herself a week to feel giddy. And, she admitted, smug. So she floated through the days, and the nights as August waned.

The contract for another book cover pumped up that area of her life. She settled into designing the look for a fantasy romance—one that included witches.

Some good, some not. But none, in her opinion, who could hold an evil candle to Dobbs.

On the point of shutting down for the day, she reached for her phone, and a call from Trey.

"Hi, good timing. I'm just—"

"Anna's in labor. Now. I mean now. I went over there to—doesn't matter—and she—it all started happening. Right there."

"Where are you now?"

"Where? At the place—the birthing center. Seth was out on a boat with some VIPs, and he's on his way. He's coming, but we had to get here. I don't know—"

The phone bobbled, then Anna spoke. "I'm fine. Contractions still about five minutes apart, and I'm fine. Except when the apart ends, then wow! But they said it'll be hours yet probably. Everything's good, but it's early. Seth's coming, and we called Mom and Dad."

"And you've got Trey right there. You're going to do great. If you need me and Cleo, we're there."

"Cheer me on from the manor. Uh-oh, I think the apart's over."

"It's happening again," Trey said. "I've gotta be here. I don't know when—"

"Concentrate on Anna and the baby. Just text when you have a niece."

"Right. I gotta go."

Thrilled, Sonya ran down to tell Cleo. And Cleo ran out of the kitchen.

"Anna's having the baby!"

"I was coming down to tell you. Trey's with her."

"And Owen's heading over there because he says Trey's all at once a basket case."

"I heard that for myself. It was kind of cute."

"I'm lighting candles for Mama, and for Fill-in-the-Blank Kate Miller. We're going to be honorary aunties. And you'll be able to drop that *honorary* soon. It's going to be soon."

"God, that's right! Let's light a whole bunch of candles."

"That's what we'll do. After, we go up to the widow's walk, have some wine to toast them both. Then we come down, light a veritable shitload of candles, make one of our big salads."

"A most excellent plan. Anna said they said a few hours yet at least."

"Bringing a human being into the world takes time. So we add popcorn and a movie."

"I'm for all that. You can bug Owen for updates. I think I shouldn't distract Trey."

Cleo chose some wine. "So, what's a flustered Trey like?"

"Adorable."

Owen's updates throughout the evening largely consisted of: Not yet.

They left the candles burning until midnight, through dinner, popcorn, a double feature.

The final text as one day became the next had a little more.

> They're saying a couple hours more. Everything's doing what it's supposed to do. They kicked everybody out but Seth, his mom, and Corrine until it's wrapped up.

After Cleo read off the text, she started to answer. "I'll tell him to text me, have Trey text you when the baby's here."

"You'll never hear a text once you're asleep. Tell him to have Trey call me."

"You're right, and that's better. You can come in and wake me up with the good news."

They blew out the candles, headed to bed.

"Almost to the finish line," Sonya said.

"It's a marathon. Wake me up."

"I will. I'm going to let Yoda and Pye out one last time. I want a quick walk anyway."

Because she wanted the sea, she took them out the front. On the cool, cloudy night, the twinkle of lights in the weeping tree broke through the dark.

She thought of Anna, laboring to bring a new life into the world, and patted the phone in her pocket.

As she walked toward the seawall she heard music. The piano in the parlor—not Astrid's sad song, but something livelier, happier. A man and woman's voice sang a duet.

Even as she turned back, the light of a sky full of brilliant stars and the bright half-moon washed over her. The sea breeze blew, but warmer than it had.

The couple, he in formal black, she in a long, pale green dress with white, elbow-length gloves, strolled across the lawn. She wore her dark hair up in a high knot, which added to her statuesque silhouette. A tall comb glittered above the knot.

As they walked past her, close enough to touch, Sonya recognized Owen, a young Owen Poole, and Agatha, the fourth bride.

"It's somewhat cooler tonight than I realized," he said. "Are you warm enough, or shall I fetch your shawl?"

"My constitution is strong, and I am comfortable, thank you. It's quite a pleasant evening. My parents and I are always grateful for an invitation to Poole Manor."

"My father very much enjoys their companionship. As I very much enjoy yours."

"And I yours, of course."

When he turned to Agatha, Sonya thought of the day she'd seen him and Moira walking together. Not the same, she thought. His smile? Pleasant, yes, but not joyful.

It seemed to her both of them carried themselves with the stiffness of formality rather than any sort of friendship.

"My dear Agatha, as our families are tied together, I have hope that you and I may unite our lives in marriage. My feelings for you are strong and true. I vow to be a devoted and faithful husband, and to provide you with a comfortable life. Will you do me the honor of becoming my wife?"

Even the sea went silent as Agatha turned to Sonya.

"I believe he would have kept that promise, as Owen Poole was an honorable man."

"He was. Everything I've learned about him says he was an honorable man."

"I would have been a good and faithful wife to him, a good and honorable mistress of Poole Manor when it came to him."

"Yes, I know you would have."

"We suited, Owen Poole and I, in the ways that matter in such arrangements. We were a very fine match. She stole that from me. She took my life on the most substantial day of it."

"I'm so sorry."

Agatha inclined her head. "I believe you are, but sorry is no matter. You must restore my ring, and all the others. This is your duty."

Then she looked beyond Sonya to the manor. "I would have been a conscientious mistress of this manor, and a good and faithful wife."

Then she looked back at Sonya. "He did not love me, nor I him. But we made a fine match. And this night, when I believed I saw my future? I was happy."

Waves crashed against the rocks as Agatha turned back to Owen. He took the hand she held out to him.

"I accept your proposal of marriage with a full heart."

Then they were gone, and so were the stars and the moon.

As she took the pets back in, Sonya wondered why it somehow seemed sadder that there had been no love, only duty.

Upstairs, Sonya took time to write out the experience. She'd seen them all now, not only on the day of their deaths, but beyond that.

Another step toward the answers? Maybe, she thought. At least steps in understanding each woman.

Then put it aside, think of Anna instead. This was now, and she'd put her mind and energies, for tonight, on the now.

She took her phone into bed with her. Yoda flopped into his bed, and they both fell asleep almost instantly.

The phone startled her awake at two-twenty-six a.m.

"Is the baby good, is Anna good?"

"Everybody's good. Everybody's great. Especially Fiona Kate Miller."

"Fiona Kate Miller." Swiping her hair back, Sonya sat up in bed. "That's beautiful."

"She's beautiful. Seriously. I'm sending you a picture. I've got a million of them, but I'll start with one."

"Wait. Let me get it, let me see. Oh, oh, she *is* beautiful. Fiona, the raven-haired beauty. So much hair!"

With the phone, she scrambled out of bed. "I'm going to tell Cleo."

"Seven pounds, twelve ounces. Okay, one more picture. The new family."

She brought it up as she pushed open Cleo's door. Anna, tired and glowing, Seth wonder and tears in his eyes. And both beaming down at the baby cradled in Anna's arms.

"You need to frame that one. It's a perfect moment."

"There were a lot of them. I can come up if you want."

"Go home, get some sleep. We're absolutely fine. More than. I'll see you tomorrow, Uncle Trey."

"How about that? I'm going to grab one more look at her, and go home and crash. Listen . . . I love you."

What was already warm and bright in her went warmer, brighter. "I love you, too. Tell Anna and Seth a million congratulations. Good night."

She sat on the side of Cleo's bed, laid a hand on her friend's arm. "It's Sonya. Cleo? Want to see a picture of Fiona Kate Miller?"

"Hmm? What? Oh, baby?"

"I'm turning the lamp on low. Get ready. Fiona Kate Miller has entered the world."

"Fiona? I love it." Cleo blinked against the light, then looked at the phone Sonya held up. "Oh, isn't she gorgeous? Couldn't you just lap her up like ice cream? With hot fudge and whipped cream and two cherries on top. How's Anna?"

"I'll show you." She swiped to the next picture.

"Well, my heart just melted. That's what it's all about, isn't it? That right there. The birth of a family. I can't wait to meet her."

"Trey said he has lots of pictures, so I'll ask him to send more tomorrow. And maybe find out when we can visit." Sonya took one more look, gave one more sigh. "Since you're awake, I saw Owen and Agatha."

"What? When? Where?"

"When I took the pets out, before I came to bed. Outside. The night he proposed."

When she'd told the story, Cleo leaned back against the pillows.

"It's just sad, isn't it? A fine match, that's what mattered. They probably would've been good together, both of them settling, doing their duty. She didn't love him, but she didn't deserve to die."

"No, she didn't. She knew he didn't love her, but she accepted that. I felt sorry for her. Anyway, today's a happy day, and I'm not going to think about that. I'm going to bed."

She started back to her room, jolted a little when the door opened another inch. Then laughed when Yoda came out.

"You scared me. Did I wake you up, too? Let's go back to sleep."

But he whined, wiggled, gave her that look.

"Really? Now? Well, if you've gotta, you gotta."

She took him down, or rather he took her, running ahead down the steps to the door. He darted out the minute she opened it.

Yawning now, she leaned against the jamb, drifting a bit as she breathed in the night, lulled herself with the sound of the sea. The wind had blown the clouds away so now, a thousand stars glimmered in a glass-clear night. The air held a chill that spoke just as clearly of summer's end.

Yoda didn't take long to bound back to her, wagging now.

"Feel better? Now I have to pee."

Since it was closer, she walked down to the powder room.

When she came out, Yoda stood down the hall, staring into the music room where the light shined out from the open doorway.

"We didn't leave that on. What do you see?" Her pulse began to pound as she walked to her dog. Astrid, she wondered, at the piano, ready to play her sad song?

The clock would soon chime three. Dobbs would stand on the

seawall. Carlotta would weep in the nursery. Molly would die in pain, alone in her room.

Braced, she walked to the doorway. The room, the air in it, seemed to throb like a wound. Nothing there, no one there.

But something . . .

Then the portraits changed.

Instead of a wedding gown, Catherine wore a thin robe over a thin nightdress. Her skin turned a cold shade of blue. Marianne, her hair matted, her nightgown wet with sweat and blood, stared sightlessly. Beside her, Agatha's eyes bulged. Raw scratches scarred her throat. Blood, her own blood, smeared her fingers.

Lisbeth, gown in tatters, red welts raw on her body, stood with wilted flowers falling from her limp hand.

Clover, God, Clover, naked but for sweat and blood, her face stripped of all joy in death. Johanna, her head turned to an impossible angle, mouth lax, eyes filmed, her gown splattered with blood.

None wore a wedding ring.

The wall where she hoped to hang Astrid creaked open, and bled.

"It's not real."

But it was real, she thought as her stomach clutched and roiled. Because all of that had happened. All of that had been real.

From the piano came a dirge, a crash of notes and chords booming through the room, banging inside her head, her heart.

In the wave of cold air, ice-tipped air, she saw her breath stutter out.

The doorbell bonged, the same notes as the piano, so the music of death and grief ran through the manor.

With horrified eyes, she watched the faces of the brides melt into skulls while their bodies decomposed.

I gave them this. The voice whispered, close, so close, Sonya felt the breath of the words on her shivering skin.

Death, painful death, a bitter end. I twisted their joy into sorrow so deep there is no bottom. So I will with you.

Something vile began to spill out of the paintings, pool on the floor, then stream like a river toward her.

Run, or meet that fate.

She might have. She might have snatched up her trembling dog and fled to Cleo. And in that moment of terror and revulsion, might have dragged Cleo out of the house.

But the clock struck three.

The house went still. For one long moment, all went quiet. She felt the warm trickling back, pushing against the cold so that a mist rose in the room.

Behind it, the portraits were as they'd been painted. Brides in their finery, wearing their rings, holding their flowers.

She jumped when the music started. Not the dirge, but Astrid's nightly song. Breathless, in wonder, she watched the keys depress and release, but saw no one.

Yoda seemed to as he hurried to the piano, sat at the stool, thumping his tail as he looked up.

Knowing he'd be safe now, she walked back to the front door. She opened it again.

No Dobbs on the wall. She's already jumped, Sonya thought. Already thrown herself on the rocks to escape the hangman's noose, to seal her curse with her own blood.

"A painful death and a bitter end for you, too. I'm going to find the way to make it stick. I'm going to rip those rings off your murdering fingers."

Clover dug back with Curtis Mayfield with the Impressions and "Keep On Pushing."

"Don't worry. I'm going to. She made a mistake. She made a mistake showing me how she turned the wonderful into the awful. She did that to you, to you and all the others, and I never forget that. But tonight? She vandalized—real or not—she vandalized art. My father's art. Collin's, too, but she should never have used my father's work that way.

"She made a very big mistake," Sonya said, and closed the door.

She slept poorly, but she slept. At her desk, she worked in fits and starts, but she worked.

When Cleo came out, Yoda got out from under the desk, anticipating his next outdoor romp.

"Coffee first, but then I want to see those pictures again. I've got an idea about . . ." Eyes narrowing, Cleo stepped closer. "Something's wrong. Not the baby, Anna—"

"No, no, in fact Trey sent a couple more pictures."

"Then what? Something's wrong. It's all over you."

"Get your coffee."

"Screw coffee."

Sonya shook her head, and pushed away from the desk. "Let's go down. I could use another hit myself. We can have coffee in the garden. I'll tell you what happened."

"Shit. More than seeing Owen and Agatha? What did I sleep through?"

"Outside." Sonya patted her arm. "Coffee and air."

"All right. You've got shadows under your eyes."

"I didn't sleep very well."

As they passed the servants' door, they heard the distant ringing of the bell. Though it felt like a weak salute, Sonya just shot up a middle finger and kept going.

But she stopped at the music room as she had on her first trip down that morning. As it had then, everything looked perfectly in place.

"Something in here then," Cleo murmured. "Go on out, sit in the air. I'll bring the coffee."

"Thanks."

And the air felt wonderful. Sitting in the sunlight with the scent of flowers eased some of the fatigue.

When Cleo brought out the coffee, Sonya took the first sip, then nodded. "Just what I needed, sunshine, flowers, more coffee, and Cleo."

"What did Dobbs do?"

"Cleo, she's so cruel. That's not news, but something like last night just cements it. When I left you to go back to bed, Yoda needed to go out," she began.

Cleo didn't interrupt, just reached out, took Sonya's free hand in hers.

"Not just to scare you," Cleo said when Sonya finished, "but to hurt you. To wring your emotions, to shock and hurt and frighten. To make you see, not just their death, but what death does. And to do it through your father's art, Collin's and your dad's art."

"There's a bull's-eye. I wanted to run, Cleo."

"Of course you did. I wish I'd come down with you. I wish you hadn't gone through it alone. The sound effects? I didn't hear anything. I know I sleep good, Son, but not that good. What you described? It would've woken, well, the dead."

"Just for me then. She didn't want you to wake up and look for me, to be there with me. She did exactly what you said. Shocked, frightened, hurt. I was sick, Cleo, nearly physically sick right there in the doorway."

"It stopped at three?"

"The clock chimed, and it stopped. Everything stopped, for a few seconds anyway. Then, it was like all the other nights. Only I watched the piano keys play. It was like—"

Pausing, she shifted to face Cleo.

"Tell me if this is crazy—the control switched. From her to the manor."

"It doesn't sound crazy."

"Good. Now try this. I don't think she can hurt me—I mean seriously, physically, fatally. Because she had me on the ropes, Cleo. I was wrecked, and no defenses there if she'd struck out. She wants me out, clearly, but she can't do to me what she did to the brides. I think she can't because I'm outside the curse. Maybe if she did, it would break the curse, and she knows that? Do you think that's possible?"

"We've thought that before, and I'm more convinced of it. But it's still a theory, a good one, but a theory. She's also crazy, so we know we can't be sure she might not just lose it enough at some point. You're going to be careful, as careful as you can be."

Cleo reached out again, took Sonya's hand in a strong grip. "You won't leave. I've known you too long and too well to think otherwise. You're committed, and damn it, so am I. We're going to remember, and we're going to use the knowing there's only one source of evil in the manor. The rest?"

"It's a damn good house. She used the portraits. Collin said there was something about them."

"Well, they have magic. They're beautiful work, but beyond that, they have magic. Dobbs used that in her ugly way to defile them. But it didn't hold, it didn't last. The light, the beauty came back. And that's what holds."

"I knew I'd feel better once I talked to you."

"Which is why you should've come straight in and told me after it happened."

"Honestly? I needed to think, and to settle down some. And I really hated she chose such an important night for this. Such a happy night."

"I doubt that's a coincidence."

For a moment, Sonya just stared. "Now I'm wondering why I didn't think of that. Of course it's not. She wanted to ruin something beautiful."

"But did she?"

"No. She had her moment, but that's it. I'm going up to the gift room, saying *Fuck you, Dobbs*, then putting together those sweet things we got from Baby Mine for a welcome home."

"We'll put them together, along with the pastel we're going to do of Fiona Kate Miller."

"Oh, a pastel, from one of the pictures."

"That's right. A collaboration. Now give me my fix and show me some more baby pictures, and then we'll both go up and say *Fuck you* to Dobbs."

"He sent so many I put them in an album." Sonya pulled out her phone, scrolled down, clicked.

"Enjoy."

"Aw, here's one of Corrine holding her grandbaby, tears on her cheeks. Happy, happy tears. Now I'm tearing up."

"You love it."

"I do." Cleo pressed a hand to her heart. "Babies just get me. I swear, looking— Oh my, this is the one, I think. See how she's got that otherworldly look in her eyes. That one where she's between where she was and where she is. I think they remember everything at first."

"I love that one, too."

"This is making my clock tick-tock, tick-tock."

"Right there with you."

"We'll get there, Son. We've got a job to do here first, then a few details to work out. Like getting married, or not, getting pregnant."

"Married or not?"

"I'm all right with *or not* as long as there's love, commitment, fealty. No duty or fine match for me like Agatha. Cleo doesn't settle, so I want all those things. And one of these. Or three or four of these precious little babies."

She glanced over at Sonya. "The *or not* doesn't work for you, and nothing wrong with either way. And, Son, we're going to get there."

"Finish the job first."

"Damn right. Let's go up and show Dobbs who's boss around here."

PART THREE

The Seven

Love is strong as death;
jealousy is cruel as the grave.

—*Song of Solomon*

Chapter Twenty-One

Trey arrived that evening with more photos, and stories.

"It was fine when I got over there, even when she says, really casual, 'I think I'm in labor.'"

He sat with Sonya and Cleo, looking out at the sea and waiting for Owen.

"I'm 'Okay, I'll call Seth,' then she tells me he's out on a boat excursion, and she thinks it's too early anyway. I want to call Mom, because Mom, but Anna's just 'Wait awhile.' I'm going to do that. I'm not just going to leave. Then one hits her, and she's puffing, and gone pale."

"And you panicked," Sonya finished.

"Not yet. It's more 'We'll handle this, but I'm calling Seth, and the midwife,' and yeah, she thinks that's probably a good idea since it's not the false stuff, or indigestion like she thought—and that turns out to be a couple hours before I got there. I get word to Seth, get her bag, get her in the car. All good. We got this."

He shook his head, heaved out a breath. "We get to the birthing center, and everything's happening all at once. Seth's a couple hours out, and my mom's doing a photo shoot and can't get back to the village for an hour."

"So it's just you." Cleo laughed. "Then you panicked."

"I wouldn't say *panicked*. Next door to panic. I have to call Seth's parents, my dad, you—because I'm going to be really seriously late. And they leave me alone in the room with her. Like just her and me. I kinda needed some backup."

He took a sip of wine. "Anyway, once Owen got there, and my dad, then finally Mom, all good. Then Seth. Anyway, it was an experience."

"And all's well," Sonya said.

"All's incredible. But it didn't hurt my feelings when they kicked me out, and I'm not ashamed. Jesus, I mean Jesus, it's a lot. After, you'd think it was nothing. She's holding the baby, and we're taking pictures and videos, and Anna's laughing. Like it was nothing. It wasn't nothing."

He drank again. "Swear to God, it makes you wonder how the human race survives."

"Because . . . Who runs the world, Clover?"

The phone shouted it out: *Who run the world? Girls.*

"After this? No argument from me. I need to start sending my mother flowers every week. Maybe daily."

"We've got a welcome gift for the new family," Sonya told him. "You could take it to her tomorrow."

"You could take it. I mean, they sent her home today." He could only shake his head. "Like it was nothing."

"We're giving them a few days. Because it wasn't nothing."

"It sure as hell wasn't."

Mookie and Yoda sent up the alert, and seconds later, Owen's truck pulled up.

"And how did he handle it?" Cleo wondered.

"I gotta say, he was a rock."

"Good to know." Cleo rose, sauntered over to greet him and Jones.

"I haven't even asked how everything's been here."

"It was fine. Cleo and I lit bunches of candles, had a girls' night. Later? Well, there was later, and I'll tell you. Cleo wants to use the grill, because September means not much more time for that. I'll tell you while that's happening."

And once they'd moved to the deck, once the grill smoked, she told Trey and Owen about seeing Agatha.

Then about the portraits.

"Cold-ass bitch" was Owen's opinion.

"She wanted to tear at you, and that was a surefire way to do it. She's not going to win this."

Grateful, she looked at Trey. "I don't think she could've done anything that would have made me more determined to take her down. But it's more. I've said before I don't think she can really hurt me. I'm more sure of it. More sure that she can't or she loses her hold here."

"Because you're not a bride."

She nodded at Trey. "Because I'm not a bride, and that's where she boxed herself in. And the portraits matter. Someway, somehow, and we'll figure it out.

"It did tear at me," Sonya admitted. "And going through that so soon after seeing Agatha, and feeling for her, for everything she lost. But that was temporary. She made a mistake using my feelings for those women, my connection to them. I won't let her hold them hostage forever, and I sure as hell won't let her take another."

"She's misjudged you, cutie."

Smiling, Sonya lifted her glass to Trey. "That's fucking-A right."

Owen had never known anyone who slept like Cleo. When the woman was ready to sleep, she was gone in seconds. And once gone, slept soundlessly and still. So soundlessly and still, it bordered on spooky.

Yet, he knew, she'd wake in that same finger snap if Sonya walked down the hallway. Oddly enough, so would he.

But Sonya didn't walk, and Cleo didn't wake.

He didn't know what woke him, not at first. Still shy of three when he checked, so not the chiming clock, not the music, not the weeping or the murmurs.

He lay for a moment, listening to the dark, the sea, the sighs of an old house in the night. He started to roll over, just grab onto the sleep again.

He swore he heard his name. Not a whisper, not a murmur of a call, but some low, smoky sort of sound inside his head.

But not.

He listened, and it came again.

Owen. Owen Poole. Owen. Owen Poole.

He wondered if what he felt was like Sonya with the mirror. But he wouldn't have called it a pull. It was more of an . . . invitation.

Intrigued, he got out of bed, yanked on his jeans. Jones lifted his head, waited. He started to go to the window, to look out. But no, that was wrong, so he turned and walked to the sitting room, and the dog, as always, rose to go with him.

He went out into the hall, and the intrigue became a kind of dreaming. But he wasn't dreaming. He knew himself awake, aware.

And yet, instead of turning to go down the hall, alert Trey, he turned the other way.

And walked to the stairs, then up into a kind of thin fog that spread through the third floor.

It smelled like secrets. Dark, female secrets. Irresistible. With every breath it aroused, sparked something in the blood so it ran hot under his skin.

His pulse began to pound.

Beside him, Jones growled, but he didn't heed the warning. He didn't notice or care.

The fog thickened over the doorway of Cleo's studio, like a wall blocking the room, the windows. And like a wall it seemed to close behind him, so he heard nothing but the voice calling his name.

In that moment, he wanted nothing more in the world but to answer.

The door to the Gold Room swung open, and light, smoky like the voice, poured out so the fog glittered with it.

Jones growled again, followed it with a series of throaty barks, wet, warning snarls. Owen barely heard it.

Fire smoldered in his blood, in his belly, in his loins. No power on earth could stop him from reaching that open door.

Where she stood, lit by a thousand candles, her hair streaming, her dress molding her body like skin.

When she smiled, the wanting was pain, and the pain welcome.

"Owen Poole. I welcome you."

He stepped inside.

Jones leaped, but the door slammed, and the dog rammed against it.

Candlelight swayed in shadows. In the air wafted a perfume so seductive, Owen could barely take a breath, and when he did, the taste of it filled him with a kind of crazed hunger.

"I've waited for you. Waited for you to take my body, to ravish it, to sate yourself with it." Watching him, she ran her hands from her breasts to her hips. "You want this body. You crave it."

Desire all but strangled him.

"I know what you are." The words tore at his throat. He swore he tasted blood. "What you've done. What you want."

"It's you I want, Owen Poole." Her voice was a cold hand on a hot wound. "This manor, they wrenched it from you. Yours by right of blood. She is no true Poole. This manor is mine, by right of the blood I took, the blood I gave. We will share it for eternity, you and I. You and I alone. You will have me to do all the things you wish, for all time. We are and will be master and mistress of the manor.

"Say it."

Her eyes burned into his.

"Say you want me. Say you want only to give me what I need and take all you need."

"I want you." More than he wanted his next breath. Rock hard, sweat slicking his skin, he reached out.

The shock stunned his hand, raced through his whole body, and left him gasping.

She laughed, and in his swimming vision was the most beautiful creature ever born.

"Oh, but not so easy, my love. Such glory as I will give has a price. You've only to pay it, and I will give you an eternity of pleasures beyond any you've known. Do as I bid you, Owen Poole, pay this price, and I give you forever."

"What do you want? What's the price?"

"I must have blood. There must be blood to pay. Take what I give you. Take it, give me blood. Kill them. Kill them all, and everything you desire is yours."

"Kill them," he said, looking down at the knife in his hand. "Kill them all."

"And be quick about it. Kill them. The cousin, her lover, then the friend. Let their blood flow over your hands, warm and thick. Taste it, one by one, you must taste their blood, so sweet, so fresh. And when what must be done is done, take their bodies out of my manor. These I will burn to ash. Then, only then, will you have me."

Something changed as she leaned toward him, but he didn't know what. Then her lips brushed over his.

"A taste," she murmured. "One taste only. Do what needs doing, then come back for all. Forever."

He turned toward the door.

"Owen? Kill the animals as well. Clear my manor of all of them."

He walked out. Jones scrabbled at his legs, and the blood on his muzzle where he'd rammed against the door smeared on Owen's jeans.

He walked on through the mists, the knife gripped in his hand.

Kill them, she'd said. Kill them all.

He walked down to the second floor. The need, so great, all but swallowed him whole. The taste of her lingered on his lips, the scent of her covered him, and her voice pounded in his ears.

His vision narrowed on the doors at the end of the hall. The turret room. The master.

It will be ours, Dobbs murmured in his head. *It will all be ours.*

As he reached the doors, music blasted, and the dogs sent up a howling.

He pushed inside.

Trey stood by the bed; Sonya scrambled out of it.

Throat dry as dust, pain screaming in every cell, Owen turned the point of the knife toward his own throat

"I'd do myself first, you fucked-up bitch. Take it, Trey. Jesus, take it before I end up doing just that. I can't let go of it."

"I've got it. I've got you."

Trey twisted the knife out of his grip, then tossed it on the bed. When Owen swayed, he grabbed him.

Something screamed, something that hadn't been human in over two centuries.

"Sonya, get a blanket. He's freezing."

"No. No, I gotta . . . Sick."

When Owen lunged for the bathroom, Trey went with him. "Get the knife, get downstairs."

Cleo rushed in. "What—"

"I've got him. Go!" He slammed the door to the bathroom.

"Sonya, what's happening?" She turned to the door and the sound of Owen's retching.

"Trey's with him. We'll go down, make tea. He was so cold and pale."

She picked up the knife, shuddered. "Dobbs killed Astrid with this knife. I recognize it."

"What's it doing here?"

"Owen had it." Sonya took Cleo's arm, pulled her from the room. "We'll go downstairs. He'll tell us what happened when he can. But I think, God, Cleo, I think Dobbs tried to get him to kill us."

"He would never. No matter what she did."

"And he didn't."

She glanced up as they reached the stairs. It sounded like a war waged from the Gold Room. And thin tendrils of fog tore apart and dissolved in the light.

"I think she drew him up there. He'll tell us," she said again, and looked at the knife she carried.

"I'll make the tea. We need to put that somewhere safe. Somewhere she can't get to it again."

"Out of the house," Sonya agreed. "It can't stay in the house. I'm taking it out now, out to my car, locking it up."

The front doors slammed open, shut, open, shut. Lights flicked on and off.

"It goes out now." Striding to the doors, Sonya yanked one open, shoved through. More screams chased her as she ran to her car. The Gold Room windows crashed open.

She turned with the knife, ready to use it if anything flew out at her.

"But you don't have that much left tonight, do you?"

She put the knife in the glove box. The screams tapered off as she went back inside and hurried to the kitchen.

"I slept through it, Son. Whatever happened to him, I slept right through it."

"We all did. I can only think whatever she did targeted him specifically."

"Because Poole. At least she's finally shut the hell up."

"Agreed. Though I like knowing she was really, really pissed off. Let's do this outside. I'm betting he could use the air, and so could the pets."

They left the back doors open to the night, set tea out on the deck, and a bottle of whiskey.

When they finally came down, Owen looked steadier, his color back. But his eyes looked haunted.

"Sorry, needed a shower. She was all over me. The smell of her all over me."

He shook his head when Cleo held out a glass with two fingers of whiskey.

"Better stick with that." He gestured toward the tea when he sat. "Where's the knife?"

"I locked it in my glove box. It shouldn't be in the house. It's the one she used to kill Astrid."

"Of course it is." Owen pressed his fingers to his eyes. "Of course it is."

"Drink some tea." Cleo rubbed his shoulders before she sat. "Take your time. Tell us when you're ready."

Tea wasn't something he'd choose to drink, but despite all the heaving, his guts still felt cold. So he picked it up, drank. Since it soothed his raw throat, and all the way down, he drank again.

"I woke up, just bang, awake. I checked the time, and it's—what? Around one-thirty, something like. It's blurry. Then in my head, my name. Over and over. I felt something."

He looked at Sonya. "Not like what you describe with the mirror, but something pushing me to get up, check it out, right?"

"You didn't wake me."

"Didn't even think about it," he said to Cleo. "Probably wouldn't have anyway, because, at first, it was more like, what the hell? I went out in the hall, and maybe I thought about getting Trey, but I just didn't. I knew I wasn't dreaming, I knew it, but it was like that. Not really real."

He stared at the tea, trying to bring it back, but it kept going in and out, in and out.

"I know I started up to the third floor, and then it just isn't clear. Fucking brain fog," he muttered, and rubbed at his forehead.

"There was actual fog," Sonya said. "It was thinning, dissolving, but there was a kind of mist on the stairs and up."

"That was real? Because it felt like that. Like pushing my way through a wall of fog. And the smell . . . It had me by the balls. Jones was there."

He looked down to where Jones sat beside his chair like a sentry. "Part of me knew that, but . . . It just didn't matter. I had to keep going."

Closing his eyes, he tried to see it.

"I think the door was open. Her door. I could hear her, I could smell her. Jesus fuck."

He put his head in his hands.

"I wanted her. Like I wanted to breathe. More. Then I was in there with her. I don't remember going in, but I was in there. And . . . there was part of me, not a whole lot, but part, that knew what she was. But the rest? The rest just wanted her. I don't remember what she said, not at first, or what I said, because it was all just feeling, needing."

He dragged his hands through his hair, breathed it out. Drank more of the tea until he could settle again, at least a little.

"There was something . . . Master and mistress of the manor. Sonya was no true Poole, but I was, and she'd give me forever. And I could have her. I wanted that. It felt like I'd die for that. Anything she asked me to do, I'd do, just to have that. Have her.

"Then the knife, in my hand. She said—I got this clear—'Kill them. Kill them all. The cousin, her lover, then the friend.' Get them out of her manor, and she'd burn the bodies. And we'd have forever.

I could do whatever I wanted with her, if I did that one thing. Kill them all."

As he struggled through it, he fisted his hands on the table. "For a minute, or however long, I wanted it. Do that and I'd have all of it. Her. Then she kissed me."

Fighting not to be sick again, he breathed through his teeth. "She tasted like death. It made me sick, made me hard, then I was in the hall again, and that smell was everywhere. The taste of her was in my throat, and—wait."

He bore down. "Blood. There had to be blood—she said. I was supposed to taste your blood, all of you. Animals, too. Some part of me kept saying no. Holy fuck no, but I felt like if I didn't . . ."

He put his hand down, laid it on Jones's head. "I walked into your room, saw Trey, saw you, Sonya. Whatever she did to me, it wasn't enough. Just wasn't enough. I swear to God, I'd have slit my own throat first. And the part of me that thought, just do it? Even that part got smothered in that smell. She was still in my head, that smell, her smell, all over me. But I couldn't do it. I wouldn't. I swear to you, I wouldn't have done it."

"You didn't." Near tears, Sonya reached out to grip his hands. "Owen, she couldn't make you."

"Give yourself a break." Cleo nearly snapped it out. "She bespelled you. The fog? I'm going to say like a drug. You were in a trance, and still you pushed back through it, so give yourself a goddamn break."

When he started to speak, she snapped again.

"She used you. Like she did Collin Poole all those years ago. And you know what this tells us?"

"That you're right, you and Sonya," Trey said. "She can't hurt us. Not the way she wants to. She tried to use Owen to do her dirty work. She failed."

"What if I hadn't seen you? If you'd still been sleeping? If I'd gone in to Cleo first? I might have—"

"Stop it! You didn't. You wouldn't. You fought back." Cleo gripped his hand. "She did all she could do. She raped your mind, goddamn it, Owen, and you fought back. You came back."

"Clover blasted music. She had your back. Ours," Sonya corrected. "And, Owen, when you came in, you looked sick, and you turned that knife on yourself. Whatever she did to you, you were stronger. Did you hear her scream?"

"No."

"Believe me, she did. You beat her, and we're all here. You're a god-damn hero."

"No, I'm not. You don't understand where my head was, where my body was."

"I know where it is now. And I know it's almost three, so here's what I'm going to say. Let's go around front and watch her die."

Sonya pushed up from the table. When she reached for his hand, he sat a moment, unable to speak or move. Then he nodded.

"Okay."

They walked around the house together, and stood united.

The clock chimed. Overhead, the moon sailed full and white.

They watched Dobbs climb onto the seawall, watched her hair, her dress blow in the wind.

Hands clasped, they watched her lift her hands to the sky as the sea crashed below her.

She shouted out her words, her curse, sealed in blood.

And leaped.

And they stood as the air cooled into the first hints of fall.

"We're here," Sonya said. "We're together. We beat her again to-night, and we're going to keep on beating her." Turning, she wrapped her arms around Owen. "Still my favorite cousin."

For a moment, he dropped his head on her shoulder. "You scare her. I believe that. And I'm with you."

"I know it. I know you are. Get some sleep." She kissed his cheek. "She's done all she can do for tonight."

Trey lifted her off her feet, held her there a moment before he looked at Owen. "We've got women like this? We can't lose."

He nodded, then glanced at Cleo. "Need another minute."

"All right."

"No, with you." He took her hand before she could go inside.

"All right."

He closed the door behind Sonya and Trey, then looked down at the dog who stayed at his side.

"She fucked with me good. This guy? I promised when I took him on, the scrappy one-eyed little bastard, we'd look out for each other. I wouldn't let him down. And I left him tonight. He got bloodied trying to get to me."

"You know that isn't your fault."

"Doesn't make it less true. I know you're going to say it's not my fault. Mostly I agree, it's not. It wasn't. But I need to say I'm sorry."

"Jones won't hold it against you."

"To you. I wanted her, Cleo, and if I'd have had the chance, in that room, at that time? I couldn't and wouldn't have stopped myself."

The sound she made mixed patience with annoyance. "What part of *bespelled* don't you get?"

"I need to say it. When I'm with someone, I'm with them. I don't mess around."

She angled her head. "If I thought otherwise, you wouldn't be with me."

"It wasn't just wanting her." Because he remembered that, too well, he scrubbed his hands over his face. "It was like survival. It wasn't just lust, it was life and death. It's not lust I feel for you."

She smiled, laid a hand on his cheek. "Oh, really?"

"Not just. Not anymore. Maybe not from the start. A good, healthy lust, sure. This wasn't that."

"Owen, of course it wasn't. She's evil. Her magic is evil."

"But until she kissed me, until I tasted her, I was lost. Even after . . . I can't explain it."

"Do you think any of us expect you to?"

Gently now, she brushed his hair back.

"She could've tried this with any of us. But she chose you because you're a Poole. And she failed because you're Owen. She'll never understand loyalty and love."

"I'm crazy about you."

"Of course you are."

"Cleo." He took her face in his hands. "I've been crazy about women before, but not like this."

"There is no one like me but me."

"That's the God's truth. I need to tell you I'm sorry."

"Apology unnecessary, but accepted. I hate her for what she did to you, for what she wanted to do to all of us. And I only think more of you because you were strong enough to fight her off."

"At the end."

"Good enough, and it's going to really get me angry if you keep beating yourself up over it."

"It might take me a little while. It was intense. Meanwhile, here's something I haven't said to another woman. Because you've got to be careful. I love you. And I'm telling you because tonight brought home shit happens, so why wait?"

"That's a really good reason, so I'll join in. I love you right back."

"I figured." He drew her close, held on. "Like I figure you're not moving out of here until you have a studio that stands up against this one. And until this is all over anyway."

"Are you asking me to, at some point, move in with you?"

"Well, yeah." He drew her back. "It'll take a while. I'd need to build on, a lot, but it's a good spot, great views, especially when we go up."

"How long's *a while*?"

"About a year, most likely, to do it right."

"All right, we'll have dealt with Dobbs by then. I'm damn well determined on it."

"Fine, after we do that, we'll get married in there somewhere. Sonya's not kicking either of us out."

"Who said anything about getting married?"

"I did. I'll build you a hell of a studio, Lafayette, but you gotta commit."

"Show me the design, and I'll give it serious consideration."

"I'll work on it. But you don't get it unless you marry me. That's the deal."

Looking at him, she decided on her scale the moment, this moment, rang the bell on romance.

"It's going to have to be an amazing space."

"I'll make sure of it. We'll look out for each other."

"Yes. Yes, we will."

"I won't let you down."

And again, the bell rang.

"I know it. Same goes. Let's go in. You have to get up in a couple hours."

When they started inside, he looked up.

"I wouldn't have gotten around to all this yet if she hadn't pulled this shit tonight."

"See that? She lost on so many levels. She's going to keep losing, Owen. I feel more sure of that now than ever."

"If I'd hurt you—"

"Stop. You didn't."

"I mean if she'd managed to pull this off? She'd have pushed me—or maybe wouldn't have had to push—into killing myself. That's what she wanted."

Because she'd thought the same, Cleo only nodded.

"And she'll never get it. None of us will ever hurt each other. You said she's afraid of Sonya."

"I felt that. Through the rest, I felt that."

"I believe she does. More, I believe she fears what the four of us have together. That loyalty and love. She can't beat those. Maybe it's a standoff until we figure out how to get the rings, but she can't beat what we have together."

She looked down the hall before they went in the bedroom and thought of long, strong friendships and love that bloomed big and bright.

Chapter Twenty-Two

Sonya and Cleo waited a couple of days to give the new family time to settle in. When they paid their visit, bearing gifts, Corrine opened the door.

"Perfect timing. Seth's just changing the baby so she's fed and fresh for company. They're all back in the great room."

"How's everyone doing?" Sonya asked.

"Amazing, honestly. Kate and I take shifts, but they barely need us."

"And how about you, Nana?"

Corrine beamed at Cleo as they walked. "I'll tell you, you think you'll never experience that breathless sunburst of love you feel when, a new mother, you hold your child the first time. But you do."

When they walked into the great room, Seth held the baby while Anna sat on the couch folding impossibly small socks.

"I don't care what they say, Anna, she's smiling at me."

"Because she loves her daddy. It says so right on her outfit," Anna pointed out.

In addition to the little pink hat and socks, Fiona wore a white onesie with the sentiment I LOVE MY DADDY inside a pink heart.

"Daddy needs to share," Cleo proclaimed, and walked to him.

Lighting up, Anna pushed herself off the couch. "Oh, I'm so glad you came! We've been waiting to show her off."

"Wait no more. Can I hold her? Please?" Cleo held out her arms.

"You have to be really careful to support her head."

"This ain't my first precious, Daddy."

"Cleo's a baby magnet," Sonya told them.

"It's true. I am."

Sonya walked around the couch, set down the basket, then hugged Anna. "You look amazing."

"Sleep-deprived, foggy-brained, and loving it."

Cradling the baby, swaying, Cleo didn't even glance up. "Of course you are. She's perfect. Excellent work, team." She brushed a light kiss over the baby's forehead. "And we adore each other already, don't we, Fiona Kate Miller?"

"I need a turn."

"In a minute. We're reminiscing."

Watching them like a hawk, Seth frowned. "You know, it sort of looks like they are. She's looking right at you."

"To my way of thinking, we've all been around before."

"That should be spooky." He considered. "But it's kind of sweet."

"Just think of it as continuity. All right, your turn, but only because I love you, too."

"Oh." With the baby in her arms, Sonya stroked a finger down one silky cheek. "She's just . . . wow. And look at these long legs!" Then she laughed, glanced at Seth. "She does smile. Don't listen to anyone who says different. She has a beautiful smile. And I hereby vow there will always be cookies at the manor."

Sonya lowered her head for a kiss of her own.

"She's going to sleep. Just like that! She's sleeping."

"We're going to take advantage of that, since she's proven she prefers awake. I'll put her down."

Anna took the baby, settled her in the bassinet by the couch.

"And while she's sleeping, there's iced tea and shortbread cookies." Corrine gestured toward the banquette. "Mine are nearly as good as Anna's."

"They're wonderful. Fiona has the most wonderful grandparents in the history of grandparents." Anna walked over to hug her mother.

"I can confirm that," Seth said. "They cook, they do laundry, run errands, give us some nap time when we need it. They taught us the essential three s's."

"Swaddle, sway, and shh."

Corrine grinned at Cleo. "You have been around before. Let's sit down."

Sonya detoured to pick up the basket. "Some welcome-home gifts from the manor."

"I'm going to say you didn't have to do that, which you already know. And add, we love presents. Seth, Mom, look! A plush pink dragon. Oh, and a onesie with pink dragons."

"The sisters of Baby Mine tell me you can never have too many onesies."

"They're not wrong."

When Anna reached for the wrapped package in the basket, Cleo tapped her hand. "That's the finale."

She oohed her way through the basket.

"This is all so thoughtful, so soft, charming, sweet. I can't even imagine the finale."

Grinning, she rubbed her hands together, then unwrapped the box. She lifted the lid, removed the padding.

Then her eyes filled. Shaking her head, she reached for Seth's hand on one side, her mother's on the other.

"I . . . can't. I can't even . . . Seth."

"Not sure I can either." As carefully as he'd held his daughter, he lifted out the double frame with its pastels of the newborn, and the facing one of the new family.

"This is . . . it's a treasure. I can look at these, and I feel exactly the way I did when . . . It's a treasure."

"We wanted to do something that captured the moment," Cleo told them, "and with the softness, the sweetness of that moment. So we worked on them together."

"We did have wonderful subjects to work with," Sonya added as Corrine pulled out tissues for her daughter and herself, then a third for Seth. "Couldn't go wrong."

"A treasure, just as Seth said." Corrine took a long breath. "The treasure of that beautiful new life, the treasure of a new family just begun, and the treasure of good friends who understand."

September held on to summer, but Sonya felt fall pushing it aside. Not just by the cooler, longer nights, but the tonal change of the light.

For now, the leaves stayed lush and green with only a hint or two of the color to come. But they basked in light that took on a golden hue. Even working at her desk, she sensed it in the way the sun slanted through the windows.

Determined to continue with her quest, she carved out a few hours during the week to work solo in the ballroom. That determination included showing Hester Dobbs she wouldn't be cowed.

She stood in the ballroom, turning a circle, looking at the notes she'd put in place. And realized she'd not only started, but finished.

She'd been through every piece.

Understanding, Clover offered U2's "I Still Haven't Found What I'm Looking For."

"No, I haven't. But I will. And in the meantime, I've got a vision for this room now. The tables, the chairs—some still in the attic, some already in here. Those two benches that look like old church pews flanking the terrace doors. Love seat over there, and another over there."

She wandered now as she drew it up in her head.

"Still have to decide on art, but there's plenty to choose from. And that room over there? We'll make it cozy."

Pulling out her phone, she checked the time and saw she'd finished earlier than she'd planned.

With Yoda, she walked out to take a closer look at the servants' quarters on that level. And came first to Molly's.

She tried not to dwell on the young Irish girl she'd come to know writhing in pain on the narrow bed.

"Will that stop?" she murmured. "Will that finally stop for you when I break the curse? I hope so. Maybe you'll go, go to whatever's next. And oh boy, we'll miss you if you do. But either way, I want that to stop."

Clover tried Shinedown and "Dead Don't Die."

"Well, at least not here, or some other places. And not the way I always thought."

She walked to the dresser, opened the top drawer. Inside, she found the butterfly bottle, the hair combs. Even as her heart warmed, her eyes stung.

"All right, Molly, this is your place for as long as you want it. I'd like to make it a little better for you. Add a couple of pretty lamps, a mirror, a nice rug. Table and chair there—scaled for the room. A couple of Cleo's garden paintings. She won't want me to buy them, but I'm going to.

"Yeah, we can make this better for you. Make it reflect who you are."

As that vision evolved, she went to the attic, went on a hunt. Delighted, she lifted a chair with an oval back framed in wood. The fabric on the back and the seat's garden pattern struck her as dreamy. She didn't want bold and striking for Molly, but soft and warm.

She placed it, then went back to hunt and found a small round table, a pretty globe lamp. She found a mirror that had the same shape as the back of the chair. Small, in a simple wood frame.

She went down for tools to hang it, let Yoda and Pye out, then stopped by Cleo's studio on the way up.

"I know you're working, sorry."

"Almost wrapped for the day. Did something happen?"

"No, all quiet. Do you need the watercolors you've done of the wisteria, the pink roses?"

"Not necessarily, why?"

"How would you price them if you did want to put them in the show?"

Cleo puffed out a breath, shrugged, pushed at her hair. "I don't know. Considering the size, the medium, I'd say a couple hundred. Maybe two-fifty depending on how I frame them. Again why?"

"I'm buying them. Two hundred each, because unframed works even better."

"If you want them, take them. You're not buying them."

"I am buying them. They're for Molly's room."

Setting aside her work, Cleo sat back. "Molly's room."

"I'm fixing it up a little, and those two small, dreamy flowers are perfect for what I've got going in there. So I'm buying them."

"Not for sale." Cleo crossed her arms. "For giving."

Because she'd already worked this conversation out in the head, Sonya had the solution ready. "You give Molly one. I buy one to give to Molly."

Cleo frowned, started to speak, frowned again. "Okay, that's silly but fair."

"Great. I'm taking them now. I have to hang the mirror I found, so I'll hang the paintings. You should come take a look when you're finished."

"Are you kidding? I'm coming now. I thought you were working in the ballroom."

"I was. It's done—as far as going through everything. I just wanted to see what I wanted in the other rooms upstairs, and started with Molly's."

Cleo got the two paintings. "It's a small room, so yeah, these are a good size for it."

"I thought if I started working through the other rooms, we'd move stuff from storage, put it to use. Sort of put it to use. And I know what I want in the ballroom, in that small sitting room off it. It means moving masses of stuff, but we can use a lot of furniture in the ballroom."

"Making progress."

"On this, but not on the reason I started this."

"It'll come."

When they reached Molly's room, Sonya gestured. "Just walk in, then give me first impression."

Cleo stepped in, and hands on hips, looked around.

"I love the chair. The size, the shape, the pattern. And the table and lamp, perfect with it. The mirror, exactly right for over the dresser."

"And look." Sonya opened the drawer.

"Oh, what we gave her! We're going to put those on the dresser after we hang the mirror. And she needs a little vase or bottle."

After turning another circle, Cleo nodded. "I'm loving this. Where are you thinking of hanging the paintings?"

"Since she's got the narrow armoire and the washstand over there—and they're charming, plus fit the size of the room—I was thinking over the bed. They'll reflect in the mirror."

"We're in tune. She needs a rug. Small. Round or oval, quiet colors or pattern."

"There must be a couple dozen between those rolled up in the attic and the ones downstairs. Different sizes."

"Then we'll get this all hung, and we'll go find the right rug."

With the mirror and paintings in place, Sonya ran down for a vase, and Cleo hunted for a rug.

Sonya decided on a pale blue vase with a fluted top, and went to the garden to cut a few flowers. When she came back, Cleo put down an oval rug in blue on cream.

"That's exactly right."

"And so's that vase. I love the little yellow and white flowers for that splash of happy. We need to get a nice duvet, some shams, throw pillows. Then this is a room that feels like Molly."

"I want to do them all, but this one? We know what Molly's room should look and feel like."

Clover showed her heart in "Daisies" by Katy Perry.

"She does so much for us. I hope this makes her happy."

"It makes me happy. Owen texted they'd bring pizza tonight, so I've got time. Let's go look at another room."

They'd done two more by the time they heard voices, dogs, and feet on the stairs.

"We're this way," Sonya called out. Hurrying to Trey, she threw her arms around him. "We've been having so much fun!"

"Doing?"

"Come see. You, too, Owen," she added, and hurried back to Molly's room.

"Nice." Owen stepped in, looked around. "Small room, furniture to scale, girly but not over-the-top."

"Molly's room, right?"

"Yes." Sonya leaned against Trey. "I finished going through the ballroom, and when I took a look in here, it all started rolling."

She pulled him out again. "And this one? Clover let us know through the Beatles, this is Rita's."

"'Lovely Rita,' meter maid?"

She laughed at Owen. "Got it in one. Then since we really don't know Rita, she gave us a clue with the Beatles again. 'When I'm Sixty-Four.'"

"So an older woman." Cleo chimed in. "We found that rocking chair, the table, the lamp. And we went with that landscape—one of Collin's—and the longer rectangular rug works with it."

"You've been busy," Trey observed.

"And not done yet. Next room, she stuck with the Beatles for 'Eleanor Rigby.'"

She gestured into the room with its curvy armchair and little footstool, the square mirror.

"Since the washstand's over here, and the armoire there, we went with the still life for that wall.

"We've got a bathroom across I'd want to update, but keep old-timey in style," Sonya continued. "And . . ." She lifted her hands. "Lots of rooms and possibilities."

Hands on hips, Cleo gave the room a look of satisfaction.

"It struck as obvious, female servants up here, males down below."

"Yes, more servants' quarters downstairs, and I hope we find Jerome's, but Collin took most of those for the theater and the gym."

"Good start, solid progress," Cleo said. "And we'll keep it up, but right now, I'm ready for food."

As they started out, Sonya tipped her face up to Trey's. "I've figured out what I want in the ballroom, how I want to set that up. And more, that I need to hire John Dee and at least one other burly guy to help move things out, things in."

Owen let out an exaggerated sigh. "Thank God for that."

"I'm going to measure, draw it out on graph paper to be absolutely sure."

"I'm going to add thank God we've got a graphic artist on it." Trey skimmed a hand down Sonya's ponytail. "And that it makes you so damn happy."

She stopped on the third floor. "It does make me happy. I know she's not going to be quiet for long. I've got that pattern. But the happier I am, the more I know I can fight back. And the more we bring the manor to life, the less it's hers and the more it's ours."

Cooler days passed in the quiet, so Sonya took advantage of the lull. She started work an hour early to justify shutting down an hour early. With that hour she worked on the servants' quarters.

Since Molly took care of cleaning, she carried tables, chairs, lamps, arranged, rearranged.

When the day came to turn her vision for the ballroom into reality, she stood with Cleo, Trey, Owen, John Dee, Manny, and Bree.

"I know it's a lot," Sonya said.

"It's a giant mountain of lot." Bree put her hands on her hips. She had a black cap over her bright red hair and wore a baggy sleeveless Metallica T-shirt that showed off her tats.

"A chunk of the giant mountain stays."

Manny adjusted his Buddy Holly glasses, tossed back his flop of hair. "Which chunk?"

"Okay, anything with blue stickies goes in the attic, red stickies go in the basement, I tagged the yellows for specific rooms, and the whites stay here."

John Dee gave her his easy smile, scratched his beard. "You're an organized soul, aren't cha?"

"Oh," Cleo confirmed, "she is. She is."

"It's the first step of successful time management. And . . . there are some pieces in the attic that come in here. Also some from the basement level that come up here."

She tried a winning smile. "Apologies in advance."

"You're sure about it, right?" Trey gave her a long look. "What goes down, over, up, wherever, stays where it's put."

"I can guarantee ninety percent sure."

On a wince, Owen rolled his shoulders. "That ten percent gives me a dull ache in the lower back."

"Well." John Dee took another look around. "Seems to me the best way is to take the blue stuff to the attic first. Clear the way some."

After the first few trips, Bree shook her head. "Did these people ever get rid of anything? Ever?"

"I think that's a no," Sonya told her. "I'm working on making use of what makes sense, and we talked Owen into taking a couple pieces, but . . ."

She noted John Dee eyeballing, for the second time, a small, single-door cabinet with curved legs and curved top.

"Pretty, isn't it?"

"Sure is. Kevin would be all over it."

"It's yours."

He waved one of his big hands in the air. "Ah, come on."

"I mean it. Take it. Move it out! Load it up!"

"Now, Sonya, I can't be doing that. Now, if you really can't use it, I'll maybe buy it."

"Okay. One dollar."

This time he snickered when he waved again. "That won't work for me. I appreciate it, though."

"Okay, let's try this. Hey, Owen."

A warning in his eyes, he glanced over. "If you're going to say you want me to move something back I just moved over here, I may have to hurt you."

"Not that. Take a look at this cabinet, tell me what you figure it's worth. John Dee's interested."

He knew her well enough, caught the look that clearly said: Lowball it big-time. But he made a show of carefully examining the piece.

"Nice. Mahogany. Solid." He opened the door, crouched. "Top shelf inside's a little bowed, but not bad." With a shrug, he straightened. "I'd call it about five hundred."

"Great. With the friends-and-family discount, that's two-fifty."

"That's not right, Sonya."

Her face showed hurt and surprise, and she loaded her voice with both. "Are you saying you're not friends and family with me?"

His eyes widened; his feet shuffled. "Well now, sure I am. But . . . I just don't want to . . . It's not right for me to . . . Three-fifty, okay? Let's say three-fifty. I wouldn't feel right about it otherwise."

"Deal." She stuck out a hand.

He shook, smiled. "Kevin's going to be all over it, even more since it comes from the manor. I'll just move it out there, so it's out of the way."

Hands in pockets, Owen waited until John Dee was out of earshot. "Nice work. More like fifteen, maybe sixteen hundred, by the way."

"Then nice work back at you."

They made good progress before the lunch break, where Cleo's cold fried chicken and Creole potato salad got Chef Bree's seal of approval.

"I could work this into the summer menu next year." Considering, Bree took another bite of potato salad. "The smoked pepper makes it."

"It's my grand-mère's recipe. I'll give it to you."

"Then it wouldn't be mine. On the other hand . . ." Lips pursed, she tipped her head side to side. "Grand-mère's Creole Potato Salad says something. I'm going to play with it, think about it."

Clover chimed in with Katy Perry and Migos to say "Bon Appétit."

Even as Bree gave the kitchen tablet the side-eye, Manny grinned, said, "Cool. See, you're talking about cooking, and it—she?—whatever plays a song about cooking."

"I got it, Manny." Now Bree gave him the side-eye before she shifted to Sonya. "Doesn't it ever just creep you out?"

"Not even a little. Thanks to Clover, my playlist has expanded by leaps and bounds since I moved to the manor."

"That'd happen sometimes when I came in to do any inside work for Collin." Shrugging, John Dee polished off a drumstick. "Didn't feel creepy so much as, well, just Lost Bride Manor stuff."

"Did anything feel creepy?" Sonya asked him. "Trust me, I won't be offended."

"Well, you got used to doors opening and closing and like that. And now and then maybe you'd hit what you'd call a cold spot. But there was a time, just last year, when I was delivering a load of fire-wood, and Collin mentioned the faucet was leaking and dripping in one of the bathrooms on the third floor, the one down past his studio?"

He smiled at Cleo. "You're using it now. Anyhow, I said I'd take a look, took my tools on up. Needed a new washer and some tightening up, so it didn't take long. But it gave me a bad feeling, kind of a sick feeling to be in there. Like there was someone who didn't want me to be."

He flushed a little. "I could've sworn there was somebody moving around in that room across the hall. A sneaky sound to it."

"We're working on that," Sonya told him.

"I guess I've been all over this house doing a little this or that for Collin, unless Trey or Owen took care of it first. But that day, down that way? It didn't feel right."

But Dobbs stayed quiet through the afternoon as the space in the ballroom spread, and the space in the attic narrowed.

She talked Bree and Manny into taking an Art Deco table as a housewarming gift, sealing that deal by assuring Bree the table wasn't haunted.

Then she brought out her graph paper.

Trey studied it, noted each piece had been drawn to scale and place. And she'd added a list on the side identifying each one.

"Did we say organized?"

"Yes, with the caveat this is where that ten percent applies."

Owen studied the graph. "Nah. This is how it's done. You've got it, so let's just get going on it."

Though she did second-guess herself, a few times, as they placed love seats, tables, chairs, Sonya saw what she'd built in her head be-coming. And leaned toward Owen's take.

They had it.

No neutrals here, but bold colors and patterns, gleaming wood, vary-ing shapes that to her eye worked together. Probably not the formal elegance the room had once held, but touches of both mixed, she thought, with comfort and welcome.

"Needs art." Sonya swiped the back of her hand over her forehead. "I wanted to see it set up before I got into that. And some tall plants. And maybe . . ."

"Forget that ten percent."

She shrugged at Trey. "It's down to five, and I think that disappears with the art and plants. I think. There's just so much open space."

"That's what this is for."

Trey grabbed her, spun her into a waltz.

"I don't know how to do this!"

"I do."

Clover added music with "Iris."

"It's the Goo Goo Dolls," Owen said, "but I don't do that."

Cleo fluttered her lashes. "I do."

"I do." John Dee held out a hand.

With a curtsy, Cleo took it.

Hands on hips again, Bree watched both couples spin around the floor.

"I had my serious doubts. Deeply serious, but holy hopping shit, this is a freaking ballroom. And Manny, Rock Hard's going to rock it hard here."

"Hundred percent. The first time we'll have played in a place with freaking chandeliers. Sign us up for the holiday bash, and we'll blow those doors off."

He grinned over at Owen. "This was fun."

"You've always had a weird sense of fun. Wait until she gets her teeth into doing a major game room in the basement, and you can have more fun hauling things around."

"We used to game in that room downstairs."

"Not big enough for what she wants. Pool table, pinball."

"Pinball?" Bree held up a hand.

"Trey's got a line on Gorgar."

"Vintage pinball!" Bree mimed pressed flippers. "We're here for that, right, babe?"

"Oh yeah, we are. Man, this place is coming to serious life."

As they circled, Trey grinned. "That's the plan, isn't it, cutie?"

"You bet your waltzing ass." Sonya threw back her head and laughed as they danced.

Chapter Twenty-Three

The next morning, Sonya rolled out of bed before Trey.

He opened one eye. "Really?"

"I've got a ten o'clock video call, and some work to make up before that. I want to get a workout in."

"Again I say, really? And add, after yesterday?"

"Yesterday is why I'm taking a page out of Cleo's book and sticking with yoga. I'm feeling all those trips up and down steps, and all the rest of it."

She pulled on a sports bra, workout capris, then walked back to the bed. Leaned over, kissed him.

"You could join me."

"I think no. I'm after a long, hot shower, coffee, breakfast. I've got a nine o'clock."

"Then I'll see you tonight. Hauling furniture is not on tonight's menu."

"Much gratitude." He grabbed her hand before she straightened. "What you're doing? What you've done upstairs? It makes a difference. Collin lost his heart, and let a lot of it go. You've brought the heart back."

Now she laid her cheek against his. "I feel that. I really feel that. But we've brought the heart back. And we're not nearly done."

She straightened. "I'll let any of our four-legged family out who wants to go in the yard. You put out the food."

She started for the door, paused, and looked back. "I really loved waltzing with you."

"And we're not nearly done."

That put a bounce in her step as she walked down the hallway with Mookie and Yoda following. Since neither Pye nor Jones came out of Cleo's bedroom, she decided Owen had already left for the day.

She tended to start hers early, but he, invariably, started earlier.

She found her assumption correct when she reached the kitchen and found a note.

All pets fed, and don't let them tell you different.

She looked down at the dogs. "There will be no second breakfast, but you're welcome to go out and play."

Clover played "Good Morning Starshine" while Sonya let them out, got coffee. Then watched them romp around while the coffee kicked in.

Color had begun to bloom in the woods. Hints of gold and orange and red splashed against the deep green of the pines.

"If I were Cleo, and since it's a beautiful morning, I'd grab a hoodie and do the yoga in the garden. But I'm not Cleo, and I need somebody telling me what to do next."

Once she'd polished off her coffee, she filled a water bottle and made her way down to the gym.

After spreading out a mat, she scrolled through programs until she found one that seemed best for stretching overworked muscles.

The fact that it started with breathing suited her, so she sat cross-legged on her mat, hands in prayer. Within ninety seconds, she feared the soothing voice and the mindful breathing would put her right back to sleep.

Then she rose, began the first gentle stretches, following along with the calm-eyed woman with the smooth ponytail on the wall screen.

By the time the instructor told her to step to the front of the mat for sun salutations, she felt relaxed but awake. And enjoyed having someone who seemed to care about her well-being telling her when and how to move, when and how to breathe.

By the second sun salutation, her muscles had loosened, her body just flowed along with the voice.

Warrior One. Inhale, exhale. One more breath. Warrior Two. Gaze over your extended left arm.

Both her body and her mind flowed with the voice, with the movements, the poses. Almost like a trance, she thought vaguely as she moved to plank, Chaturanga, Up Dog, Down Dog. Then back to repeat the whole sequence on the other side.

And the voice, so quiet, so soothing, guided her through to the next set of Warrior poses.

You're no warrior, Sonya. You fear because you're pathetic and weak. You have nothing, you are nothing.

"No." Sonya sighed it as, almost dreaming, she continued to move through the poses.

No true Poole. The manor knows it. The manor rejects you.

"No," she said again as the cold coated her skin.

I could kill you with a thought and no one would weep. I give you the gift of allowing you to take your own life. To have that moment of courage. Outside, Sonya, outside. The sea waits for you. Spare yourself the pain, and end it.

"No." Shivering, she pulled back.

On-screen the instructor continued to move, so fluid, so graceful, even while blood poured down her face, down her long, limber arms and legs.

She turned her head, grinned at Sonya with teeth as sharp as a shark's.

Inhale, exhale, you stupid bitch. Your time to breathe is almost done.

"Bullshit." Sonya grabbed the remote, hit the off button, but the image remained on-screen.

Try this.

Sonya heard bones crack as the yogi's shoulders lifted, twisted, rotated. And again as, grinning, shark's teeth gleaming, she lowered her head and shoulders between her legs, up behind her back.

She heard the neck snap, a dry twig underfoot, as her head circled.

End the fear. End the torment. Give yourself to the sea.

"That's your way, the coward's way. It's not mine."

From their hooks, the exercise bands coiled, uncoiled, dropped. She swore they hissed like snakes.

Wrap one around your neck. It won't take long, and you'll be free.

"No." Because she felt those licks of fear and knew they'd made Dobbs stronger, she turned to the door.

It slammed shut before she reached it.

Then die here, alone in the cold and the dark. No one will come to help you. And in death, so alone, to weep and wail endlessly in the manor. In my manor. Never yours. Never yours. Mine for all time.

The screen shut off, and so did the lights. All she heard in the dark was the hissing. And then the almost jubilant ringing of the servant's bell.

With a hand gone clammy despite the cold, Sonya reached for her phone, then cursed when she saw herself setting it on the kitchen island before she'd let the dogs out.

Holding out both hands, she put the angle and distance to the door in her head. Slowly, carefully moved forward. But when she reached the door, relief wouldn't come.

The door didn't budge.

The hissing grew louder, and the cold deeper.

She feared one of those bands winding itself around her throat. Feared Dobbs snapping her neck as she'd seen her snap Arthur Poole's, Johanna's.

Trey wouldn't come. He'd simply go off to work. Cleo wouldn't be up for hours.

She'd die alone, in the cold and dark.

She screamed when a hand covered hers.

Then a voice whispered in her ear.

"She lies. She lies, Sonya. You're not alone. You're stronger than she is. You have to be. Be stronger."

"Not alone," Sonya murmured, and bore down. "Be stronger."

Showered, shaved, and more than ready for coffee, Trey started down the hall toward the stairs.

The phone in his pocket blasted Buckcherry at top volume.

"Crazy Bitch."

He didn't think, didn't need to. He ran full out toward the servants' door and down the stairs. He heard the bell ringing, and it sounded like the alarm at a railroad crossing.

He sprinted toward the door of the gym, shouting Sonya's name.

As he reached for it, it swung open.

Sonya stood pale, breath shuddering. But her eyes blazing blue with triumph.

"I wasn't alone. I was stronger."

He dragged her to him. "You're freezing. Let's go get you warm."

"I'm already warmer." She wiggled away from him to turn toward the room. "Hear that, bitch? You're the one who died alone. This is my house, and I'm never alone."

She may have shouted it, may have looked fierce, but she trembled all over.

"Come on, cutie. Come on with me now."

She let him lead her away, and glanced over as the ringing bell snapped to silence.

"That's right," she muttered. "That's right. Go curl up in your hole. You won't have even that for long."

As they started up the stairs, the adrenaline began to recede. When her legs went weak, she leaned against him.

"You came looking for me. I didn't think you would."

"Clover let me know you needed me to."

"She's the best. Need a second. Legs are a little shaky."

To solve that, he picked her up. "I've got you."

"Yeah, you do."

When he pushed open the servants' door, they saw Cleo, hair wild, rushing toward them with the cat slinking behind. Then doubling her pace when she saw them.

"What happened? Are you hurt? What—"

"Not hurt. Just catching a ride. Downstairs, okay? Because I could really use more coffee. You can put me down."

"I've got you," he repeated as Cleo reached out.

"You're cold. I'll get a blanket."

"No, no, trust me, this isn't cold. Did Clover wake you up?"

"I'll say." Cleo knew her friend, and her friend needed a couple of minutes. "I heard some blast of music. That didn't really register."

"'Crazy Bitch.'"

At her half-amused look, Trey shook his head. "Not you. The music."

"If you say so. Then my phone's blasting 'Hell's Bells.'"

"AC/DC, good choice." Trey turned at the bottom of the stairs.

"Well, that woke me up. Add the Gold Room bell clanging like a fire alarm. Then there you are. I'll get the coffee. Lots of coffee."

Cleo hurried ahead.

"Dobbs is running scared."

"Is she?" Trey turned his head to brush his lips over Sonya's hair.

"Yeah, she is." As they passed the music room, she looked in at the portraits. She wasn't alone, she thought again. And neither were the brides. "Crazy bitch ruined my yoga practice, and I was into it."

In the kitchen, Cleo took the first mug off the machine, added Sonya's preferred dollop of milk.

"Just what I need."

"I'm scrambling eggs. We'll have eggs and toast."

"Sounds great." Trey set Sonya on a stool at the island. "Just let me make a call and reschedule."

"No, don't. How long was I down there?" Sonya grabbed the phone she'd left on the counter. "It's still early. You have time to eat, and hear me out, before you leave for work."

"Let's take step one. On my list that's hear you out."

"Same as my list." Cleo got out eggs, then a bowl before turning to get Trey's coffee.

"I wasn't down there nearly as long as I thought." Sonya set her phone down again. "As it felt. I came down, got coffee, let the dogs out. They're still out. Maybe we should—"

"They're fine," Cleo assured her. "I just let Pye out with them."

Trey took the stool beside Sonya as Cleo whisked eggs in the bowl.

"You went down to the gym."

"Right. Yoga, stretch out yesterday. It felt great. The instructor— the blonde, ponytail, flowing white outfit."

"Yeah." Cleo nodded as she poured eggs into the melted butter in a skillet. "She's got a voice like warm cream."

"Exactly, and I was sort of floating on that, into the Warrior poses. Then that voice said I wasn't a warrior. I was weak and pathetic. That I was nothing, had nothing."

She took them through it while the coffee warmed her inside and out.

"I was scared, really scared, when I realized I'd left my phone right here. When I couldn't get the door open. And I don't think I'll ever use exercise bands again in this lifetime. All I could think was Trey would go on to work, and Cleo wouldn't be up for at least two hours. And I'd be alone in the dark with her, with that hissing.

"Then Clover. She took my hand." Sonya looked down at her hand as Cleo set a plate of eggs and toast in front of her.

"She said Dobbs lies. That I wasn't alone, and I was stronger than Dobbs. I had to be stronger. So I turned around, and I just started spewing insults.

"God, these eggs are good. I'm starving."

Cleo set a plate in front of Trey, then brought her own to sit on Sonya's other side.

"I said things like, 'Is this the best you've got?' Did she think I was afraid of the dark, of her? Of some crazy, dead, half-assed witch who'd had to drug a man to get him to fuck her? I let my crude flag fly. She thinks I'll jump off the wall because she wants me to? Oh, hell no, because I get off watching her jump night after night. Gives me a thrill almost better than sex. Which I can have when I want, no drugs or spells required."

She shoveled in more eggs. "Then I dared her. Jesus, I was wound up. I dared her to turn on the light, face me." Sonya balled her fists. "I was ready to punch her in the face, kick her in the crotch. Give her a goddamn beatdown. 'Turn on the lights, you fucking coward, and we'll settle right here, right now, who's mistress of Poole Manor.'"

Revved, she bit into toast. "And I heard Clover laugh, but more . . . I think they were all down there with me. I heard them laugh. I heard them laugh, and it was mockery extreme. It was the whole damn room, full of laughter. Maybe, I think maybe, not just the brides, but more. Like the manor and everyone in it was making her a joke.

"Then the lights came on and I was ready, God, so ready, to take her on. But she wasn't there. I think I said, really snotty, 'Yeah, that's what I thought.' Then I opened the door. And you were right there," she said to Trey. "You were right there."

He gave her a long look, his deep blue eyes full of everything a woman in love needed to see. He flicked a glance at Cleo, said, "Me first."

He rose, then plucked Sonya from the stool. He wrapped around her, and with her feet inches from the floor, kissed her as if both their lives depended on it.

Head swimming, Sonya gave Trey a dreamy smile. "Maybe you should reschedule after all. For several hours."

"What you did? It was ill-advised, risky, and not just a little crazy. And I love you. I love everything about you. I freaking adore the ill-advised, risk-taking, a-little-bit-crazy woman."

He kissed her again, then set her on her feet.

"Your turn, Cleo."

"Well, I can't match that, but." She rose, hugged Sonya hard, and held on, swaying. "You, Sonya MacTavish, are an Amazon. You're a goddess. You're an evil-dead-witch destroyer. You're a motherfucking woman."

"I really wanted to punch her. I've never punched anybody in my life. I wanted her to be my first."

Clover hit it with the Queen of Soul and "Respect."

"I don't know how long I'd have trembled down there if Clover hadn't given me that boost. If they all hadn't. But there's more."

She gripped Cleo's hand, then Trey's. "If she could kill me—just take me out—she would have. She needs me to do it myself, and not a chance there. I'm not saying she can't hurt me, or any of us, but what we tossed around as a solid theory I see as a one-hundred-percent-solid fact now."

"She said the same thing to you she said to Owen about you," Trey pointed out. "No true Poole."

"Because my father wasn't chosen, because he became, and he was, a MacTavish. So am I. But that doesn't change bloodline, or DNA."

"She fears that," Cleo added. "She fears you. If she didn't before, I guarantee after your demonstration, she does now."

"Makes her more dangerous. But then?" Trey lifted a hand to Sonya's cheek. "So are you. A dangerous woman. People who are afraid, angry, lash out. Don't leave your phone on the counter."

Sonya picked it up, pushed it into the slash pocket of her yoga pants. "That's a promise. But you can go to work knowing Cleo and I aren't alone. We've got a whole tribe standing with us. And we stand with them."

"Damn right we do. Son, we're going to get those rings back."

"Count on it. I just hope I can punch her in the face first." She gave Trey's hand a squeeze. "Go to work."

When he hesitated, she let go of Cleo's hand to take both of his. "I'm not just fine, I'm seriously gloating. Feels good. And if you postpone your meeting, it takes just a little shine off the win. You were there just at the right moment, and I know you will be again. That's only one reason I love everything about you."

"You'll call if there's trouble."

"Solid promise. But I'm pretty sure we're clear for a while. She pulled out a lot of stops, and she lost. She'll need to regroup."

Because he felt the same, it eased his mind.

"And I'm going to make a celebration dinner."

He looked at Cleo. "I was going to suggest we take you out to celebrate."

"Not tonight. Let's just rub it in her face. The four of us," Cleo said, "and all the rest of us, celebrating in-house. Hell, I might just bake a cake."

"Talked me into it." He leaned down to kiss Sonya again. "Dangerous women all around. I'm going to get some coffee to go and leave you to it."

When he had, Sonya turned to Cleo. "It matters that he can do that."

"It does. It matters he believes in you enough to trust you'll handle what comes. Add that to the way he carried you downstairs, like you were so precious to him. Oh, my, my.

"Now, what the hell am I going to make for dinner?"

"Whatever it is, I'll help. And, Cleo, I'm sorry about the early-for-you wake-up call."

"I'm not. After the jolt, the rest just gave a lift to my day. Telling her she had to drug a man to get laid. I think that's my favorite."

"I really went off. Once I got started . . . I'm pretty sure I used the *c* word, and I don't mean *crazy*. I hate that word, but I'm pretty sure I used it."

"If the dildo fits."

Sonya snorted out a surprised laugh. "Cleo."

"Can't let you get ahead of me on the crude scale. I think lasagna. And we've got some tomatoes ripe, so I'll do something with them. And you know what? I'm going to try my hand at making Italian bread."

"From flour?"

"Yes, I am. And I'm baking a cake, too."

"I'll help, but that's a lot."

"I'm in the mood. Plus, Jesus, it's not even nine o'clock. Go, get your shower, get to work. I'm going to look over this bread recipe before I do the same."

"Send up a flare when you need a chopper/stirrer/fetcher."

"I'll do that."

Sonya let Pye and Yoda in. The cat leaped onto a chair to wash. Yoda followed Sonya upstairs.

Alone, Cleo laid a hand on the kitchen tablet. "Thank you. You were there for her when she was afraid. You were there before we could be. You were there to remind her how strong she is."

Clover answered with Selena Gomez's "Me & My Girls."

Sonya worked through the morning until she felt the Bayside Lotions and Potions website was ready to go live. Hogan, she thought with a smile, had ideas, and in the end, his mother and aunt let him take the lead.

He'd taken the photos himself, and done a damn good job of it, in her opinion. He'd wanted the addition of a Lotions and Potions crew drop-down, with headshots and bios. She'd tightened up the text a bit, but again, damn good job.

She'd consulted with him throughout the building, and thought, if her business continued to grow, she'd offer him an internship the next summer.

But since he'd be in school at this time of day, she contacted his mother. By phone, as texts and emails didn't always get a prompt response.

Patiently, Sonya guided Carrie to the website, explained the drop-downs, the online product ordering, and the rest.

"Take all the time you need, look it over, play with it. It's only live for you. If you see anything you want changed, added, taken off, just let me know."

"I'll do all that, but, ah, maybe let Hogan take a good look when he gets home from school."

"That's just fine. He can text me if it's a go, or if he wants to discuss anything first."

"I'm going to say, it looks really pretty. And professional. And I can see it just didn't before."

"I think you'll find it functions well, too. Not only for you, but for customers and potential customers. And venues like Gigi's can order, at their price, directly from the site, from the wholesale area. And no," she added, though she'd explained it before, "regular retail customers can't access that area. It requires a special log-in you approve."

"I don't understand all that, but Hogan does. It really looks— Oh my goodness! I clicked on something, and there's the family. Look at us!"

"You should be proud, of your family, and what you make to-gether."

"I am. I really am. This is wonderful. I'm actually tearing up. Thanks for helping talk me into this. Hogan's going to be so excited."

"Tell him I'm ready to go live when he is."

"I will. I will. Oh, just look at this! Thank you, Sonya."

"You're welcome."

Thoroughly satisfied, she hung up. "Okay, Yoda, time for a walk. And if Cleo's in the kitchen when we're done, we're on duty there. Otherwise, it's back here for me."

But the rest of the week, she decided, without a celebration dinner to help prepare, she'd start on the basement storage areas.

"Rub her face in it just a little more," she muttered.

She went out the front, threw open her arms to embrace the air, and turned a circle.

When she did, she noticed the leaves on the weeper had a blush of color instead of their summer green.

"It's happening, Yoda."

Part of her felt a pang that the summer, the really wonderful summer, had come to an end. The rest felt the tingle of anticipation. The crisper air, the glorious fall foliage, the fires crackling, the scent of woodsmoke and nights made for snuggling.

She'd experience and appreciate yet another season at Lost Bride Manor. And before long, she swore it, that name would no longer apply.

While Sonya and Yoda took their walk, Trey managed to grab a quick lunch with Owen. Since it was handy, they hit the sandwich shop and split the sub special—ham, salami, and provolone with a basket of house-made chips.

"What's the word?" Owen asked once they'd ordered. "I get something went down this morning."

"It turns out Dobbs did in the end, but I'll take you from the start."

As he did, he paused only when the server delivered their Cokes, then again when their food arrived. Poole's Bay, he knew well, enjoyed its gossip. And the manor was always a highlight.

"She's been down there with me a couple times. Not like that." Owen sprinkled some Tabasco on his sub before biting in. "But you can feel her. I don't use the streaming. I've got a routine and a playlist. But I can tell you, if I heard that shit instead of Metallica or M83 or whoever, I'd freak.

"In a manly, fuck-you sort of way," he added.

"A given, and she clearly did. She said the exercise bands hissed like snakes, dropped down, and slithered."

"My freak-out might not have been as manly."

"The lights go out, and the door won't open."

As Trey told him the rest, Owen munched on chips, sat back.

When it was done, he lifted his glass in toast. "First, you've got yourself a stand-up woman. Dobbs wanted her curled in the fetal position, screaming, and crying. Instead, she brought it. And Clover, not just a hot babe, but another stand-up. They laughed. Not just Clover, not just the rest of the brides."

"She thinks more, yeah. And Sonya's standing there." Trey raised his fists. "Ready to take her on. Dobbs does the retreat. Lights on. And I got there just as she opened the door."

He paused again, gave the server a quick smile. "No, we're good, thanks."

Waited a beat.

"God, Owen, she was so pale, shaking from the cold. I could feel the blast of cold pour out of the room when the door opened. Meat-locker cold. But she looked fierce. Just fierce."

"We need to end this. I want to make a life with her."

"You are making a life with her."

"One where she doesn't have to worry about these goddamn ambushes. Where none of us do."

It ground in his guts like broken glass.

"I see her like this morning, I see you ready to stab yourself rather than hurt her or Cleo or me. I want to go into that room and take Dobbs on, take her out. And I know that's not the way."

"Well, you can't do it your way, the lawyer way, so it's hard not to wish it were. I'm right there, too."

"I can't ask her to leave the manor, to give up her inheritance, or to desert Clover, the other brides."

"I get that, and it's another right there." Idly, Owen picked up one of the remaining chips. "I might be able to talk Cleo into giving up that studio, especially if I can promise something equal. But she'd never leave Sonya. And like Sonya, she wouldn't leave the rest."

"So that's where we are."

"Yeah. That's where we are. Until."

Trey hissed out frustration. "I can't figure a way through to the until."

"And you're used to figuring your way through. I'm not much on the whole fate business. That's Cleo's deal. But, man, I don't think we'd be where we are, and that's all four of us, unless there was a way through."

"That's what I keep telling myself." And it helped to hear it, but.

"She's darker than she was, Owen. The more they . . . lighten up the manor, the darker she gets. I think it's right, she can't do real damage to Sonya, to any of us without breaking her own curse. But."

"Yeah, I've gone there. She's a lunatic. She could lose it."

"Curse broken, but Sonya's the sacrifice. That's not going to happen."

"It's fucking not."

Owen shifted forward.

"Look, I'm going into Cleo territory again, but it feels like Sonya's made—don't ask me how, exactly—but she's made to be the one to find the way through. A Poole, but not. She's had choices from the time Deuce told her about her dad, the inheritance. She made all the choices that brought her to this point. She's going to make the ones that get through to the until."

"That's what I'm counting on."

Chapter Twenty-Four

When Sonya came back in, she didn't find Cleo in the kitchen. But she saw the top oven light on, and a bowl inside covered with a cloth.

Curious, she opened the oven door, peeked under the cloth. Then looked down at Yoda.

"Best guess? This is bread dough. Why it's in an oven, that's not turned on, but the light is, I can't say."

After she closed the oven door again, she got out a beef stick for Yoda. Like a very good boy, he sat, took it politely, then ran wildly away to enjoy it.

Grabbing a Coke for herself, she headed back to the library.

In just under an hour, Cleo came down from her studio.

"Kitchen duty?"

"It's time to punch down the bread dough. If it did what it's supposed to do. And I'm going to get the sauce on for the lasagna."

"Sounds like kitchen duty to me."

Sonya rose to join her.

"I can handle it if you're in the middle of something."

"I'm in a good spot. I picked up another book cover job, and I want to think about that one anyway. How come the dough's in the oven with the light on?"

"It said that's a good rising temperature. Now I punch it down, it rests a bit, then I divide it into three, let it rise again."

"Why?"

"I don't know. I'm just doing what I'm told. It's science, and that's not my area."

"Mine either. You don't have to know anything about carburetors or manifolds to drive a car. I don't even know exactly what they are. Any movement upstairs?"

"Not a sound. Usually there's some banging or bumping, but it's dead—get it?—dead quiet."

She gave Sonya an elbow bump as they walked into the kitchen. "You knocked her flat."

"I did, but honestly, I think the laughing was the knockout punch. Bullies hate being laughed at."

Cleo took the bowl out of the oven, set it on the counter. Crossed her fingers, and removed the cloth.

"Look at that!"

Sonya did. "It's a lot bigger than when I looked."

"Now I do this." Cleo balled a fist, punched it into the dough. "Strangely satisfying. Now while it sits, maybe recovering from the shock, you can mince the garlic for the sauce. I'm going out for herbs. Oh, and I'm baking a cake," Cleo added as she started outside. "I need a Bundt pan."

By this time in her life as kitchen assistant, Sonya considered herself an excellent garlic mincer.

When Cleo came back in, Sonya looked up. "You didn't say how many cloves."

Cleo took a look at the tidy minced pile on the cutting board. "One more. Great, you found the Bundt pan."

"I didn't . . ." Sonya saw the pan on the counter. "I didn't put that there, and that wasn't there, which still gives me a little wow. But thanks, I guess that would be Molly."

"She's a time-saver." Cleo washed her herbs, set them out on a towel to dry. "Okay, dough first. You're not supposed to tear it, but cut it in three. Don't ask me why. They make a tool for it, but until I have it, a good sharp knife does the trick."

She lifted the dough onto another cutting board, and to Sonya's eye looked at the pile of it with genuine affection.

"Slice it through," Cleo murmured as she worked, "roll each into a kind of ball, and back in the bowl. One, two, three. Cover, and back in to rise."

Once done, she set the timer.

"After this time, I shape them into like long footballs, put them on a greased, cornmeal-dusted baking pan, and let them rise again."

"Three times?"

"Yeah, how does it know to do that? It's fascinating."

After getting out a pot, she added olive oil, swished it around, then set it on the stove, turned on the heat.

"And I really liked the whole kneading process. It's meditative. You should try it."

"Maybe. Someday. With adult supervision."

In the butler's pantry, Cleo chose a bottle of red, opened it for the sauce.

"Nice mincing, by the way."

"I do have that skill."

"Use your skill on the herbs now. Chop 'em up."

Cleo added the garlic to the hot oil, gave it a stir.

She couldn't claim fascination, but found it nice, very nice, to chop up herbs they'd grown themselves, to spend some time with Cleo.

She stopped to let them out when both cat and dog wandered to the door. And that? Also nice. Having a dog, a cat, a big yard with the late summer/early fall flowers blooming.

"Herb time, Son."

"Coming right at you."

She brought over the board where she'd carefully chopped herbs into tidy, separate piles, then looked in the pot where the sauce simmered gently.

"Well, wow, that looks great."

Cleo swept all the neat piles together in the pot, stirred. "Now it looks even better. You know you can make the sauce from actual tomatoes instead of tomato paste. I'm just not ready to go that far. Yet."

Sonya's phone signaled a text.

It's Hogan—Lotions and Potions.
It's awesome! All the way extra. Go live!

Give me five minutes. Stand by.

"Got the seal of approval. I need to go up, go live with the website. Be right back."

"Take your time."

By the time she got back, Cleo had the stand mixer going and had started on her bread dough footballs.

"All right, fascination is beginning."

"Want to do one?"

"Well, maybe. Yeah, actually."

Sonya washed her hands, came back, and picked up a dough ball. After a study of the shape Cleo formed, she started.

"I actually consider Hogan the primary client, which makes him my youngest client ever. I'm thinking of offering him an internship next summer. Depending on how the business goes."

"I think that's a great idea. You've got this. I need to get back to the cake batter. You know you could do that every year with a high school or college student."

"That's a thought." Pleased with it, Sonya set the second football on the pan. "And I like it better than a full-time assistant. I really like working alone. Which is strange, I guess, since I loved working in an office, with a team. The structure," she said as she formed the third loaf.

"You've made your own structure."

As she formed a bread dough football, Sonya gave herself a mental pat on the back.

"Looks like I did. And I honestly think I'm more creative on my own. I really like bouncing around from little jobs like Hogan's, to solid accounts like Baby Mine, and hey, let's do a book cover, or bag ourselves a major, national client like Ryder Sports.

"You're the same."

"Completely. And thanks to Collin Poole, and you, I've got more freedom than ever. Taking the summer off to paint?"

Cleo paused to smile and sigh. "Just paint what I wanted, when I wanted? I can't tell you how that pumped me, and at the same time relaxed me."

"Under two weeks till your show."

"And I'm ready for it. It'll be fun. Those go in the lower oven now. I'm preheating the top for the cake. Just set the timer for twenty minutes for this last rising. It needs thirty, but I want to take it out for the last ten to preheat that oven."

Sonya carried the loaves over. "There's a bowl of water in here on the second shelf."

"It needs the steam when I bake them. And no, I don't know exactly why. I didn't want to forget, so I stuck it in there."

"Twenty minutes. Done. What else can I do?"

"Go ahead and spray the stuff in the cake pan. And you could get out the cooling rack for the bread. Oh, and you could go out, pick a couple of tomatoes, get some basil."

"Sure. What for?"

"I'm going to slice the tomatoes, put basil on them, then drizzle them with olive oil and some pepper. You could just put the basil in some water till I'm ready. It'll save me a trip."

"I'm here to serve."

She sprayed the pan, got the rack.

"Are you done with the measuring cups and all that?"

"I am now."

Sonya carried them to the sink on the way outside.

Still marveling they'd actually grown them, she plucked two fat red tomatoes, snipped basil. Sniffing both, she took them inside.

She put the basil in water. "Next?"

"You're relieved of duty."

"If you're sure, I'm going down to start poking in the basement."

Carefully pouring batter into the pan, Cleo paused and looked up. "Really?"

"I said I was in a good place, workwise. I'm going to take an hour or so to get started down there."

"Let me put the cake in, and I'll go down with you."

"Cleo, you've got bread, sauce, cake. Your current mode is kitchen goddess. And I'll be fine."

To prove it, Sonya squared her shoulders.

"She's got one room. I'm not giving her any more. Plus, she's up there sulking or brooding or whatever she does. And I have my phone."

"Clover's going with you. Right, Clover?"

She instantly answered with Bruno Mars and "Count on Me."

"See? Not alone. I'm taking a sketch pad." Sonya pulled open a drawer for one, took a pencil. "I'm going to take a good look at the area where we want that game room. Sketch out a basic layout."

To placate a little more, Sonya went to the back door. Yoda romped across the yard and into the house, and Pye followed at her leisure.

"I'll take them with me, too."

"All right. When the bread's done, I'm coming down to check. I might have some ideas about the game room."

"Fair enough."

When the oven timer dinged, Sonya walked over. "Take them out, right?"

"And set the temp to 450."

She set the baking sheet on the counter, set the oven.

"I have to peek." Then lifted the cloth. "They puffed up!"

Now Cleo had to look. "They really did! Before I put them in to bake, I score them three times diagonally across the top. I don't know why."

"They look fat and fantastic. I'm loving this celebration dinner. Just text if you need any more help."

"Everything is under control. I'll be there in about a half hour."

She waited until Sonya had walked out. "You tell me, Clover, if I need to go before that."

Sonya checked herself at the door before going down.

Not afraid, she decided. Really just not afraid.

Downstairs, she made herself go into the gym, walk around. She wouldn't give up the room, wouldn't let Dobbs ruin it for her.

Studying the line of exercise bands, she stepped closer, reached out.

Pulled back.

"Okay, we'll work on that."

The main storage area would stay the main storage area, she thought. And in a couple weeks, she'd dig out the Halloween decorations. But before that, yes, she'd do a similar hunt down here as she had in the attic, in the ballroom.

She moved through what she thought of as the downstairs world of servants and staff.

The space she'd chosen held, like the attic and ballroom, far too much. Organization would be key, which, she knew, meant organizing that main storage area in a way that made room for some of the rest.

It might mean moving some pieces to the attic, and hopefully finding others they could use upstairs.

In her mind, she emptied the space, removed everything inside it. Then slowly, began to place what worked for her through her sketch pad. She didn't consider it overconfidence to believe they'd find everything they needed—save the pool table, pinball machine, whatever other games they wanted—right in the manor.

An old jukebox, she decided. Wouldn't Clover have fun there? Keep it all as vintage as possible, at least in looks.

She heard Cleo on the stairs.

"I'm back here. It's a great space, and I don't want to make it modern and shiny. I really wish I could see it the way it was. Maybe we'll find some photos. Then I'd get a good sense, be able to pay a little homage to the staff. And wouldn't it be a kick to see Molly down here?"

"You forget how big this place is," Cleo said as she worked her way through.

"Tell me about it." Sonya turned to smile, and when she turned back, the mirror stood in front of her. "Cleo. The mirror."

"Wait! Wait for me. Don't go through."

"It's not pulling. It's not like that demand."

Moving fast, Cleo found her, took Sonya's arm.

"Cleo, it feels like . . . an invitation."

"You can say no, Sonya. Send your regrets. You've had enough for one day."

"I . . . I want to go in. It feels like welcome. Don't worry. It's never hurt me."

"I can text Owen. He'll come, go with you."

Sonya shook her head. "It's for me. It feels like it's for me. I can see movement. I can hear voices. Someone's laughing. I have to go."

"I'm texting Owen and Trey."

"Don't. Give me a few minutes first." She handed Cleo her sketch pad. "I'll be back."

She stepped through.

And into the servants' hall.

As they were now, the walls were paneled. But instead of white-draped furniture, the space held a long table. Two women in black dresses and white aprons and caps sat there, chatting away as they polished silver.

Another, older, wore gray like her hair. She sat in a chair by a small table sewing. Darning? Sonya wondered.

The older woman shook her head at the younger girls.

"You sound like a couple of chickens clucking. And over the new footman."

"He's very handsome," the girl on the right said. And they both giggled.

A man walked in, wearing a black suit, a stiff white shirt. "I'd best not see streaks or spots on that silver."

"No, sir, not a one." The one with blond hair and freckles answered respectfully, even as she slid her gaze—with a little roll of her eyes—toward her companion.

A man—no suit jacket—sat across the room polishing boots. He sent the girls a cheeky grin, then quickly lowered his head when the suited man looked his way.

"The master had enough mud on these boots to build a dam." His voice sounded British, but without the round tones of the older man. "But he'll be able to see his face to shave in them when I'm done. I can promise you that."

"See that's a promise kept."

A woman dressed in black came in, her hair in a tight, no-nonsense bun. She brought in a girl in a simple straw hat, a dark blue coat over a brown dress. Her brown boots looked well-worn but shining clean.

Under the hat, her deep red hair was held back and up in a thick roll. She had bright blue eyes, a scatter of freckles over a pretty face.

She carried a single small suitcase.

"Miss Molly O'Brian has joined the staff of Poole Manor as an undermaid. She's just arrived from Ireland. Molly, Grimes is head butler."

"Molly," Sonya murmured as the girl—sixteen at a guess—gave a little curtsy.

"Welcome to Poole Manor. We have the highest standards, and trust you'll meet them."

"Sir. Sure and it's a grand house, and I'm privileged to work in it. My best it will have, I promise you."

The woman introduced the others. Mrs. Steele, Rory Bates, Gracie, and Frances.

"I'm pleased to meet all of you."

"Grimes, I'll take Molly up to her room, then bring her down to show her the kitchen and the rest."

"As you say, Hobson."

"Come, Molly, we'll get you settled." There was a kindness in her gesture. "Then you'll meet more of the staff, and have a bite to eat. You've had a long journey."

"Aye, ma'am, that I have, and an exciting one."

"Molly," Sonya said again as Hobson led her away.

Sonya heard her say, with awe in her voice, "Never have I seen such a grand and beautiful house as this. I'll be doing my work with great pride, my word on it."

Mrs. Steele went back to her darning as Grimes followed them out. "Another clucking chicken, I wager."

"A pretty one," Rory said with a grin.

"Just off the boat, from the sound of her," Gracie commented.

"Her hat looked new," Frances noted. "But that dress. A terrible color, and you could see where it had been let down."

"And you're the fashionable one?" Mrs. Steele snapped.

Gracie stifled a giggle. "That coat won't keep out the cold once winter comes around. But she looked nice enough, and we can use another pair of hands, especially since Alice ran off."

"Alice wasn't any better than she had to be, and not often that. We'll see how this one fares."

Mrs. Steele set the darned sock aside, picked up another.

Wanting to see more, Sonya started forward. And the mirror, instead of standing behind her, blocked her way.

Now she felt a pull, this one drawing her back.

"All right, that's all I get. But it's a lot."

She moved to the glass.

"What happened?" Cleo gripped her hands. "You weren't gone two minutes."

"Really? It was longer than that in there."

"In where? No wait. Let's go up."

"Yeah, I could sit. Just a little dizzy. The servants' hall. I saw it the way it used to be. It had to be a hundred years ago. The bells on the wall, all polished up. The lamps on the wall. Gaslight? I'm not sure."

When she put a hand to her swimming head, Cleo took her arm.

"The walls were paneled, like they are now. A long table. Two maids were polishing silver. Gracie and Frances. Rory, a boy—couldn't have been twenty—in a chair polishing boots. An older woman, Mrs. Steele, across the room darning. Smaller tables and chairs. I'll know them if we find them."

She blew out a breath. "Yeah, I could sit."

"You'll sit. I'll get you some water."

With an arm around Sonya's waist, Cleo led her back to the kitchen.

"The head butler—he struck me as a stickler. Grimes. And Hobson—she seemed kind under it. I think maybe head housekeeper."

When she sat on a stool, Sonya let out another breath. "Better, already better. But Cleo, Hobson brought in another girl, young, so pretty. It was Molly."

"Molly?" Cleo hurried back with a glass of water.

"I saw her. I heard her voice. She was a teenager, still in her traveling clothes, I guess. Dark red hair, bright blue eyes. When I've seen her in her room, when she's dying . . . I didn't recognize her. You could just feel how happy and excited she was. She already loved the manor, and that was clear, too."

"That's—" Cleo dropped down on the next stool. "That's amazing and wonderful."

"It was. She was so young, so fresh, just glowing. I don't know how long she lived and worked here before she died, but I absolutely believe she was happy."

Clover used Bowie's "Five Years" to answer.

"Five years. I hope they appreciated her like we do. It was different, Cleo, than most of the other times. I wasn't pulled in, but invited. And not to see death or Dobbs. But just to see daily life in the servants' hall, and Molly's arrival at the manor. Still, coming back leaves me a little woozy."

"It has to cost you energy, doesn't it? You're actually moving through time. So, you come back a little depleted. But I swear, you were only gone about two minutes."

"Longer over there, and that's different, too. I would've been longer. I wanted to look around some more, but the mirror blocked my way, and then I felt a pull, but to come back through."

"Then you saw what you needed to see."

"Molly. The way the hall looked, but especially Molly."

"Sketch her." Cleo pushed the book over.

"Great idea. I can do that. Let me get a Coke first."

"Sit. I've got it."

"Something smells so good. Is that the bread! Wow, just wow." Three golden loaves cooled on a rack. "Talk about amazing."

"I'm feeling seriously smug about it." Cleo handed Sonya a Coke, sat back down with her own.

"You know you can never go back to the routine of takeout and delivery."

"And oddly, I'm okay with that."

"For which I'm grateful. I'm going to say Molly's about five-three, very slim. I'm guessing her hair's long," Sonya continued as she sketched. "But it was up in a roll. A heart-shaped face. She has freckles over milky skin. Pug nose, big, bright blue eyes, ah, just a little bit of an overbite."

"She's pretty. She's got a sweet look about her."

"Yes. Still a bud, you know? She hadn't bloomed yet. More girl than woman when she first came here. Imagine leaving everything at that age to come to another country."

"It takes courage."

"I was nervous leaving home for college, and it was right in Boston. She crossed an ocean."

"Now do one of her full-length, with these." Cleo pulled open a drawer, got out colored pencils. "I'm going to put the water on for the pasta."

"Is it that late?"

"I have to put the lasagna together, then it has to cook, then it needs to rest. So close enough."

"It's been a hell of a big day. I honestly believe we're getting closer to real answers."

Since Yoda sat by her stool, Sonya rubbed him gently with her foot as she drew.

"She had one suitcase, Cleo. The size I might pack for a long weekend. A new country, a new life, and she took everything from her before in one little suitcase."

"Which means something I'd pack for an overnight."

Sonya had to laugh. "Pretty much."

"I admire that." Cleo put a pot of water on to boil. "I admire her courage, what had to be a sense of adventure. And God knows her dedication to this house."

As she spoke, she got out ricotta, mozzarella.

"I wonder if she'll move on when the curse is broken. I've wondered if those who stay here, or at least some of them, are somehow caught up in that, and can't move on."

"I've wondered the same. I'd miss her." Sonya drew the hat over the dark red hair. "Not just because we don't have to even think about cleaning, or hiring a crew. But because there is that sweetness to her. You can feel it."

"You can. Okay, I'm going out for more herbs. I want to put some in this cheese mix. And yes," she said as both pets got up at the word *out*, "you can go."

Alone, Sonya did her best to put Molly's image on the page. She kept at it when Cleo came back, dealt with the herbs and cheese.

When the oven timer went off, she blinked, looked up.

"Cake's done!"

"I forgot about the cake. It really is a celebration, and now we've got more to celebrate. This is Molly. As close as I can get."

After setting the cake pan aside, Cleo came around the island to look.

"Sweet, pretty. There's a sparkle to her, and you brought that out. We're going to frame that, Son, put it in the gallery when we boot that bitch out of here."

"That— Well, I love that idea. She belongs there. I'm so glad I got to see her, to hear her. I'm going to sketch out the servants' hall, too. I'd started to sketch how I wanted it to be, and began thinking out loud how I wish I could see it the way it was, so we could pay some homage. And I wish I could see Molly in there, so . . ."

It struck, the simplicity of it struck like lightning.

"Cleo."

"You wished it, and the mirror came to grant that wish. That's a major holy shit, Sonya." She gripped Sonya's arm. "That's why it invited you, that's why it felt different. You asked for something."

"And it didn't let me go past that. It gave me a gift, but the gift had limits." Sonya rubbed a hand on her chest. "It makes me a little breathless."

"Join the crowd."

"I think I have to be careful, not abuse it. Not be frivolous. This wasn't frivolous. It was about the manor, wanting to honor it, about someone who takes such loving care of it. Now I've seen it, at least how it was in Molly's time."

"And I think that's perfect."

"So do I. We'll take that back, too, and make it a happy place. I think it was, Cleo. I think it was a happy place."

Sonya began to sketch again. "It's a really big day."

"And it's not over yet. Here comes the rest of us."

Chapter Twenty-Five

Joy burst into the room in the form of floppy-eared, tail-wagging Mookie. It was matched by a happy Yoda. Jones acknowledged both, accepted the licks and sniffs as Pye looked on with dignity. The wrestling match started quickly.

"Okay, boys and girl." Trey set a bottle of champagne on the island before walking to the door. "Take it outside."

"You brought champagne."

"We figured outmatching a crazy dead witch earned the bubbly. Kudos," Owen added.

"Since you're filled in on that, I have to say: But wait, there's more."

Trey paused in the act of lowering his head to kiss her. "She came at you again?"

"No." She curled her finger. "And when you finish that thought, I'll tell you." She rose on her toes to meet his lips.

"Is the champagne on hold, or am I popping it?" Owen asked.

"Oh, definitely popped."

"Great. And something smells amazing in here."

"Several things," Cleo told him. "I need a cake plate. Son, champagne flutes."

"On that. Pop that baby, and we'll get this started."

The dumbwaiter motored its way from the basement. Sonya immediately thought of red-eyed rats.

"I've got it. And the glasses."

"It's going to be a cake plate. From Molly. That's what it's going to be." But Sonya kept her distance.

"And that's what it is." Trey took out a white pedestal dish with a glass dome.

"That's perfect." Cleo took the plate as Owen released the cork with a muted pop. "You can always count on Molly."

"You can." Sonya waited until Owen poured all the glasses, then lifted hers. "And here's to Molly, the magnificent housekeeper of Poole Manor."

She sipped, then beamed. "I saw her today. I saw her, heard her voice—a lovely, musical Irish voice. I saw Grimes, the head butler when Molly first arrived from Ireland, and Hobson, the head housekeeper, Mrs. Steele, in charge of laundry. I saw Rory—not sure of his position—and two maids, Gracie and Frances."

"You talked to them?"

She shook her head at Trey. "No, I was the ghost."

"Took a trip through the mirror," Owen said.

"Yes, but not like the other times. I was downstairs. I wanted to take another look at where I want the game room, get an idea of exactly what I want, how I want it. Cleo was just coming down—taking a break from creating a magnificent feast—and I was wishing out loud that I could see that space the way it had been so we could, well, pay homage. And wouldn't it be great if I could see Molly in there."

She took another sip, gestured with her glass. "Here's what happened."

Once she'd taken them through it, she opened the sketchbook. "This is Molly, the day she came to the manor."

"Cute kid," Owen said.

"Yes, a very pretty girl. Clover let us know she worked here for five years before she died. I know she was happy here. She loved the manor."

"And she still does," Trey murmured. "The mirror came to you."

"Yes, and like I said, it wasn't like the other times. I had a choice, and it felt good."

She lifted her glass, sipped again.

"It felt as if I was being invited. I wanted it, and it gave me a choice because it wasn't something I had to see, but wanted to see. But only that much. When I thought I'd look around more, it blocked the way. I got my wish, but that was it."

"And on this side," Cleo added, "it was two or three minutes, tops."

"At least ten, and I think a little more over there. It was a good space, so clean and well-appointed. Lamps lit, a fire simmering low, comfortable-looking chairs, the servants' bells all shining."

"You were still a little shaky when you came back."

"But not for as long, Cleo. And I think you're right about it sucking up some of my energy. Anyway, it was an amazing experience."

"You want to do it again."

She looked at Trey. "I do, but I think—or feel, anyway—that it has to matter. Not just a whim. Today, it was because I wanted to do something for the manor, and wanted to see someone who does so much."

"It could be a conduit to the rings."

"Maybe, and I'm hoping maybe. But I don't want to make a mistake and screw it all up."

"You need to wait for Astrid's portrait." Owen shrugged. "You need all seven, or why the space for the seventh portrait?"

"Manor logic," Trey muttered. "Yeah, that fits. So we wait. And if you find it when we're not here?"

"We tell you, then and there," Sonya finished. "And wait for both of you. All of us hang Astrid's portrait together."

"Not just manor logic," Cleo put in as she checked on the lasagna. "Common sense. About five more on the lasagna."

"You made lasagna. And a cake. Where'd you get the bread?"

Smiling at Owen, Cleo mimed kneading dough. "From yeast and flour and so on."

He wrapped an arm around her waist, yanked her in for a long kiss. "Lafayette, when the time comes, I'm going to build you one hell of a kitchen."

"And butler's pantry. I've gotten used to having one."

"Seriously?"

"Completely."

"I'll make a note."

Sonya let out a sigh. "This has been a beautiful day. A really big, beautiful day."

They extended it with Cleo's celebration dinner.

After his second helping of lasagna, Owen looked at her. "It's a good thing you've got another job or I'd be building you a restaurant."

"This was fun. I don't think a restaurant would be nearly as much fun as cooking for family."

"Grateful family," Trey added. "Everything was terrific."

"Why don't we walk some of the terrific off?" Sonya suggested. "I'd really like to show you what I have in mind downstairs."

With the pets joining in, they went down.

"This is how it looked." Again, Sonya opened her sketchbook. "I think all the lights, the lamps, the wall sconces, were gaslight. Whenever they put in electricity, they changed the fixtures."

"You don't want to go back to gaslight," Trey said. "Just something that reflects that era?"

"Exactly. I want that vibe. The floors are in really good shape, and so's the wall paneling. I like style. Actual wood panels. I'd put art up there, and leave the bells."

"Get down to the reason." Owen put his hands in his pockets. "Screen for the gaming. Best place for the pinball."

"Pool table where they had their big, long table. It was bigger and longer than a regulation pool table. Screen, sofa, a couple of chairs over there. Pinball, jukebox over there."

"Jukebox." Owen flashed a grin. "Now we're talking."

"Card/board game table and chairs there, cabinet for games, shelves for display."

"You can probably come up with the rest of the furniture from inventory."

Cleo pointed at Trey. "I'm with you on that. Let's do a quick pass down here. We can always go through the attic again, but there's more down here. I'm not saying the Pooles were hoarders, but they sure didn't let go easy."

"Let's backtrack a minute. Do you know anything about vintage pinball?" Owen asked.

"No."

"That's going to be our thing, me and Trey."

"You can trust us," Trey assured her. "I know a guy."

"He knows a guy," Owen verified.

"Friend of my dad's. He used to own a bowling alley back when, and he still has a bunch of old machines. He restores them, repairs them—like a hobby now. He's got Gorgar."

"And that's what I'm talking about."

Sonya looked from Owen's happy face to Trey's. "Who or what is Gorgar?"

"The first voice-synthesized pinball machine. I've already tapped him. It'll be ready when you are."

"Happy to take that off my list."

"He might have, or have a line on, vintage jukeboxes."

"I can cross that off, too, if so."

"You might put a foosball table over there." Owen gestured. "Because, really, what's a game room without foosball?"

"Sadly lacking, obviously. I'll add that on."

They went through as a group, separated, wandered. The house always held more than Sonya remembered. But nothing seemed quite right to her until she uncovered another area.

"Well, God, these are the chairs! These are the chairs that were around the long table. Look, look at my sketch!"

Trey looked over her shoulder. "Yeah, they are."

"I see six, no, seven. There were more, and maybe they're still here. But we could put four of them around the table, store the others for when or if we have more people. They'll go back where they were. That's just what I wanted to do."

"There's a nice chair here—if you wanted something like this. Fabric's worn some," Cleo added. "But you know, Son, it looks like one of the two you had in the sketch."

Sonya worked her way over. "Cleo! It's the one Mrs. Steele was sitting in. There were two flanking a table with a globe lamp on it. This is her chair."

Owen stepped over. "The fabric's worn on the arms." He gave the cushion a push, sat a minute. "Pretty sure that's horsehair."

"We could have it redone. If we find the other, we could have them redone. New fabric, new cushioning. It's in good shape."

"You've got this sofa drawn in over here." Trey tapped the sketch, frowned. "I think I've seen that before, somewhere."

"If we can find it, we can put it over in the gaming section, flanked with the chairs, add a coffee table, buy a TV, and that's perfect."

They went back to the hunt.

"Here's the other chair." Owen signaled. "I'm guessing when they shut the place down, they just pushed everything wherever down here. The table in your sketch? No way that's hiding down here, so that's something they must've gotten rid of. Too bad. I'd like to've seen how it was made."

"Stains on this one. But we can pick a pretty fabric, Sonya. Something with the same feel."

"It's a game room," Owen reminded her. "No going too pretty."

"There, you have to trust us," Sonya told him as she studied the chair. "This is just what I hoped for, and more? I think it's what we're meant to do. Do you know a guy, or gal, who reupholsters?"

"Got me there. I'll ask Mom. And here's that sofa. I knew I'd seen it."

Owen studied it. "Fabric's toast, cushions are crap. But it's got good bones."

"That's settled. We get them fixed, put them back into use. This is honoring what came before."

"And when it's done?" Cleo continued. "Ownership of another room."

"We've been down here about an hour, I'd say." Trey stepped back over, glanced toward the bells. "Not one ring. Good job today, cutie."

"And that's what we'll keep doing. Let's see if we can find the right coffee table. Then, I say, it's time for cake."

After Owen found exactly what she wanted, they decided to have cake and cappuccino on the lawn. As the night ran cool, both Sonya and Cleo grabbed jackets.

Then everyone, pets included, sat and watched the half-moon shine over the rolling sea.

Sonya leaned her head against Trey's shoulder. "Best celebration dinner ever."

She ended her big day in his arms, not just content, but energized. Dobbs would strike again, she had no doubt, but Sonya felt, truly felt, the momentum—and the light—were theirs now.

"I wonder if, when this is done and she's gone, if Carlotta can move on. How many others can and will. But I hope she can instead of spending her nights in the nursery, weeping."

"You could reclaim that room."

She snuggled in against him. "Not until she has that choice. It doesn't feel right. I don't know why, exactly, since it felt right to fix up Molly's room, and the others. I just hope, when we have the rings, Carlotta can move on. Or if she stays, the grief doesn't."

"I think, like you do, she'll at least have the choice."

"And that's enough." Closing her eyes, she felt his heartbeat, steady, under her hand. "If I need to walk tonight, stay close, will you?"

"Always. I love you, Sonya."

"Knowing that? I feel like I can do anything."

When the clock sounded three, she slept through the weeping and the music and the murmurs.

He didn't. Trey lay awake, imagining Dobbs leaping off the wall. Imagining a time when that leap would be her last.

More leaves began to turn in a slow waltz from summer to fall. Blushes of color, a striking splash of it here and there, all hinting at the symphony to come.

As the air cooled, it brought a freshness with it. In the mornings,

Sonya found her bedroom fireplace simmering. By the time she settled to work, the library fire crackled.

Sonya considered the occasional door slams, window slams, doorbell bonging, bell ringing as Dobb's pique, and found she didn't mind it at all.

In fact, she decided on amusement.

She prepared herself for whatever came next from that quarter, but refused to dwell on it.

Instead, she worked through those last days that blended summer with fall. She carved out time to finalize her plans for the game room. Through Corrine, she found an upholsterer.

Maddy Black turned out to be a cousin of Lucy Cabot, who'd fostered Mookie, Jones, Yoda, and Pye.

A woman on the far side of fifty, she had deep brown eyes behind red-framed glasses. She wore her gray-streaked brown hair in a single thick braid down her back.

Her Birkenstock boots showed considerable wear, as did her Levi's. A collection of colorful braided bracelets decorated her right wrist, and dangles of moons and stars—and a curve of three red studs—her ears.

She had a trio of chains around her neck, each bearing a crystal.

When Sonya greeted her at the door, Yoda immediately fell in love.

"Well, look at you! Do you remember me?" Maddy hunkered down to rub and stroke. "I met you for about five minutes one day at Lucy's. She said you'd found a good home."

Maddy looked up at Sonya. "I don't remember what his name is."

"He's Yoda."

"Of course he is."

"I really appreciate you coming to take a look at the furniture."

"That's what I do. And I start off repeating what I told you on the phone. It's usually cheaper to buy new. I'm all for restoring, but I want the customer to know."

"I do. But these pieces have been in the manor for generations. I want to give them a fresh look and purpose."

"That's what I like to hear." Maddy straightened up, looked around.

"I've never actually been in here before. It's all I've heard and a bushel of apples. Nothing like a good old house, is there? All that character, all that history, all those lives lived."

"That's exactly how I feel."

"I didn't really know your uncle very well, but Corrine set store by him, and she's a good judge. Sets store by you, too."

"I hope so, because she's wonderful."

"She's that, and no one to trifle with. Look what you've got here."

Hands on hips, Maddy looked into the main parlor. "Beautiful pieces, and well tended to. These aren't what you want redone."

"No, those pieces are downstairs. They've been in storage for . . . I don't know how long."

"Let's take a look."

"We'll go up to go down. Through the servants' door."

As they started up, Maddy continued to look around with approval, and stopped, hands on hips, when Sonya opened the servants' door.

"There's something you don't see every day."

"There's a whole world down here. Collin remodeled some of it—put in a home gym, a home theater," she continued as they went down. "I want to keep that going. I'm doing a game room in what was the servants' hall."

"My, my. It just keeps going, doesn't it?"

"It does. We pulled out the three pieces so they're not as tricky to get to. The sofa and the two chairs."

With a long *Mmmmm*, Maddy walked over to examine the sofa first. She walked around it, poked, prodded, got down to study the frame.

"This is going to be horsehair."

"So I'm told."

"I'm going to tell you something else." She turned to one of the chairs, did the same examination. "You're a smart girl, and one that hits me where I live. They don't build them like this anymore, and that's a fact. Preserving these? Not just decor, not just something to sit on, but history. Imagine the butts that have sat on these over the decades?"

Standing, she nodded. "They're beautiful, and we can make them good as new while keeping that history. I'm going to get measurements."

As she reached into her huge bag, pulled out her tape measure, the Gold Room bell rang, and rang, and rang.

Maddy glanced over. "Somebody want something?"

"Somebody would prefer nothing changes in the manor. I assume you know the legend. The Lost Bride Manor legend."

"Except for a few years of wanderlust, I've lived in Poole's Bay all my life. Not everybody agrees on all the details, but everybody knows about Lost Bride Manor."

"That's Hester Dobbs." Sonya nodded toward the bells. "She stays, well, pissed off."

"Is that so?" Maddy fingered the crystals around her neck. "Doesn't seem to bother you much."

"I've had my moments. If you'd rather, I can have the pieces brought to you."

Maddy shoved up her glasses, as they'd slid a bit down her nose.

"During my wanderlust, when I was, oh, twenty-two or so? I worked in housekeeping at this castle hotel in Scotland. A genuine castle, not a place built to look like one. It was full of ghosts." She shrugged, started measuring. "We learned to coexist.

"I tended bar for a while in an Irish pub, lived in the flat over it. You haven't lived until you share space with drunk Irish ghosts. And damn if one of them—they called him Seamus—didn't leave the toilet seat up every blessed night."

Sonya laughed with real appreciation. "I'm glad to say we don't have a Seamus type here."

With her tape, and an app on her tablet, Maddy measured, calculated, measured, and calculated.

"All right. I'll go out and get my sample books out of my truck."

"Why don't we do the selections in the kitchen? I'll get my housemate. Would you like coffee?"

"I never turn it down. You know it's not just that Dobbs, don't you? This place is full of spirits."

As Maddy started to put her tablet away, it played "We Are Family."

"My grandmother," Sonya explained. "Clover. She runs the house music. She was married to Charlie Poole, and died after giving birth to my father and uncle."

"I've heard something about that recently. How she married young Charlie, then the old bat, Patricia Poole, gave one baby away, kept the other as Gretta's kid. That was Collin. My mother knows Gretta some—I guess everybody around here of a certain age knew her some. Strange woman."

Having Maddy take it all in stride made everything easier. When she went out to the truck, Sonya texted Cleo.

With the sample books on the table, Sonya made introductions.

"Beautiful crystals," Cleo said.

"I'll say the same. Is that black tourmaline?"

"It is. My grandfather gave it to my grandmother, and she gave it to me."

"We're having coffee, Cleo."

"I could use some. Juggling work," she said with a smile for Maddy.

"I hear that. You're the one having the art show at Bay Arts this weekend. I plan to come by. Tried my hand at fine art once. Well, tried my hand at most everything. Nothing stuck until I started working with fabric and furniture."

She sat.

"Well, you said nothing modern so I don't have to talk you out of that. More Victorian patterns for the chairs, a solid for the sofa to coordinate. Maybe some pillows."

"That's exactly right."

As Sonya got the coffee, Cleo sat, opened a sample book at random. "These are lovely. This isn't going to be easy, Son. We have a lot that would work, and this is only one book."

"If you let me know a budget, I can whittle the choices down for you."

"I'm not thinking budget yet," Sonya told her. "I want to see what strikes us. And I'd love something that picks up what was, if you know what I mean. It doesn't have to be a match, just . . ."

"You want to honor what was."

"I think Maddy gets us, Son."

Marianne Faithfull sang from the kitchen tablet. "File It Under Fun from the Past."

"I bet she keeps you entertained" was Maddy's opinion. "I got something here. It's on the high side."

Maddy picked up another book, flipped through samples.

Sonya brought the coffee to the table, and as she set it down, beamed.

"Not hard after all. That's just it. It's not exact, but it echoes. I love the rich bold colors here. The deep green, the purple, just hints of cream, almost like a tapestry. Nothing floral, just rich and bold."

"Well, I love it. And dare I say we go bold? Purple couch."

"Purple couch!" Sonya hooted out a laugh. "Who does that? We do!"

"Victorian era liked its bold colors and patterns. Still," Maddy added, "you might want to look at more choices before you decide."

"And we will," Sonya assured Maddy. "But I don't think we'll top this."

In the end, they went back to the beginning, and went bold.

"It's a game room," Sonya said. "It's for fun. And we're honoring its past with the pattern on the chairs."

"I can promise you, it'll be striking. And I'm looking forward to working with this fabric. So let's talk cushions."

They talked cushions and pillows.

With all decisions made, and the cost tallied, Sonya sat back.

"It's just exactly what we want, isn't it, Cleo?"

"Honestly? Couldn't be better."

"You do custom window treatments, bed coverings and so on, don't you, Maddy?"

"I do."

"We don't need anything like that—yet. But after Corrine recommended you, I took a look at your website."

Maddy frowned into her second cup of coffee. "Corrine warned me about you."

Laughing, Sonya lifted her shoulders. "You're going to make those three pieces beautiful, functional, and uniquely ours. I can do the same for your social media and marketing. Just give it some thought."

Clover went obvious with Bachman-Turner Overdrive and "Takin' Care of Business."

And made Maddy laugh. "Okay, that's a good one. My kids have been at me about my out-of-date website. So I will think about it. Meanwhile, I'm going to order this fabric, and I'll let you know when it's time for us to pick up the sofa and chairs. This has been a pleasure." She glanced toward the tablet. "And an experience. I do enjoy an experience."

When she rose, they rose with her.

"I'll do my best to get them done by the first week in December, but that's going to depend on how soon I can get the materials."

"We won't hold you to that date. But I'm going to get to work on the rest of the room so we're ready for you when you're done. We'll help you carry all this back out."

"I appreciate it. You've got a really special home here. I like knowing some of my work's going into it."

After they'd waved her off, they stood together in the breeze while Pye and Yoda wandered.

"Here's something I never thought I'd say. Cleo, we're going to have a purple couch."

"I love it. And I think I'm a little in love with Maddy."

"She worked in a haunted Scottish castle in her twenties, and in a haunted Irish pub."

"Now I know I'm a little in love. Oh, Son, look at our tree. It's that gorgeous golden orange, nearly at peak. This weekend, next week for sure, I'll start painting it in its fall colors."

"And tomorrow, I'm going to help you hang your first show in Poole's Bay. It won't be the last, but this is the first."

She wrapped an arm around Cleo's waist.

The window of the Gold Room shot open with a boom like thunder. Sonya shoved a hand in her pocket, closed it over the stone.

What flew out wasn't the huge bird, but a bolt of lightning, black as midnight, that shot like an arrow into the ground, where it snapped and sizzled. For a moment, the world shook.

And the air turned fetid with the stench of sulfur.

"Jesus." Now Sonya gripped Cleo's hand. "That's new."

"She could've hit the pets."

"But she didn't. They're right here with us." But shaken, Sonya reached down to pick up Yoda as Cleo did the same with Pyewacket.

"She's just evil, Sonya. Just fucking evil."

"Evil, but limited. Look over there. Where that bolt hit? The grass should be scorched. At the very least. But it's not. She wants to scare us, and good job there. But she can't scare us off."

Lowering her head, Sonya kissed Yoda's nose. "And we'll all be here, Cleo, after she's gone. Whatever it takes."

"You're goddamn right. I've been working on something in the studio. I'd like you to come up and see it. I think it's finished."

"Your secret project? You understand my exceptional willpower? I haven't even snuck a peek all this time."

"I count on that." After giving the cat a snuggle, Cleo put her down. "So let's go have a reveal."

Chapter Twenty-Six

The minute they closed the door behind them, the doorbell bonged. After one quick jolt, Sonya just rolled her eyes.

"That's what they call weak sauce. Anyway, is this painting going in your show?"

"No. Not for sale."

"Now I'm even more curious."

As they passed the servants' door, it swung open, and the bell below rang, rang, rang.

Cleo simply shut the door and kept going. "She does that one a lot when you're working and I'm going up or down."

"I liked that Maddy just shrugged it all off. She goes on the invitation list for the holiday party."

"Absolutely. You know she's going to check out your work, talk to some of your village clients. And she's going to get back to you about redoing her website."

"I'm not going to say a hundred percent, but I give it a ninety-five."

As they reached the third floor, doors swung open, slammed shut.

"Does she do that a lot, too?"

"Off and on. Mostly it's just banging around. Like that," Cleo added when the slams and thuds issued from the Gold Room. "Plus, I don't think she likes it when we're up here together."

"Then I'll have to come up more often."

They stepped into the studio, where the turret windows opened to sea and sky.

"Look, rain's coming. You can actually see it, like a wall sliding over the water. I get too caught up in work, and don't look out the library windows often enough. But I hear the ocean, and wonder how I ever worked without that sound."

She turned to the easel. "You still have it covered."

"I wasn't sure if you'd bring Maddy up. Whenever I worked on it, I told Clover it was a surprise, and asked her not to look."

Clover joined in with Soundgarden's "She Likes Surprises."

"Good, because here it is."

Cleo took a breath, held it—a sign, Sonya knew, that meant an important moment.

She removed the cover.

"Oh my God. Oh, Cleo. Oh my God."

Because her heart had leaped into it, Sonya crossed her hands over her throat.

"It's—it's—I need a minute."

The seven brides stood, shoulder to shoulder in their bridal white, on the lush green lawn. Flowers spread like a carpet at their feet. Behind them, the manor rose majestically into a deep and dreamy blue sky with wispy hints of soft white clouds.

Astrid, her body angled slightly to the right, held Catherine's hand. Catherine, lips curved, had a hand on Marianne's arm while Marianne's hand lay on Agatha's wrist.

They formed a unit, all connected. Agatha's hand on Lisbeth's shoulder, Lisbeth's hand in Clover's, Clover's and Johanna's arms linked.

The light illuminated their faces, and those faces held joy; they held life.

The wedding dresses seemed to shimmer. Seven rings sparkled.

"Cleo. Cleopatra. I'm groping for words, and I can't find any worthy of this. It's beyond beautiful. It's magical. It's glorious."

Tears clogged her throat, then she turned, wrapped around her friend, and pressed her face to Cleo's shoulder.

"I couldn't finish until we had Catherine's portrait. So I could see her, the details. I wanted to give them this moment of beauty and strength and solidarity."

"You're such a treasure to me. That you'd think of this. That you'd do this."

Clover said thank you through the Beatles and "In My Life."

"Yeah." Sonya swiped at tears. "We're so glad you're in our lives."

After kissing both Cleo's cheeks, she stepped back. "It's beautiful work, you know that. Every detail, Cleo. Every detail of the dresses, and the flowers at their feet from their bouquets."

"I wanted them physically connected to each other, and the rings part of it. But the flowers are symbolic so I spread them out there."

"And Clover married Charlie in a meadow. Sisters. Under it all they're sisters."

"Like we are. It's yours, Sonya. Yours and theirs and the manor's."

"Cleo. There I go again." This time she let the tears roll. "*Thank you* doesn't cover it."

"Living here gave me a summer of painting. Through you I met Owen, and I love the holy hell out of that man. I learned to cook and garden, and more, found out I'm good at both and like it. I'd say we're more than even."

"This means so much. I know we can't frame it yet, but it could finish drying on the wall in the music room, across from the seven portraits."

"I was hoping we'd have that same take on that. After we have Astrid."

The doorbell sounded again, doors slammed. What sounded like a wrecking ball hit the wall so the whole room shuddered.

Sonya gripped Cleo's hand. "She really hates it."

"I take that as the highest compliment."

"Is it safe here? Are they safe here?"

"I've used every trick my grand-mère gave me, and added more."

As she spoke, something screamed, something shrill, inhuman.

A shadow, huge and dark, swept by the windows, and screamed again.

It circled, the wide-winged bird, and eyes gleaming red, flew straight at the window.

Still gripping Cleo, Sonya stumbled back. Instinctively, she threw up a hand to protect her face as the creature slammed into the glass that had the half turret shaking.

It left an ugly smear of red-streaked black on the glass.

Cleo closed her free hand over her tourmaline. "It's circling again."

"I see it. It's stronger than it was before. If it breaks the glass . . ." She pulled the stone out of her pocket. "Will this be enough?"

She couldn't quite swallow the scream when it bashed into the glass again. It held there a moment, wings all but blocking out the sky, eyes gleaming, its razor-edged beak opening and closing as if to speak.

Then once again it circled.

"It's going to try again. We'll take the painting, go out—"

Where? Sonya asked herself as a glance behind showed her fog creeping on the floor in the hall outside the studio.

They braced for the next attack. The rain washed in from the sea, gusting hard in the wind.

And the bird went to smoke.

For a moment, a long, breathless moment, everything shook, walls, windows, floor, ceiling.

In the sudden scream of silence, they heard shouts, running feet, wildly barking dogs.

"Up here!" Because her voice trembled, Sonya called again. "We're in the studio. We're okay."

Dogs went streaking by to set up a din of barks and growls at the Gold Room door. Owen and Trey rushed in behind them.

Pride didn't stop Sonya from burrowing in Trey's arms.

"It was that bird, that horrible bird."

"We saw it hit the windows." Holding her, he looked over her head at the smears on the glass. "What the rain doesn't take care of, we will."

"No cracks." Owen held Cleo against him as he examined the glass. "We could hear it hit, like a freaking bomb, but no cracks in the glass. Your protection voodoo works, Lafayette."

"I'm going to do it all again, to make sure it keeps working. That wasn't weak sauce, Son."

"Not this time. She's been doing some of her usual," Sonya explained. "Making noise. Add a bolt of lightning that wasn't really.

And then she brought out bigger guns. Mixed metaphor. I'm a little shaken up."

"I wonder why." Trey kissed her forehead as the dogs, and Pye, hurried in. "I think that's all she's got for now. You're okay."

She appreciated he'd made it a statement.

"I bet this is what set her off. Holy shit, Cleo."

"I'll second that." Trey stepped over to the painting. "This is . . . just a lot of wows. They're together. A wall of together. If you're putting this in the show, I'm putting in a preemptive bid."

"It's Sonya's. It's Astrid's, Catherine's, Marianne's, Agatha's, Lisbeth's, Clover's, Johanna's. It's the manor's."

Owen turned her. "Come here, gorgeous."

When he'd finished kissing her, Trey brushed him aside. "I'm seconding that, too."

Cupping Cleo's chin in his hand, he brushed his lips on hers.

"I have to say, all this? Especially that." Sonya gestured toward the painting. "Seriously overshadows the fact we're getting a purple couch."

Owen's expression caught between appalled and stunned. "A what?"

"Game room? Purple?" Trey managed to look less of both, but not by much. "Seriously?"

"You're going to love it."

"You'd think that," Owen muttered.

"And we'll tell you all about it, but I want a glass of wine. It's been anther really big damn day."

On the way out, Sonya checked the closet.

"I guess it's not going to get any bigger. Maybe tomorrow."

The next morning ran on routine until Sonya shut down to help Cleo pack and load paintings into what she still thought of as Collin's truck.

"I appreciate this, Son. Kevin and I could handle it, but you've got a really good eye on placement."

"I love being part of it. It's all so much fun. And tonight, I just know you're going to pack people in."

"Either way, I'm good. I got to paint my way through the summer, and now I get to show my summer off. Kevin's keeping the show up for two weeks."

On the last trip out, Sonya paused at the door. "Jack, I'm counting on you, and everybody, to look after Yoda and Pye."

The answer came in the sound of a bouncing ball, and Yoda scrambled toward the back of the house.

"And that takes care of that."

With the last paintings loaded, Sonya got behind the wheel. "Okay, it's been a while, but I remember how to do this. I think. I hope."

She remembered well enough to get them into town and parked behind Bay Arts.

Kevin hustled out to meet them. "We've had people calling or stopping by since we opened. Those flyers, Sonya, they've really worked. I'm going to pick up more wine. We've already cleared other art off the walls."

He all but bubbled as they began to unload.

"This is turning into our biggest event since our May Day. I hope you don't mind me saying that having one of the ladies of Lost Bride Manor featured hasn't hurt."

"How could I mind? That's who we are, right, Son?"

"That's just who we are."

It took time, and more time, as Sonya was fussier about placement than either the artist or Kevin.

"I'd thought to intersperse seascapes, still lifes, the landscapes, and so on."

"So had I." Lips pursed, Cleo watched Sonya hang another. "But she's right, Kevin. There's a flow to it this way. I'd worried grouping like this would be boring, too much the same."

"You don't do boring," Sonya said, and stepped back. "And you never paint the same thing twice. There's always different movement or light or focus. These? The studies of Poole's Bay from different angles, the individual buildings like the old school—and future museum? They tell a story. Just like the lighthouse studies, your floral work."

She scanned the result, nodded. "Okay, seascapes, marina, the man and boy sailing."

She pointed. "Let's start there."

Cleo smiled at Kevin. "She's right again."

When they finished, Cleo took a turn behind the wheel, and a satisfied Sonya settled back.

"You'd have done it the way I did. You'd have seen the flow."

"Maybe, but I didn't have to. I could just have fun with it."

"Aren't you even a little nervous?"

"I'm really not. This is icing, Son. It's just delicious icing. I'm going to put on something boho, I think, do some glam makeup, and have nothing but a good time. If anything sells, that's the sprinkles on the icing."

"I have a feeling you're going to enjoy a lot of sprinkles."

When they arrived at the manor, they were surprised to see Owen's truck and Trey's car.

"I didn't think they'd be this early. We've got more than two hours."

"I hope they brought food, or don't expect me to throw anything together beyond some stir-fry. I need about half of what we've got to get my boho on."

Cleo pulled into the garage, turned off the truck, then nodded in satisfaction. "If we need to drive this thing during the winter, we've got it."

"I used to think of it as just a big bastard. Now it's a big, beautiful bastard."

The dogs ran around to greet them. Pye more sashayed, then noting who'd arrived, just wound her way toward the front door.

When they went inside, Clover hit it with "The Boys Are Back in Town."

"Since you're going boho, I'm going for a contrast—simple, subtle," Sonya said as they walked through the house toward the kitchen. "Boots?"

"Definitely."

"Me, too. I can be sorry summer's done, but never sorry when that means boots."

Sonya sniffed the air. "Smell that?"

"I do. Something's cooking."

When they stepped into the kitchen, they found Owen at the stove, Trey at the island.

"Men at work," Sonya declared.

"We figured you didn't have time to cook, so we decided to." Trey pushed off the stool to kiss her. "Or he's cooking. I'm chopping."

"It's pasta with that vodka sauce. I've got it down." Owen stepped back as Cleo leaned over the pot.

"Looks like you do. Thoughtful." She kissed him. "Thank you."

"How'd the load-in go?"

"Smooth, thanks to Sonya's good eye. Any activity?"

"A couple of doors slamming when I got here," Trey told her. "By the time Owen came in, nothing."

While Sonya fed the pets, Cleo set the table.

Teamwork, Sonya thought. The four of them had that down, too.

They settled down to salad, pasta, and red wine.

"You should know Ace has made some serious progress on the museum project."

"I do know." Sonya scooped up some penne. "We've been emailing. We've got an architect and an engineer on board. Once they've drafted plans, designs, we take that to the village council, and go through that process. Then hold a community meeting where fingers will be crossed that people like the idea, and the design."

"The idea, they'll go for it," Owen said as he ate. "Agreeing on the design, expect some back-and-forth. But? You've got an Ace in your pocket."

"Sonya should design the signage. You paid attention," Cleo added to Owen and tapped a finger on the side of her plate.

"To you, Lafayette? It's hard not to. And you're right about the signage."

"I don't want to push in."

"You wouldn't be," Trey said quickly. "It's what you do. They'll need a website, social pages, the works. I know Ace assumes you'll take that on."

"I would. I will if the town leaders agree. Ace and I have already talked about building a site to follow the remodeling, and help generate fundraising. But one step at a time."

"Now you sound like the lawyer."

Sonya laughed at Owen. "He must be rubbing off. Ace told me he and Paula will be there tonight."

"He wouldn't miss it. My mom and dad, too. And depending, Anna and Seth and Fiona at least want to drop by."

"Gonna have a packed house." Owen went back for seconds. "A lot of the Pooles will show. A lot of buzz about the artist lady up at the manor."

"Then I'd better not disappoint them."

"You've made a place in the community, you and Sonya. It counts." Trey lifted his glass to both of them. "Some will come to support that, and Kevin, and some will come out of curiosity—and for free wine and finger food. Either way, you'll have a crowd."

"More sprinkles. She's not nervous," Sonya explained. "The show's icing, and sales are sprinkles."

Trey polished off his pasta. "You may end up in a sugar coma before it's done."

After dinner, they went up to change. Sonya came out of the shower to find her dark green dress—cowl-neck, long sleeves—laid out and paired with her black stacked-heel boots.

"You must've heard me, and this is perfect. I honestly wonder what I did without you, Molly."

The bedroom fire simmered low, and as she dressed, Clover boosted her ego with Roy Orbison's "Oh, Pretty Woman."

"I feel that way, too. Now, Cleo? She'll be just ravishing. I don't have to hope she shines tonight because she will. But I admit it, I'm nervous. Art's so personal, and hers is so much a part of who she is. I just want everyone to love it."

She studied herself in the mirror. She'd given her hair some curl for what she thought of as a touch of festive, added her braided hoop earrings. And she'd wrapped Clover's beads around her wrist as a bracelet for that emotional connection.

"Job done. I'll go check on Cleo."

She walked down the hall, knocked. "It's Sonya."

"Come on in. About done."

Cleo's fire simmered as well as she stood, putting on her earrings—long dangles with multiple strands of crystals.

"All right. Nail. Hit. Head."

Cleo gave her head a little shake, watched the crystals catch the lamplight. "I think so. Molly and I consulted, and I think we hit the mark."

Curving patterns of old gold and silver covered the copper field of the dress with its swinging mid-calf skirt. Soft boots in the same copper hue laced to under the hem. In addition to the black tourmaline, she'd added silver chains.

The tones made her skin glow against the wild glory of her hair.

"And you?" Cleo turned toward her. "Perfect. The ladies of the manor are styling tonight."

Doors slammed, the doorbell bonged. The window glass shook.

"Oh, up your butt with a cactus," Sonya snapped, and made Cleo laugh like a loon. "It's your night." Reaching out, she hooked her arm with Cleo's. "She's not spoiling a second of it."

Cleo grabbed her purse off the bed as they headed out.

Trey and Owen rose from their seats in the parlor as they came down.

Owen shook his head. "Talk about hot babes."

"Poole's Bay may not be ready for the pair of you."

"They'll have to get ready." Sonya took Trey's hand. "'Cause here we come."

She bent to scrub at whatever pet came to hand. "We should be home by ten, maybe ten-thirty. Be good."

The lights of Bay Arts shined, and through the display window, Sonya saw people milling. Several more gathered outside, chatting in the cool autumn air.

"We're early, as planned, but there are already people inside."

"I'm going to drop you off. I'll find a place to park."

"It's a lot of icing," Owen commented as he got out, reached a hand for Cleo's.

"Who doesn't love icing? Marcia, good to see you."

And in her Cleo way, she began to mingle.

"She's great at this," Sonya murmured.

"Go be her wingman. I'll find you."

Though she doubted Cleo needed a wingman, she gave Trey a quick kiss, then slid out.

When they made their way inside, Linda, Kevin's assistant manager, hurried over. "I'm glad you came early. Some came earlier. You've already sold a painting."

"Really?"

"*Sailing Pals.* The wife/mom of the father and son on the sailboat came in with a couple of friends. Saw it. Recognized them and the boat. Sold!"

"Sprinkles!

Cleo laughed. "Is she still here? I'd love to meet her."

"She is. I'll take you over."

"Go," Owen told her. "We'll hang for Trey. She'll have them eating out of her hand," he added to Sonya when Cleo went with Linda.

"She will. And it's natural, genuine. I think I'm more excited than she is."

"How about I get you a plastic cup of what's bound to be cheap, crappy wine?"

"I'll take it. I actually know some of these people."

"Go, do the small-talk thing. I suck at it, which is also natural and genuine."

She sipped crappy wine, made small talk. Eventually she reconnected with Trey, then his family.

"We can't stay long." Seth had the baby in a pack on his chest.

"We really can't, but we wanted to at least come by. It's wonderful. It just looks wonderful. Congratulations, Cleo."

"Thanks. So does she, look wonderful."

Owen tipped his head down toward Fiona's. "Fe, Fi, Fo, Fum. Somebody has to say it."

"And you would." Corrine shook her head with a smile. "I ran into Clarice a minute ago. She's down that way. I think you've got a sale, Cleo. The painting you must have done from an old photo of Poole Shipbuilders. One before they expanded."

"I didn't see that."

"You don't see everything," Cleo told Owen. "Collin had several photos from the late eighteen hundreds."

"Show me. Sorry," he added when he grabbed her hand and pulled her away.

"I'd say it's lucky for Clarice she got there first." Ace beamed at the groups of people. "This is what we like to see, isn't it, my own darling?"

"It is. And speaking of sales, Ace, I've found my anniversary present. That series there. The hydrangea, the wisteria, and the lily. I have just the place for them."

"So she always says, and she's never wrong. Let's go find whoever's dealing with the dealing."

"And I've got my eye on another."

Surprised, Corrine turned to Deuce. "You do?"

"I do. I know you're the one who picks out art and so on, but I asked Kevin to hold one until I showed you."

"No time like the present. Excuse us, this is a moment."

"He showed me earlier. It's the cove," Trey said. "He proposed to her there."

"Pirate's Cove." Sonya just sighed. "That's so romantic."

"Want some more crappy wine?" Trey asked her.

"No, I really don't. I'm basking."

Sonya basked. Cleo socialized and talked art. Kevin, a little wild-eyed, grinned like a crazy man.

As the crowd began to thin out, Bree shot in like a bullet.

"Kitchen just closed. I've gotta get back, but I wasn't missing this. Manny said we should get something for our place. Tell me what I should get."

"Oh, Bree, you need to pick your own art. It's—"

"Bullshit." She just grabbed Sonya's arm. "What the hell do I know? Show me stuff."

Sonya did her best, and found herself surprised when Bree fixed on a dreamy watercolor of the bay. A single boat, bright white with red sails, glided toward the horizon.

"It makes me feel calm. It's hard to make me feel calm, but this does. I want this. I like how the sun's coming through the clouds, like God fingers or whatever. Yeah, it makes me feel calm. Thanks. I'm getting it."

She shot off.

"I did absolutely nothing," Sonya murmured. "But glad to help."

"Talking to yourself?"

Sonya turned, laughed when she saw Maddy. "I do that."

"Me, too. Sonya, this is Hector, my partner in all things."

He looked like Willie Nelson, braid and all, and cupped her hand in both of his. "So glad to meet you. Maddy showed me pictures of the pieces she's redoing for you. You're a smart woman. History and heritage."

"And I'm going to get in touch tomorrow, probably, as Hector and our kids voted with you on a new website."

"You won't be sorry."

"That's what I hear, so I figure you're as talented in your way as Cleo is in hers."

"We never miss an art show," Hector put in. "But this one? Total wow factor."

"I couldn't agree more."

At the end of the evening, it became clear many agreed.

"Lucky thirteen." Kevin loosened his red bow tie. "Thirteen sold just tonight, and there's a lot of interest in several more. Cleo, it's the most successful fine art opening we've ever had."

"It's the most successful show I've ever had. You did an amazing job."

He gripped her hands. "You have to promise me to do another."

"I'd love to. Maybe next fall."

"Perfect." Now he kissed both her hands, left, then right. "I can't thank you enough. And remember, anytime you have something you want displayed? We're here."

"You're my man, Kevin."

"The car's a few blocks down," Trey told them as they left. "I'll go get it, pick you up."

"I could use the walk." Cleo looked at Sonya.

"Absolutely. It got seriously crowded in there for a while. The air feels great. Thirteen paintings!" Sonya pumped fists in the air. "And he's counting the series of three Paula wanted as one, so actually fifteen. That's a lot of sprinkles."

"Well, you have to consider Trey's parents, Owen's cousin—"

"She beat me to it. I'm bitter."

"Bree," Cleo continued, "all bought— Who am I kidding? I *crushed* it! I'd do a cartwheel, but—"

"You can do a cartwheel?"

Both Cleo and Sonya sent Owen pitying looks. "Of course I can do a cartwheel."

"Prove it."

"You want me to do a cartwheel, here, on the sidewalk? On High Street?"

He shrugged. "Unless you're too dainty for that. Or can't do one."

"Dainty? Them's fighting words."

Cleo handed Sonya her purse, shook back her hair. She shot Owen one last smug look, then did not one but two cartwheels on the sidewalk, on High Street.

A couple coming out of the Lobster Cage applauded.

Dusting off her hands, Cleo took a bow.

"Can you do that?" Trey wondered.

"Yes, but not in this dress." Ridiculously happy, Sonya smiled at him. "I'll show you later."

Chapter Twenty-Seven

On her Saturday hunt through basement storage, Sonya ignored the ringing bell, and found a treasure.

"Look at this!" She held up a framed photo she'd unearthed from a broken dresser drawer. "It's the staff, house staff. A lot of house staff. Oh, this woman, this man? That's Hobson and Grimes. The head housekeeper, the head butler!"

Cleo reached her first, peered down. "That's . . . twenty-three people. I don't see Molly, so before or after."

"Take it out," Trey suggested. "Look on the back. They may have dated it."

"Let's hope."

Owen took a multi-tool out of his pocket. "Let's see it. Old frame, backing's wired down."

"It needs a new one. I can—"

"It's a good frame." He continued to work. "Just needs cleaning up."

He pulled out the backing. On the back of the picture, they found not only the date, but a carefully written list of names.

"January 10, 1933. So after Lissy, before Patricia married Michael Poole Jr. Yes! Mildred Hobson, James Grimes. Look, Cleo, there's an Eleanor Gruder listed. I wonder if it's our Eleanor."

Lynyrd Skynyrd rocked "You Got That Right" from Sonya's phone.

"Seated row, third from the left."

Easing the photo out, Sonya scanned across the front row of staff.

"There she is! She looks well into her sixties, maybe into her seventies. It's a really formal shot, so they're all a little stiff. But she looks happy. They all do, really."

"I wonder how long she worked here."

"I Saw Her Standing There" replaced Lynyrd Skynyrd.

"The Beatles say she was just seventeen." Owen grinned. "Clover's quick, man. She's a rocket."

"All those years in service here," Sonya murmured. "I think the Pooles were good people to work for. We'll clean up the frame. It'll go in the gallery."

Owen crouched down to examine the drawer. "I can fix this. Hell, Trey, you could fix this."

"Sounds like damning with faint praise to me. It looks like a nice piece, though."

"Walnut, probably from the same era as that photo."

"And since it's here, it was probably in the servants' quarters, the men's section."

"Most of those rooms came down for the gym, the theater," Trey told her. "I can't see you needing bedrooms here."

"Nope, this whole floor is fun and entertainment. Possibly a place for it on the third floor at some point. Unless you can use it, Owen."

"No, I . . . Well."

"Hesitation is assent!" Sonya wrote *Owen* on a sticky note, slapped it on the dresser.

In the hunt, they found a collection of crocheted doilies, table runners.

"Beautiful work." Cleo unfolded piece by piece. "Son, we could frame some of these. You want to pay homage. Since they're down here, I think it's a safe bet someone on staff crocheted these."

"I love it. God knows we'll have plenty of wall space down here once it's fixed up."

"Yarn, thread, whatever it is for making that stuff's in here. With the needles."

"Hooks," Cleo corrected Trey. "I feel a display coming on."

"A craft or sewing spot, yes. For display, since we don't sew or craft." Sonya took a large spool of crochet yarn from Trey. "Just an area of interest, a display cabinet or bookcase."

"You'd want this in there." Owen gestured. "It's a sewing machine thing."

"Would you look at that! It's got a big iron pedal thing. You had to pedal the sewing machine. Oh, and it's a really pretty table. The machine lowers into the table! How cool is that? I wonder if it still works."

Intrigued, she dragged over a chair, sat. And pushed down the iron pedal.

The needle pumped up and down with a clackety-clack.

With a laugh, Sonya eased off the pedal, leaned in. "We could figure out how to thread it. Maybe even find a manual around here. Set it up, a piece of fabric under here."

As she started to slide her hand toward the needle, something shoved the pedal down. She barely snatched her hand away before the needle stabbed her.

Trey grabbed her shoulders, pulled her back and up as Clover played "Evil Woman."

"It didn't get me. You missed, you vicious bitch! I'm fine. I'm okay."

The needle pumped up and down faster and faster until it blurred. Then stopped.

The bell rang.

Saying nothing, Trey took Sonya's uninjured hand to his lips.

"We're going to do just what we said." She needed a breath to steady herself. "Frame some of the crochet work, make a display, use the adorable old sewing machine. And, um, whew. We're bound to find some old cooking tools down here, stuff from the old kitchen. We'll do a display there, too."

"They'd have had offices down here, wouldn't they?" Cleo wondered. "The head housekeeper, butler. They were in charge of the staff, so they'd have needed office space."

"Desk and chair over that way." Owen pointed. "The chair's a beauty. Solid oak, swivel chair. Not a squeak."

"Desk, chair, maybe an inkwell if you want real old-timey," Trey suggested. "One of those seals for wax."

"Okay, brilliant. Yes, all of that." The ideas, the possibilities had Sonya's nerves leveling again. "Bringing it back to life, top to bottom. That's what she hates."

"Only makes me love it more." Cleo put her hands on her hips. "Let's keep going, make her crazy."

"Too late," Owen added. "She's already there."

They hunted, gathered, carried out, carried up, shifted.

Sonya took another long look at the future game room.

"It's going to be great. It's going to work. In fact . . ."

"I hear my back whining."

She gave Trey a hug. "We'll help. But if we could get the pieces we've earmarked in here, it'll be great. And piss her off."

"It's that part that makes me want to," Owen admitted.

"And once we do that, I'm ordering the big-ass TV, the pool table, deciding on the jukebox from the sellers the guy you know provided. I need the right lights, too. So putting stuff in helps me see it."

It took the weekend to move, adjust, consider, and decide on purchases.

Having so much to look forward to started Sonya's week on a high note. A meeting with Maddy about the website kept that going.

By the end of the week, she'd created a new mood board and started work for her newest client. She had lights, an enormous wall screen ordered, and an electrician lined up. Since Owen wanted one, she ordered a foosball table, and selected the original versions of classic board games.

In a nod to Collin and Deuce, she added a chess table to the mix.

September rolled on toward October. Anticipating, Sonya and Cleo gathered the last of the flowers from their garden. And Cleo, following her grand-mère's advice, froze chopped fresh herbs in ice cube trays.

Sonya woke to a fire simmering, and the first frost.

Cleo gave herself an hour each day for her autumn painting of the tree as Poole's Bay rioted with fall color.

Despite threats from Dobbs, Sonya took time for a walk every afternoon. Nothing would make her miss fall at the manor, its whippy breezes carrying the scent of the sea and woodsmoke. The dazzling color that peaked into the breathtaking.

"It's another kind of claiming, Yoda." He pranced along beside her as she glanced up at the windows of the Gold Room. "I know she knows I'm out here. I know she'd love to hurt me, but I have to show her, show her every single day, she won't push me out."

She looked down at his adorable face. "It's practically October now, Yoda. I think it's time to pull out the Halloween decorations, buy us some pumpkins. No way you live in a haunted manor if you don't go all out for Halloween."

Her hand shot into her pocket and her head shot up when she heard a window open.

But Cleo called out of the studio: "Hey, when you finish your walk, if you're not too busy, can you come up?"

"Sure."

"I want to show you the book illustrations. I think I'm done, but . . ."

"Give me ten. I'm grabbing a Coke when I come in. Do you want one?"

"Might as well, thanks. God, it's gorgeous out there. I need to get out. Later."

She walked Yoda around the house. It didn't make her as sad as she'd anticipated to see the gardens put to bed. Thanks to Jerome.

Turn, turn, turn, she thought, thinking of one of her father's favorite songs.

She knew they'd bloom again. They'd plant more, learn more.

"And look at our woods. The pines so dark and green, and the hardwoods—whatever they are—just so rich. That's a blooming, too. We're so lucky, Yoda. I need to pay it all back. I need to find the rings and earn all this."

She turned toward the house, and inside, gave Yoda a treat before grabbing Cokes.

When she walked by the music room, she paused.

"Where are you, Astrid? Where's your portrait? You're the next step. I know it."

As she walked upstairs, the servants' door slapped open. She closed it on the sound of the ringing bell.

Except for Cleo's music, something with a lot of harps and strings, the third floor held quiet.

She found her friend at her desk, the cat perched on the top of her cat tree. But the painting drew her forward.

"You finished the tree!"

"This morning, before I started work. It was all but done."

"The colors, Cleo. Not really gold, not really orange, but a beautiful mix of both. And I love it just bursts against a broody sky."

"Three seasons down, one to go. It's the actual work that has me on edge. You read the book. It's so out of my comfort zone. I know it's important. Major author. I thought, once I committed to it, I was confident. I'm not."

"I'm happy to help there. You've run these by the author, the publisher."

"Yeah, the drafts, of course. But . . ."

Sonya picked up the stack of drawings. "I'm taking these over to the sofa."

"I'm going to pace. Oh, shut the hell up," she snapped when Dobbs banged against the wall. "You're nothing against possibly screwing up a major job."

"There's no screwing it up, because if these don't hit the mark, you'll fix them."

"That's the thing. I'm out of ideas on how to fix them. Monsters, terrified teens, evil teens, teens battling monsters or each other?

"Not my comfort zone."

Sonya sat, sipped her Coke. Then set it aside and began.

She'd read the book—enjoyed the hell out of it. Then had read it a second time knowing Cleo would ask just this.

She studied each sketch, nodding at its position in the story as she ran through that story in her head. From the quiet town on the title page straight through to the final illustration of a single, bloody shoe beside an abandoned shack, she noted the details, the tone, the mood.

Then, though Cleo made a frustrated argh sound, went back to the start and went through them again.

She set them down, drank more Coke. She made a gun with her finger.

"Bang. And that's a bull's-eye, Cleopatra."

"Are you sure? One-hundred-percent-positively sure? I mean, the one for chapter twelve with the boy—he's still shy of eighteen—holding up the severed head?"

"Is genius." Sonya paged through, pulled it out. "You made Will look triumphant and appalled. Yeah, he knew the now-headless guy, who was another teenager. But Chuck had been infected. It was kill or be killed. That's what shows. That's what needs to show.

"And this?"

She went back to the stack. "Chapter two. The classroom scene. Oh, doesn't the teacher look nice? Doesn't he look like a good guy, all casually dressed, hands open, palms up as he teaches the class of teenagers. But you've got this faint shadow, an aura going, very subtle, and when you look, you get the feeling something's just not right.

"And it wasn't. Face it, Cleo. You've just illustrated a bestselling YA horror novel. And you'll be doing the next two in this trilogy."

"I can't decide if that's good news or bad news. But okay. Okay." Lifting her hands, Cleo pushed them out as if pushing something away. "You wouldn't tell me they're right if they're wrong."

"They're not right. They're fabulous. Now send them, and take a walk out in this beautiful fall day. It won't last much longer. In fact, we need to decorate for Halloween."

"It's not October yet."

"Close enough." Sonya rose. "I'm going back to work on Maddy's job." But she walked over, hugged Cleo first. "Good work, Cleopatra. And get me that second manuscript as soon as it comes. That cliff-hanger's killing me."

In the morning, Sonya woke to a simmering fire, and snow.

She stood at the windows staring out with a mix of knee-jerk thrill and simple shock.

"It's snowing."

"You'll have this," Trey mumbled as he tried for five more minutes.

"But it's still September."

"Says the woman who wants to put up ghouls and goblins."

"It's so pretty. But I'm not ready for snow. We haven't got our pumpkins."

Since five more minutes wasn't going to happen, Trey got up, walked over. And laughed.

"It's not snowing. That's barely a flurry. That's a snow sprinkle."

"In Boston, we call white stuff falling out of the sky snow."

"You're in Maine now, cutie. It'll be over before you finish your first cup of coffee. And crap, I need mine. I've got court this morning."

"Lawyer suit."

"Yeah, yeah."

Knowing he'd shave it clean for court, she rubbed the two-day stubble on his cheek. "Wear the gray one. It brings out your eyes."

"That'll bring the judge around to our side."

"You never know."

"It's also the only suit I have here, so that makes it easy."

"How many suits do you have?"

"Three. Black, gray, navy pinstripe. That's enough for anybody. Unless you're Ace. He collects them like stamps."

"And no one looks more dashing. I'm going for coffee, and we'll see if you're right about the snow."

A fire already crackled in the library. She'd get there soon enough, as she had a video conference with the Ryder group at nine-thirty.

Downstairs, she paused as she often did now at the music room. But the paintings didn't change.

In the kitchen, a fire simmered in the little hearth, a warm welcome to the day. She walked over to let the pets out, and stood in the quick wash of cold air.

A man wheeled a barrow toward the shed. He wore a rough brown jacket and peaked cap, scarred brown boots. Both dogs ran over to him, tails wagging. He turned, his lined face creasing deeper with smiles as he gave them both quick rubs.

Then he wheeled the barrow into the shed, closed it. He turned to Sonya, tipped his cap.

And was gone.

"No. No, I'm never going to get used to it. Just never." Shivering, as much from the moment as the cold, she stepped back into the warmth.

The kitchen tablet broke out with the Beatles' "Good Morning Good Morning."

"Yeah, it is. Just a little surprising."

By the time she made coffee, toasted a bagel, Trey's prediction proved true. The snow vanished as quickly as Jerome, and the sun shot through the clouds.

Trey came down when she let the pets back in. She calculated he'd managed to shower, shave, dress like a lawyer going to court in just under thirty minutes.

And she found it mildly annoying.

She got him coffee anyway.

"Thanks."

"Since it'll take me about twice the time it took you to look presentable, I'm going up to get ready for my video conference."

"You'll hit way over presentable."

She considered. "Mostly mollified. I saw Jerome."

Trey lowered the mug of coffee. "Where?"

"By the shed, putting the wheelbarrow away. The dogs obviously know him because they ran over to him, didn't bark, just ran over so he'd pet them. And he did. Then he, you know." She gestured. "Tipped his cap and vanished."

She shrugged. "I was going to say just another manor morning, but you look . . . I'm going to call it concerned."

"It's a kind of escalation."

Now that concern puzzled her. "I think—hope—it's that they're all getting more comfortable with me. With us. And that we're all getting stronger. Don't you?"

"I can go with that." He walked over to look out at the shed. "That's the plus side of it."

"And the minus?"

"Dobbs pushes harder. And she has been. Having that vulture of hers attack the studio windows, the bolt of lightning, trapping you downstairs. She's escalating, too."

"It hasn't done her much good so far."

He turned back to her. "I think about that first day, and how I was half amused about how you might react to finding out you'd inherited a haunted house. Benignly haunted, so I thought. And I wonder, if I'd known all of this, what I'd have done differently. If I'd sat with you at that table and told you all of this, what you'd have done differently."

So he carried that, she realized. And shouldn't. The best way to ease that weight, to her mind, would be plain and simple truth.

"First, I wouldn't have believed you. Most likely, since we'd just met, I'd have been polite about it. But I'd have thought: So the hot, flannel-shirt-wearing lawyer is a little bit crazy."

"I can be pretty persuasive."

"I've noticed. And I can be pretty determined."

"Also noted."

He stepped toward her, freshly shaved, lawyer suit and tie, all that black hair not quite tamed. And a world of trouble in his eyes.

"If it were an option, Sonya, I'd pack you up and get you out of here. This house means a lot to me, too, but you mean a hell of a lot more."

"It's not just the manor, Trey."

"I know that, and still. It's just a feeling, a bad one, but there's something building, something coming. There's a chance we could head it off."

"You want to go back in that room."

"It's a chance to stop it. To stop her."

She had to turn away, walk away, walk back. "I'm trying to put myself in your place, and I know I'd be angry and frustrated. I wouldn't handle either one as well as you do. That's your nature. It's how you get things done, and over these past months, I've really come to rely on that."

"But."

"It's not time to confront her like that. I know it. I swear I know it down to the bone, Trey, and I'm asking you to trust me there."

She laid a hand on his heart. "I can't tell you not to take that chance. That shouldn't be how we work. But I'm asking you to trust me on it. To stand by."

"I do trust you. And there's going to come a time, Sonya, when I'll expect you to trust me on this same thing."

"All right. We need Astrid's portrait."

"You don't hang it without me. If you find it, you don't put it up without me and Owen here."

Meeting his eyes, she skimmed a finger down his tie.

"That's a promise. It's for the four of us. I know that, too. Since you've got court, why don't you leave Mookie here? Then I'll have two fierce dogs looking out for me."

"Fierce, right. Go get ready." Leaning down, he kissed her. "Text me if."

"If. Good luck in court."

When she went out, Trey looked at the dogs. "Go on. Stick with her."

Since his coffee had gone cold, he poured it out, made another for a go-cup.

Clover assured him with Rascal Flatts and "I Won't Let Go."

"I know. And neither will I."

Promptly at nine-thirty, Sonya joined the video conference. With only weeks left before the Portland store's grand opening, the final layer of advertising came into play.

And her part in the campaign approached the finish line.

As the meeting wound down, Burt Springer asked her to stay on after the rest of the team signed off.

"Expectations not only met but exceeded."

"It's been a pleasure, Burt, as always."

"I know Miranda will contact you directly, but I'm authorized to tell you the Ryder family will offer you a contract as consultant for our digital marketing."

"Oh. You have such a solid team."

"We do, and we'd like you to be part of it. As consultant, you'd continue to work remotely on an as-needed basis. Something to think about."

"I can promise I will. Burt, thank you for trusting me, for giving me this opportunity."

"You earned it, and it didn't hurt my feelings when you proved me right. You take care, Sonya. We'll talk again."

"Wow. Wow and more wow."

Shuffling down the hall, Cleo asked, "Wow what?"

"Good morning! What a morning. In order: It snowed for about five minutes, I saw Jerome, I just finished a very upbeat meeting with Ryder, and Burt told me they're going to offer me a digital media consultant contract."

"All that? Before I have coffee?"

"All that."

"First, congrats, but I'm not surprised. You, my pal, took Ryder into the future while honoring its past. Second, snow? You Yankees start that way too soon. And last but definitely not least. Jerome?"

"He tipped his cap to me after he put the wheelbarrow away. And after, I assume, bringing in more firewood."

"I need that coffee, but unless I change my mind after that kicks in, plan on jambalaya tonight, since it snowed for five minutes."

"I'll help. With what's on my plate, I can knock off by four, no problem."

When Cleo went down, Sonya took a moment to just bask. Then, with both dogs snoozing by the fire, got down to work.

Later, when both dogs came over to sit and stare, she looked down at them.

"Time to go out? No problem."

She walked them down, let them out. She considered getting a jacket and taking her walk, but she wasn't quite ready to break. Instead, she got a Coke, set her mental alarm for an hour.

She settled back at her desk to polish up some holiday ads for various accounts.

"One by one," she murmured.

She didn't notice when Clover went with Metallica's "Here Comes Revenge."

The cold broke through her concentration, and rubbing her arms, she sat back.

As she did, her screen went black, and the TV on the second floor erupted with screams.

"Got my attention," she murmured, then noticed the fog creeping through the doorway toward her desk.

She rose slowly while slipping a hand into her pocket and closing it over the hag stone.

The library doors slammed shut; the windows went dark. In the hearth the simmering fire spiked to a roar.

As a wind gusted, as the fog crawled, Hester Dobbs glided down the curve of stairs.

"I have given you time. I have given you warnings. You will pay for not heeding those warnings. Your time here is at an end."

"No, but yours is."

As Sonya pulled out the stone, Dobbs swept an arm through the turbulent air. It struck like a fist. The shock of pain radiated as the blow lifted Sonya off her feet, and shot her back.

With her face on fire from the impact, she hit the floor hard enough to steal her breath. And the stone flew harmlessly out of her hand.

"Blood. I will bathe you in Poole blood. Generations of it. As you beg for mercy, you'll drown in it."

As Sonya started to scramble up, another blow slammed her back against a bookcase. She tasted blood as her vision grayed, as she slid bonelessly to the floor.

Then she was lifted off her feet, higher, higher, until her body rammed into the ceiling. Desperate, dizzy from the pain, she tried to crawl, tried to kick, but her body rotated until she dangled helplessly.

Like a panther toying with its prey, Dobbs circled below.

"How shall I end you, I wonder? Shall I conjure a rope, slip a noose over your head? Shall I simply snap your neck?"

Stunned by pain, frozen in fear, Sonya saw her blood drip, watched

Dobbs hold out a hand to catch those drips. Then smiling, lick the blood off her palm.

"Kill me, you break the curse. Break the curse, you lose."

"Will I? Will I?"

Her eyes darted as she began to pace. "No true Poole," she muttered. "Imposter, usurper."

Survive, Sonya ordered herself. Just survive.

"You tasted my blood. You've tasted Poole blood. You know I'm a Poole, and I'm not a bride."

"A whore then. Just a whore then."

Smiling, Dobbs circled a finger in the air. Sonya felt herself slowly lowering toward the floor.

"There are ways, so many ways, short of death to bring the blood, to bring the pain. And when I show you all of them, you'll leave my house."

Chapter Twenty-Eight

Cleo considered working on the illustrations for a children's book the perfect palate cleanser after a horror novel.

Since the goal she needed to hit required everything bright and happy, fun and silly, she set her mood to match.

And she enjoyed the quiet as Dobbs didn't bother to slam and thud. As the sun continued to break through the clouds, blue skies won over gray, and her studio filled with light.

The fire simmered, her sweet orange inspiration candle added more layers to the cheer.

She smiled as she drew her main character peering through an oversized magnifying glass with a bright purple handle. The intrepid, curly-haired little girl searched for clues, one eye huge in the circle of glass.

Then she jumped in her chair as Clover—it could only be Clover— stood in front of her desk. Her wide blue eyes looked as urgent as her voice when she spoke.

"Sonya. Dobbs has Sonya in the library. She's hurting her! We need help! Hurry!"

Even as she vanished, Cleo pushed up. She started to run, stopped, and yanked open a drawer. She grabbed the BB gun, sage, her lighter. Then she ran.

She'd nearly reached the door before the screams inside penetrated. Not Sonya, she thought in a panic, because the screams weren't human.

Fingers of mist crawled under the library doors.

She yanked, pulled. She shoved the sage and lighter in a pocket, the gun in another. And put all her strength into dragging the pocket doors apart.

"Help me!" Her muscles pinged and burned as she strained to part the doors. "I can't do it by myself. You have to help me get them open."

She braced, gritted her teeth, then nearly pitched forward when they flew open.

Blood on her face, pain alive in her eyes, Sonya dangled a foot from the floor. With her hands curled like claws, Dobbs laughed.

She turned sharply to Cleo, and her madness shined like a beacon through the fog and dim light.

"Both of you then. A treat for me!"

"I'll give you a treat."

When Cleo lifted the gun, Dobbs threw back her head with a laugh. "Do you think such a thing would harm me? What a pleasure it will be to—"

Cleo fired. As Dobbs stumbled back, her face frozen in shock, Sonya spilled to the floor.

"I think what's in it will."

Cleo fired again, and now Dobbs screamed. On the third shot, then a fourth, still screaming, Dobbs whirled, whirled, whirled until nothing was left of her but a thin stream of fetid smoke.

"Sonya!"

As Cleo rushed to her, Sonya pushed to her hands and knees.

"Gonna be sick."

Instinctively, Cleo gathered back Sonya's hair as she retched.

"She's gone. She's gone now. I've got you. Can you make it to the couch?"

"Yeah. Yeah. I'm so cold."

"I'll build up the fire, and get you water. And we'll see where you're hurt. You're bleeding."

"She hit me." With Cleo's help, Sonya limped to the couch. "Or something did because she was too far away for that. But it felt like a punch in the face. I've never been punched in the face, but I'm sure that's what it feels like."

Cleo tucked a throw around her, then rubbed Sonya's hands between hers. "I'm getting your water bottle."

She dashed to the desk and back. In that short moment, the fire roared up.

"Your nose is bleeding. It's not broken—I know what that looks like. Your mouth, too, but I don't see where it's cut."

"I bit my tongue. Hard."

"Okay, where else?"

"Banged up." Closing her eyes, Sonya let her head drop back. "Slammed me around. I'm going to have some bruises. It would've been worse, Cleo, if you hadn't come. I tried to fight back, but—"

"Don't worry. I'm going to get water and a cloth, then take a look at the rest of you. And if I say *doctor*, you're not going to argue."

"You won't, but I won't if you do."

"You're not alone, Son."

"I'm okay. Need to get my breath back. And you could add some Motrin to that cloth and water. I hurt everywhere."

"Done."

When Cleo hurried back, she saw the spot where Sonya had been sick was clean. It made her eyes sting, that small show of support.

"Here, take these. We'll fix you up. Where are the dogs? Pye?"

"I'd just let them out. Pye came down as I was heading there, too. She waited for that. I'm betting she waited for that, Cleo."

Cleo used the warm, wet cloth to bathe the blood from Sonya's face. "She thought you were alone. We know better."

"Clover warned me, but it was too late. She closed me in, and she was there."

As Sonya told her what happened, Cleo looked over every inch.

"Bitch. Vicious bitch. You're right about the bruises. You've got plenty. Including one right here." She brushed a finger over Sonya's left cheek. "I want to see if you can walk. You limped before."

Sonya indulged herself with a long breath, then stood. "Ankle, the right one's a little sore, but I can put weight on it. That knee hurts a little, but not like it did."

She went to the desk, picked up her Coke. "I feel like I took a hard fall. Which I did."

"We're going down, and you'll elevate that leg. Do some ice."

"How did you know to come? Clover?"

"Ice and elevation, then I'll tell you."

"You had the BB gun. It worked."

"Yes, I did, and yes, it did." Once again, Cleo put an arm around Sonya for support. "And I'll tell you about that, too. We need to tell Trey. And Owen."

"He's in court, and I don't want to—"

"I, for one, am not facing his justifiable fury if we don't tell him and right soon. We'll get you settled in the kitchen, and you'll text him while I make us a little lunch and some soothing tea."

"All right, because you're right."

She had to bite back a groan as, with Cleo's help, she hobbled down the stairs.

"It's just that he was a little upset this morning when I told him I saw Jerome. He called it an escalation, and said—he damn well said—she'd escalate, too. And she did. Ow, Jesus, she really did."

Because she felt weak, she let Cleo fuss, and dutifully texted Trey when she had her leg up, her knee and ankle on ice.

> Don't be smug, but you were right. Dobbs escalated. We
> fought the bitch off. Cleo did a marksman's job with the BB
> gun. And now we're having some lunch, so don't worry.
> Jambalaya's on tonight's menu.

She added a heart emoji.

His response came in under ten minutes, as Cleo let the pets in, handed out treats.

> Are you hurt?

She thought: Shit. Just shit, and gave herself a minute to think of the right answer.

Got a few bruises, nothing serious. Nurse Cleo instructed me to ice my knee, so I am. Trust me, she got the worst of it, so satisfaction outweighs the bruises. I promise I'd tell you if I were really hurt. And if I didn't, Cleo would. She's already texted Owen. We'll give you both all the details when you get here.

As soon as I can. Owen's closer, so anything else happens—anything—get him. I love you, Sonya.

She acknowledged that with another heart, one that pulsed. Then sighed.

"Now he's going to be distracted in court. He wants us to get Owen if anything else happens."

"Already arranged. Now eat," she said as she set down the comfort of peanut butter and jelly sandwiches.

"You need to tell me your side of it."

"Clover. Only she didn't say it with music. She was right there, in the studio. Obvious now, she didn't want to take the time for a song or chance I wouldn't clue right in."

"You saw her."

"I did. Right at my desk. She said Dobbs had you and you needed help. They needed help. When I got to the doors, I couldn't open them, and I needed their help. They were there for it."

"After you ran down to the closet to get the BB gun."

"About that. After Trey brought it, I mentioned it to my grand-mère. She said BBs might annoy her, but she didn't know if they'd stop her. So she sent me beads."

"Beads."

"Crystal beads, BB size. After that goddamn bird smashed itself into the studio window, I got the gun out of the closet, loaded it up with the beads. I hadn't bothered to take it back down yet. You wouldn't even practice with it anyway."

"You obviously didn't need to. They hurt her. I was pretty dazed, but I could see that. They hurt her, shocked her. And they scared her."

"My grand-mère knows her business."

"We're sending her flowers." Reaching out, Sonya gripped Cleo's hand. "I was afraid. No, I was terrified. I couldn't not be. But when I saw you, I knew she wouldn't win."

"When I saw you, dangling up there, bleeding? I knew she couldn't win. But, Son, it's coming down to the time we have to take the fight to her."

"I know it. I just don't know how."

"One thing? I'm going to reload my magic BBs."

It made her laugh. "Only you, Cleo. And I'm leaving that to you." Sonya lifted the ice pack from her ankle, laid it against her sore cheek. "This was my first ever physical fight, though I can't say I landed any punches."

"Here." Cleo took off one of her multitude of bracelets. "Wear this."

"Pretty, but why?"

"It's fluorite. Think of it as a shield against dark forces."

Sonya slid it on, admired it. "Got one big enough for my face?"

Lifting her hands, Cleo fisted them. "Keep your dukes up."

Clover lightened it up with "Kung Fu Fighting."

On a half laugh, Sonya shook her head. "Maybe I can stream a workout for that. Meanwhile, it may hurt some, but I need to move or I'm going to stiffen up. It's also the first time I've been thrown across the room like Yoda's red ball."

"How about a hot bath and a nap?"

Both sounded wonderful, but.

"If I went that route, it's like she won. Thanks to you, she sure as hell didn't. So, wearing my shield, I'm going to take my walk with two fierce dogs and a fearless cat. She's done for now, Cleo. You know it."

"I've got the look on her face when I shot her ass engraved on my brain, so I do know it."

"Go reload your weapon of evil destruction." When she rose, Sonya said, "Ow. But definitely better. I'm going to walk, finish my workday, help you make jambalaya. And, hopefully, manage to settle Trey back to his usual calm self."

A little sore, a little stiff, she took her walk. And felt better for it.

She had a moment when she stepped back into the library, and quashed it. She would not let Dobbs spoil her amazing workspace.

And scattered on the floor she saw crystal beads. They'd gone through her, Sonya realized. They'd gone right through her.

And carried traces of her blood.

Because she didn't want to touch them, Sonya got tweezers to pluck them up, put them in a little bowl.

She'd give them back to Cleo. So thinking, she gave Cleo's bracelet a rub as she sat down.

Clover added Sia's anthem "Unstoppable."

"Damn right we are."

But she felt a little more secure when the dogs settled down in the library with her.

When Trey pulled up to the manor, calm didn't ride with him. He knew Sonya had downplayed whatever had happened. And if he hadn't reached the end of the line, he was fast approaching it.

Whatever she'd gone through, he hadn't been there. Instead, he'd been miles away in court over a case that should never have reached litigation. And wouldn't have if the plaintiff hadn't been so goddamn dug in.

The fact the judge clearly agreed with that assessment didn't negate the wasted hours. And he'd waste a few more the next day before the judge ruled, he had no doubt, for his client.

That was the job.

As if to shed those wasted hours, he tugged his tie loose as he got out of his truck. Action, he thought, it was past time to take action, to stop playing defense.

His head snapped up when he heard a window open.

Clover, sunny hair shining, her young, lovely face projecting sympathy, leaned out.

"She's okay, big guy. I know you had to worry, and you're a little pissed off, too."

"Delete *little*."

She grinned. "Okay. But you need to be proud of her, and Cleo, too. They handled that twisted butthole of a bitch. I wanted you to know that before you go in. I love her, too, right? It's way weird because I don't feel like a grandma, but I really love her with all I got. And Cleo, too. We're doing all we can to help, I promise."

"It's time to stop it. To stop her."

After brushing back her hair, Clover leaned on the windowsill like a chatty neighbor. "Time's like, you know, different for me, but yeah, I get that. Something's happening, but I don't know . . ."

She shook her head, lifted her shoulders.

"Something's changing, but it started changing as soon as she got here. I feel more . . . I just feel more. You're a good guy, Trey. Strong and steady. That's what she needs. You, and your strong and steady. I just wanted you to know. Here comes Owen."

She shot out another smile. "He's a good guy, too. None of us feel so alone since you all came. Don't go away, okay? Don't give up on us. We need you."

She faded away; the window closed.

"Damn it." He rubbed at the tension in the back of his neck as Owen pulled up. "Goddamn it."

She'd hit the target, and he couldn't deny it. Nothing pushed his buttons more firmly than someone asking for help.

"Are we making an entrance?" Owen asked as he and Jones walked over.

"Clover interrupted mine."

Owen glanced up. "Yeah?"

"Yeah. Let's go find out what the fuck Dobbs pulled this time."

"How pissed are you? I ask because on my gauge, you're hitting about seven out of ten. High for you."

"It was heading for nine before Clover. Seven's about right. I'm in court handling a nuisance suit against my client while Dobbs goes after them."

Trey paused at the door. "You're not pissed?"

"I'm waiting to be pissed when I get the details. Hey, are we doing a Freaky Friday deal?"

Trey didn't really want to laugh, but he did. "Okay, level down to six."

The dogs rushed out to greet them and Jones. Mookie bounded with joy as if Trey had left town for a month. So the adoration and goofiness took Trey down to level five.

Until they got to the kitchen.

Cleo stirred something in a pot. Sonya chopped something at the island.

And she had a bruise on her face.

Before he could speak, Sonya slid off the stool and went to put her arms around him.

"I could've hid it with makeup."

"Because I'm blind or because I'm stupid?"

"Neither. Because I'm really good with makeup. But I didn't."

After giving Sonya one long look, Owen stepped over. He turned Cleo's face to his, studied it.

"Never laid a hand on me," she told him. "Pour us some wine, get a beer if you'd rather that. We need to get this going, then we'll tell you everything that happened, start to finish."

"It was a hell of a finish." Sonya grinned.

Trey's level decreased fractionally when he saw it reach her eyes.

"Where else are you hurt?"

"Since I'm not going to strip down in front of my favorite cousin, I'll show you later. Bruises here and there, but that's starting in the middle."

Clover went with Lizzo's "Good as Hell."

"Yeah, we were."

Sonya carried the cutting board over to Cleo. "Chopped, minced, diced. I'll start. You guys want out again? Okay, okay."

"Sonya," Trey said when she walked to the door to let the pets out.

"I was having a really good day," she began. "I think she likes to take swipes on my really good days. I'll tell you why it was, and is, a really good day after. I'd been up in Cleo's studio, where she was also having a really good day. Then I'm back at work, moving right along, when Clover sounded the alarm.

"I'd barely noticed the cold creeping in, or that damn floor fog she likes to do. Thanks." She took the glass of wine from Owen. "And she was there, like when I went through the mirror and saw her with Patricia. Sort of gliding down the library steps. Like something with no feet. Like a snake."

She drank some wine and told her tale.

Trey moved over, ran his hand over the back of her head. "You've got a bump here."

"Do I? I missed that one."

"Did you lose consciousness? Any double vision?"

"No, and no. I hit hard, and it hurt, but no concussion, no broken bones. Bruises, Trey, just bruises. You're making me want to jump ahead, and we need Cleo to take over because it's a 'meanwhile, up in the studio' sort of thing."

"Meanwhile, up in the studio. Clover. Actual Clover, standing in front of my desk."

Cleo dumped some of the wine Owen had opened into the pot, gave it a stir. Then she picked up her own and turned to the others.

"She told me Dobbs had Sonya trapped in the library, and was hurting her. She said: 'We need help.' Not Sonya needs help. We. I got the BB gun out of the desk—"

"You had it in your desk?" Owen interrupted.

"Since the last bird incident, yes. I ran down, but I couldn't open the doors. I said they had to help me get them open, and they did. That crazy bitch had Sonya dangling off the floor, and she freaking smiled at me. Said she'd take two for one, and actually laughed when I pointed the gun at her."

"She didn't laugh long."

Cleo grinned at Sonya. "She sure as hell didn't."

"The BBs worked."

Now Cleo turned her grin to Trey. "My grand-mère's magic BBs did. I shot her four times."

Turning, she picked up a little dish from the counter. "Obsidian, two black tourmalines, selenite. Sonya found these when she went back up to the library."

"Got tweezers, not touching them, because ick. Dead witch blood on them."

"They went right through her," Trey murmured. "Did some damage first."

"They hurt her," Cleo confirmed, then smacked Owen's hand away. "Don't touch. We may be able to use the blood on them. They scared her, and on the third and fourth hit, she went screaming into a panicked whirlwind, and poof."

"And not a sound out of her since. Trey." Sonya reached for his hand. "She hurt me, she scared the living fuck out of me. But I'm sitting here drinking wine. And dead witch aside, I'm betting I'm a hundred percent before she is."

"You could've been here alone."

"I never am. And I honestly believe if Cleo hadn't come to the rescue with magic BBs and dead aim, the others would've found a way. They're stronger, Trey, you have to feel that, too. They're just more here."

He thought of Clover leaning out the window. "All right, I do feel that."

"She knows she can't kill me—any of us—as much as she'd love to. She loses if she goes too far. She can only hurt and scare, and yes, she's escalating there."

"There's gotta be a reason for that."

Cleo looked at Owen with approval. "Yes, there does."

"You've got an idea on that, Lafayette?"

"I do."

Enjoying her wine, she leaned back against the counter. "She feels it, too. They're getting stronger, not just the brides, all of them. So are we. Nothing she's thrown out has worked in the long run. We're all here, together."

"There are four people, maybe not officially, but essentially, living in this house now. When's the last time that happened?" Sonya asked, then answered. "Since Patricia, since before Patricia. Clover and Charlie with some friends for a while, but what kind of friends were they to leave Clover at that point in her pregnancy?"

Gucci Mane expressed Clover's opinion with "Fake Friends."

"And that, the man I love, my best friend, my favorite cousin, isn't us. She feels that. We're more of a threat to her than she's ever faced."

"And you're the biggest threat in that group," Trey pointed out.

"No slap at female power," Owen put in, "but it's fucking hard to be somewhere else and know, at any time, something can come down."

"And no return slap at male ego, because I know it is. But . . ." Sonya lifted a hand, let it fall. "That's part of who we are, too, isn't it? And I know, I just know, when it comes down to it, the end of it, we'll be here together.

"It's not just me, Trey. It's never been just me."

"Things started changing when you got here. That's something Clover told me before I came in tonight."

"Oh! Twice in one day? That's—"

"A sign of something stronger," Trey finished. "She said something was coming. She didn't say, or didn't know, what or when."

"Samhain." Cleo checked her pot, stirred, nodded. "The night the veil thins between the living and the dead. A high holy day, a major Sabbat."

"That's a witch thing, right?" Owen took a sniff at the pot himself. "Wouldn't that be a big night for her?"

"Light kills dark," Cleo said simply.

"Halloween," Sonya murmured. "It seems really . . . apt."

And it gave Trey what he felt was a solid bargaining chip.

"October thirty-first. That's the line. If we don't have the rings, or a clear and solid path to them, Owen and I go in."

"The Gold Room? But—"

"It has to end sometime, Sonya. And at some point, you have to go on the offense. Add, for all we know, that might be the way to get the rings. Taking it to her. That's as logical a method as any."

"I might go along with that," Cleo considered, "with one amendment. We all four go in. Sonya's right. It's going to be all of us."

Since he'd expected that counter, Trey flicked a glance at Owen, got a half shrug.

"Agreed," Owen said. "We've got that piece of her dress Jones ripped off. You've got her blood on those stones. I don't know dick about that kind of thing, but there should be a way to use them."

"She's strongest there," Sonya began.

"That could be the point," Trey argued. "Up to now, it's mostly been fending her off."

"Excuse me," Cleo put in. "Sonya and I both made her bleed."

"So just think of what four of us, together, could do. And where she feels strongest and safest. We'll prove her wrong."

"We need Astrid's portrait. I swear, I know we need that first."

Trey brushed a finger over Sonya's bruised cheek, and found his level had settled at about a simmering three. "If we do, and I trust your instincts there, then we'll have it."

Chapter Twenty-Nine

In spite of, or maybe because of, all that happened, Sonya insisted on decorating for Halloween.

They bought pumpkins and gourds, and hauled out Collin's collection.

In that collection, she found a long string of lanterns that spelled out SPOOK CENTRAL.

"How perfect is this!"

Because he remembered it from his childhood, Trey felt a quick pang. "Where the hell are you going to put it?"

"It should hang under the half turret. Just the right length."

"That's where Collin always put it."

"Is it? See, perfect."

"It did look pretty cool." And Owen finished with a mutter: "I'll get the ladder."

"Not yet! We have to see what else. Look, here's a trio of broomstick-riding witches."

"Some consider that insulting."

Sonya barely glanced at Cleo. "But we won't. And there's this vampire on a stake. Oh, oh, look at this skeleton guy with the tattered cloak. You put him in the yard, right, so he's clawing out of his grave. And these ghost things light up! We can hang them on the tree."

She stopped herself.

"I've just become my mother. And I don't care. This is so much fun! When we're done, I'm going to send her a video. She'll love it."

It took most of a weekend, but Trey considered it worth it. Not only did Sonya simply sparkle throughout, but it did bring back memories of his childhood.

"We'd always come here." Trey stood with the others in the brisk October wind, watching ghostly wind spinners whirl and goblin lights glow in the magic of dusk. "We'd do trick-or-treat in the village, that was a must, then come up here. Anna and me, Owen and Hugh, plenty of other kids."

"He'd always have this going on. He had that fog machine for a while, Trey, remember? And creepy music blaring. He'd mix it up, too. One year, a severed head on a platter, or that time he had a coffin out here. Must've had a remote because the lid would creak open and the bwah-ha-ha and a skeleton hand came out of it."

Picturing it, Owen hooked his thumbs in his belt loops. "He'd always answer the door in costume."

"And had a ton of serious candy," Trey added.

"Damn right. No stingy little bags of candy corn or bite-sized bullshit. Full-size Snickers, Milky Ways, Hershey bars."

"We could do that. We could do all that. Not this year, I get that, but next year? We could do all that."

Catching Sonya's enthusiasm, Cleo chimed in. "We could make up some flyers. *Would you dare a Halloween visit to Lost Bride Manor?*"

"*Your trick is our treat.*" Sonya pushed at her blowing hair. "Next year. But this year? It looks great. I'm going up to send the video to my mother. Then how about a Sunday night movie?"

"Not a spooky one."

"Man, Lafayette, it's October. There's horror movie marathons for a reason. And that doesn't count Collin's collection, which is righteous."

Clearly seeing she was one against three, Cleo drew her line.

"Not a gross spooky one. I draw the line at gross and spooky. And if I'm going to sit through any kind of horror movie, I'll need wine."

"*Get Out.* The movie," Owen added quickly. "It's not just horror, it's funny and socially relevant."

"He's right," Trey said.

"And that's three for it." Sonya clapped her hands together. "I need to watch it again anyway. Get the wine, popcorn, and I'll run up and send the video."

She ran up to the library to edit the video, add music, a few sound effects. Then added a tag.

Greetings from Spook Central. Capping the evening with a scary movie, talk soon! Love you.

Pleased, she sent it off.

When she stood, she turned to the steps up rather than down.

Not a peep out of Dobbs since the attack. Workers had come for the game room, and still nothing. The pinball machine had arrived, and they'd tested it out with a competition.

Trey nipped Owen by a handful of points, and both had trounced her and Cleo.

They'd practice and change that.

She still needed to arrange the display cabinet, set up the jukebox, wait for the pool table. And the reupholstered furniture. But with the rest of the furnishings in place, the new lighting, the wall screen installed, it was happening.

Still, all through the progress, the work, and the fun, Dobbs stayed silent.

But Sonya wanted to go upstairs. Not a pull, not exactly, but more of a sense.

Her phone played "Time Has Come Today."

"For what?"

She wouldn't go in the Gold Room. Not only a breach of trust, but stupidity. When they went in, and time was ticking down there, they'd go together.

Then she paused at Cleo's studio.

"Of course. Jesus, of course."

She walked to the closet, opened it.

And found Astrid.

She stood in her white gown with the sea, calm and blue, behind her. Her eyes, reflecting that warm blue, seemed to look into Sonya's. She carried her flowers in the crook of one arm, with her hands crossed at the wrists beneath them.

Her wedding ring shined gold.

The painting didn't replicate the one in the foyer, as the bride's body angled, her head tilted. Much, Sonya realized, as Cleo had painted her.

And the style of the artist, of course. The style . . .

She made a sound caught between grief and joy as she saw Collin's signature in one corner, her father's in another.

She stood where she was and wept.

In the kitchen, wine opened, corn popped, Trey glanced toward the hallway.

"She's been up there awhile. Maybe she decided to call her mom. I'll just go check."

Halfway down the hall, he heard her on the stairs.

"She's coming now," he called back, and waited for her.

He saw the painting she carried; he saw the tears.

"Astrid," she said as he went to her. "It's Astrid."

He laid a hand on her damp cheek. "Here, let me take her."

"I felt I needed to go up. Felt I needed to look." Another tear spilled as Cleo and Owen came out of the kitchen trailed by the dogs and Pye. "It's Astrid."

Cleo put an arm around her. "Let's take her into the music room."

"They painted her together. The signatures . . . The mirror. It had to be."

Cleo's arm tightened around Sonya when Trey set the portrait against the wall. "She's only more beautiful because they did."

"She's standing facing the house, back to the sea, but the angle's more like how you painted her, Cleo. We have to get your painting."

"I'll get it." Owen started out.

"Hold it by the edges. It still needs drying time."

"I'm not sad." With a quiet sigh, Sonya swiped at tears. "Just emotional. I know we've waited for this. For her. So it's a relief to have that wait over. Knowing they painted her together? It's just . . . My heart's so full. Then there's the bookend. When we hang her, will that open some door, turn a key in some lock? Or not?"

"It's going to matter." Turning from the portrait, Trey took Sonya's hand. "We're about to find out how. You want Cleo's painting on the wall facing them. I'll take that art down."

As he did, Owen carried Cleo's painting in, and nodded toward the wall. "That's where you want them, right?"

"Yes, but not until Astrid's up. She should come first. Sorry." Cleo shoved at her hair. "I should've gone for the hammer, the hook. I couldn't stop looking at her."

"I'll get them."

As Trey went out, Owen yanked tissues out of his pocket. "Here, I brought these down. Figured you could use them."

"Thanks."

He pulled some out of his other pocket, handed them to Cleo.

"In case. Another beauty," he said, studying the portrait. "I'm going to say, she doesn't look as regal as she does in the big one in the foyer. More, I don't know, approachable."

"You're right." Cleo tucked the tissues in her own pocket. In case. "I like that she's facing the manor, where she should have been mistress. They're all painted with such skill, such wonderful detail. And more."

"With love," Sonya finished. "There's love in the brushstrokes."

When Trey came back, they measured, they marked. They nailed in the hanger.

"It's for you, cutie. You put her in place."

"Okay." She gripped her hands together first. "Here goes."

She lifted the painting, positioned it.

"Might need a little help with getting the wire on the hook."

"I've got you." Moving to her, with one hand on her shoulder, Trey reached behind the framed portrait to slide the wire on. "She's secure."

Sonya didn't hold her breath because it was already trapped in her lungs as she looked into Astrid's eyes, adjusted the painting as Cleo instructed.

And stepped back.

The seven brides filled the wall.

Sonya waited, gripping Trey's hand on one side. Cleo's on the other.

Her breath expelled on a half laugh. "I think I expected a crescendo of music or bright, flashing lights. Maybe a voice whispering: *To retrieve the rings, click your heels together three times.*"

She jolted when her phone rang out with Journey's "Don't Stop Believin'."

"No, Clover, we won't stop believing. I know you're right, Trey. It matters they're all up there together. But I guess we're going to have to wait to find out how."

Owen stepped back. "Help me get Cleo's up, Trey. Maybe they just need a boost."

"Edges," Cleo reminded them. "Maybe we have to wait until three. Or something's changed somewhere else in the manor, and we don't know it yet."

She turned. "Up a half inch on your side, Trey. Another smidge. That's got it."

"Wait!" Sonya waved her hand back, bumped it against Cleo's shoulder. "Did you see that?"

"What? See what?"

"I thought . . . Yes! Did you see that? The rings."

"Where?" Trey moved to her.

"In the paintings! The rings in the paintings. I saw— There! Johanna's. It glinted. Sparkled. Clover's. Now it's Clover's."

"I saw that!" Thrilled, Cleo gripped Owen's arm. "Lisbeth's. Now hers. One, two," she counted. "Agatha's."

"Now Marianne's. Wait a beat," Sonya murmured. "Wait two, yes! Catherine's. Oh, oh, and Astrid's. Did everyone see that?"

"Hard to miss if you're looking." And because he wanted a closer look, Owen moved forward.

"It's starting again. Johanna's." Trey watched each ring sparkle in turn. "From the last bride to the first. The last ring to the first ring."

In silence they watched as the pattern continued. Then stopped.

"Seven times. It happened seven times." Sonya pressed a hand to her lips. "Not exactly bright flashing lights, but close enough."

"And nothing from Dobbs," Owen pointed out.

"I'm going to guess she's either still recovering, recharging, or . . ." Trey liked his second option more. "She can't do a damn thing about this, about them."

"Because they're together now," Sonya agreed. "And they want their rings back. That's as clear as it gets. Just not how."

"You know the order you need to go to get them back," Trey pointed out.

She frowned a moment, then pressed her hands to her head. "Last to first. Of course! I was just caught up in the moment, and didn't think through it. Message also clear, and received."

"You're thinking it through now." Trey could see it on her face. "And you know what you have to do to get them."

Sonya gave herself a moment to just breathe. "I have to go through the mirror. I have to go through the mirror seven times, in that order, and, somehow, take the rings from the brides before Dobbs does."

"You won't go through alone. She won't be alone," Owen repeated. "I'm ready whenever you are."

"Not tonight. I mean that," Cleo insisted. "This is the answer. I feel that, too. Take the rings before Dobbs can, bring them back through so you can give them back. But there's a lot more to get ready for, and I still believe, absolutely, it needs to be on Samhain."

"We can wait, and we should," Trey agreed. "No rushing in. Plan first. Looks like instead of a movie, we're going to sit down and figure out what to do, and how to do it."

They chose the dining room, and Sonya brought in the kitchen tablet to take notes.

"Silly, maybe, but I see things better if I write them down."

"Not silly," Trey disagreed. "Sensible. And let's be sensible on this aspect. Clover, if you know, is it safe for us to talk strategy here, tonight?"

When he heard Harry Styles and "Late Night Talking," Owen lifted his shoulders. "I'd take that as a yes."

"Okay then." Because she wanted to stay sharp, Sonya had traded the idea of wine for a Coke. "We know, obviously, getting the rings back is, well, the mission. Now we know the order—we know it's one at a time, from Johanna back to Astrid. So, it's not a matter of going after Dobbs in the Gold Room—yay—but for me to go back through the mirror to each day each bride died, in turn."

"For us to go back," Owen corrected.

"Actually, I think it's best if I go—"

"No." His interruption was flat and final.

She tried again. "The reason for that is—"

Now all three at the table said, "No."

She looked hard at Trey. "I should be allowed to state my case."

"You're outvoted, Son."

"Let her lay it out," Trey suggested.

"In four of the cases, I'll be going into a bedroom, and two of those while women are in labor, giving birth, or have just had twins. It's going to be shocking enough to see me, another woman."

"If they see you."

"Okay." She nodded at Trey. "If they do see me. Marianne and Clover did, I know they did while they were dying. How would those women react with Owen popping in?"

"There's a reason I can go through."

"Agreed," Cleo said. "Who was there to smash the evil spider before it took a chunk out of you?"

"That was the first time I knowingly went through. I'm more prepared."

"More prepared, but," Trey qualified. "The facts are, you have to go through, get the ring, get out before Dobbs can stop you. You might need help with that. Seven times," he said before Sonya could object. "And each time saps you. If you miss any one of those times? Well, we don't know what could happen."

"We don't know what's going to happen if I don't miss either. You think I'm being stubborn."

He smiled. "Do I?"

"Look, Sonya, I'm going whether you like it or not. Might as well get on board with it."

Clover chimed in with "You Can't Always Get What You Want."

"Listen to Mick," Owen added.

"Step one," Trey began.

"I call the mirror. Or I want or wish to go somewhere, see something. Which I am actively not doing now, because not now. Johanna first. She ran in the house and upstairs to change her shoes because they were killing her. Dobbs waited until she came out, and they were at the head of the stairs when . . ."

And it twisted in her belly.

"I know I can't change what happened to her, or any of them. I know I have to accept that. I know after I take the ring, she'll die. They'll all die."

"What you'll do isn't just breaking the curse, which is enough. It's helping them." Cleo reached out. "And everyone. Everyone who comes after us, too. That's the focus, Son."

"I'll stay focused. I know I have to. I don't know how I'm going to talk a new bride out of her wedding ring, if she sees me. If she doesn't, it seems to me pulling off someone's ring is going to give them a big-ass jolt."

"Get it, get back," Owen said. "No hesitation, no regrets."

"Seven times, cutie. And we have to assume that's one after the other. It's a lot on both of you."

"I don't get spinny the same way Sonya does."

"Seven times," Trey reminded Owen.

"And it's different this way, Owen, when I, sort of, pull out. It's a little rocky. It didn't last as long, but we'll have to go right back through again."

"Ever sailed in twelve-foot seas? I can handle rocky. Seven times. Lather, rinse, repeat. We've got that."

"Will she know?" Sonya wondered. "When we bring back the first ring, will she know we have it?"

"How could she? For her it's then," Cleo pointed out. "Once you bring it back, it's now."

"Which is why it makes sense going last to first. Trickier," Trey conceded. "We know the rings add to her power. She'll still have six before you go through again."

"So we can't waste time. We won't," Sonya promised herself. "If they see me, I just take the ring. I'll hate it, but I'll do it. And you're all right. I might need help with that. This has to be right, doesn't it? This has to be the right way."

"I'm listening to Mick, too. What I want?" Trey picked up his coffee. "I want to go in, take her down, yank the rings off her hands, and kick her ass. But."

Cleo danced her fingertips on the table. "You might still get a chance to do that last part."

"Don't toy with us, Lafayette. I owe Dobbs a good ass-kicking."

"Then I'm going to weigh in. We agree Sonya and Owen go through the mirror, seven times. And yes, one after the other, as close together as they can manage. We can't know exactly what's going to happen on the other side. I trust they'll get the rings because they're meant to. But we can't know how that affects the now, not really. Another reason it makes sense to go last to first."

"If I started with Astrid, it could make changes down the line. I hadn't thought of that."

"And time runs different there than here," Trey pointed out. "That's another factor to consider."

"So is the three o'clock loop." Linking her hands, Cleo rested them on the table. "It has to be done, all the way done, before three. If we start at midnight on Samhain, just one second after midnight, that's three hours to do it, and to finish Dobbs. Because breaking the curse, that's a lot. That's monumental. But it doesn't end her. It ends her curse, but not her."

"And it's not over, not done, until we end her. Got something for that?" Owen asked.

"Maybe. It's something I've been thinking about. And I want to consult with my grand-mère. Another reason we wait until Samhain."

"It'll be the four of us. It'll take the four of us." Sonya looked around the table. "If I'm sure of anything, I'm sure of that."

"We all wear protection. Don't give me that look," Cleo said when Owen rolled his eyes in her direction. "I'm coming down firm on that. I'm asking my grand-mère to send something for you and Trey."

He may not have subscribed, but Trey shrugged. "It couldn't hurt. We need to bait her. Assuming she doesn't come hard that day or the day before? We need to bait her into blowing some of her power, energy."

"Drain the battery some." Owen nodded. "Good call."

"And that's for you and me."

"Even better call."

"Now, wait—"

"No. Sonya, how many times have you and Cleo, or just you, had to deal with her on your own? Let her come at Owen and me. It'll distract her, put her on the defensive, and weaken her. That gives you and Owen a better chance, then the four of us a better chance.

"We're ending this, and her." He gripped both of Sonya's hands. "Then we're going to live our lives. You, me, Owen, Cleo. The brides? They go, they stay, who the hell knows. But they're free."

"What if she hurts one of you before we can do all this?"

"No risk," Owen said. "No reward."

"You just want to smack her."

He shrugged at Cleo. "She'd be the first woman for that, but I don't really think of her as a woman. So yeah, I'd like to smack her. I'll settle for pushing her crazy buttons and taking her down some before we get the rest going."

Now he looked around the table. "Sounds like we've got most of a plan."

"Needs some fine-tuning, some gaps filled, but yeah." Trey polished off his coffee. "We've got most of a plan."

They sat another hour doing that fine-tuning, filling what gaps they could. During the hour, Owen let the pets out, came back with the forgotten popcorn.

"Why waste it?"

"I'm with you." Cleo took a handful. "This is better than a scary movie anyway."

Before they went up for the night, they stopped at the music room.

"I need to tell my mother we found her, and that Dad and his brother painted her. I wonder, did they talk, did they laugh, did they tell each other things brothers tell each other?

"I like to think so."

"Will you tell her the rest?"

She shook her head at Trey. "No. She'd worry, and she'd insist on coming here. I don't want that. I'll tell her everything when it's done."

When they went up, she walked to the window.

"One night soon we'll look out here and we won't see her jump. She'll be gone."

Trey wrapped around her, looked out over her shoulder. "It's human to be nervous, Sonya."

"I am. Nervous I won't be fast enough or smart enough. Nervous I'll let them down."

"That's the last thing you should be nervous about. You will be fast enough, smart enough. You won't let anyone down."

Words mattered, she thought. And his of faith and support meant everything.

"I thought, when we had real answers, I'd just plow ahead. But it's not that simple. I know I have to take the rings. I know it's what they want, what they need. It still breaks my heart."

"You'll give them back."

"Do you think so?" She turned to him, held on. "Do you think I'll be able to, somehow?"

"I do. They're not yours." He pressed her hands to his lips. "I'm going to give you yours. What do you say to June, when summer's just coming on? Here at the manor. Small and simple, big and flashy, whatever you want. Just marry me, Sonya. Build a family with me. Build a life with me."

"Yes, so much yes." Framing his face, she pressed her lips to his. "I want the ring you'll give me, and I want to give you yours. I say yes to June."

She kissed him again as he swept her up to carry her to the bed. "And I want just big enough and simply beautiful. I want the manor filled with flowers and people and music. Most of all, I want you."

She rolled over him, rained kisses over his face.

"And I'm not listening to Mick. I'm going to get just what I want. Nothing's going to stop me."

Later, she dreamed of walking on a moonlit night in air scented with flowers. The sea rolled, split by the beam of the fat white moon.

She heard music, soft and dreamy, and in her long white dress swayed to it, turned a circle. Lifting a hand, she watched the band on her finger sparkle in the moonlight.

She was a bride. She was a wife.

She loved, and was loved.

As her happiness soared, she turned another circle.

And saw Hester Dobbs.

"No."

"Did you think you could take what's mine? My home? My world?"

When she spread her hands, Sonya saw the seven rings glint and glimmer.

"You thought you could take these? See how they shine, see how they sparkle. For me! And you dare to become a bride? Like them?"

They lay on the grass, white gowns blood-soaked, faces gray, dead flowers around them. The Seven.

"And like them, I take the symbol from you."

Unable to run, unable to loose the scream caught in her throat, Sonya stood paralyzed. But she felt the icy grip on her wrist as Dobbs wrenched the ring from her finger.

"You will join them now. Now there are eight. More will come, more will come, more will die. Only I am forever."

Though she struggled, Sonya couldn't stop herself from walking to the seawall, couldn't stop climbing onto it to stand over the rocks and thrashing waves.

"You love the sound of it. You love the sight of it. So there be your death. Now leap, and leap every night for a thousand years."

Against her will, against her heart, she jumped.

As she felt herself falling, saw the rocks waiting, she woke.

When she bolted up in bed, Trey woke beside her.

"Sonya."

The scream in her throat turned into a gasp for breath.

She was here, whole, alive.

"A nightmare." Gulping in air, she tried to slow her speeding heart. "What time is it? What time?"

"It's nearly five."

Not three, not Dobbs's hour, she thought, grateful as she burrowed into him.

"Stress dream, that's all."

"Tell me."

Because she didn't want to revisit it, couldn't bear to, she shook her head. "Gone now."

She curled against him, closed her eyes.

Gone now, she thought again. And she wasn't.

Chapter Thirty

Since the last attack, Trey shifted his schedule so when Sonya hit the gym, so did he. Because she understood his reasoning, she didn't mind, not really. But it did remove that solid hour of me time.

Plus.

"You're over there bench-pressing five hundred pounds, and I'm over here curling fifteen. It's demoralizing."

He finished his last rep, racked the weights. "One-fifty, and I'm bigger than you, cutie."

When he went with thirty for curls, she repeated, "Demoralizing. But you make up for it looking all sexy when you flex and sweat."

"Back at you there."

"I'm about finished sweating sexy for the day. It's cooldown stretch time for me."

He had to admit, he did enjoy watching her bend and stretch.

He finished his reps, was about to stretch it out himself.

The Gold Room bell clanged.

"Looks like somebody woke up. Been a while."

"It's colder in here."

"Yeah, I feel it." Calm as a lake, he did a biceps stretch. "If you're done, go on up. I just need a few more minutes."

"You stay, I stay."

As he continued to stretch, more bells rang.

"Sounds like she's hitting them all." Trying to mirror his calm,

Sonya bent her leg, held her foot to her butt for a quad stretch. "She hasn't done that one before."

The music changed from upbeat to a hard, harsh drumming. And the volume soared.

"Just being a nuisance." Trey shrugged his shoulders, then stretched his triceps.

Baiting her, Sonya realized. She steadied herself, braced herself. She could do the same.

"It's getting easier to ignore her tantrums. I used to babysit for this two-year-old boy who threw more impressive ones."

A dumbbell tumbled off the rack, rolled toward her. Sonya side-stepped it as another hit the floor. The exercise bands sprang off their hooks, flew through the air. When Trey caught one on the fly, it hissed. When it snapped toward his face, he used his other hand to force it back, then both to twist it, tie it at the handles.

Sonya grabbed for another and barely avoided a twenty-pound weight that sped toward her, end over end.

"We get a little more of a workout." Trey snagged the band himself, looped it around the other, tied it off.

To Sonya's fascinated horror, the bands wiggled, seemed to snap at each other. Trey hooked his hands under her elbows, lifted her up when another weight rolled.

The wall screen came on in a curtain of blood, with piercing screams behind it.

He felt her shiver, not from fear—or not much of it, he decided. But from the bitter cold.

The lights flashed on and off, on and off. The doorbell bonged, echoed, and bonged again. Doors slammed like gunshots, and the sound of the dogs barking answered.

"Trey, Cleo's upstairs. She's alone."

"We'll go."

The door resisted him, then swung open so fast he narrowly avoided a hard hit to the face. Then nearly lost his grip as it tried to slam again.

"Go."

He had to bear down with all he had to keep it open for her. Sonya put her weight against it to help as he slid through the opening.

The newly installed pinball machine rang and clanged. Gorgar's throaty voice shouted: *Beat you! Beat you!*

Sonya might have run, but Trey held her arm and walked at an easy pace toward the steps.

On the steps, tendrils of smoke curled up between the treads. Sonya heard the wood sizzle as the servants' door swung open, slammed shut.

"It's not real," Trey murmured to her. "They're your steps, in your house."

She hesitated when she saw a flame lick up between the treads. Then she heard Cleo scream. That was all it took to have her bounding up.

At the top, Trey outpaced her.

From the library came the screams and wails of the tortured and books flew like missiles. All the doors bowed out, and behind them roars sounded. Both dogs scrabbled at Cleo's door, issuing guttural warning barks.

Blood trickled through widening cracks in the walls.

Just ahead of her, Trey shoved against Cleo's door. Through the terrible sounds inside, Cleo screamed again.

"Don't touch the knob!" he snapped when Sonya reached for it. "She's iced it. I'm going to try to break the door down."

As he stepped back to kick, everything stopped.

"Wait!" After yanking off his shirt, Trey wrapped it around his hand, turned the knob.

The second the door opened, Sonya ran through.

Cleo lay on the floor, the cat caught in one arm. Sonya all but dived down to her.

"Cleo, Cleo." Sonya pulled her up to cradle as the dogs milled around them, whining, licking.

"Give her some room. Come on, boys, get back." Trey crouched. "Are you hurt?"

She shook her head, but the gesture was more confusion than denial.

Her gorgeous face had gone sick and gray with her eyes too wide and bright against it.

Her windows, all opened, let in the blowing chill of late October. Trey straightened, pulled a blanket from the bed. "Put this over her."

He tossed the blanket to Sonya, and despite the stench in the room, shut the windows.

"Let's get you up on the bed."

Curled into Sonya, she shook her head at Trey. "No, God, the smell. Downstairs. Hot drink. So damn cold."

"I've got you. I've got her," he said to Sonya as he lifted Cleo into his arms. "Go down, get some tea going. Strong. Can you tell if you're hurt?"

"I don't think so." But she let her head fall onto Trey's shoulder. "Cold. Winded. Shaken up. It—it sounded like the house was falling down around me."

"It's still standing." He pressed a kiss to her hair.

"Everybody's okay. Nobody's hurt. I don't even know what time it is."

"Just after eight."

"God, one more thing to hate her for."

In the kitchen, Sonya had the kettle on, and a mug of coffee waiting.

"To warm you up until the tea's ready. In the dining room, Trey. The fire's bigger there."

When Trey set her down, the cat settled in her lap, and the dogs flanked her chair.

"Drink that, get your breath back. Does anything hurt?"

"I think I fell mostly on my ass. Maybe rapped my head a little."

Moving behind her, Trey ran his fingers through her clouds of hair, checking for injury.

"Not hard enough to bring up a lump."

"Lucky me." Cleo closed her eyes, sipped. "I just need another minute."

From the tablet, the Eagles sang "Take It Easy."

"That's right. Take it easy. There's the kettle."

"The ashwagandha, Son."

"The what?"

Cleo smiled a little at Trey as Sonya walked back to the kitchen. "It's good for stress, anxiety, emotional trauma. Sonya knows."

"Okay then." Trey laid a hand on Cleo's shoulder, relieved she no longer shivered. "I'm going to put these guys out awhile."

"I heard them barking. It helped knowing they were there." Closing her eyes, Cleo stroked the cat, who stayed in her lap. "She's fine here."

"We let the dogs out when we went down to the gym," Sonya murmured as Trey led them to the door.

"I know. Somebody let them back in to try to help."

Metallica roared out with "The House Jack Built."

"Thanks, Jack."

While the tea steeped, Sonya made more coffee.

She brought it all in, then nudged what was left of Cleo's coffee aside. "Half a teaspoon of honey, just the way you like it."

"Thanks. And thanks for the lift down, Trey. I don't think my legs would've handled it."

"You tell us," Sonya suggested, "then we'll tell you. What happened, Cleo?"

"A rude awakening. I'm sound asleep, and the next thing I know, I'm floating three feet in the air. Then the banging, the crashing, the fire's roaring like a furnace, but the room's cold as a meat locker. Noise everywhere. Blood running down the walls, then she dropped me. I think I screamed before it knocked the breath out of me. Pye's hissing, her back's arched."

She sipped some tea, then squeezed Sonya's hand. "Just exactly the way I like it. I was going to go down, find you, because it was everywhere, the banging, the bonging, the howling. Then the windows slammed open, and I saw it. I saw it coming."

Unable to stop the shudder, she paused.

"That bird of hers," Cleo continued. "And the windows were open this time. I've tried putting some protection around the house, but I'm no Imogene Tamura. I didn't have the damn BB gun."

She paused, drank more tea. Steadier for it, she continued.

"I got up, fast as I could, and grabbed my labradorite ball. The big one. About softball size," she told Trey. "It's coming, and I knew I'd never get to the door even if I could get out. So I threw it, just as that thing came through the window. I screamed and I threw it as hard as I could.

"It went right through it." Stopping, she shivered, drank more tea. "I saw it go right through, and I thought—at least I think I did—maybe it can't kill me, but it's going to do some serious damage. And that bastard's going to kill my cat."

She set down the tea, covered her face with her hands.

"Jesus, holy Jesus."

Rising, Sonya wrapped her arms around Cleo.

"It poofed. Oh God, the stench. It went to smoke. It couldn't have been a foot away from me. I went down. Legs gave way. Everything gave way. I heard you calling, but I couldn't get air for a minute. Then everything stopped, and you were there. You were both there. And the dogs."

She sighed, gave Sonya a squeeze, then eased back. "I really loved that crystal ball."

"You said it went through the bird. Did it go out the window?"

She frowned at Trey. "I don't know. I guess . . . yes."

"I'll go find it."

"Oh, do you think . . . Thanks."

"No problem. Sonya will fill you in on our part of it."

"No damage," Sonya began. "To either of us."

Cleo listened, sipping tea while Clover hit it with Queen's "Another One Bites the Dust."

"You made fun of her. That was smart, and that was brave."

"Trey started it. And he never flinched. It's easier to be brave when you're standing there with a man who just doesn't flinch. Then we heard you scream. When we got to your room, he was going to break down the door. You know how thick those doors are? But I swear, I think he could've done it."

She closed a hand over Cleo's. "This cost her, and there's only a couple of days before Halloween."

"No need to bait her into doing all this again. And let's give thanks there."

Trey came back with a small cardboard box. "Got your ball. Looks like it bounced and rolled nearly to the seawall. Nice arm you got there. It's got a lot of black ooze drying on it. I'd take that for a blood substitute."

"You didn't touch it?"

"Got it with my shirt." He held it up, showing some streaks of black on the cotton.

"Okay, good." Cleo nodded. "Toss the shirt in there, too. No washing, no cleaning. More potential use for our side."

"It was a pretty nice shirt." But he tossed it in the box. "Odds of her causing more trouble today are pretty slim. Owen's going to check in later."

"Owen."

"I let him know. I'm going to go grab a shower. I can reschedule things if you want me to stick around."

"No." Sonya shook her head. "You're right, and we thought the same. She's done for now. We're good. We're good until one second after midnight October thirty-first."

The closer it came, the more brutal the wait.

Work only held her concentration an hour or two at a time. And even then, she made mistakes she had to go back and fix.

She took aimless walks, in the house and out.

And played endless games of what-if.

What if she couldn't pull it off? What if the mirror wouldn't let her and Owen through seven times in three hours?

Two hours, fifty-nine minutes, and fifty-nine seconds, she corrected.

Because every second counted.

What if, oh God! What if it wouldn't or couldn't let them *back* through every time?

Dobbs would continue her reign of blood and terror, and they'd be stuck in another century.

And even if they accomplished all that? What if Cleo's plan to end it all failed?

Would it somehow start all over? How did it work?

And how the hell could she know?

With only hours left to wonder and worry, she paced her office while Clover played rah-rah songs.

She heard Imagine Dragons tell her she was "On Top of the World." She wanted to tell Clover it wasn't helping, but didn't have the heart.

Downstairs, Jack bounced the ball for Yoda. Even the sound of the boy's laugh, the dog's happy yips didn't cut through the anxiety.

She caught the scent—the familiar cologne—seconds before she heard the voice.

"You've got so much on your shoulders."

She turned, thought: Collin, in paint-stained jeans, high-tops, hair tumbled. Then.

Everything leaped.

"Dad. Dad!"

As she rushed across the room, he held up both hands. "You can't touch me. I wish, oh, baby, I wish I could hold you. I'm not altogether here. This isn't my place. I'm just . . . a reflection."

"I can see you. I can hear you. I miss you so much."

"I'm sorry I had to go. Sorry I couldn't be there with you, with your mom. I'm sorry you're going through all of this, but I need you to know, my strong, clever, beautiful girl, I believe in you. I love you. My heart grew ten times bigger and richer the moment they put you in my arms. And every day I had you was a joy.

"I want you to do one thing for me."

"Anything. I love you, Daddy. Anything."

"Believe in yourself. Do that one thing for me, Sonya. Do you remember what I used to tell you about believing?"

"'Believing is more than half the battle. You'll never get there, you'll never win, if you don't believe you will.'"

He shot her the smile that made everything inside her light up.

"That's my girl."

She could see him fading, stepped closer. "Dad."

"Part of me's always with you. Remember that."

When he was gone, his scent remained just a few seconds longer. While emotions swamped her, she breathed in that scent.

"That was a gift. An amazing gift. And I will remember."

She heard the door open downstairs, and Mookie bark a greeting to Yoda.

She went out, started down. Trey glanced up, and his smile of greeting shifted into concern.

"Oh." She patted her damp eyes. "No, gratitude tears. I saw my father. Or what he called a reflection. I talked to him."

"Your dad, not Collin?"

"My dad. He gave me a kind of pep talk. It worked. It worked," she repeated, and looked at Owen. "We're going to do this."

"Never doubted it. Cleo?"

"Still in the studio, I think. Or what I think of the last week or so as the demi-witch's lair."

"I'll go get her." He passed the pizza boxes he carried to Trey. As he came up the steps, he stopped beside her, gave her arm a light punch. "Never doubted it."

"Now I don't either."

Trey waited until she'd walked down to him. "Neither do I. Cutie, you look ready for anything."

"I'm ready for this." They started back to the kitchen. "And not only because I have to be. I want to be. Just under six hours now."

In the kitchen, he set down the pizza boxes, then laid his hands on her shoulders. "This isn't how I figured this would go. No candlelight or romantic spot, but here in the kitchen, pizza waiting, and you ready for anything? It fits pretty well."

He reached in his pocket, took out a small black box.

"Trey."

"I was going to wait until after, then I realized, hell no." He flipped open the box to a square-cut diamond on a band sparkling with brilliants.

Clover reached back and played Cyndi Lauper's "Time After Time."

"I believe in you, Sonya. I'm hoping you'll take this, wear this, a symbol of that belief when you go through. You'll come back at the end with seven more, but this one is yours if you'll have it. And me."

"And I'm crying again. Trey." To steady herself, she took his face in her hands to kiss him. "Yes, I'll wear it. Yes, yes, yes, I'll take it and you."

"I love you." He slipped the ring on her finger. "Now and always."

They heard the rumble from the third floor, a kind of stirring. Then a flash, but not of cold. Warmth spread like an embrace.

"She thinks this opens a door for her, but she's wrong. It's another closing. It's beautiful." In the warmth, she wrapped around him. "And it's perfect. The perfect time, the perfect place."

The kiss filled them both with love, with hope, with trust.

"You'll be with me," Sonya murmured. "When I need you most."

She turned when she heard Cleo and Owen coming.

"I had to tell her to keep her up there long enough for you to do the thing. You'd better have done the thing," Owen added.

"Let me see!" Cleo grabbed Sonya's left hand. "All right, Trey! Good job. Damn good job."

As Cleo embraced Sonya, then Trey, Clover went upbeat with Queen and "Crazy Little Thing Called Love."

"I'd say break out the champagne, but—"

"After," Sonya finished.

"After. Now we do it with pizza and Cokes."

Time ticked away. They spent the last of it outside, in the seats facing the sea. A three-quarter moon sailed the sky as they went over plans, steps, contingencies yet again.

"And still," Sonya said, "we won't know until we know. Each time, every time."

"But we're as ready as we can be," Trey pointed out. "Cleo and I will deal with whatever she throws out on this side."

"Counting on it. And Owen and I will do what we have to do on the other."

Still she clung, one more minute, to the here and now. The four of them together, the brisk air, the sailing moon, the restless sea.

"We've got to start doing what we gotta." Owen rose, reached for Cleo's hand.

When they went in, the dogs followed them up the stairs. Pye ribboned her way through them.

"It may be easier on Owen and me to go through where it happened, each time. Johanna came up these steps so . . . this is the place."

Nerves threatened again; Sonya fought them down.

"All right. I wish I could see her again, Johanna, on her wedding day, when she ran up these steps to change her shoes. We need to go there, Owen and I, to take her wedding ring so we can return it to her. We—"

The mirror was there, as if waiting.

"God, okay. Owen."

"Yeah, I see it. Not really movement, but shapes. I hear music."

Quickly, Sonya turned to Trey. "Look out for each other, and the dogs, Pye."

"Count on it."

"Cleo—"

"You don't worry about us." She shifted her gaze from Sonya to Owen. "You don't worry."

"Ten seconds until midnight." Trey gripped Owen's hand as he kissed Sonya.

Then he let go.

"Time."

They went through. Trey clicked the stopwatch he held. Cleo touched a hand to the sheer glass, then dropped it.

"They're going to do this. They're meant to do this. And still."

"Right there with you."

On the other side, Sonya and Owen stood on the same spot in air scented with flowers.

The door burst open, and Johanna, radiant, ran in and started up the stairs. On a laugh, she stopped, and pulled off high, sparkling heels.

"She doesn't see us," Sonya murmured. "I'd half hoped she would."

Laying a hand on her belly where the hope of a new life slept, she hurried up the rest of the stairs. She spun in a circle, her happiness like a wave that swept everything in its path.

"She'll go to the main bedroom, put her wedding shoes away."

"You have to move in."

"In the bedroom, I will. When she's there."

They followed as Johanna all but danced down the hallway and through the doors of the bedroom.

She put her shoes away, stood smiling, glowing as she scanned her choices.

"Well, the hell with shoes," she began.

And everything froze.

"Oh. That's how it'll be then." Struck with sorrow, filled with purpose, Sonya stepped to her. "I'm sorry, so sorry I can't do more. I'll get it back to you. I swear."

"Cleo said to put it on."

Sonya slipped it on her middle finger where, for an instant, it glowed.

"Move." Owen grabbed her arm, pulled her away. "Don't think about it now."

"In just a few minutes, she'll—"

"We can't stop that."

"Dobbs is coming. Can you feel her?"

"Yeah, I can feel her."

Owen all but tossed Sonya through the mirror, and leaped behind her.

Trey grabbed her. "Eleven minutes, forty-two seconds. You're pale."

"A little dizzy." But she held up her hand, where Johanna's ring sparkled beside hers.

"We weren't over there more than three minutes," Owen said. "Anything on this side?"

"Nothing." Cleo put a hand on his cheek. "You're a little pale yourself."

"Rough ride. We good?" he asked Sonya.

"Yes. It's Clover now." Because she knew this would take the biggest toll, she shut her eyes. "We need to go to the bedroom. Where she had Collin and my father. Where she died."

Clover's understanding came through with "In the Name of Love."

As they walked to the bedroom, a scream sounded on the third floor.

"She missed the seventh ring," Cleo said as something boomed like cannon fire.

"We need to see Clover and Charlie, the birth of Collin Poole and Andrew MacTavish. We need to be there, take back what was stolen so we can return it."

When the mirror came, Owen saw movement in the glass, and the flash of fire, heard music—"I Only Want to Be with You."

"Watch your backs," he said to Trey and Cleo. Grabbing Sonya's hand, he pulled her through just as the fire in the now roared to life.

Cleo pulled the sage stick from her pocket, lit it. "I put protection in every space Sonya laid out. If it's not enough—"

"We'll handle it."

For the second time, Sonya saw her father's birth, heard his first cry.

"Well, Jesus" was the best Owen could manage.

"It's my dad. Charlie's holding my dad." Streaming tears blurred her vision. She wanted to touch, just once to touch the tiny new life that would grow into the man she'd loved so much.

For a moment, she swore the infant looked at her with her father's eyes. Reaching out, she brushed a finger over the soft cheek.

"Man, I'm sick with sorry, Sonya, but you have to get the ring."

"I know. I will."

As she put her hand over Clover's, the tableau froze.

Or so she thought.

Clover's hand moved under hers. Her head turned and she offered a weak smile. "Did you come to see the babies? Me and Charlie have two beautiful boys. Hey, you've got Charlie's eyes. You, too."

"I know. They are beautiful, and so are you. I'm sorry. I have to take this for now. I'm going to get it back to you."

"I'm so tired," Clover said as Sonya took the ring, slid it onto her right-hand ring finger. "But I have to nurse the babies. They need me. I'm going to be such a good mom."

"The best."

The exhausted eyes cleared for a moment. "She's coming soon. You have to hurry."

Before Sonya could speak again, Owen pulled her back through the mirror.

"She knew." Sonya covered her face with her hands. "She knew."

Trey put his arms around her. "Eighteen minutes flat. We need to keep going." When he started to pick her up, she pushed back.

"No, I can walk. I will. She knew, and she told us to hurry. It's the ballroom next."

Fires roared in every room, and lights flickered on and off. In unison, the dogs growled when they reached the third floor. Jones turned with a guttural bark toward the door where hard red light pushed through into an outline.

"Jones!"

At Owen's sharp command, the dog snarled once but followed.

Breathless, more than a little dizzy, Sonya began to call the mirror before they reached the ballroom.

"We need to go back to Lisbeth's wedding day. To where the band played and people danced. We need to take what was stolen from her so we can give it back."

The mirror waited.

"If you need a minute."

"No." But she squeezed Cleo's hand. And this time, she led Owen through.

Lights gleamed while women in glorious gowns danced with men in formal black suits, in shirts with stiff white collars. Sonya saw Owen Poole, the proud father, beaming while he led his young, beautiful daughter in a quick fox-trot.

"I'm so happy, Daddy. It's the happiest day of my life."

"I know I have to give you back to your husband again."

"My husband!" And throwing back her head, Lisbeth laughed. "I'm a wife."

"But you'll always be my little girl."

"It's going to happen soon," Sonya remembered.

They had to wind their way through the dancers, then through servers who passed glasses of champagne.

When they reached Lisbeth, Sonya tried not to focus on that shining young face, but on the ring that rested on her father's shoulder.

The music stopped, as did all movement.

"I'm sorry, Lissy." She slid the ring off the bride's finger and onto her own.

They'd barely started back when the music sounded again. Sonya stumbled through a pair of dancers. She caught herself, but thought she'd lost Owen.

She stopped, looked behind her.

"She's coming. Go!"

Through the laughter, the dancers, then the screams, Sonya ran. She caught a glimpse of Dobbs gliding into the ballroom as she and Owen all but fell through the mirror.

And into a ballroom where cracks had begun to form on the walls.

When Sonya swayed, Trey hooked an arm around her waist. "She's taking it up a notch."

"We saw her, she was just coming in." Owen spoke leaning over, head between his knees as the dogs whined and licked. "A little space, guys. Time?"

"Eight-twenty-three."

"Weird. That took longer over there than the other two." He straightened. "Still good?"

"Good enough. We stay here this time at least." And here where it seemed the floor rocked under her like the deck of a boat in an angry sea.

"For Agatha. We want to see Agatha on her wedding day. We need to go back to the ballroom on that night, before she died. To take what was stolen from her so we can give it back."

She heard Dobbs's scream of rage as the chandeliers began to sway. "Please be careful."

Candlelight filled the ballroom. The music, more refined, drew couples into a waltz. A young Owen Poole, now groom rather than father of the bride, danced with Agatha.

The bride, regal, aloof, looked very pleased. Her wedding ring shot fire.

"He'll ask her to go sit with Jane, his twin. Pregnant over there."

"I see her. You holding up?"

"I've got to. Pretty queasy now."

"I hear that."

As Owen led Agatha toward Jane, Sonya swayed again. "Sorry. Room took a big spin."

"I can get this one."

"I have to. You know that."

She felt more than half drunk as she started over. Her ears rang, and for a second, her vision doubled. Before movement stopped, she reached for the ring.

Agatha jerked as if struck, then froze, eyes wide, lips parted.

"Sorry," Sonya muttered, and pushed the ring onto her finger.

This time she and Owen hooked arms and, weaving, made it back to the mirror.

"Shit, here we go."

He went down to his knees when they passed through. Trey managed to catch Sonya before she did the same. "They all fit," she said as her head spun. "Whatever finger I put them on, they fit. Funny. A little sick."

"Little's relative," Owen managed. "We may need a bucket before this is done."

"They're bleeding. The walls are bleeding."

And the doorbell bonged, fog had begun to creep. A war sounded from the third floor.

"How much time?"

"That might've been the longest twenty-one minutes, fifty-six seconds of my life. And you both need to take a few more. You're sheet pale now."

"Here. I ran down for these." Cleo passed Sonya a Coke, knelt to hold the other to Owen.

"Might sick it right back up."

"You won't." She brushed her hand over his clammy face. "Four down, three to go. Then the real work begins."

"You kill me, Lafayette." But he drank. "Bedroom next, another push-the-babies-out deal. Jesus, why do women ever agree to that?"

This time Sonya didn't object when Trey carried her, nor did Owen object to Cleo taking some of his weight as they went down.

Now the door of the Gold Room glowed red, and had begun to pulse.

"Marianne." In the bedroom, Sonya bore down as Trey set her on her feet. "We need to see Marianne when she gave birth to her twins, Owen and Jane. We need to . . ."

"Take what was stolen from her," Owen finished. "So we can give it back. I'll hold you up, cousin. You hold me up."

With a nod, Sonya went through with him into the room where a roaring fire heated the air and candles flickered for light.

And two women attended the one crying out in pain.

"Jesus Christ, there's gotta be a better way."

The midwife knelt on the bed between Marianne's legs. The infant Owen, already delivered, squalled.

And the newborn Jane slid into the midwife's hands on a shrill cry.

Weeping again, she couldn't help but weep, Sonya walked to the bed. This time when movement stopped, she wasn't surprised when Marianne looked at her.

"Poole green. Your eyes. Who will mother my babies when I'm gone?"

"Their father will love them as he loves you. I have to take the ring, Marianne."

"They're Owen and Jane."

"I know. I'm from them. We're from them. I'm sorry I couldn't save you."

"Save my babies."

"They live good, long, happy lives."

Sonya stepped back as the midwife cupped the infant. With five of the seven rings on her fingers, she turned to Owen. They held each other up as they went back through.

Chapter Thirty-One

In the manor, in the now, books flew off the shelves of the library. Windows slashed open, and a storm, raging, whipped in. With the dogs barking wildly, the cat hissing like a snake, Trey and Cleo rushed to the terrace doors, pushing, pushing against the whirling wind.

Cracks opened in the ceiling, and blood dripped through them.

"She won't stop now," Cleo shouted. "She can't."

"We're going to stop her."

They managed to close the doors, and when Trey moved to deal with the windows, Cleo's side flew open again and knocked her flat.

"I'm all right! I'm all right! Close it if you can."

As she spoke, Owen and Sonya spilled out of the mirror and slid to the floor.

Trey pulled Cleo up before he rushed to them.

"Need a minute. Do we have time?" Her hand trembled as she lifted it to Trey's face. "You're soaked."

"It's nothing." He gathered her into his arms, rocked.

"Time," Owen managed.

"Shit. Distracted." Trey hit the stopwatch. "Twenty-eight minutes, three seconds. You look like hell."

"Feel the same. Two more," he managed as Cleo dropped down to hold him. "We've got two more in us."

"Let me get the doors shut again."

"Forget them. Let her blow." Shoving at her hair, Sonya pushed to her feet. "The cold air's waking me up. Catherine's next. It's okay, Yoda. It's okay. Downstairs."

Fog laced the floors, but the cold didn't sting. She's not as strong as she was, Sonya thought. But neither am I.

She looked down at her hands, at the rings. The one Trey had given her, and all the others.

Not as strong as I was, she thought again.

But she would be.

"Catherine." Sonya spoke over the banging, the clanging bong of the doorbell, the rush of wind, the snap and sizzle of lightning.

"We need to go to Catherine on her wedding night. Here where she wandered in a trance. Here before Dobbs drew her out into a blizzard and her death. We need to take back what was stolen from her so we can give it back."

She pressed one hand to her spinning head while Owen gripped the other. With a nod, she went through with him.

The manor held dark and quiet.

"Can't see a fucking thing," Owen began. "It's as dark as dark gets."

"She came down the stairs, and—"

Then they both saw it.

The single light from a single candle illuminated the woman coming slowly down the stairs. In her nightdress, Catherine walked in her trance, her eyes open and blank, her lips curved in a dreamy smile.

Sonya didn't hesitate, and didn't wait, but moved through the dark toward her. "I'm sorry I can't save you."

She took Catherine's left hand, slipped the ring off, then onto her own.

Catherine continued to walk, dreamlike, toward the massive front doors. Opening one, she stepped out into the thick wall of snow.

Owen took Sonya's hand. "One to go."

Sonya's knees wanted to buckle, but she refused to let them. And forgot the weakness when they came back to the dark cut through by a pair of flashlights.

She saw the blood on Trey's face.

"You're bleeding."

"She aimed at me. He got in the way."

"Just a flesh wound, cutie. Winged a vase at me."

"At me," Cleo corrected. "The man moves fast."

"When I need to. One more, okay, cutie?" He pressed kisses to her face. "Just one more."

"I know." Then she let out a surprised laugh. "I feel better. I feel . . . good."

"That's one of us," Owen said. "How long?"

"Fifteen and forty-seven. Plenty of time left."

"Whatever's left, it'll be enough. We've got to get back upstairs."

They moved through the curling fog. The front doors slammed open as they started up the steps.

"Watch out for flying objects," Cleo advised. "She's weaker, I really think she is, but she's a lot angrier."

"She doesn't understand what's happening, not really." Buoyant now, Sonya took Cleo's hand. "She had seven rings, and now she only has one. She doesn't understand."

"And maybe doesn't remember. We're intruders, that might be all she knows."

"Keep your bitchfork handy because we're nearly done."

Smoke filled the hallway, smoke that stank of sulfur. Through it, they walked to the bedroom.

She did feel better, Sonya realized. No, not just better. Energized.

"Astrid." She had to shout over booms of thunder. "We need to see Astrid on her wedding day when she comes here to take a moment to herself. To study herself in the mirror . . . God, this mirror. I didn't think—"

"Keep going," Owen said.

"We need to take what was stolen from her so we can give it back."

"This is the last time." Trey kissed her. "We'll be waiting."

They stepped through, and stood face-to-face with Astrid Grandville Poole.

In her bridal white, she reared back, eyes wide as she gasped.

"What witchery is this!"

"Astrid. No, don't run. Owen."

"Take it easy," he said, and took her arms.

Terrified, Astrid struck out, shoved. Weakened, Owen tumbled back through the mirror.

"Knocked down by a girl." He lifted a hand so Trey could pull him up.

But when he tried to go back, the mirror's glass proved solid.

"Goddamn it, it's not letting me through. It's not the same. It's not letting me go back."

"She's alone over there." Trey pressed a hand to the glass. "She's alone."

On the other side, Sonya held up her hands. "Astrid. Look at my eyes. I'm from Collin. I'm Sonya Poole."

"No, no. What manner of dress is this? You came through the mirror. It's sorcery!"

"But not my sorcery. You play the piano. You play 'Barbara Allen' when you're sad. You had a party and you played the piano. Collin turned the pages. A woman knitted."

As she described the scene she'd witnessed, Astrid backed away.

"Go back. Go back where you came from."

"I will. But I need something first. We don't have much time. I'm sorry. I'm so sorry."

She gripped Astrid's left wrist.

Astrid went still. She looked in Sonya's eyes.

"Death upon death, she brings to us. The brides of Poole Manor. Take the ring, the first she stole when she spilled my blood, when she took my life. Know it frees us, but does not, it will not, end her."

Astrid took off the ring herself, held it out. "I give it, and freely. Seven were taken, seven are found, seven are given."

"Thank you."

"She comes. And time runs out. Go quickly, end her reign of death. End her."

"We will. I swear it."

When she went through, Trey scooped her up, held her hard and close. "You're back. You came back."

"Woo. What a ride."

Like a mile-long descent on a wild roller coaster.

"It wouldn't let me in. I couldn't get through again."

As she held just as tightly to Trey, she turned her head to Owen. "I guess the last—or the first—was meant for just me."

"That's what I told him." But Cleo wrapped around Sonya.

Owen rolled his eyes. "First knocked down by a girl, now giving a group hug."

One he couldn't quite admit felt good.

"How long that time?"

"Thirty-six brutal minutes and six seconds."

"We should hurry."

"We've got time. Here." Cleo passed Sonya a fresh Coke. "Recharge some. She has been."

"I'm so charged!" But she gulped down Coke. "She hasn't been raging like this the whole time?"

"She shuts it down for five or six minutes, then starts it all over again. I think the pets are going to need therapy. Let's get your jacket." Cleo kissed Sonya's cheek. "And we'll take it outside."

"Astrid. Something changed when I touched her. It was like she knew—like Clover and Marianne."

Words tumbled out. Where she'd felt weak, queasy, dizzy, she now felt pumped with pure adrenaline and an espresso chaser.

"She knew so she gave me her ring. She said it would free them, but wouldn't end Dobbs. Just as you said."

"We're going to do that—all of us."

"I promised her we would. So, Cleo, this better work. Let's go, let's do this! Wow, I feel a little drunk, a lot high, but in an amazing way. Let's go send that bitch back to hell."

"Okay, cutie." As he took her hand to slow her down, Trey shot a look at Owen and Cleo.

"It's the rings." Much more delighted than concerned, Cleo shot out a grin. "It's having all seven. It's power."

Cleo tossed a jacket over Sonya's shoulders while Sonya turned to Owen. "I'm traveling at the speed of light."

"Seems like it." Trey bundled her into the jacket, though with the heat pumping off her now, he wondered if she'd need it. "No keeping the dogs and Pye in the house. She's still in here, and—"

He snagged a candlestick out of the air. "She's only going to get worse."

Owen carried the copper pot Cleo took out of the closet. "We may need them anyway."

Trey kept a firm hand on Sonya, and felt her vibrate. "I don't like leaving her alone in the house when she's peaking like this."

"She's not alone." As they stepped out, as the wind struck, Sonya lifted her face to it. "They're all here. All of them. Can't you feel them?"

The door slammed, a bullet from a gun, behind them.

"And they're stronger now."

The dogs raced as dogs will as they walked to the seawall.

"Circle first." Cleo took the bag of salt from the pot, and used the words her grandmother had given her. "Here before the three o'clock hour, we four cast our circle of power. Within its ring we abide to break the curse on manor and bride.

"Light the candles. One for each of us."

She took her own, and the globe to shield the flame.

"Against the dark we bring the light to end the witch's reign this night."

They looked up as something flew out of the Gold Room window. It screamed, set the dogs to barking. Then simply sputtered into a thin smoke.

"She's weaker there," Trey murmured.

"She won't be when she comes here." Sonya looked up at the three-quarter moon. "We'll be in her world then. But . . ." Almost giddy, Sonya held up her hands so the rings caught the moonlight.

"She doesn't have these. Seven rings and mine makes eight. Circles of love stand against hate. The blood she spilled through generations leads to her eternal damnation."

Sonya blinked. "Wow. Where did that come from?"

"I'd say these." Trey folded his hands over hers.

"This is getting seriously weird."

"It's going to get weirder," Cleo warned Owen. "We need to call the dogs and Pye in here. I don't know if they'll stay through this, but we have to try."

"She's coming." Sonya pressed a hand to her heart. "Oh. I feel like I could jump right out of my skin. Do you feel that? Do you feel her?"

"I do now." Trey gripped her arm. "Stay close."

She came out of the dark. Not gliding, no, Sonya realized. Walking slowly, effortfully as the now-full moon hung white over the sea.

Alive, human, weary. And still completely mad.

"We can't let her jump." Cleo spoke softly. "Whatever happens, we can't let her jump."

The dogs growled almost in unison, but—for now—obeyed the command to stay. When Pye arched her back, hissed, Owen picked her up.

Dobbs looked up at the house where the entity she'd become still raged. Then she stared at the group inside the ring of salt.

"Who stands on what is mine? Who dares? Begone from here or face my wrath."

Trembling a little, Cleo knelt and began the ritual.

"Your blood." She poured the stained crystals into the copper pot. "The blood of your creature." Then added her labradorite ball, Trey's shirt.

She looked up at Owen.

"Yeah, I got it."

He passed the cat to Trey, then took out the knife Dobbs had used to kill Astrid.

"This is mine!" Dobbs swept out a hand. Outside the circle, wind swirled. Inside, Owen felt a sting across his cheek.

"Need to do better than that," he said, and earned a hiss from Cleo. Shrugging, he held his hand over the pot and scored his palm with the knife.

"Blood of the innocent, blood of a Poole."

"Poole. A Poole. You thought to hang me! I take what is mine. You have no sway over my life, my death. I bring death!"

Lifting her hands, Dobbs curled her fingers. "I bring death to

Pooles but first the pain. And in the manor I will remain. Mistress here for all time. Bride after bride their lives I'll take, and with one twist your neck I break."

"Tickles some." Owen wiped his bloody hand on the bandanna in his back pocket.

"I'll say." Sonya rubbed at her throat.

Dobbs screamed, by the seawall, inside the house. As she charged the circle, Trey shoved Sonya behind him.

But filled with fury, and more, Sonya pushed back. And held up her hands. Moonlight flooded on the rings.

"I'm mistress here, and so are the seven before me."

"Mine!" As if mesmerized, Dobbs rounded the circle of salt. "You. You I know. How do I know? In the glass, in the cauldron. In the blood. Give me what's mine!"

As she started to strike out, Trey grabbed Sonya, prepared to take whatever blow got through. And Jones charged.

Lightning bolted out of the manor, lanced into the ground even as Jones snapped.

As before he tore the black dress.

"Jones!"

At Owen's shouted order, Jones, all but steaming with reluctance, went back.

And Dobbs struck out with fire.

"Going out weakened the circle, but good boy anyway. Let me have that." Cleo took the swatch of black cloth, folded it with the first. "One from each of them. One from then, one from now."

"The fire's eating at the salt," Sonya warned.

"Blood you spilled, blood we took, and blood given free."

The clock struck three.

Dobbs stopped, smiled. "Blood. My blood to seal the curse. There will be no hangman's noose for Hester Dobbs."

"Speed it up, Lafayette."

"I blend them here with water from the sea."

Before Dobbs could climb onto the seawall, Sonya ran out of the circle.

"Come and get them!" she shouted as Trey cursed and rushed after her.

Behind them, from the manor, thunder roared. With one hand on the seawall, Dobbs turned. Sonya wiggled the fingers of her lifted hands.

"You killed for these. Now I have them."

"Eight, eight. Seven, eight. Where was the whore's? Astrid Grandville. She had no ring. But a bride, still a bride."

"That's right. She gave it to me." Sonya tapped Astrid's ring.

The wind, coming from all directions, might have knocked her down as Dobbs turned from the seawall. But Trey held her upright.

"It better be now," he called out.

"Damn wind!"

Crouching, Owen cupped his hands, nodded at Cleo. And this time the flame held.

"Gotta improvise a little. This cloth from then, this cloth from now, together burn."

Owen adjusted his hands as the black cloths caught fire.

"As their flames rise higher, I cast into the bloody sea their fire. And with this token, your curse forever broken. With this spark, we cast out the dark. With your greed and hate, you seal your own fate."

She tossed the burning cloths into the pot.

"Go, go, we have to help them. If this doesn't work—"

Shrieks cut through the thunder. Owen lifted Cleo to her feet.

"I think we've got it. Nice work, Glinda."

Flames licked up the black dress. As Dobbs shrieked, as she swatted at them, Trey pulled Sonya back.

"God. My God."

The wind Dobbs had whipped fed the flames. Her screams tore through the greedy crackle of them as she ran in circles, beating at them still as her hands began to burn. Her hair caught, sparks flying from the fiery ribbons of it as she stumbled, fell.

"I didn't expect . . . I didn't know she'd . . . burn."

"She sealed her own fate," Owen reminded Cleo.

She burned, she burned screaming with a fire that blazed toward the moonlit sky.

Then the screams died, and the wind with it. The manor went quiet so the only sounds came from the roll of the sea and the voice of the fire.

The flames died.

"There's nothing left." Her heart still hammering, Sonya stared at the grass where Dobbs had fallen. "Nothing at all."

"Because she's gone." Trey lifted her hand, kissed it. "We ended her then, we ended her now."

"Go team. High fives all around." Owen looked down at his wounded palm. "Maybe later on that. And well, Jesus, we've got company."

Trey spun around, ready to defend again.

The seven brides stood together, the manor behind them.

"It's like your painting, Cleo. It's just like your painting." Sonya looked down at the rings on her hands. "They've come for these. I need to . . ."

"Go ahead. We'll wait."

As Sonya walked toward them, Clover took a step forward. "Everything's cool inside. We took care of it. You sure took care of us. And her."

"Clover."

"Some of us—most—want to stay if that's okay with you. I know Charlie'll want to when we can really talk again."

"This is your house, all of you, all or anyone who's stayed and wants to stay, for as long as you want."

"We knew you'd say that, but we wanted to ask. You should start with Astrid this time, okay?"

With a nod, Sonya walked down to Astrid, held out her hands. "Take yours."

Astrid slipped it off Sonya's finger, onto her own. "Thank you. Grief is over, and Collin waits for me in the manor."

She walked through the open doors.

Sonya held out her hands to Catherine.

"No one waits for me, but this has always been my home."

"It always will be," Sonya told her as Catherine put on her ring.

"I had strong, beautiful babies." Marianne slipped on her ring.

"Hugh and I had a strong and beautiful love. We'll be happy here again."

Agatha took her ring. "I was to be mistress here, and that was taken from me."

"You're welcome here as long as you like."

With a regal nod, Agatha walked into the manor.

"I can't have Edward, but I want to stay, at least for a while." Lisbeth took her ring, admired it, then slipped it on. "I was really happy here."

"I'm glad."

Sonya stopped at Clover, and this time took the twined heart ring off, put it on Clover's finger herself. "My favorite of the seven."

"Aw. It's really sweet, isn't it? So's my Charlie. I really love you, Sonya. Now I'm going to go kiss Charlie until his eyes roll back!"

She raced to the house, and shouting for Charlie, ran in.

And Johanna smiled. "She helped me through the first terrible fears and grief. And then you." She took both Sonya's hands, then looked past her to where the others waited. "All of you."

She took her ring.

"Because of all of you, I'm the last who'll know those terrible fears and grief. Thank you."

She kissed Sonya's cheek, then walked into the manor.

Trey bolted forward when Sonya swayed.

"Whoa. I'm okay, just . . . The rings, they really packed a punch. All gone now. Except mine."

"And you're chilled again. Let's go in."

"Yeah. Who's for breakfast?"

"Owen." Cleo laughed, linked her arm through his. "Only you."

"Actually, I could eat. I'm empty," Sonya admitted. "Eat, sleep for thirty or forty hours, hope it seems real after that."

"It's real," Trey assured her. "Nothing's left of her, not even back where she started."

"I know it, I saw it, I feel it. But before we do anything else?"

"The Gold Room." Cleo looked at the stairs as they went inside. "I feel the same way."

"Then let's go up. We've been wanting to get back in there for a while now. Right, Jones? You witch-biting maniac."

"I think that was meant, too." Cleo leaned down to give Jones a rub as they started up the stairs. "Having a piece of her from then to add to what we had from now. We thought—my grand-mère and I—that if we could break the curse and keep her from jumping until we broke it, until the hour passed, she'd just fade away."

"She sealed her fate," Owen repeated. "No regrets."

"No, no regrets."

When they reached the third floor, Sonya paused.

"The door's open. The door to the Gold Room."

"It's time to go in." Taking her hand, Trey walked down the hall.

Then reaching in, turned on the lights.

It was just a room, with walls papered in gold, a bed with an elaborate head- and footboard. Lovely old furnishings covered with dust.

"Needs some serious cleaning," Cleo observed, batting away a spiderweb. "And clearing out. Then."

"The Poole Family and Friends Gallery. She's gone." Sonya walked through, her steps leaving footprints in the dust. "There isn't a trace of her left. Despite the shape of this room, I have to say it. This house is clean."

"And you're mistress of Poole Manor."

She threw her arms around Trey, then pointed at Owen. "Kiss Cleo. And you, kiss me. Right here, right now. First thing we do in here? Bring the love and the light."

"If you insist."

When their lips met, when Clover added some Huey Lewis and the News with "The Power of Love," Sonya felt it burst through her.

The love and the light.

Epilogue

In June, the flowers bloomed. The air softened, sweetened. Music played in the garden where dozens of chairs with white covers faced the pergola. Wisteria spilled like waterfalls.

And in June, Sonya became a bride.

She stood in her sleek and simple white dress as her mother adjusted the circle of rainbow-hued rosebuds over her hair. Sonya thought of the flower headpiece as an homage to Clover.

She wore the diamond-and-sapphire earrings Collin had left her mother, covering old, borrowed, and blue all at once.

"You look so beautiful, baby."

"You can't cry before it even starts."

"Yes, I can."

"Have some of this." Cleo, in her bold red gown, handed Winter a glass of champagne.

"And you're next."

Cleo smiled, smugly, at the ring—vintage, flashy—on her finger. "Plenty of time yet there. But the house is coming along. Today, we drink to the magnificent bride, and her handsome groom. Which he is, as I had a peek when I went out before."

"I wish your dad could be here. He'd be so proud."

"He is, Mom. I know he is. He'll be with us when you walk me down the aisle. So this toast goes to my mom and dad, who gave me everything I needed to get me right here, where I want to be, where I belong, where I'm happy."

"And you expect me not to cry?"

Sonya just hugged her. "If you ruin your makeup, we'll fix it. I'm having the wedding of my dreams, surrounded by people I love. I'm marrying the man I love, a man who sees me, hears me, loves me. A man I already know will walk through fire, not just for me but with me."

"You fought for it, Son."

"We fought for it." They clinked glasses. "I love you both, so much."

After the toast, Cleo took Winter's hand. "Give us five minutes in the bathroom to touch up Winter's makeup. Then it's time we went down."

"I'm ready. Whenever you are."

Sonya turned to the mirror, then around again when she saw Clover.

"I didn't want to, like, get in the way."

"You're never in the way."

"You look completely wow. I just wanted to say . . . I'm going to blubber some. I'm really happy, really proud, really so much of all kinds of stuff. Anyway, when Trey sees you? Socks knocked off."

Clover blew a kiss, and was gone.

When Cleo and Winter came out, Sonya angled her head. "Beautiful, both of you." She picked up her bouquet. "Let's go knock some socks off."

As they went down, Cleo texted to cue the music.

After a last hug, she stepped out as Etta James soared on "At Last."

"Nervous, baby?"

"Not even a little." Holding her mother's hand, she walked out.

She felt her father, caught his scent, and as her mother's hand tightened on hers, she knew Winter felt him, too.

She saw friends, Trey's family and hers, Cleo's.

And the seven brides with the grooms who'd stayed. She saw Molly and the staff who'd stayed.

Love and light, she thought. So much it seemed to fill the world.

Then she saw only Trey, waiting for her. She saw his heart in those deep blue eyes.

So she kept her eyes on his as she walked to him to exchange the symbol of rings, and to promise him a lifetime.

A lifetime, together, building a life and family in the grand old house the locals called Lost Bride Manor.

NORA
ROBERTS

For the latest news, exclusive extracts
and unmissable competitions, visit

f /NoraRobertsJDRobb
www.fallintothestory.com

UNLOCK THE LATEST CRIME AND THRILLERS

Sign up to our newsletter for criminally good recommendations, exclusives and competitions.

www.thecrimevault.com

𝕏 f ⃝

@TheCrimeVault